MW00577726

Also by Doug Richardson

Dark Horse
True Believers

THE SAFETY EXPERT

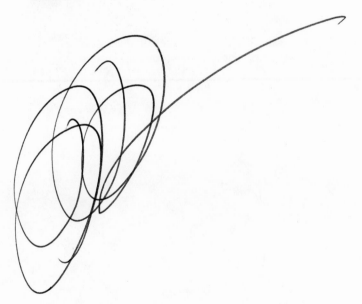

DOUG RICHARDSON

THE SAFETY EXPERT

velvet elvis entertainment

los angeles

VELVET ELVIS ENTERTAINMENT
13547 Ventura Boulevard
Suite 126
Sherman Oaks, California 91423

Copyright © 2011 by Doug Richardson
Cover design by Karen Richardson
More information at http://www.dougrichardson.com
ISBN: 978-0-9848071-0-9

Library of Congress Control Number: 2011942976

Printed in the United States of America

Richardson, Doug, 1959-
The Safety Expert / Doug Richardson.

For Kate

prologue

TICK. Tick. Tick.

"So there it is. I've made my confession. It's off my back. And now it's on yours."

Old man Pratt shut his mouth and sucked back some fresh O_2. Tick. Tick. Tick. The oxygen meter continued. It sounded every bit like a death clock counting down to his very last moment on earth.

"I don't care what you think about me, who I am or what I done. I said what I said for me 'n' me alone. You understand?"

Tick. Tick. Tick.

The goddamn oxygen meter—always talking over Pratt while he was thinking. Some days he would stare at it for hours, watching the tiny indicator arm vibrate with every merciless tick. Other days the meter reminded him of the gas gauge attached to the north side of the one and only house he had ever owned. Stockton, California. '63 to '69. There was that one time, he recalled, his pet Rottweiler nearly tore the legs off one gas company employee who came to read the meter. What the hell was that dog's name? he thought. Good dog. Fat prick of an animal. The name came to Pratt. He had called the dog *Gutter*, on account of where he had found the poor thing, its leg busted by a passing car. *Best three-legged dog ever*, thought Pratt. Good damn guard dog too. After the incident with the meter reader, the gas company wisely provided a set of field glasses for readers to track Pratt's gas consumption from the street. Nowadays, figured Pratt, he would have been sued by the meter reader and lost or had to settle. The thought made him glad he no longer owned the house. In Pratt's rulebook, owning anything was for losers.

"Where the hell was I?" he grumbled. "Ain't got no regrets, neither. You can't live with that shit . . . Hell. You can take regret and flush it for all I care."

Ribbons of plastic hoses coiled around him, each neatly affixed to him with tabs of white sweat-resistant tape. There were two bags of IV fluids hanging from what could have passed for a hat stand. What was in those damn fluids, only God and chemists knew. The contraption on Pratt's head was elastically fit, the nipples releasing the precious oxygen into his nostrils. The rest was up to Pratt. As long as he kept breathing and his heart kept pumping, the fluids would flow and the O_2 meter would tick, tick, tick. All charges paid for by the Indiana State Bureau of Prisons.

"So if I got no regrets and don't give a shit what other people think, why'm I tellin' you this? That's a good question and I don't know the answer just yet. Maybe I won't send you the tape. That'll prove I don't give a rat's piss."

Rat's piss or not, Pratt kept talking. With every lung-load of fresh O_2, he watched the microcassette player rise and fall on his goiter-like stomach, a round orb of a gut that was his own work of art.

"Just so you know, I got no proof. Just what the guy said. But lemme say this: I've been in the joint long enough to know bullshit from what's real. And this guy, believe you me, was real as real gets. No shit. I believe him to this goddamn dyin' day —"

"Will you shut the fuck up?" barked the black con. "Jeesuz

H. Christ, man. All you do is beat your fuckin' gums."

The black con was two empty beds over to Pratt's right. The infirmary was at a low population. The sixteen beds were separated into two rows of eight, divided by a double-lane causeway and cut up with vinyl curtains hung on roller track. Only four of the sixteen beds were occupied. And the two other cons were so narced on sleep meds that Pratt would have laid bets that the Second Coming wouldn't have roused them.

That left Pratt and the black con.

"Shut your cotton pickin' ears and go to sleep," said Pratt.

"Shut your mouth . . . cracker fuck."

Pratt figured correctly that the black con was new to the joint. The con hadn't yet learned the martial art of doing time. Prison was never quiet. And nights were a series of terrible noises. Cries, grunts, pain, dementia. Pratt called the noises *coyote sounds*. Beasts barking at the dark. Or carnivores fighting over the last remains of a dead carcass. He assigned each horrible sound to its place in nature, turning prison into his own Wild Kingdom. Suddenly those awful noises fell naturally on his ear. And sleep became easier.

"You can either shut your ears or shut my mouth," said Pratt. "Your call, nigger."

Big words. But Pratt knew the black con was strapped in with Velcro and duct tape. *Some failed suicide*, figured Pratt. Probably buggered-up on his first night in the dorms and certainly not able-bodied or willing to take on the older con lying just twenty feet away.

"Next time he'll kill himself right," Pratt found himself saying into the tape recorder. "Twist a rope out of a bed sheet and take a dive off the top tier. Save good taxpayers like you some dough, I expect."

Click. The tape player shut itself off. Pratt griped to himself, "Cuz I'm fuckin' ramblin' on and on . . ."

Side 1 of the microcassette tape was exhausted. Pratt fumbled with his drug-swollen fingers to extract the tiny cartridge, flip it and reinsert it into the recorder. It felt as difficult as performing ocular surgery with a pair of chopsticks.

Fuckin' cancer drugs.

Side 2. Pratt thumbed the RECORD button, then calmed himself with a deep breath. If he closed his eyes he could use his imagination and make the canned oxygen smell like just about anything. Cigars. A woman's sweaty musk. Bacon frying. This time it was spearmint. Wrigley's Doublemint. What Pratt would have paid right then and there for a pack.

"What I was sayin' was just this. You don't know me from Adam. And I sure as hell don't know you. For all I care, you can toss this tape in the incinerator."

Pratt found he was holding his breath, weakening his voice to a whispering rasp. Why? He had burned half a cassette, running on like a broken valve. And still he hadn't told it. He hadn't delivered on the promise he had made at the start of the tape. Pratt pulled another two liters of oxygen.

Tick. Tick. Tick.

"Like I was sayin' before. I was his cellmate. L.A. County. Eleven years ago? Twelve, thirteen? Back around them riots. All them fires, you know? We were poppin' these little blue grinders. Good stuff somebody had scammed off a guard. Anyways, he was inside on this three month pop for beatin' on his girlfriend. Gave him giggles that it was such a short pop considering the shit he had been doing outside. Home invasions, follow-homes, shit like that. Big money house cleaning. Had a partner, he said. In, out, jewels, cash. Said it was easier than robbin' banks."

Pratt paused, finding his own silence unnerving. The black con had returned to the land of tranquilized slumber. The distant babble from the nursing station had faded. If he strained his ears, Pratt wondered if he would hear the old plaster cracking beneath the ward's new paint.

"Guy said all the jobs was slick but for this one time... one time where some soccer mom decides to fight back. Killed her and the two little girlies 'before anybody could say, *Puff the Magic Dragon.*' Them's his words, not mine. And won't never forget 'em. *Puff the Magic Dragon.* You know what I'm sayin'. You know who I'm talkin' about, too. Soccer mom and the little ones was yours, fellah. Your own wife and kiddies, man."

Pratt found himself on pause. And for half an instant imagined himself as the man for whom the tape was intended.

"Sorry, partner. Kinda harsh words. But I suppose that's the shit you had to live with ever since. Guess that means I feel sorry for ya. Kinda hell a man goes through. Just since then, ever so often, that damn song comes into my head and I think of that SOB and what he did to you and what he said to me. *Puff the Magic Dragon*, man. Fuckin' cold, you know?"

Click. Pratt turned off the recorder. His eyes swirled to the back of his skull. The fuck am I thinkin'? reasoned Pratt. Probably never lived with the shit. What kinda man could? Probably swallowed a bullet by now. Nobody's ever gonna hear this. So why even try?

With that sole idea stuck like a knife between his eyes, Pratt gave up by flinging the microcassette player. The recorder shattered against the wall and fell to the floor in broken bits.

"Fuck that guy."

1

January 5. Interstate 118. Eastbound at Tampa. *The damned diamond lane,* griped Ben to himself, where two or more passengers in a vehicle constitute a legal carpool. That was the law in California. Just two people per car. Any people. A pair of pot-smoking teens. A van carrying two plumbers to their next appointment. A mother with an infant riding in a rear-facing car seat. Each a legal carpool. Hardly what state traffic and safety administrators had planned when carpool lanes were originally introduced back in 1985.

Ben checked the traffic in front of him, then his speed. It was just south of twenty-five mph. The temperature indicator to the right of the speedometer read ninety-two degrees Fahrenheit. It was the beginning of a second steaming mid-winter week. Not that irregular for Southern Cal. Still, all the news was abuzz with more nauseating talk about global warming. That alone was enough to make Ben sweat.

In the diamond lane to Ben's left, a blue Camry surged by at something close to eighty mph.

Nineteen-eighty-eight, recalled Ben, shaking his head. Back then it took *three* passengers to make a carpool. Back then it was reasonable to hope drivers would want to spare themselves the hassle of slow bumper-to-bumper commutes in exchange for ride-sharing and maybe some conversation with neighborhood co-workers. Back then any person violating the three-passenger rule would be hit with a hefty two-hundred-dollar traffic ticket.

But as it so often is with government plans, things worked out just a bit differently. For months and months those left-hand lanes of unencumbered promise remained practically deserted during the morning and afternoon rush hours, squeezing more traffic into fewer lanes. The average commute increased over one minute per highway mile. Traffic planners had never imagined that drivers would choose the increased expense of greater fuel and time consumption over a shorter commute with two caffeinated friends.

Before scrapping the mega-million dollar highway project and returning the "extra" lane back to the freeway at large, someone in Sacramento suggested "two." Not three, but two passengers to constitute a legal carpool. And just like that, along with the cost of changing a few freeway signs, daily commuters took to the "two passenger" restriction like ducks to water. Within weeks traffic eased by four percent as the left-hand lanes filled with willing participants. Commutes decreased. And the powers that be were redeemed and rewarded for their calculation and collective genius.

If they had only asked me, thought Ben. *Or anybody with a teaspoon of common sense. They could have saved California millions in start-up costs and more than a year of nearly empty diamond lanes. I would have told them two was wiser and suggested authorities apply a simple and ancient axiom: three's a crowd.*

Ben employed his turn signal for a safe lane change. It wasn't yet 9:00 A.M. and eastbound traffic on the 118/Ronald Reagan Freeway was inching through the Los Angeles County community of Chatsworth. The January sun was angled perfectly to create annoying reflections off the Sunday-waxed hood of Ben's new Volvo S80. The sedan was an upgrade from his last Volvo four-door and the Volvo four-door before that. Ben would recommend getting a new car every two years to his clientele, just to keep up with the latest advances in vehicle safety technology.

Ben lowered the visor to protect his eyes from the glare. Each squint cut deeper lines into a nearly forty-year-old face that was clean-shaven and blue-eyed under a conservative cut of short brown hair. Still handsome enough—or so teased his wife Alexandra.

The diamond lane hugging the center meridian was, as usual, breezy and unobstructed. Drivers pushed their cars well over the sixty-five mile per hour speed limit. But not Ben. He knew better. It was his job to know better about lots of things.

Ben's cell phone trilled in a very phone-like manner. Not one of those customized pop-music ringtones. Just a normal, dental office ring. He pressed SEND on his mobile and let the hands-free Bluetooth do the work. Both hands back on the wheel, he could now safely talk and drive.

"Hello," he answered, despite knowing full well who was calling.

"Hey, Ben," answered the familiar voice of Josie Jones, Ben's gal Friday.

"Morning, Josie," said Ben.

A Nissan Z screamed down the diamond lane, low to the ground, customized for illegal street racing. Ben mentally clocked the rice rocket at better than 90 mph. Josie never heard the speeding Z, but could almost make out the sound of creaking leather as Ben firmly re-gripped the steering wheel.

"Do you know why diamond lanes are a mistake?" asked Ben.

"Uh, no. But you're gonna tell me, aren't you?"

"Not if you don't want to know."

"I don't want to know," teased Josie.

"Okay. What's on you mind?" asked Ben.

"I was kidding," said Josie. "I wanna know."

"You really want to know?"

"I super seriously really wanna know," said Josie. "If it's your business to know, then I should know."

"Fine," said Ben, pleased. "It's a three-factor error. Factor one is the open highway theorem. Put Lucy behind the wheel on an unobstructed highway and she will often unconsciously drive at an unobstructed pace regardless of the speed limit."

"I didn't know that," Josie said patiently.

"Factor two, Ethel is in the lane closest to the diamond lane. That lane is usually obstructed and the difference in pace during rush hour between the diamond lane and the obstructed lane can sometimes be fifty or sixty miles per hour.

"And factor three?" cued Josie.

"If Ethel has a passenger, qualifying her to drive in the diamond lane, and if Ethel gets fed up with her slow commute, sees the speed at which Lucy is getting to her destination, Ethel is likely to want to switch lanes."

"That's what I'd wanna do . . . Correction, that's exactly what I do. So what's wrong with that?"

"What's wrong is that you'd glance into your side view mirror, see if it's safe and pull into the diamond lane. Right?

"Right."

"By looking into your side view mirror, can you gauge the difference between a car driving at fifty-five miles per and eighty-five miles per?"

"I dunno. I suppose—"

"Stop supposing. You can't. CHP can't. They've tested it. In a side view mirror, those speeds look the same at a glance. And a glance is all most drivers in heavy traffic can afford to give without smashing into the car in front of them."

Ben was rolling now, picturing the situation in his mind, reeling with evidence and spewing without regard for time or usage minutes. "What kind of car you drive?"

"I drive a Jetta," answered Josie.

"Average car, average acceleration. Zero to sixty in seven or eight seconds. It's roughly the same differential if you're driving at fifteen to twenty miles per hour. To accelerate to the speed of the oncoming car takes about eight seconds."

"Okay. This is higher math territory. I still can't determine all those seventh grade problems where the train is going so many miles per hour and the car going the other direction is driving a different speed—"

"I'll make it simple," interrupted Ben. "Statistically speaking, Ethel can't accelerate faster than Lucy can safely apply the brakes. Big wreck happens. People die."

Ben's summation had the tonal finality of a surgeon delivering the bad news. The patient has expired.

"Okay," said Josie. "Important safety tip. Now, why I was calling was—"

"It gets worse."

"Of course it does," said Josie. "It always gets worse."

"Josie?" asked Ben in a smiling tone. "You wouldn't be mocking me?"

"I would never mock the man who signs my paycheck."

"Now you're kissing my ass."

"Dying to know why it gets worse," said Josie, sarcasm between a drip and a trickle.

"During normal traffic jams, fatal accidents are minimal because of slow-moving cars. Factor in a fatal accident during rush hour and how the hell are emergency services going to respond in a timely manner? Traffic is already backed up. It triples the time of first responders to the accident."

Ben took a much-needed breath and suddenly worried if he had missed his exit, then added, "The whole diamond lane thing is a first-class government fuckup."

"What isn't?" quipped Josie.

"You're calling about the Carson plant," guessed Ben.

"How'd you guess?"

"I'm a good guesser."

"Some assistant plant manager keeps leaving voicemails. He sounds pretty anxious."

"Tell 'em I called my guys at OSHA and got their inspection pushed until I submit my recommendations."

Of course you did, reasoned Josie. If Ben Keller informed the Office of Safety and Health Administration that he was a paid consultant for Foster Farms, they would put inspections on hold under the direct assumption that Ben would convincingly keep any and all chickens out of harm's way.

"Anything else?" asked Ben.

"Not much. Jack Stein had to cancel lunch tomorrow, it looks like that tire recall is going to go through, and World Toys has a question about a shipment of kids' jewelry they just got from China. Oh, and you got a weird-looking, registered letter that says PERSONAL all over it in purple Sharpie. Want me to see what it is?"

"Nah. It can wait. Probably nothing. Gotta go now," said Ben before smoothly merging his Volvo to the right and into the paired traffic lanes earmarked for the southbound Interstate 5.

By the time Ben finished the commute to his Burbank office he had forgotten about the curious letter. It was an uneventful low-key day. With no big fires to put out he was able to catch up on returning emails and touch base with some clients about recent legislative changes. With ever-changing government regulations there were always new and higher standards that his clients had to meet. They trusted Ben to keep them safe from consumer and employee lawsuits and stiff federal and state penalties should they be found in violation of any codes or policies.

Before folding his laptop promptly at five, Ben went to Google Maps to see what the drive home had in store for him. He scrolled along the 5 and 118 freeways and mercifully saw nothing but green and yellow lines. He should be home by six. All red and that would have meant anywhere between seven and nine and a cold plate waiting for him in the microwave.

Ben made his way to his Volvo. As he pulled his keys from his shoulder bag he also happened to pull out the forgotten and unopened padded envelope marked PERSONAL. The package tumbled down in an arc and landed behind the car's front tire. Ben stooped to pick it up, sat in the car, buckled his seatbelt and turned over the engine. Curious, he unzipped the envelope's pull tag and discovered a CD along with a handwritten note.

He shoved the disc into the CD player and unfolded the letter.

> *Dear Mr. Keller,*
>
> *My name is Debbie Pepper. It is with a heavy heart that I write this letter. I am enclosing a recording made by my father, Arthur Pratt on his deathbed at the Indiana State Prison at Michigan City He mentions a crime which may unfortunately be of interest to you.*
> *May God Bless you and keep you,*
>
> *Debbie Pepper*

Ben felt chilled. He wondered just how long he had been sitting there rereading the succinct letter. At some point, the Volvo's air conditioner had mysteriously switched to full arctic blow. The temperature in the car had to be sixty-two. Yet Ben was sweating. He finally guided the setting back to AUTO and the fan slowed. That's when Ben heard the voice. Arthur Wayne Pratt's voice, barely audible, as if whispering through his car speakers. Without thinking, Ben jammed his index finger at the eject button. The whispering stopped and the player gently spit out the CD.

"Christ," said Ben aloud.

Ben knew instinctively that listening to the CD while driving would certainly be unsafe for him. Not to mention the other drivers on the road. The CD would have to wait.

⁊⁊⁊

Alexandra Love Keller was a true blue Valley Girl. Born and raised in the suburban hills overlooking Tarzana, she was the youngest of three children born to Maurice Keller of the famous Keller Karpet and Flooring. One of her earliest memories was a television image of her late father pitching wall-to-wall shag. For a time, her old man was a genuine Southland celebrity. "As recognizable and tan as a TV weatherman," Maurice would often boast to his youngest child. Of course little Alex was only four and at that tender age, there were no TV stars bigger than Big Bird and Elmo.

Unfortunately for Maurice the celebrity factor, fueled by a thousand dinner-hour commercials, proved to be the downfall of his first marriage. With Keller Karpet and Flooring showrooms expanding as far away as San Diego, Alexandra's beloved father was spending so much time south of Disneyland that he felt oddly compelled to start a second family. At the time of Maurice Keller's death-by-heart-failure he had garnered eight children, two ex-wives, and a mountain of red debt. What leftover assets not picked over by banks and the government were eventually held in trust—the Keller Family Trust—shared equally by the thirty-eight-year-old Alexandra and her seven siblings. Alex's stake was by no means a fortune. But the trust did provide her with enough of a stipend to provide an early retirement from her not-quite-flourishing singing career and a small college fund for her three daughters: Elyssa, Nina, and Betsy.

"Nina!" barked Alex. "Where's your sister?"

"Which one? I've got two," quipped Nina, only nine but a wiseass in the making. She wouldn't look her mother in the eye, preferring to mentally catalogue the miles of breakfast cereal choices.

"Betsy," answered Alex. "Just find her, will you?"

"After I make my choice."

"Now or there'll be zero choice."

"Almost done."

"Cold oatmeal for the rest of your life."

"Fine!" spat Nina, trudging off down the supermarket aisle to search for her six-year-old sister.

Strange how the world has changed, thought Alex. Cold oatmeal of all things. What was repugnant to her middle child had been a breakfast favorite of hers since she could remember. "From the old country," her father would say to her. From Russia. Cook the oatmeal, chill it overnight, and serve with warm molasses on top. Like bread pudding. Alex had wisely chosen not to share the story with her girls. Not yet. Not while she could still use the threat as leverage.

Next on Alex's list were rice cakes, applesauce, and tomato paste. Like some über-organized moms, Alex had a list neatly ordered by supermarket aisle. Like Patton she refused to battle through the same real estate twice. And if she missed an item, one of her girls was there to fetch it.

"They don't have the soy milk Ben likes." Eleven-year-old Elyssa appeared from behind Alex. She was holding two different half-gallon cartons of soy milk, fully expecting her mother to choose.

"You pick," said Alex.

"No way," answered Elyssa. "Then it's my fault if he doesn't like it."

"If he doesn't like it, he won't drink it," said Alex flatly.

"That's so wasteful."

"What's more wasteful?" asked Alex. "Buying a half-gallon of soy that Ben won't like or wasting time and gas driving to another supermarket that still may not have what Ben likes?"

"Okay. So choose," the eldest persisted, pre-adolescence infecting her tone. "My arms are getting tired."

"Find Nina and Betz. Have Betz eeny-meeny-miny the soy milk. She likes to do that."

"Whatever." Elyssa spun on her Converse All Stars, tucked those cartons of soy milk under her arms like footballs, then trudged off to find her sisters.

Alex checked her watch. It was two minutes shy of six. Home by six-thirty, she calculated. Set the girls to homework, begin preparing dinner by seven. Ben would let her know when he would be home. There would be a voicemail, email, or text message. He was good that way. No mystery or big surprises. Ben was steady, stable, and predictable.

Ben was safe.

The thought made Alex smile, ever mindful of the times in her life when everything seemed unsafe. Especially unsafe were the men she had been with and the substances she had experimented with. Especially unsafe was her first husband and the father of her precious daughters. God rest his tortured soul.

By the time Alex had piled eleven bags of groceries and her

three daughters into her black Escalade, she had checked all her electronic sources for messages from Ben. So far she had received none. It was odd, but she expected she would hear from him any minute. He was that regular.

But Ben wouldn't call or text or leave a voicemail because he wouldn't need to. Ben was already home.

"I'm not a well man. Docs say the fuckin' cancer's just about everywhere. But that's just the shit they say. I never seen it. Nobody had a mind to even show me a picture. Cons get no goddamn respect."

Remote control in hand, Ben unconsciously rode the volume on the CD player. Every time that hollow voice inhaled, Ben experienced an irritating, high-pitched whistle. An audio anomaly produced somewhere in the transfer. Ben could have simply filtered out the annoying noise by reducing the high frequencies on the equalizer. But that assumed Ben could move more than his right thumb. It was volume up, volume down. Dry swallow. Then wait for the next mumble of recorded words.

Ben had the blackout shades drawn in his backyard office. The office was above a game room, roughly paneled with board-and-batten painted a country cream. The room sported an open-beam ceiling and an old school fan that never stopped turning. The furniture was a mix of warm oaks and leather. The single wide window overlooked a coral-blue swimming pool. The pool itself was horse-shoed by a 1995 two-story, stucco family home. The Kellers' home was on a cul-de-sac snugly fit into the planned community of Vista Viego. "Vista" suggested foothills and the two hundred-plus houses in the development had sweeping views of the incorporated city of Simi Valley, California.

"Fuckers use all these words. Curse words to make people sick. Like what . . . Like glioblastoma. Don't remember most big words but that ugly fucker stuck in my head. Bet if I said glioblastoma ten times on this tape you'd get the cancer too. Fuckin' glioblastoma. Hope the docs get it just so they know that the shit feels worse than it sounds."

Glioblastoma.

Ben thought maybe he had heard or read about the disease. Glioblastoma described a difficult-to-treat brain tumor. Cellular phones? wondered Ben. Maybe those university studies were on to something. Cell phones were going to kill everybody. The final human solution courtesy of Nokia and Motorola.

"Like you give a shit about my problems. You don't know me and I don't know you. Already said that, I think."

Damn straight, thought Ben. He didn't know the voice at all. Not a whisper of recognition. So why the hell was he still listening, rapt, cemented to his reclining desk chair? The gristled voice escaped from the speakers in a disembodied, poorly recorded, and cryptic monotone. As Ben listened on, he felt the sweat from his neck coagulating between his lower skull and the leather headrest.

The voice grew weary.

"Suppose you're tired of me babbling . . . Suppose you want to know what this shit's all about."

At every pause or broken thought, the automatic gain on the original recording would elevate as it sought to register the thinnest decibel. This provided an increased hiss that Ben found irritating. He instinctively lowered the volume, but then found himself leaning forward, listening more intently. He could hear the old con's breathing slow, a certain sign that either sleep or death was just around the corner.

"Tired," popped the voice. "Tired of holding it in. Tired of remembering the pictures in the papers. Just pictures. Your wife and baby girls. Twins, I think. Did I read that or was that a picture too?"

A rush of heat surged inside Ben. It was a sudden autonomic thrust of blood turning his skin pink and squeezing fresh perspiration from every pore. His stomach tightened.

"Was right around them riots. I was in County and there was a guy who'd just got popped for beatin' on his girlfriend. Happiest guy to ever get popped. Happy cuz he was inside while the cops were outside lookin' for the guys who did it."

Doors opened in Ben's mind. He could actually see them swinging free like those of a saloon. His thoughts and memories flooded through without the usual interceptors.

"Anyway. He wasn't braggin' or nothin'. He was relieved. Why he told me? Fuck knows. I coulda turned him over. Made a deal for somethin' but I figured he knew I wouldn't. I was pure convict. Code and shit."

Lunch, thought Ben. *I didn't eat lunch. Otherwise I would be vomiting.*

"Guy didn't think he'd go down for it. Said it was real clean. No evidence. In, out, cash, jewelry . . ."

Another silence came, followed by a room-shaking hiss, like a giant gas valve had blown and was filling the room with nothing but earth-moving sound waves.

"Twins. That's why I remember. It was the twins. See, I met some evil fuckers inside. Why they made the inside, man. Had to have a place to put all the evil. But this one, he got out. Free bird and hell if anybody ever knew what he did. Hell if you knew what he did. Maybe he got caught. I just never knew. Was those little twin girlies that stuck in me. Those sweet little faces."

Those sweet little faces.

"Lea and Mae," uttered Ben.

Names he hadn't spoken in years. Not a single whisper. Twins. His precious girls.

"Mom looked kinda pretty. And young, I guess. Were you that young? Suppose we all were once."

Sara, thought Ben. This time his lips didn't move. Surprisingly, he remembered her often. More so than the baby girls. He wondered why that was. *First real love? Only real love?* Questions he had learned not to ask. Not if he wanted a real life again. Not if he wanted to move on.

"Stu," said the voice. "Guy's name was Stu. Stu Raymo. Cons called him Stuey. I might be old, but I didn't forget that one. Evil fucker killed those sweet faces."

Stu Raymo didn't register for Ben. He was good with names and phone numbers. Faces too. Ben was so good at matching the faces with the names and the numbers he would often see the face, think of the phone number, then pull up the name. Stu Raymo had no face or number. He was just a name served up by a faceless voice. *Why?* wondered Ben. *Why that voice, that name, and that moment? Why now? Why me? Questions without answers,* thought Ben—*anchors that keep life from moving on.*

"Stooo-ey," said the voice, purged and groggy now, inviting sleep. "Stooo . . ."

"Evil fucker!" shouted Ben, kicking over a nearby floor lamp before succumbing to tears. He wrapped himself tight with his arms and pulled his knees up. The sobs came faster and harder than Ben could ever remember. Painful wrenchings, eventually bringing on an involuntary sleep.

Ben would later calculate that he was out for nearly an hour, snapping to from what he thought was an earthquake. His chair was vibrating as was just about everything else in the office. The loudest racket came from a wastebasket full of recyclable diet soda cans. Wall to wall, the room itself was physically buzzing. As Ben reclaimed consciousness he soon discovered the remote control still in his fist, the volume maxed. Five hundred watts of electronic nothing were surging through the 5:1 speaker system. The subwoofer had caused so much vibration that objects in the room had seismically shifted.

Ben stiffly rose from the chair, ejected the CD from the tray and with shaky hands, repacked it and buried it deep in the back of his top desk drawer. It was 6:16. Alex and the girls would be returning home any minute.

Ben managed to get through the rest of the evening on autopilot and after lying about having post-lunch-food-poisoning, none of the girls expected him to sit at the dinner table.

The evening assumed the usual tag team effort. Ben drilled Nina on her spelling, played good cop to Alex's bad cop on the subject of Elyssa's failed pre-algebra exam, and cuddled with Betsy for the umpteenth reading of *The Runaway Bunny*. Ben did his evening rounds without any indication whatsoever that there were stirrings underneath his usual sunny demeanor. Nobody, not even Alex, suspected a rearrangement in Ben's inner chemistry—that an emotional wrestling match raged just beneath his skin. He seemed merely himself. Ben. And for a short while even Ben believed it too. That he was himself.

Until, of course, the bedroom lights were extinguished and Alex curled into him. After Ben complained that his stomach was still cramping, Alex kissed him good night, wished for him a better tomorrow, then quickly sailed off into seven easy hours of sleep. She was magic that way. A true talent. No matter what her workload or level of anxiety, Alex could go horizontal, flick a mental light switch, and be snoring before Leno's opener.

As Ben twisted toward the flat-panel screen, he upped the volume two notches before surfing the TV He was searching for a program engaging enough to occupy his mangled brain, but narcotic enough to lull him to sleep. The exercise proved fruitless. For no matter what channel he rested on, at the precise point his body gave in to sleep, his subconscious would come alive with the same soul-jarring propaganda. Sounds, faces, snapshots from the past rushed in. Smells even. Crime scene photos. Not to mention the voice on the CD. Who was that anyway? Was he dead already? Did the cancer kill him? Ben hoped so. Ben wanted the voice dead. Wished for it. Even prayed.

"Who's Stu?"

Had Ben imagined Alex's voice? He could feel her breathing, slow and steady, and was certain she was asleep. That was until Alex asked, "You awake, hon?"

"I am, now," lied Ben.

"I asked who is Stu?"

"Don't know what you mean."

"You said some names. Sounded like you said Stu and Sara."

Had he actually fallen asleep? How else would Alex have heard the names?

"Musta been talking in my sleep," said Ben.

"Sounded kinda creepy."

"I don't remember."

Alex folded herself in closer to Ben, molding her body to fit his.

"You're warm and sticky."

Ben took her hand, briefly fondled her wedding ring then pretended he was going back to sleep.

"Anything you wanna talk about?" she asked.

"No . . . Everything's okay."

"Mmmm. Awake now." Alex stroked Ben's thigh, knee to hip. "Wanna fool around?"

"Stomach's still a little . . ."

"Okay. Feel better. G'night."

And then she was gone. Asleep again. Her gift at work. The invitation for sex, he reminded himself, was her conditioned response to anything that was "Sara." Psychologically speaking, it was perfectly normal. Healthy even. As long as Ben didn't use his dead wife as emotional leverage, Alex could express her natural possessiveness with sexual affection without recrimination.

Funny, thought Ben. *When the subject of Alex's dead husband bubbles up, the last thing I want is a 1:00 a.m. screw.* He made a mental note for their next couple's session, then slid from bed. Sleep was no longer an option that night. Or denial. Ben needed to go back out to the office, dig the CD out of his desk, and listen to it again. Not all of it. Just the bits at the end. The hard parts about Sara, the twins, and the stranger named Stu Raymo. If he had learned anything from twelve years of grief counseling it was the following: the only way out of an emotional wreck is a good road map.

No time like the present, thought Ben.

2

"SAFETY FIRST!" answered Josie. Those were the exact words that Josie Jones used to answer the office phone. Every time. Even if caller ID informed her that it was her own mother at the other end, Ben's instructions were crisp. Every call should be answered identically. She thought it was a bit silly, but of course she had said *yes*. After all Josie wanted to keep her job. Soon after she had rationalized it all as a branding thing. Like with TV commercials or advertising. That and it could appear extremely unprofessional if clients were waiting in the lobby and she answered the phone with a simple *hello*. But that assumed clients actually waited in the lobby for Ben and they usually didn't. Ben's Burbank office was rarely visited by anybody other than overnight delivery men.

"I'm sorry," Josie continued on the phone, "Mr. Keller hasn't checked in yet." She was lying. "No, sir. But when he calls, I'll give him the message that you've called twice."

Josie hung up, spun to her computer, then tagged the phone

sheet with a note to remind Ben that Mo Lessberg from Cramp
and Freed Metal Stamping had both called and emailed twice
without a response. Precisely three mouse clicks later Josie had
returned to her task at hand: rockin' to a homespun playlist
on iTunes and "Googling" every conceivable variation and
permutation of the name Stu Raymo.

Stuart James Raymo . . . Stuart John Raymo . . .

A mere twenty-three years old, Josie didn't really mind her
job. After nearly a year, she had discovered she liked the autonomy
of it, the daily research challenges, changes in pace, hours, not
to mention the serious lack of dress code to fit her post-punk
proclivities. She was dyed and pierced, and tattooed with her
favorite Looney Tunes characters and when asked, would insist
that Sex Pistol Sid Vicious was murdered by Britain's MI5.

Stuart Raymo, Sr. . . . Stuart Raymo, Jr. . . . Josie had even
grown to like the three-story, post-fifties office "cube" where
Ben leased a fifteen-hundred-square-foot office suite. With its
dungeon-like underground parking, switchback stairs, and an
elevator reserved for deliveries and the handicapped, the 3rd
Street building was, at first, a turn-off for the UCLA graduate.
Strike one, she had thought. After all, it was Burbank. And
Burbank was uncool. So working in Burbank would, most likely,
be equally uncool.

Strike two for Josie was her interview with the safety-fixated
Ben Keller. Her initial impression was that he was anal, paranoid
and unbending, but sort of funny in a dark way. She forgave
Ben his obvious afflictions and annoying traits only because
she was aware of her own front-office shortcomings. During
their three meetings prior to her appointment, he hadn't once
made mention of—or reference to—her piercings and body
art. Of course, since Josie Jones had taken the job Ben hadn't
stopped referring to, inquiring about, or needling her about her
counterculture appearance.

Stewart Raymo . . . Steward Raymo . . .

In the end, Josie liked her job. And she was good at it.

"Safety Thirst," answered Josie in a chipper tone. The LCD
readout on the phone had shown that it was Boss Ben phoning

from his mobile. She grinned widely to herself and waited to
find out if he had heard her answer the phone right . . . or wrong.

"It's me," said Ben.

"And how are you today?" asked Josie.

"Did you just say Safety *Thirst*?"

"*Thirst*? As in *Thirsty*?"

"Yeah. Safety *Thirst*. Did you have dental work this
morning?"

"No. Why would I have said Safety *Thirst*?"

"I dunno," said Ben, shrugging off the bother. "Must be the
cell connection. Did you get my email?"

"Stu Raymo. Got it."

"You found him?"

"Oh… no," said Josie. "Got it—as in the email. Not him.
Sorry. Google's got loads of Stu Raymos. If this is a new client,"
Josie anticipated, "maybe if you gave me his business I can refine
the searches."

"Not a new client," said Ben. "Just a favor for a friend. Work
comp claim."

"Why not give it over to Woody?" Josie asked.

Woody Bell was the private investigator Ben kept on
retainer. Woody specialized in workmen's compensation claims
in work environments already under Ben's consult. If there was
fraudulence in a claim, Woody Bell would find it, document it,
and serve it up cold.

"Woody's too expensive for—"

"I thought Woody was on a retainer," argued Josie, sounding
altogether as if she was trying to pass off the chore. "Sorry. You
gave me the job and I'll do the—"

"Different kind of friend," answered Ben. "That and
Woody's working on something else for me. Just see what you
can find, what he does, where he is, boil it down to something I
can read tonight."

"Fine. But which Stu Raymo?"

"All of 'em," said Ben before hanging up.

"No problem. Talk later," answered Josie to the dead phone
line.

She lowered the phone to the cradle and examined her nails. The punk-styled press-ons were hot-wax black. Each bore a skull and crossbones. *Shit*, she thought. *Skulls were punk. But skulls with crossbones were abso-fucking-lutely not punk. Skulls with crossbones were all about pirates. Kid stuff*, she thought. *Johnny-Depp-Jack-Sparrow-Pirates-of-the-Caribbean-kid stuff.* As Josie began ripping each plastic nail from her cuticles, she rewound the conversation she had just had with Ben. There was something off about her boss. Oh, and Ben was odd enough. She was certain of that. But he was never, if ever, rude. Ben always said, "Goodbye." Ben always left her with a feeling that the glass was half-full.

Strangely, Josie's stomach felt empty. And as suddenly as the craving for a glazed Krispy Kreme and coffee came over her, she put the phone on "voicemail" and skipped all hundred and forty-one pounds of herself out the door, down two flights of stairs, and paid little mind to oncoming traffic as she rushed headlong across 3rd Street to satisfy her urge.

Indeed. "Safety First" may have been Ben's credo. But it wasn't hers. Krispy Kreme, coffee, then find more Stu Raymos.

While Josie was digging up whatever she could on the cornucopia of Stu Raymos in the world, Ben was neatly trying to bury the idea of Stu Raymo deep into a more manageable part of his psyche. To accomplish the feat, Ben accessed his unfinished second book, *Ben Keller's Guide to Grief Relief, Version 9.0.*

A coping counselor had once warned Ben that consuming all available information on the subject of grieving amounted to eating a battalion of African elephants with a single toothpick. Hardly Confucius, thought Ben, who was still undeterred in seeking the wisdom of others. Within the untold volumes of conflicting philosophies on coping, Ben was determined to find the answer to his uncertain solace. In time, he had absorbed so much written advice he thought he might add his own tome to what he had come to call the "Library of Lament."

Chapter Eight. Subsection 22. Exercise.

The sleepless night that Ben had listened over and over to the unwelcome CD had been followed by an early-morning exit.

He had left a sweet note encased in a pink heart for Alex and the kids on the kitchen chalkboard. Pink was still Betsy's favorite color. Ben had rolled the Volvo out of the driveway at dawn, drifted quietly out of the cul-de-sac, then surged down Tapo Street. He had bypassed his regular gym, the Simi Valley Fitness Club, in favor of the 24 Hour Fitness in nearby Northridge. There he could pay a daily fee and be pretty certain to avoid stumbling into someone he knew. Ben wasn't emotionally prepared for conversations, bullshit or otherwise.

At the gym he had furiously pounded on a treadmill while sandwiched between what appeared to be an age-impeded rock musician and a reality TV wannabe. Ben had ignored the wall-mounted TVs with their closed-captioned early-morning news, tuned out the piped in pop music, and concentrated on squeezing out as much sweat as his body could muster. Ninety minutes and a steamy shower later, Ben was back on the freeway.

Chapter Seventeen. Subsection 7. Reboot Your Emotions and Make a Plan.

The plan had been formed long ago. All Ben needed to do was resurrect it and execute it in order to fully reorganize his emotional structure. By no means was he attempting to purge everything. This would be a mere spring-cleaning—sweeping the cobwebs out and gently placing the dark memories and sick feelings back in their respective closets. So Ben proposed for himself a day of spot-visits to some of his manufacturing clients.

It was a five-factory circuit. Ben would drop in unannounced, put on his former OSHA inspector's hard hat, and conduct a surprise safety review. He called it *ambush and frisk*. And if it was good for clients, it was even better for Ben. The day would be all about number 2 pencils, checklists, ratings, flowcharts, subtotals, and final scores. Ben would even find good juice watching the Volvo's odometer tick over each mile.

Five factories, five cities. There was the window manufacturer in Santa Clarita, the solid rocket fuel plant in Glendale, the hardware wholesaler in Monrovia, the freight distributor east of downtown Los Angeles, and the airline seat subcontractor in Van Nuys. The circuit took nine hours. Each plant scored a passing grade.

Chapter Five. Subsection 1. Feed Your Wounded Soul.

For Ben, feeding meant eating healthy. And eating healthy meant gathering, prepping, and cooking a large meal. Between ambushes, he had sent a text to Alex, informing her of his plan to cook that night. The text back was a vintage jab: *about fucking time!* She had later followed with another text consisting of nothing more than Xs and Os. Alex understood the general subtext of Ben's occasional need to cook. After all, she had been there too. She had often joked they should coauthor a book and call it *Coping with Cooking.* That was until one Christmas when an unthinking relative gave them a glossy book bearing the exact same title.

Once again, Ben avoided running into anyone he might know by visiting a supermarket in nearby Moorpark. He packed his shopping cart with enough food to feed his entire cul-de-sac and drove back to his Simi Valley home where he busied himself in a kitchen that Alex had so well-appointed and stuffed with gourmet quality appliances it appeared ripped from the pages of *Bon Appétit.* Ben efficiently served a meal of herb-roasted chicken smothered in a pineapple and tangerine chutney, baby asparagus tips, a mixed green salad with glazed walnuts and mangos, and a wild rice pilaf. Of course, as an accommodation to young Betsy, there was also hot Kraft macaroni and cheese and steamed broccoli with Heinz ketchup.

Then came the post-dinner roundup of homework, baths, and bedtime stories. The rejuvenated stepfather energetically hummed through his routines, even clowning for his children with an impromptu impression of Pee Wee Herman. Ben lovingly refused calls for an encore and kissed the girls good night before retiring to the master bedroom suite and the thick manila envelope that lay on one of the twin fireplace chairs.

Alex was already at her nightly post, a corner desk built into a wall-length custom cabinet unit stuffed full of books, DVDs, and a built-in entertainment center. As the volunteer editor of the Simi Canyons Country School monthly newsletter, she was shuffling photo files on her widescreen iMac.

"You seem extra-chipper tonight," said Alex.

"As opposed to . . ." prompted Ben.

"Last night."

Ben lied, "Don't feel any different."

"Right. You're the same exact guy."

"Yup. That's me." Ben was peeling the tape off the large envelope, winding it around his fingers.

"You cooked," said Alex. "Anything we need to talk about?"

"What's to get? I needed to cook so I cooked."

"And it was yum. Did I say thanks?"

"You just did."

"Had a good day?"

"I did. You?"

"Usual."

There was a quiet comfort in their conversational shorthand. A contained brevity that spoke volumes. Alex remained focused on her computer screen while Ben prepared to read. There was little, if any, eye contact. The comfort was in their proximity to one another and the quiet found in their respective chores.

Ben slid the printed stack from the envelope the courier had dropped off just before dinner. He didn't count, but by weight he guessed it to be just shy of two hundred pages bound for easy perusing. With all her piercings and body art, Josie might look the part of a flake. But damn was she thorough. A born researcher.

He fanned the pages, stopping on occasion to browse the content. Clearly there were many Stuart Raymos, including variations on both first and last names. So Ben began skimming from page one. There was Stuart Raymo, the Cadillac dealer in Secaucus, New Jersey. Stuart Raymo, the author of military history texts. One Stuart Raymo in Michigan was listed as having scored a hole in one on a 137-yard par three at West Lakes Country Club. There were Stuart Raymos in Arizona, Mississippi, and South Dakota—all three, teachers. Two Stuart Raymos were listed as deceased, one of them single, the other a loving husband, father of four, grandfather to eleven, a twice-decorated Vietnam veteran, and loyal Notre Dame fan to his death.

Ben suddenly slammed on the brakes.

What followed was a sudden eye-peeling examination of one particular Stuart George Raymo and his arrest record. This Stuart Raymo had been arrested twice for sexual battery. He had served time in prison. The rapist Stuart Raymo—according to Josie's research—was born in Carson City, Nevada. He had a spotty arrest record dating back to 1985. He had last been arrested in Reno and was currently serving a twenty-two year sentence in a California state detention facility in Oakland. His last arrest was in 1998.

Ben drifted. Oakland. As an OSHA inspector he had spent a fair amount of time in the Bay Area. Oakland had a significant manufacturing base. In his mind, Ben drove stretches of road he could recall, searching left and right for any tall barbed-wire fences he might have missed. A guard tower even. He tried to imagine what a modern prison would look like from the outside. Concrete and razor wire. Not unlike most Oakland industrial parks. He could have been next door to Stuart George Raymo without so much as a clue.

Included was a mug shot of the villain. Stuart George Raymo, as last pictured, had a drawn, jowly face, long ears, and an Adam's apple large enough to stuff in the mouth of a Christmas pig.

Did you kill my wife and baby girls?

"What'd you say?" asked Alex?

Ben twisted in his chair. Alex hadn't turned around, only queried from her perch.

"Did you ask me something?" asked Ben.

"I asked what you said." Then Alex turned, looking directly into him. "Sounded like you asked me something."

Ben hadn't asked a thing. Not out loud. At least he thought he hadn't.

"Must've been reading aloud," said Ben.

"Bad enough that your lips move when you talk," teased Alex.

Ben ignored her, masking his rush of guilt by flipping pages. It wasn't verboten to speak of his ex-life. His deceased family. They weren't forgotten. Just rarely mentioned. Not ignored. Just in the past. Ben had moved on.

Hadn't he?

Ben stuck a mental Post-it to his brain. And before turning off the bedroom TV, he emailed Woody Bell and passed on his questions about Stuart George Raymo of Carson City, Nevada. When he finally closed his eyes, darkness closed in quickly and he was asleep before he could utter a prayer. Ben never felt Alex climbing into bed, nor heard her gentle belly laughs during Jay Leno's interview with comedian Carrot Top. His sleep was hard and dreamless, interrupted only by the trill of his cell phone at seven-thirty.

"Yeah," Ben answered, paying no mind to how groggy he was. After all, it was seven-God-damned-thirty!

"Gimme somethin' harder," said the voice. Woody Bell, Ben guessed. It wasn't that Woody's voice was so easily recognized. It was his unmistakable timing and manner.

"Just woke up," grogged Ben.

"Seven-thirty, man. That house of yours? Everybody's up but you."

Ben rolled over. Sure enough, Alex was nowhere in sight. As his senses sharpened, he could smell bacon and oatmeal cooking. He could hear the distant whine of a gardener's leaf blower. All that was missing was the sound of girls arguing.

"Ben?" said a voice from the doorway. Ben twisted and focused. Nina had her arms crossed. The middle child was about to tattle on one of her two sisters. Even Las Vegas odds makers would have had trouble determining the likelihood of which sister had harmed dear freckled Nina.

But Ben guessed anyway. "Got a fifty-fifty shot. So lemme guess. It was . . . Elyssa."

"Betsy!" stamped Nina. "She took purple markers and drew hearts all over my composition book!"

Ben was holding up his cell phone to Nina, twisting it in his fingers so the child couldn't mistake his priority. It was the universal sign of stepdad's-too-busy-to-arbitrate-your-silly-sibling-conflict-right-now.

"Fine!" said Nina. But instead of leaving the room and taking her argument elsewhere, Nina just stood her ground and waited.

"You still there?" asked Woody.

"What was too easy?" asked Ben.

It was an honest question. For a moment Ben had forgotten what task he had assigned the private investigator. The good night's sleep had momentarily scrubbed his brain of all concern.

Mental note to Ben: *You've moved on. Bravo.*

"Stuart George Raymo."

The name snapped Ben back to consciousness. His stomach turned slightly. Or was it just morning hunger triggered by the sweet smell of breakfast cooking?

"You wanted to know what this Raymo guy was doing in August of ninety-five," confirmed Woody. "The email?"

"Yeah, that's right," remembered Ben.

"Stuart George Raymo of Carson City was doing eighteen months in an Idaho pen for possession and burglary."

"Sure about that?" asked Ben.

"Already faxed the sheets to your office," said Woody. "Should I refax 'em to the house?"

"No," said Ben. He was sitting up now, legs hanging off the bed with his toes brushing the hardwood floor. The hard sleep had left him with a stiff neck. He unconsciously kneaded it with the knuckles of his right hand.

"August ninety-five," Ben repeated, wondering if he had his dates right. As if Ben could have forgotten the date of the most horrific event in any person's life, let alone his.

"What happened back then?" asked Woody.

"Just . . . something," answered Ben. Instinct told him to end the discussion. He sought help from Nina. "Look. One of the girls needs me so I gotta go."

"Rest is in an email. Talk to ya." Woody hung up. Ben shoved his mortal memories and plastered on a smile for the near-ten-year-old.

"What about blue markers?" asked Ben.

"Purple markers!" barked Nina.

It was morning. A radiant new Southern California day. And Ben was driving. He slowed at the corner of Alamo and Stearns. It was 8:14 on a Wednesday. Ben had the red light at that intersection timed to forty-eight seconds. He looked on his dash. There sat his BlackBerry that held his phone book, calendar, and email. He knew that in the forty-eight seconds allotted by the red light he could safely check his email. Or he could dial a number and let the Bluetooth do the rest so he could drive and speak hands-free, reducing the risk of accident to himself and others. That was the smartest option. The one recommended by everyone from Triple A to Arnold Schwarzenegger.

Safe was always an option.

Ben's daily credo. He repeated the same ad nauseam to clients and friends at nearly every opportunity.

Ben chose to review his email. It was a three-click move. All with his thumb: button, scroll, button. It took all of two seconds. Then three more seconds to scan the little yellow "unopened mail" icons and their senders, leaving forty-three seconds to choose a message and read it. Ben unconsciously chose an email from Woody Bell. Only Woody's missives were always sent as attachments. The speed documents downloaded depended entirely on the quality of the mobile connection. In those quiet seconds Ben watched the phone's progress bar and remembered a study that claimed drivers were far less distracted by their cell phones than other things such as reaching for items in the glove box, applying makeup, wolfing down a Jumbo Jack while keeping the secret sauce from staining a dress shirt, and—worst of all—maintaining a state of peaceful détente between backseat-riding siblings.

Ben hadn't planned to actually read Woody's email while waiting for the signal to change. He only wanted to peruse it for importance then determine if he needed to pull off the road so he could safely digest it. The connection appeared clean and efficient. Ten seconds to download. Ben glanced upward to make certain the signal was still red, then down to the screen on his BlackBerry.

47 . . . 48 . . . 49 . . . 50 . . . 51 . . .

The light remained red as Ben counted in his head. *I must have miscalculated.* Either that or an emergency vehicle was bounding down Alamo Street. The local firemen and cops had transponders in their vehicles that automatically extended the "green time" of traffic signals, thus extending the "red time" at the intersecting boulevard. Ben looked left, then right. He saw no emergency vehicles nor heard any sirens. Still that signal remained cherry red.

So with his BlackBerry still in his right hand, Ben glanced downward at Woody Bell's delivered email. The note was succinct and easily read without so much as a single blink:

Found something Josie missed. Stew Raymo Remodeling and General Contracting. North Hollywood. 818-555-5999.

Ben blinked and reread the twelve-word message. He found himself stuck on the word *Stew. As in goulash*, he thought. A mishmash of meat and vegetables. Josie had fine-tuned her searches on everything from Stu to Stewart. But not the definition of last night's mélange sealed and refrigerated in Tupperware.

Stew? What kind of man calls himself Stew?

Then came the scream. It was Ben's scream. A sharp shock-of-a-noise that escaped his lungs—a result of the auto-electric jolt served courtesy of his central nervous system in response to the giant air horn blowing at his rear bumper. When Ben's eyes finally found the rearview mirror, all he could make out was the chromium grill of a semi-tractor trailer rig with the name "Peterbilt" spelled backwards.

The traffic light had somehow clicked to green while Ben was in a fog. Exactly how long had it been since the signal had turned? Two seconds? Five? Ten? Before Ben could switch from the brake pedal to the accelerator, the air horn blew again. And this time Ben heard every frequency. The sonics of the air horn made the Volvo's windows hum while sending another bolt of adrenalin directly into Ben's foot. The pedal hit the floorboard and rocketed the car forward. Normally, Ben's good driving habits would have had him checking both directions before pulling into the intersection. But history had taught Ben that habits, good or bad, were easily nullified by a hasty helping of primal fear. His lizard brain had ordered his body to get away—and fast.

Ben eased off the gas only after he had spun the Volvo onto the freeway on-ramp and the diesel rig had disappeared from all his mirrors. The interior temperature of the Volvo was a cool sixty-seven degrees Fahrenheit. Still, Ben twisted the air conditioner hard to the left until the arrow was pointed at the snowflake icon. He needed it cooler because he had already sweat through his dress shirt.

"Hello," answered a voice that sounded hurried and out of breath. Ben had pulled off the freeway at Tampa Avenue and found a parking space in the shadow of a Whole Foods Market. Without planning what he was going to say, let alone his true motive for making the call, Ben had dialed the number Woody had emailed him. After five rings a woman answered. When Ben asked to speak with Stew, she informed him that Stew was on site and could be reached by his cell phone. She politely paused, breathing heavily into the phone until Ben said he was ready to write down the number. Then in the nanosecond before Ben was about to say "ready," the out-of-breath woman asked, "You a client?"

"Just lookin' to talk to Stew," Ben answered, almost too cryptically.

The lull that followed sounded anything but patient. The woman's heavy breathing had vanished, replaced by an air of suspicion as she delivered the number. *Wife*, thought Ben. *Or jealous girlfriend*. Ben's vague response to her simple question had set off alarms in the woman.

"Why don't I take a message for him? Just in case you don't catch him on site."

"I'm sure I'll get him," Ben assured her. "No big deal. Thanks a lot."

Ben clicked off.

In the near silence of his car he could still hear the tone of the diesel's air horn in some auditory memory synapse buried deep in his brain. And the poor woman, he thought. He had cold-called a number with little forethought, asked to speak with her husband, and then made it sound like he was trying to make a drug deal.

Sometimes you're a real dumbass, Ben.

The cell number was scribbled across the front of a gas station receipt. Ben pressed it up to the windshield, letting the daylight bleed through, further blending his quick scrawl with the thermal printing on the paper. What Ben was hoping for—wishing for even—was a feeling, a divining rod to his gut that would tell him the truth. That by simply staring at a phone number he would instinctively know if the possessor of that phone number, the man attached to that one cell phone, was the same man who had butchered his family.

But no such feeling happened. *How could it?* reasoned Ben. *It was just a stupid phone number.* Only by meeting the actual man would Ben be able to tell. He would shake the man's hand and look him in the eye. God knows he had seen it in countless movies. Like Christopher Walken in *The Dead Zone*. Then Ben laughed at himself. What were the odds, anyway? Of all those Stus and Stewart Raymos Josie had unearthed, what were the chances that "Stew" Raymo, General Contractor, would be any kind of killer, let alone the man who had personally flushed all that Ben once thought he would ever love.

"This is Stew," answered a voice that sounded like a mixture of ground glass and a lifetime of Marlboros.

"Hi. This is Martin Benjamin," Ben lied. "I'm looking for your site but I think I have the wrong address."

"One-three-nine-eight-eight Camellia," said Stew. "Studio City. That do ya?"

"Yeah, I gotcha," said Ben before Stew hung up, ending the connection as quickly as it had begun. *Easy*, thought Ben. The lie he had prepared would remain unwrapped. *Soon enough,* thought Ben. Studio City was just off the 101. A ten-minute drive. With rush hour traffic? Twenty minutes.

Then Ben would shake Stew's hand and know.

Pamela Raymo's stomach was grinding up a storm after the weird phone call. She chewed two Tums and chose to carry on with her self-assigned chore of cleaning out the garage. Sure, it was a guy's job. Something the man was supposed to do on weekends between church and ball games. Pam even had a strapping hubby who swung a hammer for a living. A classic man's man. Still, when the marital duties got divvied up in the Raymo household, somehow Pam got the garage. It was mostly her mess, anyway, Stew had argued. Old shopping bags loaded with everything from discarded kitchen utensils to years of old tax files. Quarterly, Pam would pick a sunny day, empty the garage of clutter, toss out half the junk that had built up and find shelf addresses for everything else.

But damn that Stew!

That phone call had pissed her off. The caller was cryptic and way short of forthcoming. The trust button in Pam had been pushed again. And by whom? In the aftermath she tried to convince herself that the unfamiliar voice could have belonged to anybody. A subcontractor. A lumber supplier. A building inspector. Or maybe just an old chum who didn't think he needed to answer to his old drinking buddy's suspicious wife.

So Pam used the garage to work up a sweat. She checked her heart rate. One hundred thirty beats per minute. *Faster*, she thought. Her goal was two hours at 140 b.p.m. That's the kind of burn she could dine out on. After finishing up, she would shower and call up Stew, suggesting they eat out that night. Don Cuco's in Toluca Lake. They would order a pair of Diet Cokes and a tub of guacamole as a starter. Then as Stew sucked the salt off the tortilla chips, he would watch the platters of margaritas roll past and recount his twelve steps to sobriety.

And count all the women you fucked that I don't know about.

For all Pam knew, the unknown caller could have been another pissed-off boyfriend or angry husband, looking to hang

Stew for his Happy Hour conquests. There were days when she wondered if Stew was going to die with his own claw hammer buried in his skull.

The phone rang. Pam reached and picked up the cordless unit on the half-ring.

"Hello."

"It's me," said Stew.

"So it is."

"What's that supposed to mean?"

"Nothin'."

"Bullshit," called Stew. "What'd I do now?"

"I said nothin' and that's what I mean," calmed Pam.

"Okay . . . So what are you doin'?"

"Garage."

"Finally," said Stew.

"You could come home and help."

"And you could get me Mikey's new shipping address," goosed Stew. "Think it's on a Post-it next to the computer."

The garage was detached from the house. *And for good reason*, thought Pam. In most single-family dwellings, a garage was built for one or two cars and served as a shield against the elements. But in Pam's world of calendar-year sunshine, the garage was brimming with junk and clutter so she could keep her house neat and free of consumer chaos. Though on the smallish side, the Raymos' single-story house was a postcard for *Martha Stewart Living*. Pam even subscribed to the magazine. Every month when a new issue arrived, she would secretly puzzle over who she had become, who she wanted to be, and what the "old honeys" would think of her now.

"You got it yet?"

"No," lied Pam.

The house had three bedrooms. A master suite add-on in the rear and two bedrooms that faced the street. One was a converted office—aka "Stew's Room." The other was for the baby that hadn't yet found its way into their lives. "A room filled with hope," Pam would call it. She had even furnished it with the fundamentals of a newborn's necessities. If only their baby lawyer would call her back. He teased her with tales of young Russian mothers who, for a fee, were happy to give up their unwanted children to American couples. Pam cursed herself for all the abortions that had left her body able to conceive, but unable to carry a baby to term.

Stew's Post-it was right where he said it would be. "So who called you?" Pam asked.

"Who called me when?"

"I dunno. Thirty minutes ago. Some guy. Wouldn't say why."

"Not a clue. Wanted to know where the site was," said Stew, sounding incrementally annoyed. "Got plumbing inspections today. Probably him. You got Mikey's address yet?"

Pam swiveled in Stew's desk chair, the Post-it stuck to her chipped nails. She thought of having a mani-pedi as a reward for her efforts in the garage, but that would require first showering the stink off and applying some makeup. Not that she needed any. Her skin was tan, thirty-years-old going on ageless. Her hair was naturally blonde and short enough to be called low maintenance. All she ever needed was to shampoo it and shake it out for her to look like a million bucks. The rest of Pam was small enough to dance in a teacup. She stood barely five feet tall, but was so perfect, yet cartoonish in her proportions that in photographs, she could easily be mistaken for a six-foot swimsuit model.

Pam fanned herself with the Post-it as she guessed whether or not Stew was telling her the truth.

"Your office is a mess."

"My office," said Stew. "If it's not next to the computer, try the phone."

"You know that guy who called. His voice sounded a lot like that Pilot Guy—"

"You on that again? Jesus, Pam!"

The Pilot Guy, remembered Pam. He was shacked up with the Cheesecake Factory Hostess Girl who Stew was conveniently pounding during the hours he was supposed to be playing twilight golf with a client. When Pilot Guy suspected Hostess Girl was cheating on him he began secretly dialing every number stored in her pink, designer mobile phone. The Raymos' home number was saved under the give-away heading, "Stew's Ex-Porno Wife."

"Not the same exact guy," saved Pam. "Just the same kinda cryptic I-don't-wanna-give-my-name-tone—"

"You wanna start a fight? Is that what this is about? C'mon, P'Amazon."

P'Amazon. That was Stew's pet name for his beautiful wife. When he used the word it usually sounded like he was begging for mercy. He didn't sound guilty. So Pam decided to cut him some slack.

"Got it," she said.

She read Stew the address on the Post-it. Before neatly replacing it next to his computer screen, she grabbed a Sharpie and drew a red heart on it. "Let's go to Don Cuco's tonight."

"Sure," he said. "Gotta go, babe."

"Love you," said Pam.

But Stew was gone. That was his way. Gotta go and hanging up. Getting on with the next phone call or nail he had to drive. And certainly never waiting around for the gooey "love you" part.

3

STEW SNAPPED HIS Nextel shut and holstered it into the clip on his belt. For the briefest of moments he was enveloped in his bubble, his ears plugged by the sound of his guilt and rage. *I should've just played golf*, he vexed to himself. The shaming thought was counterbalanced by another more common inner voice that screamed: *That nosy fucking ball-busting bitch! She fucked how many men before she met me? Five hundred? A thousand? Inside out, upside down, two ways, three ways, in one hole and out the other?*

But Stew loved Pam. That much he knew. He loved the way her hair smelled at daybreak, the way she would fuck him any way he demanded, and the way she had made the second act of his life seem almost normal.

And she's still pissed at me for banging some Cheesecake Factory girl instead of playing stupid twilight golf?

The sounds of pounding hammers penetrated Stew's skull.

Agreeably so. To him, it was the sweet cacophony of progress. A constant pitch of metal against wood, driving steel, circular saws, and hydraulic nail guns. Stew purged his anger, then with his long legs, strode across the small residential street to stand at the bottom of the ramped driveway. Once there he briefly stopped to admire his biggest venture yet. This wasn't one of those fast buy-it-and-flip-it remodels that had been his recent stock in trade. This was far more ambitious. The next level.

What had once been a classic pre-war San Fernando Valley ranch was gone but for the original dirt, a flat rectangle corralled on three sides by a rickety ivy-covered fence. The modest eleven-hundred-square-foot house had been replaced by a wood and steel skeleton that would soon be two stories and nearly four thousand square feet of a brand new five-bedroom home. The financing Stew had scraped together proved enough to beat out twenty other real estate speculators in a quick-claim foreclosure auction. Stew had obtained the design and engineering schematics cheaply from an Internet site specializing in black-market blueprints. And while the new architectural footprint ate up most of the lot, there would still be room for what most Southern California buyers demanded—a swimming pool.

Including interest on the loan, the estimated total cost of the endeavor was never far from Stew's brain. $922,000. If the current real estate market held, Stew would be able to sell his spec house for somewhere between one point eight and two million. *That's more than an $800,000 profit*, thought Stew. Not bad for a year's labor. He might even have enough left over to lease Pam that Mercedes station wagon she so dearly lusted after.

If she stops busting my fucking balls.

Stew liked to keep his crews small. "Less chatter and faster hammers," he would say in Spanish. He was surprised that at the age of forty-one, how much practical use he had made of his required two years of high school language.

The crew consisted of four general laborers and a crew chief named Henry, the only legal citizen of the bunch. Stew didn't bother to find out where any of them were from. Guatemala, Nicaragua, El Salvador. They were all beer-drinking, Tejanodancing Mexicans in his book. He paid them cash, faked their check stubs and kept his workmen's comp paid up.

Brown faces. That's all Stew wanted to see on his construction site. So who the hell's the vanilla stick? wondered Stew. Who's the nervous-looking white guy ducking the falling two-by-four stubs?

"Watch out, will ya?" shouted Stew. The man was clearly no building inspector. Building inspectors were usually retired contractors who knew their way around a construction zone.

"Are you Stew?" asked Ben. His nerves were so wrecked he had wanted to turn around the moment he stepped foot on the property. He could have too. So why didn't he? Was it because Ben possessed some strange need to follow through, no matter how stupid the idea? Pratt's audio recording had clearly rattled him. For two days now, he was off his game and out of the safety of his own safety zone.

"And don't lean yourself on my new windows!" barked Stew.

In trying to avoid the falling two-by-four tails, Ben had lost his balance and was in the process of steadying himself on a squarish tarp-covered pile that he thought was wood or sheetrock.

"All glass," said Stew. "Could put your arm right thought it and hurt yourself."

Ben stood in place and assessed the big man who nimbly bent and slipped between a window frame and wall joist. He quickly billed Stew to be well north of six feet, heavy-beamed at the shoulders, with a dwindling patch of blonde curls and a face rounded by years approximating his own.

"Not safe at all," finished Stew who, on approaching Ben, had transformed himself from annoyed general contractor to a grinning, inspector's best friend. He obviously thought Ben was some kind of official "whatever" and that it would be best to put on his most winning front with a broad smile.

"Stew Raymo," said the big man.

"Martin Benjamin," lied Ben.

And there it was, Stew's outstretched hand, friendly, wrist twisted to two o'clock, palm facing upward. All Ben had to do was grip the man's hand and he would know whether Stew Raymo was the devil. At least that's what he had reasoned an hour earlier while stuck in eastbound traffic.

But not a stitch about Stew stirred anything in Ben. Nor was there any hint of déjà vu. Stew, as he appeared to Ben, was a complete stranger. As if the two men had never, ever met. Their paths never crossed.

Ben didn't need the handshake. His heart he believed, had already weighed in. From the second he had heard that big voice and set eyes on the easy lumberjack of a man, he felt that he had truly erred. This Stew wasn't a killer. On first impression alone, the contractor was exactly the kind of man Ben would have hired to run a residential construction site. Athletic and commanding, with the right dash of authority. Stew had that air of a former college tight end who tilted brews with his old football gang on Saturday afternoons.

Ben felt plain awful. In his mind, the morning was already a huge mistake. He needed to shake the man's hand, tell a few more of his rehearsed lines, then get on with his present life as soon as humanly possible.

Move on, Ben. Move on.

"What can I do for you?" asked Stew.

With that, Ben gripped Stew's hand and shook it. And just as he expected, the only tingle he felt was from the heavy calluses on Stew's palm. While inspecting factories, Ben had shaken many such hands in recent years. The rougher the hands, he had learned, the better the intel on the factory's work conditions. Hands like Stew's rarely lied. At worst, they might spin things a bit for the management upstairs. But overall, rough palms could be trusted.

And no Dead Zone *moment*, thought Ben. *After all. It was just a frickin' movie.*

"I'm with OSHA," announced Ben, going ahead with his rehearsed dialogue.

Stew's eyebrows clinched for a moment. His eyes slightly narrowed. Then when he let go of Ben's hand, his face turned into a human question mark. Maybe he hadn't heard so well over the ringing of a circular saw spinning to a stop.

"You say somethin' about oceans?"

"Oh-Sha," pronounced Ben. "Office of Safety and Health Administration. We monitor safety and health conditions."

The rest would be easy, thought Ben. He was still lying, but from his own comfort zone. Though he had since moved on from his government job, the back-and-forth patter was second nature. A little history. OSHA overview. An eight-hundred number for Stew to call in case he had any questions. Then, maybe, Ben could crawl back to his Volvo with what little tail he had left between his legs.

"Okay," said Stew. "I got it. Isn't that for factories and stuff? I'm pretty up on all the city and county regs and I don't remember—"

"A workplace is a workplace," interrupted Ben. "Primarily, I'm just here to get a first look around, take a few notes, then I'll generate an initial summary. After that, we can talk."

"And what if I'm not up to standards?" asked Stew. "Are there fines?"

No, thought Ben, *there would be no summary report and no follow-up conversations.* Stew might sweat a week or two waiting for a fax, but after a month he would feel as if he had dodged a regulatory bullet. He wouldn't be dumb enough to follow up. No contractor would actively seek out fines or penalties. And Stew would never see or hear from Ben again.

"So far everything looks dandy fine," said Ben. "Might want to run some warning tape across the steep stuff. A couple of red flag stakes next to your pilings . . . How about your second-story guys? They got steel toes like you?"

"Unless Nike makes 'em," said Stew. "But what they don't have I'll buy. I'll take care of it."

Ben had one more recommendation and the sales job would be complete. It had to be something ridiculous only some overzealous bureaucrat in government could have concocted in the name of blue-collar concern. Something even Ben would find frivolous and dumb.

"What about cups?" asked Ben.

"Cups? What kinda cups?"

"To protect the genitals," said Ben. "Athletic cups."

"Like for baseball and shit?" asked Stew. "You gotta be kidding."

"Look," said Ben, posturing as if the advice he was going to give was about doing Stew a favor. "Let's say one of your guys is walking a beam and falls the wrong way. Takes a hard one in his junk. You don't want your workmen's comp getting sucked dry because Jose can't get it up no more. Know what I'm saying?"

"That's crazy," said Stew.

"I don't write the rules," shrugged Ben. "Good news is that athletic cups are cheap and purchased at any sporting goods store. While you're there, pick yourself up a half-dozen cycling helmets."

"My guys gotta wear helmets?"

"No actual regulations yet," said Stew. "But they're lighter than hard hats and offer more protection in a high fall."

A little added value, figured Ben. And not the worst idea. Hard hats only offered protection against objects falling from above. But nearly zero protection for falling humans. As Ben stood there with Stew, a lobby group representing cycling helmet makers was proposing new workplace rules.

"Christ Almighty," said Stew. "And I'll get all this in your—"

"Called a Workplace Safety Summary," finished Ben. "Otherwise, you're good to go."

As Stew was shaking his head in disbelief, his words were wisely conciliatory.

"Well, thanks, I guess," said Stew. Once again, Stew offered his outstretched hand. "It's Marty, right?"

"Ben," answered Ben by rote, before quickly catching his own error and correcting with, "Benjamin. Martin Benjamin. My mom's the only one who calls me Marty."

"Sorry," apologized Stew. "Lousy with names."

Stew hung onto Ben's hand. The handshake was well past the stage of formality. It was time to unclasp. But Stew kept a firm grip for an uncomfortable two seconds longer before letting go.

And once again, there it was—the curious clench between Stew's eyebrows. The puzzled look. A human question mark.

"Have a nice day," said Ben.

"Yeah. You, too. Thanks for comin' by."

Run, thought Ben. Escape. While you've gotten away with it.

Gotten away with what? Not embarrassing yourself?

Ben wondered what sick part of him was so pitifully paranoid. And what other parts were still sane and rational. His soul felt in conflict with his brain. After shutting and locking the door to his Volvo, he sat in the seat and performed a mental check. His heart was pounding but his mind seemed crisp and aware. He took a cleansing breath. He was mostly okay, he reasoned. Wise even. He had realized his mistake the moment he had met poor Stew Raymo. He had deftly danced his little OSHA jig though his conscience heckled him for going ahead with the whole cup and helmet ruse. Ben's retort was that it was a harmless prank. And he had been so rattled he hadn't had the faculties to deviate from his practiced script.

Then, before turning over the engine to his car, he cursed that evil raspy voice on the CD who had planted the seed.

"Christ, Ben. It's not healthy!" he spoke aloud to nobody but himself. "Let them go."

Jesus, please, help me let them go!!!

RIIIIIPPPP!

Ben heard the sound before realizing just what he had done. His fingers had slipped into a crease in the sunroof's veneer, his right biceps had flexed and with that, torn a piece of upholstery.

The involuntary act frightened Ben. He sucked back the sobs and drove away so nobody could see him. No one to witness his private pain. On the drive to his office he would need to rework through the critical steps of grief recovery in order to slide the heavy lid back over his emotional abyss.

Stupid ass. What can you really know from a handshake?

A simple handshake.

Stew couldn't get over his sudden flu-like symptoms. When

he touched the hand of that what's-his-name inspector, it was as if all the blood in his body had surged to his face. And it had remained there, just below the surface, pushing out beads of sweat for the morning breeze to chill.

Then his stomach turned.

A demon, thought Stew. Not the inspector. The vanilla-faced man appeared docile enough, and beyond his official role, devoid of threat. It was feeling the presence of demons of the personal kind that usually made Stew's face flush and his joints ache.

One of your own demons, Stew.

Fuck that, Stew said to himself. He had plenty of demons. All of 'em as old as he. And he had beaten them down more often than they had beaten him. The demons were the losing team in Stew's book. Ten years straight, sober, and violence-free. In his head, the score was clear. Stew - 10. Demons - 0. A good goddamned rout.

And I own your demon asses.

And with that primal notion, the blood spilled back into Stew's body. His face cooled. The pain in his bones released.

Stew found himself blanketed by the shadows of his illegal laborers. He twisted and squinted up at the rafters. One man was holding a heavy four-by-eight Glu-Lam into position while another balanced between two beams, hammer ready, waiting for the joint to be fit. Stew noted the distance between his high-wire workers and the concrete slab below. Stew's brain turned to the ever-increasing costs of his workmen's compensation insurance.

"Friggin' bike helmets," muttered Stew to himself. "Can think stupider ideas."

"What's that?" asked Henry. The crew chief was behind Stew, swirling up a fresh bucket full of Quikrete.

"Yeah," said Stew. "Lunchtime, I want you to run over to Sports Authority and pick up some bike helmets."

"Bike helmets? What for?"

"Just get 'em," barked Stew. "Helmets and some athletic supporters. Kind with the cups."

"You're messing with me, *Jefe*." Henry liked Stew's casual style. The two of them—boss and crew chief—needled each other constantly.

But Stew shook his head. "Just do it, will ya?"

End of conversation, decided Stew. He hopped off the slab into what would eventually be the backyard pool. He figured he could use a good swim.

A swim and a blowjob.

After dinner, thought Stew. A meal, a naked swim with his beautiful, porno-licious wife, maybe a little online poker, then a deep, demon-free sleep.

ᘔᘔᘔ

Woody Bell was so fat that sometimes he would tell people he bought his clothes at Home Depot. It was good for a quick laugh and dispelled the discomfort most new clients felt sitting across from the self-described inspiration for Jabba the Hut.

"Last I checked," said Woody into his handsfree phone rig, "I was four-hundred seventy-five pounds, give or take a ton."

"You are seriously joking," said his feline source inside the California State Corrections Office.

"Then again, last time I got weighed they had to use a marlin hook."

"You don't call often enough," she said.

"Stuff I usually need's just a couple clicks away."

"Anything you can't find out about a person?" teased the voice, sounding more southern belle than Nor Cal divorcee.

"Let's try," said Woody. "All I need is the name on your birth certificate and a social."

"Not me," she said, giggling softly.

"Yeah, you. Now, c'mon. Gimme some sugar."

Gimme some sugar.

That's how Woody started every damn day. He would say the words aloud when he woke. He would say them after he had broken his first sweat, wrenching himself from his heavy duty bariatric bed into his custom wheelchair. He also said them first thing as he waved his hands over his magic computer keyboard.

Ah. Gimme some sugar.

"Right now?" she asked. "I've got work to do."

"You and me both. That means my work cancels out yours so stop your stalling and gimme. Birth name and—"

"Social," she interrupted.

Over his headset, Woody heard that soft girlish giggle. Inside he tingled somewhere he could no longer touch without the aid or a nurse or a prostitute.

The back bedroom where Woody plied his trade was permanently dark, curtained with a blackout material called Duvatyne. The fabric worked two ways. It kept him focused on his three computer screens. It also blocked his view of the empty backyard swimming pool that he wouldn't have a prayer of ever swimming in again. If only his mom and dad had known someone like Ben Keller. Maybe life would have turned out differently for Woody. Maybe someone like Ben could have warned his parents of the spine-crushing dangers a backyard swimming pool possessed.

"Amy June Aitchison," she said. "That's A-I-T. . ."

He wouldn't tell, but Woody knew precisely how to spell her last name. And his fingers were way faster than her slow civil-servant cadence. If sweet Amy June could only see him, parked in his doublewide wheelchair with hydraulic lifters, docked at a u-shaped desk with three thirty-six-inch computer screens.

"What about your social?"

While Amy June quietly reeled off her social security number, a soft electronic gong sounded. This was Woody's cue to attend to the virtual chessboard on his left-hand computer screen. His online opponent, a not-so-deftly-named "bobbyfisherking7362," had impatiently put the private detective on a warning clock. If Woody didn't move within thirty seconds, he would have to forfeit the match. With two quick keystrokes, Woody snatched the queen and sent his opponent's king on the scurry.

"How long's this gonna take?" asked Amy June.

"Almost there," said Woody.

"No way."

"Way," said Woody, unashamed to sound as if he was parroting that dumb movie, *Wayne's World*. "Shame" wasn't a word reserved for the nearly five-hundred-pound paraplegic. Shame was for Catholics and boys caught masturbating by their moms.

"You were born in seventy-one. Graduated Oakmont High School in Roseville, California in eighty-nine. Junior college. You've been married and divorced twice. First was sixteen months. Second was five—"

"TMI already!" said Amy June with added exasperation. "Christ Almighty."

TMI. As far as Woody was concerned, there was no such thing as Too Much Information. The insurance policies left over from his old man's death had long been exhausted. Without an information glut, how the hell was a paralytic gumshoe like him supposed to pay the utilities, the cable bill, let alone tip the pizza delivery man?

"We're not even at the good stuff yet."

"Good stuff?"

"Credit rating, bank balances, outstanding debts, where you bought your last pair of panties."

"You do not know that!"

"Got a thirty-nine dollar charge here. August. Nordstrom."

"You put that back!" she squealed.

Nice reaction. As if he had actually opened her panty drawer and was waving her pink lacies for the world to see.

And then when she had calmed down a notch: "How in Sweet Jesus do you do that?"

"My database, their database. Some legal, some not-so. Some are subscriptions, some are offshore. Lemme put it this way, if it's intel, somebody's either selling it or buying it."

Of course, it was far more complicated and demanded more skill than he would ever let on. But boiled down, the modern private detective was a digital information whore.

"Got a picture of me?"

"You're a redhead. California Drivers License #N65748699," read Woody. "See you got a birthday coming up, too. Don't forget to renew."

"I'm soooooo impressed. But I'll bet with all the databases and stuff you still can't tell what's in a girl's heart."

"Biggest mystery to me is does the carpet match the curtains."

"Does the carpet what?"

"Match the curtains," repeated Woody.

Stumped, the sweet-but-slow Amy June asked, "What's that supposed to mean?"

"Well, the picture says you're a redhead . . ."

Woody listened to the vacuum of sound coming from the other end of the phone line. If it weren't for the sound of her phony-baloney fingernails scraping the handset as she covered the mouthpiece, he would have thought she had hung up on him.

"Amy June?"

"You know, I just asked my girlfriend what you meant and she said you're sexually harassing me."

"Do you know what I meant?"

"No. I still don't get it."

"If you don't get it," asked Woody, "Then how can I be sexually harassing you?"

"But what's it mean?"

"So what about the email?" asked Woody, instantly bored. All the fun had been wrung from the conversation. That and bobbyfisherking7362 was gonging again.

"Your email said to call," reminded Woody. "So here I am."

"Somebody just throw somethin' cold on you?"

"Icy Big Gulp," said a flattened Woody. "What do you got?"

"Somethin' you didn't get."

"Impress me."

"Your Stew Raymo?"

"What about him?"

"Didn't come up as an alias cuz it's not."

"What was it, then?"

"A partial," she said. "Old correction files that never transferred so good. Happens every so often. Lopped birth dates, criminal codes. I've seen murder ones turned into aggravated assault."

"So . . . ?"

"Stew Raymo, aka Stewart Raymond. No middle name or initial."

Bobbyfisherking7362 had conceded the chess brawl and was upping the ante for a new game. These were money games that Woody played with half his brain tied behind his back. The board was already reset and Woody was IM-ing his opponent in an attempt to quadruple the bet.

"You want the file or what?"

"Yeah, yeah," said Woody. "Can you send me a PDF?"

"Can you send me a dozen roses?"

"On the way."

"Hey, wait," she said. "I just got it . . . The carpet thing."

"Two dozen," said Woody, sparked and re-engaged. "And I'll sign it, 'with affection from Justin Timberlake.'"

From Ben's Simi Valley home his average commute time to his Burbank office was forty minutes. No short haul for a man who, if he had chosen, could have run his consulting business from the converted room above his garage. But Ben liked the locals-only feel of Burbank. It was, at its heart, a factory town, lazily clinging to the eastern slope of the San Fernando Valley. And though its own city fathers dubbed it the *Media Capitol of the World*— home to NBC Television, Universal Studios, ABC-Disney, and Warner Brothers—its true roots were in aviation. Starting in World War II, hundreds of thousands of men and women had been employed in Lockheed's Burbank factories—factories Ben had since walked through as a safety consultant—designing and assembling military aircraft from the P-38 to the U-2 spy plane to the more recent F-117 Nighthawk.

To Ben Burbank was blue-collar and homey and near perfect. If it weren't for the damned parking at his office. The underground lot had originally been designed for a maximum of fifteen cars. How and who the hell had upped the number to twenty-two cars was a mystery. So double-parking was a daily ballet. The eleven tenants divided the spaces both equally and unequally. Everybody had two spaces. But who was double-parked and who was blocked always depended on the time of day and willingness (or not) for people to get along, exchange keys, or trust one another when moving someone else's car.

For Ben the politics of the building's parking situation was too much for him to stomach. Not to mention his certainty that in a 7.0 plus Richter earthquake the parking lot would be pancaked in a heartbeat. So Ben chose the game of street parking. There were always plenty of spots available—only the streets were metered for one and two hours. Success depended on running downstairs to feed the meter before the city parking enforcers stuck him with a ticket.

"Parked on the street?" asked Josie of her boss. Ben was barely halfway inside the door. That's how Josie said hello in person.

"And good morning to you, too."

"Late morning. Gimme the time and I'll feed the meter," offered Josie.

"Thanks, but I'll feed the lollipops," said Ben, briefly recalling the last time he had left her in charge of dropping coins into the meter. As great as Josie was, her best asset was also her number one liability. Time management. Josie could get so deep in her research that she would lose track of the clock. And that had cost Ben nearly two hundred dollars in parking tickets.

Still, Josie kept on offering every day Ben stuck his head through the door.

"Sure about that? I got lotsa quarters."

"Let's work the bulletin board," smiled Ben, happy as hell to be back in a controlled environment. Pushing into his official inner sanctum, Ben was calmed by the warmth of the space. Slightly larger than the outer office where Josie had a desk, Ben's office had three walls of old pine paneling painted in a slightly burnt orange hue called *Barrier Reef.* And though Ben had never been Down Under, he liked both the name and the way his framed set of black and white family photos popped against the color of a rich autumn sunset. The entire wall was peppered with pictures of Alex and her three girls. A former client had dubbed it "Ben's Constellation of Love."

On the paneling behind the old library table Ben used as a desk was a bulletin board. Opposite were a leather couch, a chair, and a simple oak coffee table where Josie would set up shop when Ben was in the office.

The fourth wall sported a large floor-to-ceiling window hung with vertical louvers. As much as Ben didn't care for the louvers, they were part of the original building design and removing them would have been a breach of the lease agreement.

Rules were meant to be followed.

There was the usual routine. While Josie set up her laptop and notes on the coffee table, Ben would put his feet up on the desk and log in to the Internet. He would casually browse emails and a variety of news and information sites while Josie orally worked through the phone sheet, new client profiles, and outstanding consulting reports that demanded Ben's once-over or approval. She would leave the payments due file for last, knowing that clients who didn't pay their bills in a timely manner would slightly rile her usually unflappable boss.

In their late-morning session, Josie would simply read, recite, and comment as she saw fit. Ben would interrupt when he had something to add. Sometimes his comments would be acute and to the point. Other times Ben would free-associate into any number of safety concerns, personal or otherwise. Josie would never forget the time Ben rattled on endlessly about knives and other sharp objects within the reach of curious toddlers. And though there was little data to support his fear, Ben couldn't bear to be in proximity of a child near something as benign as a butter knife.

"General Machine and Electro," said Josie, working from her new client file. "They are assemblers of everything from industrial generators to heating grills."

"What kind of grills?"

"The plug-in kind," she said. "The ones that get all orangey-red."

"You know how much power those pull?" remembered Ben. "Way back when, in my other life, we had this little house with hardly any furniture. Heater was busted. So I went to a hardware store and bought one of those little units for every room. Number one, the house was pre-war and had zero insulation. Number two, you should've seen my power bill the next month. And Daddy didn't have the dough to pay it."

"Oh, dear. What did Daddy do?"

Ben laughed.

"Sara took a temp job with Accountemps. She was seven months pregnant and answering phones for some dubious CPA group. She would come home and complain. Called them all Certified Public Assholes."

Josie was wise not to press for more information. When Ben would say, "Way back when in my other life," it was his code way of referring to his first family. His wife and twin girls. All tragically destroyed in a long-ago home invasion robbery. Weird. She couldn't remember Ben having ever having called his first wife, Sara, by name. Once or twice, when Ben wasn't in the office, Josie had trolled the LexisNexis database for more information. All that she had discovered was the coroner's report and a blurb from the *Los Angeles Times'* police blotter. That was plenty enough for Josie. Her boss had a deep wound inside. *From that wound he had transformed himself into a human miracle*, she thought. A man who had taken the horror from his life and built it into a safe little niche.

Ben had indeed moved on.

Josie continued, "General's thinking of starting an assembly plant in Compton."

"Tax break deal?"

Josie nodded. Ben was briefly ahead of her. California and the Feds had created a new set of enterprise zone tax breaks as an inducement for manufacturing companies to invest in the not-so-business-friendly state.

"Guy who called said they were on the bubble after going through AQMD and Environmental Regulators."

AQMD was shorthand for the South Coast Air Quality Management District. Since 1980 they had been trying to clean up Southern California's famously smoggy air. In Ben's mind, the AQMD was slowly winning the war, making it safer for children to wind themselves on the local atmosphere.

"Okay, I got it. Wants to know if OSHA regs are going to put them out of Compton," finished Ben. "Did you send them our rate sheet?"

"Uh huh. But they wanna know if you're negotiable."

"You told them no."

"Of course. But their guy said he was sure you and he could work something out. Something about a quality bonus if they decide to move ahead with the plant."

Inducement bonus, thought Ben, rolling his eyes. Assholes. They only wanted to engage Ben if he could grease the wheels between the company and the state safety cops. Maybe show them some cost saving short cuts.

Josie understood the situation as much as her boss. She knew how Ben would respond. He would say either, "pass" or "be polite, but say no." Still, it was her job to pitch the job. It was Ben's choice to swing or not. But Josie had already made the note to call the company back and deliver the bad news. *Good for Ben*, she would say to herself. Her boss was picky and had an actual backbone.

All she needed was Ben's official word.

So she waited. Patiently hunched at the couch, knees together, elbows pinned to her side, those danger nails quietly tapping out the punk tune in her head on the coffee table's top. When enough time had passed, she looked up at Ben. What she saw wasn't at all what she had expected. Ben had a way of turning into something Josie liked to call "the man on pause"— momentarily tuning her out while reading an email or online article. None of the moments lasted long. Ben would resume by saying, "What's next?" or "Where were we?"

But this wasn't the man on pause. This was her boss— Ben—stony and as if holding his breath. His eyes were wider than normal, unblinking while fixed on his computer screen. Then for just the briefest moment—maybe two seconds—Ben swiveled to the window, let his eyes reach infinity, rubbed his face, and returned to his monitor. Josie thought she saw him swallow hard, and confirmed it when he gulped again. But this time, something caught in his windpipe and he began convulsing with coughs.

"You okay?" asked Josie, rising to help.

Ben didn't answer. He put a hand to his chest, held still for a moment, then continued with that uncontrollable cough.

"I'll get you some water." Josie sprung to the outer office. The mini fridge behind her desk was always stocked with soda pop and bottled water. She grabbed a 500 milliliter bottle of Fiji and sped back to Ben. As Josie gave the cap a quick twist, hearing the familiar snap of breaking safety plastic, she also heard Ben croaking between hacks.

"I'm okay," Ben said. "Just . . ."

Ben looked up to find Josie was stuck in the doorway, water bottle at the ready. She was frowning at him with conditional concern. As if she wanted to help but was afraid to cross some invisible boundary.

"Seriously," said Ben. Something just went down the wrong way. "Here. Gimme the water and let's pick this up later."

"You're sweating," she remarked. "You getting sick?"

"Maybe," he said.

Josie handed Ben the water and he thanked her. Next, she gathered up her notes and laptop and returned to her desk.

"Mind closing . . ." Ben had meant to add "the door." But Josie understood anyway, softly clicking the door behind her like a mother trying not to wake a sleeping child.

The central air kicked in, sending an overhead wash of cold air through Ben. It instantly mingled with his sweat and gave him a shudder. At least he was alone. Nobody to see him drowning in his moment of abject fear.

Yet the face continued to stare back at him. It was a JPEG image attached to a concise email from Woody Brown. The picture, large enough to fill most of the screen, was a color mug shot of the one and only Stew Raymo—or Stewart Raymond if Ben could have gathered enough of his wits to actually read the attached note.

The image itself was scanned and faded, depicting a thinner, mullet-haired version of Stew only six days after turning twenty-seven years old. One could imagine the stubble surrounding the thin smile on Stew's face was leftover from a birthday bender that had ended with his arrest. The eyes of the criminal appeared drained and resigned to whatever punishment lay ahead.

It was hardly the picture of the affable man Ben had met only hours earlier. Ben had shaken Stew's hand. The hearty grip had been nothing more than that, giving back not so much as a twelve-volt tingle.

The coffee and muffin in Ben's stomach were mingling, rising fast. He spun in his chair and slipped to the floor, thrusting his head into a freshly lined garbage pail, vomiting everything.

Nightmares.

Stew Raymo hated nightmares and the lost sleep that followed after one had invaded his slumber. *Nightfuckers*, he came to call them after first hearing the word during one of his two adolescent incarcerations. And they had plagued him ever since. He lay awake after disconnecting from the bad dream, reoriented himself, rolled over and over, and almost constantly checked the bedside clock. It was only eleven minutes past two in the morning. He knew that trying to fall back asleep would be useless. So he slipped from bed, careful not to wake Pam.

The hardwood floors he had installed felt smooth and perfect to his bare feet. *A great wood product*, he thought. That baked-on factory finish was loads better and more durable than the old-fashioned sand-and-varnish styles some homeowners demanded. Cheaper too. Thank God for progress.

After peeing, Stew padded along through his usual post-nightmare route. Back corridor, dining room, kitchen, fridge, snack. Then he turned himself into a big lump in front of his big flat-screen, high-def TV. While flipping channels, he touched his gut. He had gained nearly four inches on his waist since Pam had started to turn his office into "the baby's room." Gone were the treadmill, flat bench, and free weights Stew used to heft into the wee hours. He used to fight back against the nightmares with sweat and heavy reps until he ached. He would finish with a half pack of smokes and a long walk to the corner pie shop for a cup of coffee and slice of sweet cornbread. Sure, there was a twenty-four hour gym that was close enough to walk to. But he hadn't yet found the charm in all that high-tech equipment lined up in modern health clubs.

And he had recently quit smoking "for the baby."

What fuckin' baby?

Pam wanted the baby something bad. And who the hell was Stew to deny her? She was pushing thirty years old and his instincts were telling him that it was either gain a baby or lose the wife. What the fuck? Stew had thought. He sure as shit would be a better daddy than his own.

The nightmare was sticking to him. Fifteen minutes, a guzzled Sprite and a half-eaten pastrami sandwich later, even the big screen TV couldn't wash it away. Not that Stew could remember exactly what had made the nightmare so freaking disturbing. It was more like an icy reflex. As if he had woken up, swaddled in cling wrap, his muscles aching to break some invisible constraint. That and this image he couldn't shake—three amorphous human figures, their clear, elastic skin bursting with a dizzying electronic snow like television static.

Stew's ears were plugged, too. After a dozen forced yawns, he stood, pinched his nose and gently blew, hoping that a change in atmosphere might clear them. His ears remained stopped up. *Possibly a head cold*, he thought, just before settling back into the sofa. He clicked the remote to DirecTV channel 605, The Golf Channel.

All for the baby.

Screw it, he decided. If he couldn't run the treadmill and lift free weights, damn if he was going to give up cigarettes.

It took him two minutes to dress, brush his teeth, and hit the sidewalk. He was walking fast. It was one block east to the lights of Laurel Canyon Boulevard, then two blocks south to the 7-11 where a reunion pack of Marlboros was waiting for him.

Ah. Cigarettes, coffee, and hot cornbread.

Then he thought of that inspector guy from OSHA. His name was Benjamin Something or Something Benjamin. He had a *snapable* neck. Prison had taught Stew to size up every new man the instant he entered his immediate vicinity. Since then, he divided men into two categories. Men whose necks Stew could snap in two. And men with whom he should keep peace.

Simple.

And the OSHA guy was from the snapable side of the gene pool. *His bad luck*, thought Stew. Why the hell Stew was thinking of him during the short walk to the 7-11 was a mystery. Was it just some random switch in the fuse box of his subconscious? Or was Benjamin Whatshisfuckinname hiding somewhere in that lousy-assed dream? All Stew knew for sure was that the more he thought about Ben, the more the cigarettes were calling him.

So Stew began to jog.

Across the boulevard, half a block to his left stood the sputtering 7-11 sign. One of the fluorescent tubes needed to be replaced. *Going on three weeks now*, thought Stew. It annoyed him when simple things didn't get fixed right. Where the hell was the maintenance crew? All Stew needed was a ladder, a new six-foot tube, and his DeWalt power driver and he would have the sign fixed in no time.

Then again, maybe the owner was some Punjab immigrant who thought the flickering signage made his 7-11 stand apart from all the other open-all-night convenience marts. Hell if Stew was going to volunteer to help some camel jockey SOB fix his shit. Stew vowed that from this point on, he would never buy smokes from a 7-11 with flickering signage.

Ahead was a notoriously lingering stoplight. The go-green of the southbound signal appeared to ripple across the wet black pavement. A slight marine layer of ground-clinging fog had crept in from the ocean, leaving the air feeling a notch cooler than normal and every object coated in a dewy sheen.

Stew had no patience for that particular stoplight and at three-fifteen in the morning, wasn't one to press the crosswalk button to wait for a signal to tell him when it was safe to cross the street. Still jogging, Stew stretched from the curb into the parking lane and glanced left, but was more concerned about the oncoming traffic three lanes over. All appeared clear. And the signal in Stew's brain was as green as a sunlit emerald. He made a heading for the stuttering sign, sucked in his last lungful of nicotine-free atmosphere, and kicked his body into another gear.

He didn't see the car.

It was a drifting Toyota Prius, its hybrid engine on electronic stealth mode. But for the faintest hum and the sound of tires spinning over wet pavement, the car was virtually silent. In the police report it said that the driver recalled seeing a tall, darting jogger and hearing the thump of her left front bumper striking him before she had time to apply the brakes.

Stew was upended, spun in the air, and dropped to the earth with a crunching sound that made him certain his skull was crushed. The Puma that was half-laced to his right foot carried all the way to the opposite gutter. And in the slow motion rewind that followed, big Stew lay motionless, waiting to lose consciousness. Maybe even his life. When that didn't happened, he groggily started to complain.

"Just wanted a fuckin' cigarette!"

4

THE CITY OF Simi Valley. Population 119,388. Cradled on the southern slope of the Tehachapi Mountains, bisected by the 118 Freeway connecting to Route 23, and forty miles northwest of downtown Los Angeles. Home to the Ronald Reagan Presidential Library and Museum, Simi Valley is known for being one of the safest cities in America, if not the safest city in America. More police officers and firefighters call it home than any other place on earth. The valley itself, compared to its vast sister the San Fernando Valley, is more like a badly warped coliseum bowl built out of hard, craggy terrain with a suburban paradise growing in between the rocky elevations. Famous as a backdrop for countless B movie westerns, it isn't difficult to look up from any backyard and imagine seeing the likes of John Wayne or Randolph Scott, either on horseback or rising up from behind some rocky outcropping to fend off a horde of advancing Indians.

Or in Rodney King's case, looking in his rearview mirror to see he was being chased by the cops. It was late one Monday night in 1991 that the infamous motorist led police officers on a high-speed chase through Simi Valley. When he resisted arrest, his reward was a vicious baton-beating by four LAPD cops. The event was captured by an amateur videographer. Not since the Zapruder film had any moving picture been so scrutinized. Eventually, three of the four cops were later acquitted by an all white Simi Valley jury, sparking what has become known as the Los Angeles Riots.

The city burned for nearly a week.

"That beating was the best thing that ever happened to Rodney King," Ben would say to spice up an ordinary cocktail party conversation or backyard barbecue. It was both provocative and an effective counter-jab to anyone who couldn't help making jokes or sideways remarks about Ben's Simi Valley address. No matter where Ben traveled throughout the Southland, the Rodney King beating always seemed to bubble up.

"Rodney King walked away with what?" Ben would continue, knowing exactly how politically incorrect he was sounding. "A bruised face? Zero broken bones?" Then Ben would drop his kill factotum. "A high speed chase? A hundred-ten, a hundred-fifteen miles per hour? In an '88 Hyundai? If he had blown a tire, hit a wall, flipped that car at half that speed? Best case scenario, Rodney would be maimed for life, paralyzed, breathing through a tube, or dead—not to mention his two passengers."

After that kind of conversation kick-start, Ben was certain to dominate purely because he held the most interesting facts. He wouldn't need to argue the morality of America's most notorious home video, the police beating, or the race issues associated with the tragic events that followed. From his own sorry past, he had learned that personal safety struck at the heart of nearly every adult. He had morphed his losses into a great asset, using his unique ability to dissect a dangerous event or situation, reduce it to odds, tendencies and inevitabilities, separate factoids from mythology, and then sell his advice on how best to avoid injury or death, and most importantly, excessive workmen's comp claims for the businessmen who paid him.

※ ※ ※

Lydia Gonzalez was one of the many cops who called Simi Valley home. When she was but five years old, she flew alone from Mexico City to Los Angeles. From her window seat, the young girl stared in wide wonder at the never-ending blanket that was suburban Southern California sprawl. Below the cushion of air upon which the airliner floated were what appeared to be thousands upon thousands of tiny rooftops divided only by the constant peppering of sky-blue swimming pools. That's when young Lydia swore she would one day own a pool of her own.

Thirty-one years later, Lydia owned her pool and the $516,000 mortgage that went with it. Her LAPD pension would kick in in seven more years. That, and a second job, just might make that heavy mortgage an easier pill to swallow.

"Just added a second mortgage," said Gonzo. Sergeant Lydia Gonzalez preferred to be called *Gonzo* by her friends and colleagues. Gonzo had been her official nickname since she broke the single-game scoring record for the Van Nuys High School girls' basketball team.

"Price you pay for a fancy-assed private school," said Romeo Williams, Gonzo's partner, wannabe neighbor, surrogate big brother, and all around confidante. He was comfortable playing the role of the five-foot-eight roly-poly in plaid shorts and an L.A. Clippers t-shirt to Gonzo's near six feet of alien elegance. A slimming pair of black Capri pants and a Simi Canyons Lancers shirt elongated her height and grace.

"You just wait," she said. "Some girl's gonna find out Romeo's got more than a job in his shorts. And she's gonna own your ass. Then you're gonna marry her. Then she's gonna want babies. Then she's gonna wanna house for the babies. And when those babies are just out of diapers, she's gonna say, 'Romeo, oh Romeo, wherefore art thou the good schools?'"

"Simi's got good schools."

"Privates are better. It's a retail education. And you get what you pay for."

"Where's the burgers and dogs?" asked Romeo.

"Freezer in the garage."

"Costco?"

"Smart and Final. All I can afford between payments on my payments," joked Gonzo. "Make sure you toss the box or my friends might think I'm cheap."

"Your friends?" asked Romeo, referring to the eleven-odd couples either milling around the backyard, seeking shade, or keeping cool during the winter heat wave by playing lifeguard to the nineteen six-year-olds making waves in the pool. "Any other cops here?"

Gonzo pressed her lips together and shook her head.

"This many bodies at a Sunday barbecue in Simi and only two cops?" Romeo feigned his disbelief. "Where's the balance of the universe and all that shit. Must be something wrong."

"Romes," smiled Gonzo. "You're all the cop this woman needs."

Gonzo snapped the tongs she was using to turn the chicken. There were ten birds on the hot grill, hand-cut and marinated for two days in her late mother's favorite Tejada recipe.

Romeo decided to withdraw from the banter and forage for frozen burger patties in the garage freezer. He knew better than to cross verbal swords with his sarge. She had the looks and game to out-harass just about any fellow officer. And he would sure as hell suffer her wicked tongue the entire following week if he stayed and played on her turf.

"Need any help?"

Gonzo recognized the voice. But when she lifted her eyes from the grill to the woman sauntering towards her, she was lost for a name to fit the familiar face. *Ben Keller's wife*, Gonzo recalled. *But what the hell was her name?*

"I'm great. All good," said Gonzo. "How are you?"

Gonzo knew Ben. First from the gym, then two years of summer softball. But mostly she knew Ben for the kindly worded letter of recommendation he had written on behalf of her little boy, Travis. Without Ben's letter she was certain Travis would never have been admitted to Simi Canyons.

But what's her friggin' name?

"Travis in the pool?"

"Think the whole kindergarten is in the pool."

Gonzo swung her eyes over to the swimming pool. The pride and joy of finally owning a pool was lost in the mildly panicked moment. Gonzo had a horrible time remembering names. As a cop it had never been a liability because, for the most part, everybody in the PD wore a name tag. Otherwise, for Gonzo it would be to serve, protect, and "What was your name?"

"Ben was swimming with Betsy. But now I can't figure out where the hell they went."

Ben's wife, Betsy's mom! What was her . . .

"Alex!" snapped Gonzo, practically spitting the name as it popped into her head.

"Yes, Lydia?"

"Gonzo," spun the hostess, trying to bury herself in the embarrassment of the moment. "Everybody calls me Gonzo. Even Travis."

"Really nice of you to have everybody over."

"Long time coming. Everybody in the class has been so nice to us."

Of course it was code speak. Everybody in the class had, for the most part, been nice to Travis. But despite her badge and the general politeness afforded a police officer, Gonzo still felt like a misfit at morning drop-off. She in her dinged-up Chevy Suburban waiting to turn 200,000 miles, waiting in line amongst all the checkbook moms in their newly leased Land Rovers, Escalades and BMWs.

"Looks hot. Lemme take over," said Alex.

Gonzo shook her head and smiled. "Oh, I got it. Know what? I could really use a beer."

"Coming right up."

As Alex walked away, Gonzo finally grabbed an eyeful of the mom whose name she had forgotten. And though it was only a rear view, there was plenty about Alex for Gonzo to memorize. Alex Keller was just north of five feet five and looked rock solid for a woman who had birthed three children, survived the death of her husband, and remarried an oddball like Ben. Alex was both beautiful and confident without looking the part of a grown-up fairy princess, wearing her surf shorts and bikini halter under a sheer white blouse in something of a statement to the other moms. She didn't appear to sweat either. Alex was clearly socially adept, easily navigating through the crowd of Sunday wine-chilled parents, smiling with the straightened teeth of a prom queen, laughing at unfunny jokes, obligingly flirting with every drunken husband, but never slowing long enough to appear delayed from her mission.

"Stare at her any longer, people will talk."

"Asshole!" spat Gonzo, laughing at herself. She was, indeed, staring. And so very guilty.

Ben had clearly startled Gonzo, ambushing her from the smoky side of the grill.

"Don't be embarrassed," said Ben. "My wife's got hot stuff when she wants to show it and you to know it."

"I wasn't looking at her that way," Gonzo defended.

"But you're supposed to look at her that way," said Ben, holding up his half-supped plastic glass of wine. Gonzo couldn't tell if it was a gesture or a mocking toast. "Once in the spotlight, always in the spotlight," said Ben.

"She was an actress?"

"Singer, model, performer, whatever," said Ben. "Look her up on the IMDB."

The IMDB was short for the Internet Movie Database. Ben sometimes wondered if it was the most accessed website in Southern California. With so many residents claiming to either be, or have been, in show business, the IMDB was one quick, surefire way to divine a little truth from all the fiction.

Gonzo turned away from the barbecue and bent closer to Ben. At first it was to check the dilation of his pupils. Off the mark, she already knew he was drunk. How drunk? was her question. And she couldn't exactly perform a sobriety test right then and there. So it was the pupils she would go by. One point two percent blood alcohol, she guessed. Clearly over the limit. She had been watching her guests and making a mental list of who should and should not drive. Ben was her newest entry.

"Now, you're staring at me," remarked Ben. "Guess I should be flattered."

Gonzo whispered in Ben's ear. "Everybody thinks I'm a lesbian. Don't they?"

"Don't know. Want me to take a poll?" smiled Ben. "I can ask for a show of hands."

"Please."

"If you're disappointed in the result, I can also start a rumor."

"If they think I am, I get it. I'm a cop. I'm not built like most women. I'm a single mom. Travis' got no dad—"

"What about Romeo?" Ben nodded past Gonzo. Romeo was on his way back with a platter of uncooked burgers and hot dogs. "He a boyfriend or a beard?"

"He's my partner."

"Whatever," said Ben. "My advice is stop worrying. People talk. You can't keep 'em from talking. And if they are, at worst, you're popular."

"Kids talk, too. I'm thinking about Travis."

"And who knows what kids will ask?"

"Exactly."

"Like, 'Is Travis' mom a lesbian?'"

"Exactly."

"Well," braved Ben. "Is she?"

Gonzo straightened and twisted her head only slightly. In her politically correct world of the LAPD, it had been a few years since anybody had asked her so bluntly.

"Are you or are you not a lesbian?" asked Ben.

"No!" said Gonzo.

"Have you known or ever been associated with lesbians?"

"Stop."

"Ok. Be happy it's a Christian school," said Ben. "Last time I checked, we believed in the Immaculate Conception."

Gonzo laughed. It was a big, loud laugh reserved for big

women. Few humans could laugh like Gonzo.

"If you didn't know, you're drunk," she said.

"Only slightly," said Ben, who knew he was drunker than he admitted. He figured Gonzo knew, too. He was relying on that.

"What was so funny?" asked Romeo, looking for a place to set the tray loaded with frozen hamburger patties and hot dogs.

"Ben's lit," said Gonzo.

"Safety Dude's got his buzz on?" laughed Romeo. "Ain't that like the anchor guy reading the news. But backward?"

Romeo had referred to Ben as "Safety Dude" many times. But never to Ben's face. He had only made the mocking superhero remark when Gonzo was passing along one of Ben's famous safety factoids.

"Romes?" warned Gonzo.

"C'mon, man," Romeo continued. "Tell me somethin' I don't know about drunks and driving."

"Not driving," defended Ben. "And I'm only slightly drunk."

"First mistake of a drunk driver is denial," said Romeo.

"Not even close," corrected Ben.

"Okay," said Romes. "You're right. First mistake is drinking."

"Nope. First mistake is the driver putting himself in a position to drink." Ben raised his plastic cup, swirling what was left of his red wine.

He continued, "Most convicted drunk drivers, given the luxury of hindsight, would tell you they had a clear choice on the day they got busted. With exceptions to the chronic alcoholics who must drink to function, the modern drunk driver is so well-versed in the perils of his actions, he or she can usually pinpoint the precise moment they chose—not just to drink—but to position themselves in a risky situation. Alone. No designated driver. Not enough time to prearrange transportation or a place to sleep it off—"

"This is what he does," interrupted Romeo. "Right? Put a quarter in him and he just goes and goes—"

"Don't be an asshole, Romes."

"Same behavior applies to most kinds of risk-taking," Ben continued, undaunted. The wine was making him brave.

Not that he needed much moxie to get himself rolling on any precautionary subject. The alcohol, though, made the nails feel sharper and the hammer that much heavier.

"Like a cheating man," rambled Ben. "He knows the nature of risk. And every adulterer finds himself at the same crossroads as the drunk driver. Same options. Left, right, straight ahead. Should I or shouldn't I? And that's before he even walks out of the house."

"Good advice," said Gonzo, trying to pump some air in the moment. "Good thing for Romeo he's not married yet."

"You know," Ben added, "not so long ago, Stanford Medical did a study on HIV-infected men. Every one of them knew well before the actual moment they contracted the virus that they were putting themselves in a risk situation—"

"What's your point?" Romeo's tone was entirely rhetorical. He just wanted let on that he was annoyed.

"Point is that we know!" pressed Ben. "We all know when we're putting ourselves at risk. We know when we put our families, the ones we love at risk—"

"What's going on?" asked Gonzo. Instinctively, she had rotated to Ben's left, blocking him from the rest of her guests. If Ben was drunk and sketchy, she didn't want him embarrassed.

"Need to talk to you," said Ben, his voice slightly trembling. Then he caught himself. "I'm sorry. This isn't the place. I'm kinda drunk . . ."

"We already established that," said Gonzo.

"Right. You're right. Sorry."

"We can talk all you want," said Gonzo. "Later, okay. Whatever it is, we can talk."

Gonzo couldn't read what kind of emotional knife had been stuck in Ben, or the depth of his pain. Let alone how much of his dark demeanor was alcohol-induced. There was, though, that adultery remark he had delivered through grit teeth. For a nanosecond Gonzo had wondered if Ben had been unfaithful. Guilt-ridden men liked to confess to women cops. Women cops were sometimes treated like priests. As if a woman wearing a badge served as some kind of priest or Holy Madonna.

One thing was for certain. Ben wasn't himself.

He was usually sunny despite his odd rants and opinions. In Gonzo's book, he was an irregular Will Rogers, occasionally moody, but buoyed by a good soul. Gonzo felt as much from the moment she had met him. But whatever ailed her friend would have to wait. There were two more hours of pool party to hostess, kindergarten parents to schmooze, and a gifted bottle of El Conquistador Tequila waiting for her once her little boy fell asleep.

"Am I interrupting?" asked Alex.

Ben's wife looked positively posed, standing two yards beyond Romeo and outside what appeared to be some kind of triangle of conspiracy. How long she had been standing there was anyone's guess. She had one arm akimbo, and in the other, that cold bottle of beer forked between her index and middle finger, suspiciously swinging it to and fro like a pendulum.

"Hey, you got that beer," said Gonzo. "Thanks."

Alex handed off the beer to Gonzo, trying not to look too accusingly at the recipient before letting her eyes dart to her husband.

"Everything okay, hon?"

"Fine," lied Ben, throwing a fist to his mouth and feigning a cough. "Allergies are kicking up."

Ben wisely slipped his arm possessively around Alex's waist, attending to her with a warm smile.

"Having fun yet?" whispered Ben.

"Not as much as you," nudged his wife.

"Some time ago, I had another life . . ." Ben confessed. The next words choked him. He sat up in the chaise, his elbows to his knees, and tried to pull out what had long ago been massaged into a secure hiding place. "Obviously, it was before Alex. I was right outta college. Married young. Had kids. Twin girls."

Rolling the pricey bottle of tequila between her palms, Gonzo was propped on an identical lounger, her eyes stuck on a hanging moon. She was already halfway to drunk when she had answered the doorbell, a 9mm pistol bootlegged to her hip.

When Gonzo discovered Ben on her dim little doorstep she hadn't known if he truly wanted to talk—or if by feigning a need to talk, his true plans were to try and fuck her—or if she was juiced enough to let him.

But clearly Ben had other things on his mind.

"Anyway," Ben continued. "Things didn't work out for us."

Funny, Gonzo thought. She hadn't pegged him for the divorcing type. And thinking she could break the tension of the moment, almost said as much. She was glad she kept her mouth shut.

"It was a home invasion thing. Thirteen years ago. God . . ." added Ben, surprising himself. "Has it been that long?"

Gonzo swallowed. Despite the expensive tequila, her throat had turned dry. She took another sip.

"Where'd it happen?"

"Culver City. Owned us a little house off Sawtelle. Starter house. But it was ours. Our house. I remember saying that to her. The two of us to each other—all the time. Our house."

The pauses. When Ben stopped talking, if only for seconds, Gonzo thought the pain in him sounded like there was so little give inside, his head might crack open.

Ben told her about tending bar. That from the moment he turned twenty-one he had been a barman. It was all part of a master plan devised since that first restaurant job he had landed at age fifteen. Montagues. An old school steak and lobster joint. With a little hustle, Ben had graduated to a red-vested waiter by sixteen, the restaurant's youngest ever. And though it was technically illegal for him to serve drinks until he was eighteen, the management and customers had either looked the other way or didn't care. The young waiter was energetic, entertaining, efficient, and would come to the restaurant straight from school. Ben would plough through his homework before the first shift and on his breaks, pocket his tips, and be home in bed by eleven to ponder the next move in his master plan: Sports car. College. Wife. Kids. His own restaurant. And on his days off, maybe try his hand at tennis or golf.

Young Ben was always snappy. At Montagues, when a

regular customer would slap an extra fiver into Ben's palm, the reply had always been the same. "Ah. It's because you know that junker of mine don't run on good looks."

Bartending had been the path to the dream. Liquor prices were always at a premium, the customers habitual, and the tips for a smiling barkeep with a patient ear and a friendly joke, certain to be worldly enough to help pay for college and the student loans he would incur.

Then there were the women. Whether arriving at the bar single, in groups, or with a date, a talented, smiling Ben was in a prime position to pick his mark, divide her from whatever her social engagement, and have her before the clock struck 2:00 A.M.

"I was working that night." Ben wasn't so much telling the story to Gonzo. He was reliving it, coiled on the lounger and staring into the night.

"I was partnered in this restaurant over on Pico. Maybe you knew it. Was called Prague '88."

The year was 1994. After Ben had graduated from Cal State Los Angeles with a bare-knuckled degree in business administration, he threw in with his two best high school friends, Miles and George, on the restaurant venture he had long dreamed about. The restaurant was called Prague '88, after the Vodka-soaked week the three chums had spent in the Eastern European destination. The city was profoundly beautiful, the liquor cheap, and the women so very willing.

From the jump, the three never deviated from Ben's business plan. Ben would manage the bar and Miles would handle the food service. George, whose father was generous enough to kick-start his son's entrepreneurial adventure, would handle the financing.

"Before we bought it, it was a strip bar," said Ben. "Called the Jaguar Club. Cool location. North of the freeway but still on the low-rent side of Santa Monica. City even gave us a break on the license fee. Sure you never went there? Not even for a drink? Mediocre food, but—yeah—the bar truly rocked."

The food side of the endeavor was never successful. The reviews were more thumbs down than up and getting a table was rarely difficult. But the business of serving booze to L.A.'s young and trendy was a different animal. The deco-styled bar was a full forty feet long and usually stacked four deep with pressing flesh, most waving cash or newly minted credit cards in return for the premium drink du jour. It was enough to tip the restaurant into profit. Bored with his part in Prague '88, Miles soon quit and moved on to study art history in graduate school. And though George kept his stake in the business, he didn't care for the late hours. This left Ben at the helm with an increased stake and a bank loan to cover Miles' piece, but still pocketing the lion's share of the profits.

"I met her at the bar. She'd come in with some bond trader in a suit. Merrill Lynch, I think. First date kinda thing. Bad idea bringing a girl to a bar on a first date. She got bored and started talking to me. Bond guy left. She stuck around."

Gonzo's head may have been buzzing, but her vision was crystal. She could make out the age lines on Ben's face, each appearing to fade as he recalled his first wife.

"And Christ, was I so done. Coulda had a parade of supermodels walk through and I wouldn't have given ten shits . . . Man. Did I tell you her name?"

"No," answered Gonzo.

"Sara. Sara Bess Savidge. I swear, we musta been shacked up in a week. She got pregnant, we got married . . . Shit happens so fast when it's right. The twins were born in August 1996. Lea and Mae. Both with the middle name Bess. After Sara quit her job at Oppenheimer, we bought a small fixer in nearby Culver City.

"That damn house needed a lot of work. And the subs, they all worked cheap if I paid cash. So for a while, instead of doing the nightly cash drop at the bank, I'd stuff it in my pants or a kitchen bag and lock it up in a gun safe at home. Bedroom closet. Combination was my mother's birthday. 4-29-41."

Ben's eyes glistened.

"Still don't get it. Sara was so good with numbers. Phone

numbers, addresses. So why the hell couldn't she remember the goddamn combination?"

December 1997. The holiday season brought the usual foggy evenings to Santa Monica and in Ben's experience cold air turned out the drinkers. Per person consumption had nearly doubled.

That fall Ben had sent out a mailer to local businesses offering the flagging dining room of '88 to local party planners. In no time the venue was booked six solid nights a week. Prague '88 had turned into a gusher of booze and money.

"We were hosting this party. Buncha Fox TV people. Really loud. I was short a man so I got behind the bar and started mixing. I remember barely hearing the desk phone ringing and nobody answering. Had this hostess named Marti. You know, the wannabe actress type with tits out to . . . Anyway. She wasn't at her post. Shoulda been answering the phone instead of kissing ass with the TV people."

In his second life, Ben would have rated their Culver City fixer a safety index of less than three out of a possible ten. By all outward appearances it seemed safe enough. The house was in an older neighborhood where most of the homes were built in the forties and fifties. The streets had sidewalks and were well-lit. The lawns were all manicured. Just a few of the houses were rentals and Ben could recall a real pride-of-ownership feeling when he and Sara would take the twins for walks in their double stroller, often stopping at El Marino Park, conveniently located only a short suburban block to the west.

For the young couple, it seemed like a perfect place to start a family. Ben was only twenty-five years old. Sara was twenty-six.

"I shoulda known things. Like the increased crime index for living near a freeway. Or a park. Living near a park seems like a good thing. Lots of green grass. Playground for kids. But you're a cop. So you know what happens in city parks after the sun goes down. All the drug deals and gangbangers lookin' to start trouble."

"Culver PD's always been strong," said Gonzo, instantly regretting her idiotic addition to Ben's monologue. The picture he was painting was clearly grim. Something awful was about to happen in Ben's first life. Gonzo blamed the tequila and chose to keep her mouth clamped tight until Ben had finished.

"Yeah, Culver has their own PD," said Ben, "but everyone had those stupid private security companies with those stupid alarm systems. Those days, local PDs spent so much of their response time chasing faulty alarm trips, their response to real calls was no better than Inglewood's."

Sara's habit on those long holiday nights was to crawl into the master bed and flank herself with Lea and Mae. The girls would twist and burrow in as she read from a picture book, each child pretending she had mommy just to herself. Occasionally, the two would cry or fight, but mostly they would just drift on her words until mother and children were deeply asleep. So heavy was the trio's slumber that Ben would sometimes joke that he could crawl into bed with the USC Trojan Marching Band without disturbing a single one of their heavy-lidded snores.

"I locked the restaurant doors after two. Did my routine of checking the tills against the receipts. I liked to do that at the bar instead of in the back office because I could listen to the music. I'd switch to some mellow CD. Maybe have a few sips of Cognac."

As in so many other municipalities, Culver City's emergency response telephone system was having difficulty keeping up with the increased demands of a burgeoning digital society. It was antiquated and analog, suffering from a rising influx of cellular phone calls, and had only five full-time operators. Only a month prior, in the November general election, Culver voters had narrowly passed Measure C, giving the sitting treasurer permission to issue and sell two million dollars in municipal bonds in order to pay for a much-needed upgrade.

But until the upgrade, some Culver City residents dialing 911 were going to have to put up with a busy signal.

"Was two-thirty when I finally made it to the back office. I remember four messages on the answering machine."

The back office was closet-sized, utilitarian white, and stacked with files, supply catalogues, and timecards. Scheduling calendars were pinned to a corkboard. There was room for one swiveling chair, a desk fit for a college dorm room, and a menagerie of photos of Ben's young family stapled just above the two-line telephone.

Ben was exhausted, certain he was getting the flu, and weighed whether or not to play any of the messages blinking on the answering machine. Then he reconsidered, thinking there might be something important on the tape—such as a changed order that might affect the party scheduled for the next evening.

"First message was a professional party planner looking to book New Year's. Second was some drunk asshole who was supposed to be at the party but was lost somewhere in Venice . . ."

Gonzo decided she should stop sipping at the tequila bottle when she found herself tense and gripping the neck so tightly she thought it might snap off. No longer was she stargazing. No longer was she tracing Ben's moonlit profile, or wondering why he had come to her that night. Gone was any inclination that she might be stupid or drunk enough to suck his cock.

"Third message was Sara."

Ben's voice squeezed into a crunchy whisper. His hands shook as he dried his palms against his pants legs. His face was streaked with tears.

"She uh . . . she sounded really scared and was trying to be quiet. Said she thought there was somebody in the house. Said she dialed nine-one-one but couldn't get through . . . She didn't know what to do. She was begging me to come home now. Right now."

Ben wiped the heels of his palms across his eyes. Gonzo could see the snot draining from his nose. She wanted to hold him. To tell him it was all okay now. That he was just reliving bad memories. Trauma. She wanted to share her horrid experiences as a police officer in order to make him feel as if he wasn't the only victim on the planet.

But that would have been wrong. At least not now. Not when Ben was purging.

"Last message," braved Ben, clearing his throat and swallowing hard, the pressure behind his eyes close to unbearable. "Last message was Sara again. 'Cept this time she wasn't whispering. I could hear the girls crying. And a man's voice—but I couldn't hear what he was saying. Just Sara begging me to call back with the combination to the safe."

The rest of what Gonzo heard seemed scattered. She didn't know if it was because of the frailty of the man telling the tale or because her own receptors were on overload. The story had snuck past her steely cop veneer. She was on the verge of sobbing outright. Poor Ben, she kept thinking. What a weight to carry around his neck.

Ben faintly recounted the foggy drive home. Of running stop signs and red lights until an LAPD car finally pulled him over. He somehow explained himself and was placed in the back of the patrol car and driven to his neighborhood.

The front door of the house was intact. But a quick recon revealed that the kitchen door off the driveway had been kicked in. One of the cops had restrained Ben while his partner explored. Before Ben knew it, the street was a parking lot full of emergency vehicles, flashing red lights, and dumbstruck neighbors standing on neatly mowed lawns.

"All dead," said Ben. He was slowly shaking his head from side to side. Like a metronome. "Kids in our bed. They found Sara . . . found her face down in front of the safe. They'd hit her with the same hammer they'd used to try and bust the lock . . . Dumb fuckers never got the money."

The dead space that followed Ben's tale could have lasted ten seconds—or ten minutes. Gonzo didn't know. One thing was for sure. Ben was cashed out. He had nothing more to say.

And Gonzo? What could she say? The sound that finally broke the silence was the squeak of the cork twisting off Gonzo's bottle of tequila.

"Think you need this more than me," she said.

"Bet you're wondering why I told you all this."

"You don't need a reason."

"I know," said Ben. "But I have a reason. Good one."

"Have you talked to Alex about—"

"She knows most of it. What happened to my first family and all. We actually met—Alex and me—in grief counseling.

After it all happened, it was like someone turned out the lights. For a long time everything was just dark. Anyway, me and Alex, we worked our way out together. Night became day again."

"Good to hear," said Gonzo.

"But there's a part she doesn't know," pressed Ben. "'Bout a week or so ago, someone sent me this . . . recording."

"Like what? A tape?"

"CD. Some kind of . . . deathbed confession . . . from a guy in prison."

"From the perp?"

"Perp?" asked Ben.

"The perpetrator. The man who . . ."

"No," answered Ben. "This was some old guy who claimed he'd shared a cell with the guy who killed my family . . . Anyway, he gave me a name."

Ben continued on, briefly laying out the rest of it. Josie's research on the name. Woody Bell. Ben's visit to Stew Raymo's construction site. Even his harebrained handshake theory and the embarrassed feelings that followed. Lastly, Ben finished with Woody's email and Stewart Raymo's picture. He withdrew three folded pages from his shirt pocket. These were copies of the email, Stew Raymo's mug shot, and his criminal record.

Gonzo took the papers, stood, then circled around to a nearby landscaping light. She had to crouch to read the printout.

"There were never any arrests?"

"No," said Ben, clipped.

"Leads?" she asked. "You must've been in touch with the detectives."

"No fingerprints. No witnesses."

Once again, the lights were out in Ben's world.

Ben continued, "You know? You spend twelve, thirteen years getting over something horrible. Building a new life. New career. Wonderful family. Of course, the past doesn't go away. It fades a little more every day. Eventually, it starts to feel like nothing more than a bad dream. I mean, some if it's work. Therapists. Grief relief. Perspective, life picture. You work at it, and yeah, you've moved on. You survived."

Ben felt his muscles tense and watched both his hands fold into fists.

"At least you think you have. Then this shit happens. A pinprick and you find out it's all a fuckin' bubble. I'm right back there. Might as well have been yesterday—"

"This doesn't mean it's him."

Gonzo had finished browsing the printouts. She seated herself at the edge of Ben's recliner and calmly touched his knee.

"I mean, this guy," she continued. "This builder guy whose hand you shook. Yeah. He was a bad guy. Maybe he still is. But none of this—not what some dead con said on a CD—or this rap sheet—none of it means this Stew Raymo was the one who did the thing."

"The thing?" said Ben, slightly incredulous. "You mean *murdered*, right? My family?"

"Yes. Murdered," she apologized. "What happened to you is truly horrible. Unimaginable—"

"It could be him."

"Sure," she conceded. "It could be. But without any kind of proof or lead or—"

"So you won't help me?"

Gonzo's eyes closed. Her lips pressed together as Ben's new master plan had become clear. He hadn't come to her house with sex on his mind. Nor had his visit been a confessional to the Madonna police officer. Ben wanted her to run the dogs on Stew Raymo, the ex-con-turned-general-contractor.

"It's not even my division—"

"You know people," pressed Ben. "You can ask around."

"I can," she relented quickly, only because she had another tack. But not yet. "I can ask. I can pull files. I can see if anything matches up. You deserve that much."

Gonzo hooked a gentle finger under his chin.

"But first, Ben, I need you to look at me."

Ben's entire face was wet from crying.

"In the likelihood that there is no proof. No evidence or connection to your tragedy. What then? What will you do then?"

In Ben's eyes, barely illuminated by the moon's ambience

and a single pool light, Gonzo could still see hope. A hope that the old pain that haunted him would return to its ancient hole and politely shut the door behind itself.

"I don't know," he said. "I don't know at all."

"Go home to Alex. Go home to your wonderful family who loves you and needs you. Okay?"

Gonzo gave Ben an affirmative nod.

"You'll check it out?" Ben wanted a promise.

"I will check it out."

Gonzo walked Ben to the curb. They hugged under a streetlamp, holding each other for longer than either felt was appropriate. It was in that moment that Gonzo realized she had wanted to sleep with Ben that night. And would have if he had made any sort of advance. Earlier, she might have been able to resist him on principle. But she was a goner now, emotionally sucked into his nightmare. She wanted to do something more than mother his aching soul. She was willing to do just about anything that would leave Ben a little lighter. Even something as fleeting as sex.

But Ben didn't ask.

Ben crawled into his Volvo, thanked her again, shut and mechanically locked the door, and drove away.

The instant he was gone, Gonzo felt so damned alone. Strangely so. She stood in her suburban driveway and panned her view across the landscape of stucco houses, perfectly kept yards, all sparsely illuminated by streetlamps as tall as giraffes. She wondered what made her neighborhood so different from Ben's in Culver City. How random was crime anyway? She questioned if her sleep was sometimes so sound that she might not hear a deadly intruder. For the first time in many months, she feared for the safety of herself and her little boy.

Before returning to the comfort of her house, Gonzo made plans to sleep with her son that night. She would also make certain to keep her gun close. Very, very close.

When Alex climbed into bed, she was both wondering and worried. Ben's quick departure after dinner and bedtime stories had been both unlike him and so thinly excused that she didn't quite know how to process it. He had informed Alex that he had left his BlackBerry over at Gonzo's and was going back to get it. The fib would have sufficed if not for her distinct memory of Ben making one of his patented email checks at a stoplight during the short drive home. Alex didn't know Gonzo all that well. Only that she was a single mom of the alpha variety. And the body language her husband and Gonzo had displayed earlier that afternoon was, if anything, suspicious.

As Alex recounted their marriage, Ben had never cheated. Nor had he given her a solitary, doubt-worthy indication that he was so inclined. But Gonzo was an attractive enough woman. Ben was a man. And he had been gone for nearly four hours.

So Alex lay awake until she heard the dog stir. Then came faint tones as Ben let himself in the front door. There was the jangle of keys, a visit to the downstairs bathroom. The toilet's flushing. She could hear some brief puttering in the kitchen, a plastic cup filled with water, then Ben's clockwise routine of checking the locks on every door and window. Lastly, there was his soft steps up the two-tiered staircase, the room-by-room check of the sleeping girls, then before he entered the master suite, the distinct high-pitched beeps as the alarm code was tapped out on the keypad.

Then there was the dialogue in her head. She had been rehearsing it for the past two hours. Her questions first, then his possible answers, excuses, or lame rationales for not even calling. Her counterarguments. Then the big question.

Are you screwing another woman?

She couldn't brave it, though. Before Ben crossed the threshold into the room, she had pulled the covers up and curled into a fetal ball. Stillness was what she craved. Conflict at this late an hour would be unwise. Alex thought maybe she would be able to smell it on him. The sex of another woman. But that chance was washed away when she heard Ben slipping into the bathroom, discreetly clicking the door shut, and turning on the shower.

By the time Ben crawled in next to Alex, she was comfortably feigning sleep. She let him form his body to hers, kiss her bare shoulder, and whisper good night. It was his code. If she was awake and needed to chat, she would answer. If not, she would continue to log precious hours of slumber. When his left hand found hers, she let him clasp it. And as their wedding bands touched gold to gold, she prayed to Jesus it was a sign that he still indeed loved her.

Sleep came quicker than anticipated. Alex didn't wake until the alarm sounded at 6:00 A.M. Ben, she discovered, was already gone. Guilty as charged, she reckoned. Ashamed and unable to face his wife. All he had left was a scrap of paper Scotch-taped to the refrigerator door handle. The note was simple: *Factory walk-thru in South Bay. I'll call from the car. Love, B.*

"Mom!" Elyssa barked from the landing. "Nina's wearing one of my t-shirts again!"

"I swear, she gave it to me!" defended Nina all the way from the top of the stairs.

"I let you borrow it—ONCE!"

"Let her borrow it again!" shouted Alex.

"But what if I want to wear my shirt?"

"She's already dressed," yelled Nina. "She's not even wearing a t-shirt."

"BORROWED FOR THE LAST TIME, WASHED, RETURNED, AND THAT'S ALL I WANT TO HEAR ABOUT IT!" shouted Alex.

The tone was final, and in Alex's mind, ended the subject. She had enough weighing on her mind. Prepping lunches, delivering the girls to school before the bells rang, and then a long list of chores to accomplish. The painful subject of her cheating husband would have to simmer until she could dispose of it or it disappeared altogether. Alex had already lost one adulterer-of-a-husband-and-father to a heart attack. She sure as hell didn't want to lose her current spouse to something as easy—not to mention common—as divorce.

Stew woke up from the surgery with a headache. One astronomically bigger than the one he had started with. He had complained to the anesthesiologist that his head felt like a bucket of joint compound that had been left overnight. Neither doctor nor nurse was amused. Hell, figured Stew, they probably hadn't a glimmer what joint compound was.

At least I thought it was funny.

He wished that he had pressed the headache issue and gotten some meds before they had wheeled him into the operating room.

Nothing else hurt, even the left knee that had just been arthroscopically invaded. The pop he had heard the moment the silent-but-deadly Toyota Prius had hit him was the ripping of his ACL. Well-known to athletes and orthopedic surgeons, the Anterior Cruciate Ligament, Stew learned, is the knee's major stabilizing component. The surgery was routine, mildly invasive and involved drilling holes in his knee in order to reattach the ligament.

"Sounds pretty fuckin' invasive to me," Stew had said at the time of the pre-op exam.

"You're gonna be fine," Pam hushed, before whispering in his ear, "and I think it's a really bad idea to curse at the surgeon before he's about to operate."

"Curse the fuckin' hospital bill," Stew replied.

Stew and Pam had no formal health coverage. He wasn't insured under his own over-bloated workmen's comp policy. And the way the accident report had been written up by the LAPD, Stew was at fault for not crossing the street at a crosswalk. The Prius' driver was instantly absolved of all liability. Adding insult to Stew's injury, he was cited for jaywalking, a misdemeanor traffic ticket that would surely boost his car insurance rates.

The post-operative suite at Burbank's St. Joseph's orthopedic unit was comfortably new, freshly painted in green and blue pastels. The room was divided in half. Six beds on one side, each curtained for privacy. The other side had a rudimentary nursing station with two sets of synthetic leather couches and chairs for waiting relatives. Stew couldn't tell exactly how many other post-op patients were sharing the suite with him. There was, though, a large Korean family taking up most of the available seating. *They were noisy*, he thought. *And why the hell couldn't they speak*

English? Or even Spanish, for that matter? They were in America, goddammit!

"Still got the headache," Stew complained. He was louder this time, hoping a nurse would magically appear with a syringe of something chemically sweet to feed into his IV.

"Doc says the knee pain's what you're gonna need to deal with," said Pam.

Stew twisted his thumping head to find Pam at his side. She was wearing black jeans and a matching turtleneck. By his best guess, he had been awake for at least fifteen minutes.

"Don't feel shit with the knee," said Stew.

Pam put her hand on his forehead. Her palm felt smooth and cool.

"Got enough ice on your knee to cool a twelve pack." She gestured to his left knee. It was splinted and bound in plastic bags looking to burst with ice. "'For the swelling,' they said."

"Maybe they should pack my head in ice. Fuckin' kills."

"I'll ask and see if there's anything more they can do, okay?"

Pam's voice was soft. A blessing, he thought, considering the hammer in his head keeping time with pounding of his heart.

Stew closed his eyes and tried to block out both the pain and nattering voices. He could feel the anesthetic swimming in him, blurring his mind and leaving the taste of galvanized metal in his mouth. He remembered a dream. Was it during the surgery or just some playback from the night he had jogged out for cigarettes? In the dream *everybody was wearing bicycle helmets. And not just his crew. Everybody. Car drivers, pedestrians, supermarket checkers—even the schoolchildren. Why the hell schoolchildren? Strange.*

There was a crossing guard in the dream.

Stew remembered *the crossing guard as the inspector guy. Martin or Benjamin Whatshisname. There were about twenty school kids in the crosswalk, each and every last child identical in age, dress, and physical features. Girls,* Stew remembered. *Little schoolgirls in perfect plaid pinafores. Each child a carbon copy of the other, as if mechanically stamped out by machine in a schoolgirl uniform factory.*

And every child was wearing a bike helmet.

Except the inspector, remembered Stew. *That fuckin' OSHA inspector! All he was wearing was a pair of vision protectors and a smug-assed smile.*

"Mr. Raymo?" asked the woman's voice.

At last, a nurse with drugs!

Or so Stew thought in the microsecond before he pried his eyes open. Instead of a nurse, Stew discovered a tall, Hispanic woman. She appeared at the foot of the bed wearing a brown pantsuit. A shiny LAPD detective's shield hung from her pocket.

"Mr. Raymo? My name is Lydia Gonzalez," said the detective. "May I?"

With that, Gonzo pulled the curtain until she and Stew had privacy.

Stew wanted to say something like, "If it's about the accident, I'm going to protest the police report." But experience had taught him that when it came to cops, the less said the better.

"Sorry about the accident," offered Gonzo. Though like from most cops, sorry didn't sound so sorry.

"Okay," said Stew.

"Docs say you should rehab okay."

Stew tried to raise his eyebrows, as if to ask why she was there. Only his head hurt so badly he couldn't tell if his facial muscles were in tune with his intent.

"What can I do you for?" croaked Stew.

"Well . . ." Gonzo began her tale. "LAPD has a new computer system that crosschecks itself. So say, when a particular offender or witness we're having trouble finding gets, say, a traffic violation, it pings back to the desk of the detective in need of assistance."

Gonzo wasn't exactly lying. The LAPD had recently installed the new software. It was buggy, and so far, causing more technical mischief than crime-fighting shortcuts. But what Gonzo wasn't going to admit to was that she had used the system in reverse. After pulling up Stewart Raymo's arrest record, Gonzo had run the name and gotten pinged with the freshly minted accident report automatically sent from LAPD's traffic division via fiber optics.

"Almost get killed and they give me a goddamn ticket," said Stew.

"Good news for you is that you can fix that with a trip to traffic school," said Gonzo, as bright and fake as a girl working the lost baggage desk at LAX.

Stew wanted to tell her that she didn't know shit. Sure the detective understood the basic precepts of traffic school; after eight hours of mind-dulling classroom instruction, citations for moving violations could be expunged from a driver's record. What she wasn't aware of were the qualifiers. The most important being that the driver must not have received a moving violation within eighteen months of his or her last visit to traffic school. Stew had attended a traffic school run by a local comedy club just a few months ago. He distinctly recalled that the actress/comedian/instructor was neither attractive nor funny.

The post-op ward had turned so gravely quiet Stew could hear faint chords from the piped in music. Where the hell were the Koreans? When Stew swiveled his gaze past Gonzo, he caught sight of a thick-looking detective covertly ushering the Korean clan out the double doors.

Then came the question. Gonzo made sure to mentally record every tick, twitch, or bodily tell that Stew might unconsciously manifest.

"We're investigating an unsolved homicide . . ." started Gonzo.

Stew's eyes were sluggish. Gonzo had already clocked his pupils. They might not tell her a thing. She was more interested in his hands and chest. Would Stew breathe, heave, or curl his fingers towards his palms? Her tack wasn't so much from her detective training, but from techniques taught to TSA employees when questioning suspicious airline passengers.

"A triple murder from thirteen years ago."

The patient's fingers twitched slightly, but nothing resembled a contractive move inward. Stew's chest did heave involuntarily, pulling in an extra tankful of hospital air.

"Was that a question?" asked Stew, his eyes fixed solidly on the lady cop.

"Ring any bells?"

"Thirteen years ago," said Stew flatly. "That was before I got sober so I can't say I remember much before then."

"Culver City—"

"Why ask me?"

"Home invasion robbery gone wrong," pressed Gonzo. "Your sheet says you were in that business for a while."

"Only did time for burglary," defended Stew. "But you knew that, right? Cuzza the fact you read my history."

Indeed, she did know that Stew had done two turns for robbery and another for third-degree assault. But those were merely pleas that his public defender had bargained. Stew's initial indictments were for crimes more dangerous than breaking and entering an unoccupied home.

"Well, your name came up. How's that?"

"Yeah? Am I some kind of suspect?"

"Unsolved crime, Mr. Raymo. We thought you might be able to help."

Stew's fingers began to stiffly waggle, as if warming up to play the piano.

"Long time since my bad-boy days," grumbled Stew. "'Cept for some traffic tickets—some IRS shit about back taxes—I've been a good citizen."

"Got your life together?" asked Gonzo, not really buying it.

"Straight up," affirmed Stew.

"How about contacts from the old days? Know anybody who might be able to help?"

"Nobody knows where to find me or what I do. And that suits me just fine."

Gonzo bent slightly at the waist, leaning in just a fraction closer.

"Well . . . I found you," said Gonzo with the thinnest veil of incrimination. The words hung in the air like a piñata waiting for a bat. All Stew had to do was swing. Instead, his tone turned sharp.

"Next time I'll use the crosswalk."

"So no talk about the old days. Over and out?" asked Gonzo.

"Oh, I talk about it," said Stew. "In AA meetings. Call it sharing. That's when we talk about the shit we used to do that fed our abusing behaviors."

"How's that working?"

"Just had my tenth birthday."

"Sober ten years. Pretty good." Gonzo nodded and breathed deeply. "Congratulations, then. And I'm sorry for the intrusion. Good luck with the knee."

But as Gonzo turned to exit, Stew squeaked out a question. "What was your name again?" asked Stew. "In case I remember something?"

The question galled her. It was full of attitude and wholly insincere. But Gonzo returned two steps and made absolutely certain Stew Raymo clocked her name.

"Detective—Lydia—Gonzalez," she said.

"And what division are you from?" he pressed.

"Unsolved Cases," said Gonzo. "Have a nice day."

As it turned out, there was no actual Unsolved Cases Division in the LAPD. But Gonzo's story already had plenty of cover. If Stew Raymo wanted to track her down and charge her with harassment, the furthest he would get would be her boss, Lieutenant Bigelow of the Gang Suppression Unit. And Biggs had Gonzo's back. Not to mention, all LAPD detectives had the proxy to dip into the seemingly bottomless bin of unsolved crimes. They were encouraged to do as much. If investigated, Gonzo's hospital appearance was well within department protocol. She had merely sought advice from a former expert in the field of home invasion robbery.

Gonzo's educated prediction was that Stew Raymo would do what most ex-cons would do after such an encounter. Not a damn thing. Engaging the LAPD in anything head-on was a losing proposition. All Gonzo wanted was to rattle Stew's cage a bit. And she had shaken the man enough to convince her that Stew was guilty of something.

But triple homicide?

"Hey," said Romeo. "I know her."

Gonzo was exiting the post-op room with Romeo when her partner stopped hard and heel-swiveled as Pam Raymo whisked past him in the opposite direction.

"That doesn't impress me," answered Gonzo.

"No. I mean I've seen her."

Then Romeo snapped his fingers.

"Yeah, yeah," he said. "She's like this actress."

"Are you coming?"

"Misty Something."

Romeo stared as Pam disappeared behind the curtains.

"Misty Fresh," said Romeo, at once pleased with himself for remembering, yet slightly sickened that the fantasy girl was visiting the ex-con.

"Sounds like a porn star name," joked Gonzo.

"Is a porn star name," said Romeo. He unglued himself and quickstepped his way to meet Gonzo at the elevator.

"You know a porn star?" asked Gonzo, holding the elevator door for Romeo.

"Know her like every other guy knows her."

Romeo made an obscene pumping gesture with his empty fist.

"I hate when you do that."

"Do what? This?"

Romeo grinned and made the pumping gesture again.

"You're hopeless." Gonzo let the elevator doors slide shut.

"Damn right, I am," explained Romeo. "How else would I know her freaking name?"

When the former Misty Fresh returned after her failed search for a nurse who would administer headache meds, she found Stew both agitated and remote. He lied that it was due to the enormity of his headache and added that, given access to an ice pick, he would consider driving it through his own ear until it quelled the pain.

Pam didn't care for Stew's description. She calmly informed Stew what the nurse had said. His headache was likely a temporary reaction to the anesthesia. The nurse, though, promised Pam she would page the doctor.

"Think I need to sleep some more," Stew said.

He then closed his eyes and let go of her hand.

"Why don't you go buy a magazine or something?" he said.

"Okay," said Pam.

A little worried about Stew's sudden change in manner, Pam nodded and withdrew. Then she let it go, rationalizing that his mood was in concert with the anesthesia that was still in his bloodstream.

"Close the curtains, too, will ya?"

Will ya?

There was a false ring to the way Stew capped his request. Pam obliged anyway.

His eyes closed, Stew listened to the curtains glide along the runners until Pam had given him total privacy. He waited until the sound of her heels faded. He opened his eyes, raised his heavy hands over his head and balled his fists so hard he could hear his knuckles pop.

"Motherfuckers!"

Stew's teeth clenched so hard his jaw ached. He wanted to move. He wanted to swing out of his post-op straightjacket and kick something until he bled. His long arms swung around him involuntarily, like those of an octopus, fingers splayed and stretching to grab at anything. All the while he thought about nothing but cigarettes. A cigarette would calm him. *One fucking puff,* he thought, *would chill me enough so I could think through the clanging in my skull.*

Stew found a handful of the curtain. He pulled, slowly retracting his arms until all slack was gone. He heard a POP—POP—POP—POP. One grommet at a time, Stew tore the curtain from each ringlet. And when the slack returned, Stew merely twirled his arm counterclockwise, wrapping the fabric around his wrist. POP—POP—POP. With each simple snap came the slightest satisfaction. Soon, Stew's left arm was bound in yards of white muslin. A mummy's arm, ripping harder, twirling again, then pulling harder and faster. The ringlets' pops sounded like a rapid-fire machine gun until, suddenly, all tension was lost and the curtain fell.

Stew opened his eyes. There was, indeed, some small measure of satisfaction in hauling down his entire wall of privacy. He exhaled heavily, then listened to his heart pound.

"Must be some nasty headache," said the doctor.

Stew's eyes shifted down the line of his nose. At the foot of his bed was the surgeon who had operated on the injured knee. He wore green surgery garb and his hair was still netted. And though Stew recognized the man's voice, the face was foreign, distinctly Asian in origin, and resembled that of the sensei guy in *The Karate Kid*. Stew bet himself he would remember the name of the movie character before he would remember the name of his surgeon.

"Sorry," was all Stew could think to say at the moment.

"No worries," said the surgeon. "As long as you don't screw up my work."

"I'll pay for it," said Stew.

"I'm sure it'll show on your bill," said the surgeon. "Now, let's talk about your rehab."

"Rehab," repeated Stew.

Stew's last rehab was on the thirteenth-floor prison ward of County USC Hospital. Twenty-eight God-awful, gut-puking, days of hell. But Stew had survived. Kicked his drug habit in the ass and begun anew. Yet Stew didn't care for the sound of the word.

Rehab.

But the surgeon was so calm. This after he had just witnessed the beast in Stew. He had merely stood there and serenely watched his patient rip the entire curtain from the railing, loop by loop. Then it came to Stew. A voice in his head. A memory. Words with both sound and image attached.

"*Daniel-san*," said the voice.

"*Mister Miyagi!*" shouted back the boy.

Success, thought Stew. And he smiled.

※ ※ ※

In 1992 the odds of a young American male losing his spouse in a violent crime were higher than a million to one. The risks were twice as elevated for the same man to suffer the murder of a child under the age of eighteen. Two children? The odds climbed. As a pure safety issue, these were numbers Ben had never calculated. Had he ever crunched the numbers, combining both his wife and children into a single, life-shattering, triple homicide, he would have found the odds were so great that he would have a better chance of getting struck by lightning twice while standing in the middle of New York's Central Park on a nearly cloudless day.

But Ben wasn't standing in Central Park when the cloudburst happened. He was tending bar.

As Ben would later come to understand, odds, long or short, weren't important to most Americans. Otherwise, Americans wouldn't foolishly invest billions into their state lotteries. Nor would they routinely stuff themselves into ugly Aloha shirts and vacation in the gambling Meccas of Las Vegas and Atlantic City. Gaming was way up in America. To interview Joe Citizen was to hear countless tales of habitual losers who had cashed their paychecks at the local Indian-owned casino only to lose everything on twenty hands of blackjack.

In fact, Ben would sometimes pontificate, Americans by in large ignored any and all odds, astronomical or otherwise. They consumed too much fast food, abused alcohol, and helped tobacco companies stuff their vaults with cash despite the obvious and heavily publicized betting lines against their own personal benefit. Americans drove cars without buckling seatbelts, owned and stored loaded guns in unsafe places, smoked cigarettes in bed, operated machinery while tanked on cold medication, polished off bottles of wine while soaking in hot tubs, and engaged in millions upon millions of sexual liaisons without asking for proof of a single AIDS test.

Hell, thought Ben. *Soldiers in Iraq played life safer.*

Americans clearly didn't make choices based on odds. But cook the very same probabilities into a monetary context and most of those same Americans would listen. Example: What if

Ben were to explain to a convenience store owner that the mere installation and display of a closed circuit video system would not only decrease the odds of an armed robbery, but increase sales by creating an environment that made the customer feel safer? The profit motive alone would convince the convenience store owner to open his checkbook.

The very same formula worked for most businesses. Ben would work the same odds that most men or women would find reason or rationale to ignore. Except he would turn the numbers into dollar signs. Clients would always see the advantage and pay Ben well. This was Ben's unique and true talent.

A talent born from loss.

As Ben sat in his car, engine idling, parked across the street from what was once his precious Prague '88, he couldn't help but calculate the cost versus benefit in his life so far. With astronomical odds in his favor, he had still lost his family. But from the ashes of that gruesome loss he had eventually found what he considered his true calling. He knew there was nobody in his business that was as good as he at diagnosing danger, prescribing caution, and profiting from other people's fears.

Ben was the best at what he did. And he hated the ego-driven side of himself that knew it. The cost of becoming the best had been too high.

At dawn that day he had rolled from bed, called Josie and had her scrape his schedule clean. He had driven in the half-light to the downtown Los Angeles flower mart and crafted his own bouquets—three in all—then set a course for Live Oak Memorial Park in the City of Monrovia. The grass was wet and the sky, pale blue and utterly cloudless. It was a sure sign of a scorching day to come. Despite the years that had ticked away since he last visited the graves, Ben needed no assistance whatsoever in finding his way through the small knolls and valleys of rolling green and live oaks.

Lord, Ben. The things you never forget.

As he set the flowers down, Ben was momentarily dumbfounded when he saw the grave markers. The flat stones were three in a row, each daughter flanking Sara. But Ben was struck by how small his daughters' stones were—no more than six-by-eight inches compared to their mother's ten-by-twelve inch plaque. His girls would have been nearly full grown by now, he thought. Young women. It shamed him that their grave markers would forever be so diminished.

Ben prayed the Lord's Prayer, cried a little, then prayed again from guilt that his first recitation sounded too indifferent, too damned monotone.

Once back on the road, he called Gonzo on her cell phone and left a voicemail message. It was only 7:30 A.M. Ben stopped at a nearby Denny's for breakfast, tried to read a newspaper, but couldn't help wondering if and when Gonzo would return his call. Shortly after nine, he called Gonzo again. He left his third message close to ten. Ben made sure not to plead. Each message was nearly identical.

"Gonzo. It's Ben. I'm on my cell phone."

Ben checked the clock. It was 1:48 in the afternoon. He had been parked in his car outside the former Prague '88 for nearly three hours. And Gonzo hadn't returned a single call. He could reason that she had other responsibilities, primarily her child and her job. And when she had something to pass along to Ben, she would as soon as humanly possible.

But something heavy had shifted inside of Ben. As if his emotional components had been rearranged without his consent. Deep down, he knew he wouldn't be at all right until Gonzo called him with some kind of information. Anything, he hoped. Any tangible bit of intel to assist him with that plaguing question:

What to do next?

In that moment, Ben re-attacked the question more specifically.

What to do about Stew Raymo?

The mostly brick, one-story space that had once been Ben's restaurant was plastered with a large, orange and green *Grand Opening* sign strung over the pub's unsubtle name, The Sham Rock. And for a minute there, Ben thought the three pedestrians ambling toward the door were the proud new leaseholders and their pinstriped banker. He even had a thought of getting out of the car and joining them for the walk-though. Only the pedestrians kept walking.

Ben picked up his cell phone and speed-dialed Alex. After four rings, she finally picked up her mobile phone.

"Hey, there," she said.

"I'll pick up the girls today," Ben said.

"You sure about that?" asked Alex. "I'm right around the corner."

"Of course, I'm sure," he said. "I want to."

"Slow day?"

"No," said Ben. "I just want to be with my family . . . if that's okay with you."

"Of course, it's okay." Alex's voice warmed. "Maybe we can all go out to dinner."

"Fine by me. I'll see you at home," said Ben.

"I love you," she said.

"Love you, too."

"How's it goin', Boss?"

"Surgery is easy. But rehab is a cunt!" bitched Stew.

Despite the sketchy cell phone connection, Stew could hear his site foreman quietly laugh then cup the phone and say something in indecipherable Spanish. He imagined that square head of Henry's parked atop equally block-like shoulders with no discernible neck to speak of, big grin on his face while translating Stew's foul mood for the rest of the amused crew.

"Will be okay. You're tough man, *Jefe*," said Henry.

"Tough men eat morphine," replied Stew. "You forget, asshole. Once an addict always an addict. One bite of that shit and I'm back to where I was."

And I'm sure as shit not ever going back there.

What's the use? thought Stew. Sure, Henry was supposed to be his most trusted employee, but he was also known to knock back a couple of semi-cold Buds at lunch. So why the hell would or should Henry Lopez give a crap about a man's daily bout with sobriety? *Better keep the information simple*, thought Stew. Henry didn't need to know the painful details of enduring ACL rehab without drugs stronger than shelf-worn Ibuprofen, not to mention the emasculating necessity for Stew to wear medical support hose in order to increase circulation to the knee and cut down the risk of blood clotting.

"Sounds bad," said Henry.

"You know, I don't hear hammers," said Stew.

"Inspector came by this morning. Said we had to pour new foundations."

"What inspector?" asked Stew. "The OSHA guy?"

"I don't know that guy," said Henry. "The guy for the pool. Came by to sign off on the rebar job."

"So what does the rebar in the pool have to do with the foundation on the house?"

"That's what I asked. But he looked at the pilings anyway and said we have cracks in all of 'em."

"Did you see the cracks?"

"Maybe, I think."

"And you didn't think to fill in the holes with dirt?"

"They already pass inspection once, *Jefe*."

Stew wanted to hurl the phone. He imagined the device fast-balling across the bedroom and busting a hole in the television tube, effectively wrecking Judge Judy's TV courtroom. In that instant of rage, Stew hated everything he could see. He hated the perfectly fluffed pillows that propped his knee, the custom wrought-iron bed he lay in, the tartan pajamas that Pamela had purchased and altered to suit his needs, the fake French pine armoire that was really just a free-standing TV closet, not to mention the Sheetrock walls on which his wife had painstakingly applied a faux fresco, powder-blue finish with Napoleon white trim.

Where the fuck does she think we live?

Stew hated so hard that the kind of pain most men would treat with prescription narcotics became totally secondary to his getting out of bed and figuring how to put on a pair of Levi's.

"I'm coming down there," Stew said into the phone before hanging up on Henry.

Pamela caught Stew struggling to climb down the steps into the backyard. The French doors leading down from the master bedroom were wide open. Stew's left hand gripped the railing while the other held a crutch under his right arm. He had but three stairs to negotiate, but the precise tack to coordinate the crutch, the handrail, and his single good leg had momentarily escaped him.

"Where the hell are you going?" asked Pam.

"Gotta get to the site!"

"Except for the bathroom, you're not supposed—"

"Can't talk about it!"

"Get back in—"

"Get outta my way!"

"Make me, you big prick!"

And in that tiny moment, Stew wanted to strike her. A thought that rarely ever dawned on him. At least, not while they weren't screwing.

Pam knew as much. She had seen the look before in other men who had kept her. The thought even crossed her mind of how funny Stew would look after trying to swing at her. He would surely lose his balance and come crashing down the steps, maybe bloodied with a mouthful of fresh green sod.

But if he ever connected . . . thought Pam. *If he ever hit me . . . I would kill him then leave him.*

"You know what that house is costing us?" moaned Stew. "Fuckin' vig on the loan, the crews not workin', and now they say I gotta re-pour the fuckin' pilings!"

"Call Henry."

"Who do you think I just talked to?"

"It doesn't have to be today!"

Stew inched in as close as he could without tumbling head over ass.

"You like your little house?" asked Stew. "You like antiques and Baldwin doorknobs and arty paint finishes? You like that stuff?"

Pamela stood with her arms crossed and her lower lip tucked under her front teeth.

"If I don't finish the fuckin' spec house and flip it by the new year," pressed Stew, "all your precious shit's going on the front lawn for a yard sale. You got that?"

Pam got it, alright. Right down her spine. There would be no holding Stew back. No reasoning whatsoever. She saw it all in his eyes, clear and drug-free. In that short space of time, everything became so very simple. So what would be her best move? All she needed to do was step aside. But then he would continue to steamroll her, right or wrong, for the rest of their marriage.

"I'll drive you," she said.

"What?"

"You heard me, dipshit. I'll drive."

Pam held out a hand.

Agreeing to let Pam drive was easy enough for Stew. He figured once inside the truck he could wrestle the keys back from his wife, climb behind the wheel, and motor unobstructed to the site. If only getting into the truck hadn't been such an ordeal. Stew swore out loud at the asshole salesman who had sold him the off-road lift kit that raised his spanking new F-250 an extra eight inches. Between that and the oversized tires, the climb into the truck was a full foot higher than normal.

It may as well have been Everest.

After tossing the crutches into the truck bed, Stew had to balance on one leg, turn his back to the passenger seat, and using only the strength from his upper body, pull himself up onto the seat.

Pam offered to help, climbing in from the driver's side, insisting he take her hand. Stew ignored her and the pain surging from his leg into his groin, finding a purchase in the air conditioning vent. He was able to wrap his right arm around the headrest, at last gaining enough leverage to hoist his body into the seat. He swiveled his legs into the truck and slammed the door.

All thoughts Stew had of driving were vanquished in a single exhale. He could only think of those Everest climbers he had watched on the Discovery Channel and how they craved oxygen.

The ten-minute drive to the site passed silently. When the truck pulled up to the curb, Henry Lopez trotted down to greet them, twice pleased to find beautiful Pam behind the wheel.

"Here," said Stew. "Take pictures of the pilings."

Stew withdrew a disposable camera from the glove box and handed it to Pam.

"All the pilings," said Stew. "Henry will show you."

Glad to be part of the construction team, Pam hopped from the truck, momentarily leaving Henry staring glumly at his boss.

"Jefe. You don't look so good," worried Henry.

"Just make sure she gets the pictures," said Stew. "If the pilings are bad, fuckin' Morales Brothers are paying my costs."

The Morales Brothers were Stew's choice du jour in concrete subcontractors. They were a small team with five cement trucks, all painted the colors of the Mexican flag with giant sombreros stenciled on the agitating cylinders.

"Maybe you should take a look at the footings, *Jefe*—"

"Get with Pam and show her!" spat Stew.

Oh, he wanted to look at the footings. But the thought of crawling out of the truck only to suffer the climb back in was too much to imagine. Stew was already thinking of cashing in his prescriptions for Kadian and OxyContin, both morphine derivatives and a former addict's wet dream. The treated side of his brain wisely figured he could survive the drive home and the painful transfer from the truck back to the couch. Any more aggravation and he might as well take his ten-year Alcoholics Anonymous' chip and spin it into the gutter.

Stew twisted his view to make sure Henry was making as much of an effort on instructing Pam about how to photograph the footings as he was admiring her infamous ass.

Next, Stew achingly searched his pants pocket for his cell phone, checked his watch for the time of day, then dialed an old number from memory. The connection sounded clean, but the phone at the other end seemed to ring forever. Ten rings. Eleven rings. Just like the old days. Before cell phones and voicemail.

Sure, there were answering machines. But those devices were for legitimate people living legitimate lives.

Fourteen rings. Fifteen rings.

"Yeah," answered a voice, foggy from a lifetime of breathing in secondhand smoke.

"Lookin' for The Sax Man," said Stew.

"Don't know no Sax Man," said the voice.

"Just an old friend checkin' on a pal," said Stew.

"So what's that to me?" said the voice. "I don't know no—"

"Tell him Stew's got somethin' he needs. I'm sure Jerome'll take care of you after he gets his. Now take down this number."

"Wait," said the voice. "Need to find something to write . . ."

The pain in Stew had stopped at his pelvis, but seemed to be pooling between his hips with no place to run. As if it were a reservoir that might very well overflow or burst. Nothing a handful of OxyContin couldn't snuff out. Crush that shit and snort it? The pain would die even faster. Stew squeezed his eyes shut and kept his voice even.

"Who you say you was?" asked the voice.

"Stew."

"Like I said. Don't know no Sax Man but if a fellah comes in with that kind of fool name, I'll pass it on."

"You do that," said Stew. "Now here's the number."

Stew reeled off his mobile number. His silence was rewarded when the voice read back the digits in the correct sequence. Then Stew hung up without saying goodbye. There was no rudeness in it at all. If anything, it was a basic criminal signature. Anyone polite enough to engage in the banal niceties of the average civilian's telephone conversations might tip his hand that he was playing for the other side.

In other words, cops said "goodbye."

When Stew thought cop, he pictured that tall brownie-of-a-woman towering over his post-op bed. What the fuck was her name?

Stew's phone buzzed in his hand. The incoming call had an Echo Park prefix. Close to downtown, not far from Chavez Ravine and Dodger Stadium. It had to be the Sax Man. Jerome.

In some ways, the underworld still moved faster than broadband. Otherwise, the cops might catch up one day.

"This is Stew."

"It's Jerome," said the happy voice. "Man, what you been doin'?"

"Been awhile," answered Stew, relieved and irritated all at once. When visited by the lady detective, she had asked him about a crime in Culver City. A family thing. Home invasion. Triple murder. The first person Stew imagined was Jerome. The Sax Man. If the old smack-head hadn't overdosed yet, Stew would have bet Jerome was the rat. But if such were the case, Jerome wouldn't have called back. At least not so efficiently.

"How's it hangin'?"

"Swings with the breeze," said Stew. "Listen. You know how I feel about phones. I got somethin' for you."

"Man, my motor's not so good no more. Can't walk two blocks without sittin' down awhile."

"Middleman shit," assured Stew. "Got some bizness you might know how to move."

"Still know me some guys. Hey. Got a gig tomorrow night. Maybe you can—"

"Still playin', huh?"

"My horn'll quit me before I quit her. You know that."

"Some shit doesn't change. But I'm a daytimer now. Gotta be a nooner."

"Shit. I don't see noon for less than a c-note."

"Hook me up and you'll make ten times," said Stew.

"Daytimer. You got a real job or somethin'?"

"Or somethin'," said Stew. He was terse, biting his lip due to the pain under his belly. "You got an address?"

"Place you called," said Jerome. "You still know it?"

"Stink Hole. See you tomorrow."

Stew clicked off then jackhammered his head back into the leather headrest, as if the soft impact could ease his suffering. Tears squeezed out from his slammed eyelids. His mouth formed an O from which he exhaled slowly. In through the nose, out through the mouth. Stew did this over and over until—

"Got your pictures. Wanna go to a one-hour photo?"

Stew opened his eyes to find Pam had already climbed into the driver's seat and turned the ignition.

"Take me home," exhaled Stew. "Then you go out and do the pictures, okay?"

"Bad?"

"Worse than fuckin' detox!"

"How about childbirth?"

"Women got nothin' on my shit."

"Advil. Here's five."

Pam shook five gels caps from the bottle into Stew's open hand. He brought up some spit and dry swallowed the little green balls of ibuprofen.

"Baby lawyer called today."

"It's not the time, Pam."

"Good as any. Might take your mind off the pain."

Pam was driving now, clearly relishing both the wheel of the big pickup and having her husband hostage.

"Russian couple," continued Pam. "She's due in November. They're both cleared with Canadian visas and could meet us in Vancouver. All we gotta do is buy their plane tickets."

"Hurts too much to hear."

"I'll take that as a yes," said Pam, winding herself into an excited tizzy. "You don't even have to go. I'll take care of—"

"If I gotta re-pour those footings—"

"Fine. If you have to re-pour and rebuild, then no deal. Otherwise . . ."

Stew opened his left eye, catching the briefest glimpse of Pam's wide grin. Deep down, he supposed adopting would be an okay move. "Think of the upside," she had once tried to sell him. "An actual baby without all the fuss of pregnancy. No unattractive weight gain, mood swings, or depression." Stew's wife would remain Queen of the Neighborhood Hot Bodies while satisfying her undying yen to be an suv-driving soccer mom.

"Whatever," was all Stew could muster.

"Alright!" squealed Pam, bouncing on the seat.

"Just get me back into bed."

The Stink Hole was exactly as Stew remembered it. Formally called Ronny's Pub on Sunset, it was an Echo Park haunt the cops could never kill. Opened shortly after the Los Angeles Dodgers moved into nearby Chavez Ravine, Ronny's had survived floods, fires, robberies, gunfights, murder, DEA and ATF raids, health code shut-downs, name changes, and more owners than title searches could possibly unearth. But just about anybody who ever sat on a bar stool at Ronny's knew it by its easy-to-remember nickname, *The Stink Hole*. The source of the moniker was pure mystery turned into local mythology. The most popular legend was that the pub was built on a fault line that released a sulfurous plume through cracks in the foundation when the earth shook, as it so often did in Los Angeles.

The fistful of change Stew slid into the meter bought him sixty minutes of Sunset Boulevard street parking. Ought to be enough, he estimated, for the anticipated small talk and, he hoped, quick round trip to and from Bad Memory Lane. As Stew swung the crutches around and stepped himself up onto the sidewalk, he did a pain inventory. The excruciating agony of Tuesday had subsided to a dullness that, if Stew focused on better thoughts, was close to numb. This was, praise be, from a cocktail of over-the-counter analgesics, Advil and Aleve, alternated every three hours with a double-dose of Tylenol. Pain aside, the hard part was keeping his belly full with food to keep the meds from etching a hole in his stomach lining.

Also, the crutches were getting easier to maneuver. With that a sense of equilibrium had returned. Stew found he could move swiftly, swivel, and even lean on them. With his armpits stuck in the saddles and the sticks supporting him like ramparts, he looked something like an ape perched on a pair of rubber-tipped knuckles.

Stew squinted at his watch. It was straight up noon. This less-than-famous end of Sunset Boulevard snaked along the bottom of the southern slope of the Silverlake hills until it ran smack into downtown Los Angeles. On either side of the strip stood a mix of old, sun-baked apartments and modest, pre-World War II bungalows, most from the Arts and Crafts era. And as much as the area had been slowly reborn from inevitable urban gentrification, some remnants of its barrio roots remained untouched by anything but colorful spray paint.

Stew swung open the door to Ronny's and stood at the threshold, waiting for his eyes to adjust. Nothing had changed. The bar, the wooden stools, the red vinyl upholstery of the booths held together with layers of silver duct tape, and the dolphins, of course. The ancient Sea World posters were everywhere, rippled and faded in ten-dollar aluminum frames.

The dolphins. How could I forget those silly-assed, frolicking dolphins?

The bar was cast in red lights and shafts of sunlight streaking through dirty windows protected by metal bars and the joint had an orangey glow. Then Stew sniffed the air. It was, after all, the famed Stink Hole. But the only aroma he recognized was that of the rancid oil used for frying Mojo Potatoes.

"Hey Stewy," croaked Jerome. "Over here."

Stew swung his view deep into a corner of the room, and for the thinnest moment, failed to recognize his old partner in crime. As long as Stew had known Jerome, he had been a junkie. A robust sort of addict. A man of multiple appetites, including the good and greasy food found in late night jazz joints. But the Jerome that sat in the far booth was a man who resembled an AIDS patient clinging to life. The fat in Jerome's face was nearly gone along with the muscles on his bones.

"Damn, brother! What happened to you?" asked Jerome, speaking exactly what Stew was thinking.

His eyes adjusted to the light, Stew put his head down and deftly made his way through the obstacle course of rickety tables and empty chairs. The bar was empty but for Stew and Jerome. *Whoever was running the joint*, thought Stew, *must be the man in the back working the chicken fryer.*

"Lost an argument with a speeding Toyota," quipped Stew, slinging himself into the booth and resting his crutches on the back of a chair. "One of those electric jobs. Didn't even hear it comin'."

"You hurtin' any?" asked Jerome. His eyes appeared large and genuinely concerned, magnified by his emaciated face.

"Know what?" Stew began. "I'm grateful I'm not in a fuckin' wheelchair."

Truly grateful. Grateful he was no longer an addict like Jerome. Grateful he didn't have to steal quarters from cigarette machines just to buy a fix.

Gratitude.

The feeling swelled inside Stew like a birthday surprise. It was a rejuvenating, pain-relieving moment brought on by the face of the poor and dying Jerome the Sax Man. Stew had come so very far. Far from dingy, dirty joints like Ronny's Pub. Far from scraping out scores, only to settle for fifteen percent of the take from the merchandise he had stolen, and then having to divide the dough with mooks half as smart as himself just to keep someone from sticking a shiv in his back.

"So you're daytiming it, huh?" asked Jerome. "Like a real deal job?"

"You don't know the half of it," said Stew.

"You look clean, too."

"Sober, married. Own a house, got a business. All on the straight up."

"Fuck all."

"Fuck all is right. You should meet my wife. So hot she'd burn your dick off."

"Double damn, man." Jerome sat back as if to take an even wider look at Stew.

"Everybody we know'd is either dead or in the joint. You're like a wonder of modern man."

"Listen, man," turned Stew. "Why I called—"

"How'd you do it?"

"Do what?"

"Go over the wall. Get all worldly good and shit."

"That part's wrong. I'm not that good."

"Yeah, right. Nobody is. But why you?"

"Why'd I get shit right?"

"How'd you get so lucky?"

"No luck," said Stew. "Epiphany. Know what that is?"

"Fuck yeah."

With that Jerome swiveled his shoulders and stuck out what little chest he had left. He looked like a life-sized marionette on strings.

Stew stole a look at his watch, momentarily concerned about the parking meter.

"Same old shit," said Stew, tingling with the momentary satisfaction of knowing he had escaped his previous life in crime. "I was workin' scores in the Valley. Construction sites. Fridays 'n' paydays. Crews 'n' bosses."

"And bosses go to banks," said Jerome, thinking himself ahead of Stew.

Stew explained that after general contractors pay their crews and do their banking, they often make trips to suppliers. Home Depot was Stew's favorite. He would camp out at one of the Valley's many do-it-yourself stores on Friday afternoon and wait for some flush-with-Friday-cash construction jockey to appear with a stupid smile on his face.

"Boys with toys," said Stew. "Generals love new tools. And when they get a few bucks, can't wait to go shopping."

The rest was no different than following home a man who had just bought his first Rolex. Only with general contractors, the new tools weren't worn on their wrists. They were usually in the garage or shed, hidden from their bookkeeping wives. Sometimes Stew would wait for nightfall and the chance to break in without detection. Other times he would simply park behind the contractor's pickup and meet the victim in the driveway. With a smile on his face and a gun in his belt, Stew would kindly ask for help transferring the tools to a waiting panel van with stolen plates.

"Like I said," continued Stew. "Same old shit. Time I unloaded the tools it was nothing more than pocket money. Then came the moment. The epiphany."

Stew's epiphany came when he was driving through all those

nice suburban neighborhoods. Those contractors he was stealing from seemed no smarter than Stew, but they were sure living a lot better. Nice houses. Decent cars. Money to burn on new tools. Spurred by low interest rates, the construction boom in Southern California had turned the art of fixing fixer-uppers into marketable properties with a little curb appeal into a license to print money.

"I mean, there was other stuff going on, too," added Stew. "By then I'd met Pam. My wife. She was in the Program. What can I say? She pulled me into a meeting. Starting anew sounded good after breaking through the first detox. Leave the old me behind with the dry heaves and cold sweats."

"Looks like it stuck," said Jerome with a trace of jealousy.

"Most if it, I guess."

"Most of it or you wouldn't have called me."

A mild clatter could be heard from the kitchen, followed by the sound of a door swinging open. Stew skipped his view from Jerome to the old Mojo Maker, a jowly man with mostly indistinguishable foreign features. The Mojo Maker walked with a floor-scraping shuffle that Stew thought must always announce his appearance well before he ever enters a room.

"He's alright," said Jerome of the Mojo Maker. "He ain't even open yet. But I called him so he popped the lock early just for me."

"He the guy I talked to on the phone?"

"That would be him."

The Mojo Maker was just another added discomfort for Stew.

"Let's talk in the office," said Stew, gesturing toward the back.

"Seriously. He's cool."

"Yeah, well I'm not no more."

Stew slid from the seat, retrieved his crutches and moved toward the men's room.

Whatever, Jerome figured. Then he followed Stew to a men's room with an odor so putrid some regulars preferred to take relief against the rusty fence out back.

"Jesus," said Stew, finding every inch of the men's toilet as repugnant as anything he could recall.

Stew remembered using the same shit hole of a bathroom countless times for drug buys or payoffs or to just get out of earshot of all the other bad boys that were Ronny's Regulars. But the men's room was a squalid stink pit with paint-peeling walls splattered with a strange, septic residue.

"Give it a minute," Jerome said. "You'll get used to the smell."

Stew used his crutch to push the door shut. He didn't want to even touch the knob with his hands. Hardly a germaphobe, Stew was still momentarily rendered into a stiffer version of himself. He wondered if the stitches in his knee could get infected merely by his standing in the unseemly air.

Jerome found a jug of disinfectant that was kept under the sink. He unscrewed the lid and splashed some around on the floor.

"Like that did any good," said Stew.

"Improves the smell," said Jerome. "Now what you got?"

"Yeah," said Stew, recovering from his momentary worries over germs and getting down to the point.

"Old business," continued Stew. "Way back."

"And how's that supposed to get me paid?" the old junkie spat with a sneer.

"Got a visit from the heat," pressed Stew. "Detective. Talking about shit way back when. Culver City shit. Home invasions."

"Who gives a crap about old news? We did a bunch back then. Time's up on all that shit."

"Not the one," reminded Stew. "You remember the one, dontcha?"

Jerome shook his head. Either he didn't remember or he didn't want to. Stew eased closer, stuck his face in Jerome's and twisted it a tick counterclockwise for emphasis.

"How's this?" said Stew. "Remember you had to go swimmin' to get the shit off you."

Enough said. The Sax Man's grill grew slack as the ugly memory returned. The hollows in his cheeks puffed with the slightest exhale.

"Long time," said Jerome. "Fuck all . . . I'd put that one right out of my head . . ."

"Well, somebody put it into the LAPD's head! Now, besides me, only two guys coulda talked—"

"Not me, homey. Like I said, I'd, like, forgot the whole—"

"You and Bebop," hissed Stew. "You talked to Bebop?"

"Fuck all! I haven't seen Bebop since he went short on me. No good, cornhole motherfucker!"

"How'd they know then?"

"Don't know."

"C'mon. Sax Man? How'd they know?"

"I say talk to the Bop!"

"Don't think I will? And what am I supposed to say when he tells me to talk to you? Fuckin' junkie! Look at you! You're so low you'd sell your nuts for shit!"

"Stop it!"

"What'd you do?"

"Said . . . stop it . . . stop it, Stew."

"Tell me what you fuckin' did."

"P . . . P . . . Puhleeease," wheezed Jerome.

"You cocksucker junkie fuck with a big mouth! Talked, didn't you? Didn't you?! Who'd you tell, huh? Who'd you tell about it?"

It's not that Jerome wouldn't answer. It's just that he couldn't with his windpipe crushed. The man couldn't so much as gasp for the putrid air he now desperately needed.

And Stew.

He was so trained on Jerome's bulging eyeballs, searching every broken blood vessel for a grain of information, that he hadn't registered the physics of the situation. Stew's long arm was stuck straight out, but not near enough to touch Jerome. But in Stew's right hand was one of the crutches. And the saddle of the crutch, usually reserved for Stew's armpit, was neatly fitted underneath Jerome's chin. It was as if every measure of Stew's power and weight and rage had been conducted into and through the aluminum crutch.

Jerome was pinned against the sticky wall, totally defenseless. If the man's arms had ever raised themselves in surrender or resignation, Stew never saw them. Only later would he recall Jerome's eyes as they strained from their sockets—then the sudden shock of discovering that in his lost moment of uncontrolled choler he had actually killed the Sax Man.

Stew released the crutch. Jerome's body listed sideways, sliding down the wall, gaining momentum until it crashed through the stall door. All Stew could see were Jerome's lower extremities—two equally starved limbs lost in a pair of baggy jeans. Stew stared at the Sax Man's scuffed loafers.

Jerome was wearing only one sock.

Stumbling backwards, Stew found himself nearly cracking the dirty sink from its pedestal. Then it was either wits or instinct that took control. Stew grabbed a handful of paper towels and spun quickly around the bathroom while trying to remember if he had touched anything. No, he reasoned. He had been so disgusted with the foul space that he had kept his hands to his crutches. He calmed his own breathing, then used the towels to turn the doorknob. And like snapping his fingers, he was back in the bar, the Stink Hole, Ronny's Pub on Sunset.

The rest was cold, remote, and remembered by Stew as if laid out in a "how to" handbook written by incarcerated criminals. All the steps seemed defined or preordained to happen in the order in which they had come. The first cue was the sound of another batch of breaded potatoes being dropped into the kitchen fryer. Stew swiftly moved toward the sound, surprising the Mojo Maker as he was tossing a bag of sliced frozen potatoes into a soggy bag of flour. Stew's initial instinct was to radiate a worried look, inform the Mojo Maker that Jerome had fainted in the bathroom, and then flatten the old man with a surprise fist as he hurried past. But without so much as thinking of a Plan B, Stew simply executed one. The fryer was to Stew's immediate right. He quickly gripped the rubber handle and flipped the basket's bubbling contents at the Mojo Maker.

The old man cowered and screamed under the spray of hot oil and potatoes. Stew came two steps closer. A poke from the rubber-tipped crutch sent the Mojo Man writhing to the floor. The steel-tipped boot on Stew's right foot worked swiftly to the finish, finding the soft spot in the old man's neck, cutting off his vocals. Using the crutches for balance, Stew locked his elbows and lifted himself just enough to drive all two hundred forty pounds of himself downward.

He felt the man's neck snap and . . . that was that.

Next, Stew quickly latched both the front and rear doors, wiped his fingerprints clean off the fryer, and rummaged in the storage closet for some kind of industrial degreaser. He scanned the labels for three words: Contains Petroleum Distillates. Stew found what he was looking for in a junior-sized drum of Greasygone. He liberally splashed the degreasing agent along the paths he had taken through the pub, at last stopping at a bootleg vending machine that dispensed individual packs of cigarettes. Instead of smashing at the lock until the machine busted open with piles of smokes, Stew inserted a five-dollar bill and purchased a single pack of Marlboros.

Stew put a match to not one, but two smokes. To light his evidence-erasing inferno, he employed a single cigarette as a fuse. Stew placed the cigarette at the edge of the largest puddle of degreaser fluid, then put the other between his lips. He inhaled and closed his eyes.

At last, Stew breathed. *A fuckin' smoke.*

Stew barely noticed the blistering sunlight as he exited the pub. Nor did he pay much mind to the parking ticket stuck to his truck's windshield. His only thought was to escape the crime scene without using the crutches. He thought two shiny sticks underneath such a hearty frame might look too conspicuous. So when he left Ronny's Stew quickly tossed his crutches into the truck bed, stepped off the curb, snatched the ticket from underneath his windshield wiper blade, climbed into his truck, and drove the hell on.

Pain be damned.

The cigarette was his reward for the agony of a left knee that felt like it was going to buckle with every wobbled step.

Drive, motherfucker.

Drive far.

Drive yourself away from the killer you once were.

But while driving north on the 101 Freeway, Stew's stomach began to grind and his bowels felt as if they would soon turn septic. The feeling was creeping toward the surface, readying to turn to steam the moment it escaped his pores.

The killer had returned.

In an instant as quick as a finger snap, the madness inside Stew had pushed the cork clean out. *All the hard work*, thought Stew. *For what?* The weeks of detox and sweats. The twelve steps to sobriety. The minutes, hours, days, weeks, years. He had crawled so far out of himself that he was sure the old Stew was dead and decomposed. He had moved on, dammit! He had found Pam. Found love and the salvation of honest work. He owned a home, for Christ's sake. He even paid taxes. The ugly past was truly something so far in his rearview mirror that he sometimes wondered if it had been little more than a bad dream.

I've moved on, dammit. That's not me anymore.

But that was Stew Raymo in the men's room. The same Stew Raymo who set fire to Ronny's Pub on Sunset. A blaze that was just beginning to rage while Stew, driving right on the speed limit, was cresting the Cahuenga Pass and beginning his familiar descent into the safe harbor of the San Fernando Valley.

The same damn Stew who still hadn't a clue who the rat was. The same damn Stew who knew that once his past had caught up with him, it would cling like cancer until he had scraped himself clean of all malignancies. The rat would have to die. So would anyone the rat might have told.

Think, Stew. Think it out. You're not done, yet.

He needed to stay present. There's blood to deal with. Trace evidence on his body. Hairs. Microfibers. Blood specks the size of needle pricks. Everything had to be scrubbed. Clothes, the cab of the truck. All of it. Then an alibi established. Killing was work, he remembered. Harder work than anybody gave credit for.

Stew's cigarette was burned down to the filter and the pain was coming back. And to think the day was barely half done.

Stew fished for the pack of Marlboros and lit another stick.

"I'm back," Stew cursed. "Goddammit all, the beast is back."

5

WHILE JANUARY ENDED with a cold snap—by Southern California standards—February arrived with a wave of Santa Ana winds and a rash of brushfires that left Simi Valley under a constant cloud of smoke and ash. Concerned for young, developing lungs, both private and public schools asked parents to keep their children at home and indoors. Ben thought the idea was laughable. Unless a home was hermetically sealed and outfitted with a HEPA air filtration system the size of a Volkswagen, the terrifyingly tiny carbon particulates wouldn't be stopped from finding their way into the lungs of every child in Simi Valley.

The day after the winds shifted back into a normal offshore pattern, Simi Valley schools were back in business. This suited Ben just fine. By reinvesting his heart and time into Alex and the girls, the dark clouds in his soul had all but vanished. He had insisted on doing the morning driving, earning him a largesse of points from his wife. Sometimes Ben would even venture to forgo the drop-off lane and would park so he could walk Betsy to her classroom. Those days he would mingle and hang out with other school parents, mostly chatty mothers and a few unemployed fathers.

Ben never intended to bump into Gonzo.

After all his plaintive calls to her had gone unreturned, he had actually begun to hope she wouldn't call back. For if she had, the dark clouds might return. He had even rehearsed the conversation he would have with Gonzo on the day their paths would inevitably cross. She would first apologize. Then, before she could pull at the stitches on his healing heart, he would apologize back for wasting her time.

He would next beseech her to forget that awful night by the pool. He was drunk. He was melancholy. Let's put a cork in it. Keep the past in the past.

But it didn't quite work out as planned.

The Simi Canyons headmaster had kindly asked Ben to assist the school in choosing the safest artificial turf to replace the tired sod on the athletic fields. Ben's first response had been to recommend the school invest in better maintenance of the natural grass. Even before his formal research he had known that real turf was statistically the safest move. He had warned that while artificial turf might be easier to manage, it would most likely increase the risk of injuries, primarily to young ankles and toes. Ben recalled reading warnings about some bizarre condition called Turf Toe.

Unfortunately Ben was later informed that the school's board had already voted, the money had been earmarked, and it was merely a matter of choosing the faux grass surface and the overpriced contractor to install it. *Typical*, thought Ben. *Spend first, ask questions later.* A terse reminder that school boards were no smarter than most other organizations when it came to spending other people's money.

The morning was crisp and sunlit. Ben was alone and at peace, seated in the bleachers while taking in what might be his last look at the school's three acres of parched and beaten grass.

He was grateful that his primary, daily concern had returned to issues of human safety.

"Asshole got hit by a car."

Ben turned at the waist, squinting into the east. Gonzo was standing there in a t-shirt and motorcycle jacket, her long legs fit into a pair of jeans and boots. It was no stretch that most Simi Canyons parents assumed she was a lesbian. She was a tall cop, had a butch nickname and on her days off, dressed as if she were looking to rumble with a 1950s street gang.

"Who got hit by a car?"

Gonzo stepped up onto the foldable bleachers.

"I wasn't going to tell," said Gonzo. "I'd worked it all out. I was gonna lie to you."

"If this is about—"

"I'd lay awake at night and convince myself that you didn't need any more pain. That anything I said, anything I knew, all I'd be doing is squeezing lemon juice into an old wound that was better left to heal."

For Ben, the words were there. All he needed to utter was, "stop" or "shut up." After that, he could deliver his rehearsed speech and the conversation would end right then and there. All his life, Ben had read or heard about words getting stuck in people's throats. It was a figure of speech. A cliché. He never thought it would feel so damned literal. He knew what he had to say but his voice felt strangely constricted, as if someone's hands were around his neck.

"But then I thought about it this way," continued Gonzo, unaware of Ben's plight. "Who am I to decide what's best for you? I might have my opinions. I might wanna strongly advise you to drop your shit and move the hell on. Live and let live. The world isn't fair. Lord knows I'm an expert in that stuff. All cops are expert in what a cesspool our world is."

Gonzo stuffed her hands in her jacket pockets and set her eyes just about everywhere but on Ben.

"That shit—the bad things that happened to you—didn't happen to me. I have no fuckin' clue what it feels like to live inside your skin. You came to me as a friend and asked a favor. I owe it to you to be straight. I owe you what I know."

"Okay," said Ben, unstuck, his unprimed pump curious and churning words he had sworn to himself he wouldn't utter. "What shit do you know that you didn't want to say?"

"Like I said. He got hit by a car. Bad luck it didn't kill him. But it lamed him up good."

"You're talking about Stew Raymo?"

"I was digging up what there was, asking around the PD. Then his name popped up on an accident report. Would you believe that I caught up to him in his post-op bed?"

"You talked to him?" asked Ben. "You actually met the guy?"

"Think he was still a little narced from the anesthesia. But yeah. We met. I talked. I asked him questions about that night. Mostly, he just listened."

"Listened . . ."

Ben's left foot was involuntarily tapping the metallic bleacher seat, making a dull ring. It was now or never. He could dam the tide of darkness. He could ask Gonzo to go away and leave him be with the cushioned life that he had remade.

Gonzo nodded as if Ben had asked her a silent question, then sat herself one row below him.

"Ask an innocent man about a crime he didn't commit, he still feels accused," said Gonzo flatly, as if repeating something learned in a graduate criminology course. "He'll appear shocked, incredulous, curious. But never silent."

"You think he did it. You think he murdered my family?"

"Not that simple . . . Ask a guilty man about a crime he committed, he's as likely to put up the same sorta protests as the innocent man."

"But Stew said nothing. Yeah?"

"Every so often though, you get another kind of criminal. Smart guy that knows the less he says the better for him. Admit nothing, deny nothing. Give your accuser zero help, no handholds, nothing to go home with. Just a lotta silence."

"He could've been on meds. Post anesthesia."

"Do you want to know my opinion?" asked Gonzo. "If you

don't want to know just say it. We can all move on. You. Me. Stew Raymo."

No luck for Ben. The storm clouds of his first life had returned and the rain was already starting to fall. He felt flush. Angry. Abused. The rage was returning. The same damn fury that had followed his original stage of grieving.

They're not dead. Just a bad dream. My wife and baby girls. They're not gone!

Ben attempted to recall the five stages of grieving.

Denial. Anger . . .

Anger, hell. It was utter rage. And in his rage, Ben couldn't remember the other three stages.

Bargaining. Depression. Acceptance.

With that, Ben's chin moved ever so slightly, left then right, repeating itself in a primal head-shake. Ben didn't *want* to know. He *needed* to know. The rage in him demanded it.

"Did Stew Raymo kill my wife and baby girls?"

"My opinion?"

"Just say it!"

"Yeah," said Gonzo. "He's your guy. Gave me goosebumps just being in the same zip code as him."

Ben could feel the darkness infecting him all over again. He shut his eyes, brought his knees together and leaned into them until his forehead was cradled. His fists were balled and his knuckles as white as pearls.

"Ben. I've been straight with you, okay? But now I'm gonna be even more honest and direct."

Gently, Gonzo placed her hand on Ben's head and began to stroke his hair. Her voice softened, but remained resolute.

"You listening?" asked Gonzo. "Now that you know, you've got to forget you ever heard the name *Stew Raymo*. You've got to put him and all that ill stuff behind you."

Incredulity welled up in Ben, spilling over.

"Cannot believe you are saying this to me," he croaked.

"Believe me! I know what—"

"You're a cop! A goddamned cop and you're telling me you think I ought to leave it be? A capital fucking offense?"

"A minute ago, I could swear you were going to say you didn't want to hear it—"

"That's your fix? Wind me up then tell me to leave shit be? Forget I ever heard the bastard's name?"

"I know it's not easy—"

"He took my life from me! Everything I cared about. You have a clue what it took to bring me back from that place? The kind of work? Give up one life for another? Do you?"

"My point exactly!"

"You know? Just go away! Please."

"You came back, Ben. You built a life. A new life with a wonderful wife and family. Now, I shoulda said this to you that night by the pool. Don't go diggin' in the graveyard. It's just ghosts and bones and badness—"

"Asked you to go. So go, okay? Go."

But it was Ben who shoved off. He showed her his palm at the end of a stiff arm, stood and started to walk.

Gonzo snagged Ben by the elbow. Her grip instantly had the feeling of authority.

"I looked that prick right in the eyes," she said. "Some people you get a feeling from."

"You're right. I got a feeling from you. I thought you'd help. As a matter of fact, I recall you saying you would help!"

"This Stew Raymo guy," urged Gonzo. "He's a package you do not want to open! You got that? Stay away from him."

Ben didn't pull his arm away from Gonzo. He merely glared at her kung-fu grip until she released him. Gonzo watched as Ben set a heading for the parking lot without once looking back.

Damn it, she thought. If only she had been wearing the uniform. She rarely made mistakes on the job. With civilians she would always remain detached and impersonal. She never would have crossed up some poor citizen with conflicting advice. Why then, did she make such an idiotic error with Ben?

Later she would wonder why she really hadn't called him back. And why she had approached him at school, out of uniform, and dressed like a bull dyke.

Mixed signals. *Hell*, thought Gonzo. *That's all I am to men.*

Given context and a little history, the argument on the bleachers between Ben and Gonzo was easily understood. But from less than a hundred yards away, the altercation appeared altogether different. Especially when viewed through the designer lenses of three small-minded school parents. The scandal-selling troika of power moms, Layla Johnson, Rhonda Markel, and Janie Hart, also known as the Yummy Mummies, was parked and chatting underneath the crimson and gold umbrella-covered tables on the bricked patio outside the student store.

Each of the trio had a wealthy husband and shared sex and cosmetic surgery secrets with the others, not to mention trendy vacation getaways. And while their children were toiling in school, the women had far too much money and free time on their hands. Theirs was a small universe and very little escaped their keen attention.

The primary purpose of the Simi Canyons student store was to sell junk food and hooded sweatshirts to high school students. It was run by volunteer parents, mostly middle-school mothers, and served decent cappuccinos and chai lattes, thanks to the well-intended family who had donated the restaurant-quality espresso machine. Since the installation of a genuine Pasquini, the student body had taken to calling the closet-sized shop *Student Starbucks*. And not unlike its namesake, some of the more social parents had begun gathering there for their morning doses of caffeine and gossip.

The Student Starbucks was within clear eyeshot of the football field bleachers.

There was already a faint buzz about a possible affair between the odd but well-regarded Ben Keller and the suspected lesbian, Lydia Gonzalez. Thus, her "suspected lesbian" label had been replaced with that of "bisexual" through such whispers as, "she must play for both teams."

But it was just idle chatter. Ignored by most.

If Ben and Gonzo had only known. Except for a small grove of decorative palms, the view from the Student Starbucks to the athletic field was mostly unobstructed. The bright blast of morning sun put a spotlight on the bleachers and the man and woman there as they engaged, argued, and angrily separated. The body language was unmistakable, depicting affection, anger, and pain. A lovers' spat in plain view of Simi Canyons' most malicious magpies.

Layla, the former department store model, was closest to Alex. It would be her mission to artfully inform Alex of Ben's suspected infidelities without appearing underhanded. After all, her television-producer husband was known for an occasional out-of-town liaison. She would joke to her friends that he was only following the old show business axiom—it's not adultery if you're on location.

The trio agreed, though, that Ben's alleged affair was far more dangerous. It was within the school community and played out in full view of the children.

For the children's sake, something had to be done.

Once again, Ben withdrew from living in the present.

Since receiving the anonymous CD, he had felt like an unwitting passenger on a never-ending emotional roller coaster. Only the ride was in reverse. Each twist and dip sent him backward into a yet untapped depth. How deep was the bottom? How far could he actually sink?

So instead of faking his way through another day, Ben wrote himself a get-out-of-work-free pass. He asked Josie to cancel everything, giving her his proxy to make any kind of excuse she saw fit, and then buried himself in a conga line of mindless movies playing at the local megaplex. Lunch and dinner were buttered popcorn, jumbo Diet Cokes, and five-dollar boxes of Raisinettes. When one film ended, he would get up, wander into the next theater, and hope the next picture would help him forget.

Ben never called Alex to say he wouldn't be home for dinner. He assumed Josie had covered for him, which explained the lack of text messages or emails from his wife.

It was nearly eleven o'clock when Ben pulled into his driveway. He stood at the front stoop, twirling his keys on his finger, daring himself to enter. He suspected Alex would be angry. She had a right to be. He had been AWOL for the better part of the day. Totally incommunicado. That was the stuff of lousy husbands.

The fog had crept in again. Thick. The low voltage lights that lined the path gave off an appearance of glowing pods, one way leading into a domestic refuge of peace and tranquility, the opposite way pointing toward the world of the unknown. Somewhere, just beyond the glistening rooftops and dimmed streetlamps, was a man named Stew Raymo. Was he sleeping? Was he enjoying his life and liberty? Did he even recall what horrors he had committed?

And Simi Valley was supposed to feel safe.

Ben quietly entered the house and punched in the alarm code. In the kitchen he grabbed and swallowed three slices of lunchmeat to make up for his day without protein, then ascended the stairs. He slowed at the first landing, directing his eyes upward to try to figure out what was wrong with the picture. It was how the light fell on the stairs. The doors, Ben worried. All the doors to the upstairs bedrooms were usually propped open with antique doorstops. As a rule, firemen warned that doors should be closed at night in case of fire. A closed bedroom door could prevent fire and deadly smoke from spreading.

Transversely, Ben knew that earthquakes presented an equal or greater danger. If supports or sheering walls of the house somehow failed or buckled, a closed bedroom door could be jammed in the doorframe and impossible to open. Weighing the risks, Ben had decided the safest bet was for all the bedroom doors to remain open at all times. This of course didn't suit Nina at all. The budding teenager wanted as much privacy as she could extract from her parents. She wasn't beyond affixing a rude, handwritten sign, locking her door, and damning the consequences.

But Nina's door was open.

Traveling two steps more, Ben could see that it was his own bedroom door that was shut. The master suite. It puzzled Ben because he couldn't recall Alex closing the door at night—ever!

She's angry. She has a right. Asshole, you didn't so much as call.

The master bedroom door appeared as a deep rectangular shadow, inset and without much relief. Just some shine off the doorknob as a teasing invitation.

Go in, Ben thought. Just go in, wake her if she's asleep, and demand she give him what for. Then after she cooled, after he had apologized for the self-absorbed infraction he had committed, he would tell her all of it. Confess. Tell her about the audio confession, Stew Raymo, Gonzo, all of it. Even the visit to the gravesites. Tell her that he loved her more than life—that he needed her in his time of renewed grief.

And renewed rage.

Then came the cry. The slightest of whimpers in the dark. A tiny voice trying to form words from inside the black hole of sleep. It was somewhere behind Ben. Betsy's voice. Cries for help from deep within her nightmare.

On impulse, Ben hurried into her room. The pastel walls were cast with diffused gray from the streetlamps in the fog outside. Ben had to tiptoe around the clothes and tiny toys that littered the floor. Little Betsy was twisted out of her covers, not quite thrashing, but struggling as if she were bound in cling wrap.

"Sshhhh," soothed Ben. "It's okay. Daddy's here, now. Sssshhhh."

Ben lay next to her, pulling her in a bit closer, his voice hushed with assurance.

"It's okay, Bunny. Daddy's not gonna let anything hurt his baby girl."

"Scary," forced Betsy with a jerk. Her eyes were still squeezed shut. She was still in the dream.

"What's scary?"

"It's scary!"

"Well, you just tell it to go away. Say, 'Get out of here bad thing.'"

Betsy's mouth pursed and she punched the air.

"Get out of here bad thing!"

"Go away and never come back to my dreams."

"Go way."

"Never come back to my dreams."

"Never come back . . ."

"To my dreams."

"To my dreams."

And as quickly as he had heard the first cry, Betsy's face slackened into the heavenly pose of a sleeping six-year-old. Perfect. Without a world to worry for. *Just as it should be*, thought Ben. *Just as it should be.*

Ben fell asleep next to Betsy. When he woke, he was alone in the child's bed. The house was bursting with daylight, but sadly quiet and empty. Alex had left a note taped to his tube of minty-fresh toothpaste.

"WE NEED TO TALK. LUNCH?"

⁊⁊⁊

"Had this bad dream last night."

"Okay. Want to describe your nightmare?"

"Said it was a bad dream," grumbled Ben.

"Essentially you're saying that it wasn't bad enough to qualify as a nightmare," confirmed the psychotherapist.

"Weird, annoying, uncomfortable."

"Go on."

Ben rewound for a moment. He allowed his head to tilt back into the pillowy chair. His eyes unconsciously counted the knots in the open-beam ceiling. But he was thinking about the chair. A damned comfortable chair, upholstered in soft, green and gold chenille. Of course, the chair matched the rest of the mellow-voiced therapist's backyard office, a vaulted room tastefully appointed in earthy colors and textured fabrics. There was a couch to Ben's left, a coffee table with a ceramic vase that sprouted a neatly cut splay of seasonal golden wheat, and underfoot, a plush oriental rug. Everything about the room was tuned—warm, comforting, neutral. Much like the man in the matching chair opposite Ben, the noted grief guru and published author, Dr. Daniel Dhue.

It had been eight months since Ben had last visited the

Tarzana-based therapist. And years since they had talked of profound subjects like death and grief. Ben would just dial up the doctor like a patient in need of his annual physical. Most sessions quickly evolved into something akin to a social checkup. There were more laughs than anything else. Dr. Dhue was fascinated by the way Ben had turned his pain into a proud profession and profit. Danny Dhue praised Ben as his personal Safety Geek. And Ben jokingly called him Dr. Frankengrief.

This session was different. Neither man had once cracked wise. They had been talking for forty-two minutes.

"Betsy, my wife's youngest daughter," recalled Ben, "I'd say she was having a nightmare. She has about one a week. These fits. So I do what I do. I lie down with her and talk—"

"You said, 'my wife's daughter,'" interrupted the therapist.

"Yeah. We've talked about her before. She's six—"

"You've never called her that before."

"Called her what?"

"My wife's daughter."

"I was talking about the bad dream."

"When you talk about Betsy, you usually say, 'Betsy' or 'my daughter' or 'my youngest.'"

"So what's your point?" asked Ben, barely containing his aggravation. He wanted to convey the content of his lousy dream. But the shrink was digging beneath the skin where Ben was raw.

"Just pointing it out. If you don't think it's important, go on with your dream."

"You're baiting me."

"Am I?"

"You think that because I referred to Betsy as hers instead of mine . . ."

Dr. Dhue scratched his beard with his knuckles.

"I think you've regressed. Understandably so."

"So you don't want to hear about the dream," growled Ben. "You want to tell me how I feel before I tell you."

"Your time. But do I really need to hear the dream?"

No. The good doctor felt he was already miles ahead of

Ben, and no doubt, the time clock on the session was running out. Another Daniel Dhue Grief Relief patient would surely be arriving soon and Ben's time would be up.

"I think it's important," insisted Ben. "In Betsy's dream, she was fighting something. I told her to shake her fist at it. Call it a bad thing and tell it to go away."

"Okay."

"Now, in my dream, I was lying there with Betsy. Her room. Same as if I were awake. But I was sleeping and she was telling me to shake my fist and fight the bad thing."

"I see."

"No. You don't see. Because when I turned back at Betsy to remind her that I was the dad and she was the little girl, it wasn't Betsy anymore. It was one of the twins."

"Just one?"

"Yeah. Except she was older. Six. Betsy's age."

"I'm with you. And when she was telling you what to do—the twin—did you get angry with her?"

"I don't remember."

"Because you're angry now."

" 'Course, I am. That's why I'm here." Ben felt a flush in his cheeks. "We're going backwards now."

"Regressing, Ben. That's all."

"I'm not so sure."

"In order to move on. In order to put the pain behind us, what must we recognize comes after anger?"

Of course Ben knew the answer. Unlike the day before, the five primary stages of grief tripped across Ben's brain like listening to a child recite the alphabet.

Denial. Anger. Bargaining. Depression. Acceptance.

"What about blame?" said Ben. "I think that should be a stage."

"We both know the next stage is bargaining. Have you made any deals with yourself lately? Promises to God that if you're a better person or, let's personalize it, make the world just that much safer—"

"Listen to me! What if I know who did it? Who he is. Where

he works. His fucking address? Christ Almighty, I shook his goddamn hand!"

"Ben. Sit. Please."

"Why the hell can't we talk about what I want to talk about?"

"Sit and we'll talk."

Sit?

Ben glanced downward and strangely enough, discovered his legs were straightened under his body in a full, vertical pose. How the heck did that happen? A half moment earlier he had been seated, head back and resting on a comfy cushion while his eyes pinged off warts in the knotty-pine ceiling.

"You know you can't fully recover unless you—piece by piece—move yourself through the steps and stages—"

"Goddammit, I was recovered! You know it. I know it. I was over all of it. Why the hell should I have to reclaim the same territory over and over again?"

"That's life. That's grief. That's how we move on. By falling. By getting footholds. Then foot by foot, hand over hand, climbing back out."

Before the session, Ben was ready to buy anything the doctor had to sell. Daniel Dhue and his kind had resurrected Ben and countless others from the darkest of human places. Given them life and hope and even love.

But the bastard had to look at his watch.

Fucking headshrinker!

It was as if a power circuit in Ben had been thrown, redirecting the electrical charge to another part of his being. Suddenly, he couldn't stand to look at the doctor. To even smell his David Beckham cologne! Ben was instantly repelled by the man's trimmed beard and casual style. For Christ's sake, Ben screamed from inside his own skull, the man was wearing Birkenstocks. A walking cliché! Was it all just posturing and psychotherapeutic pretext? The decorated office, the whole image-thing made Ben feel sick, invaded, like he had been victimized by a con man.

"Push your next session," begged Ben. "I need more time."

"I'm having lunch with my niece—"

"Then call her. Tell her Uncle Danny's got a flat tire and is waiting for Triple A."

"I can fix my own flat tires."

"Dammit, Danny!"

"Calm down. All your feelings are normal. Regression is normal. Why don't you come back tomorrow?"

The therapist had his electronic calendar open on his iPhone. He was poised over the two-by-three-inch screen, ready to make a time in digital ink.

"I can fit you in at—"

"Please!"

"How's first thing? 8:00 A.M.?"

Ben could hear it in his head. He could see it as vividly as if it had really happened—as if Ben's mind had reached out and picked up the ceramic vase at the neck, caring not at all about the beautiful display of dried wheat, and swung it with a two-handed backhand. Ben felt the weight and stepped into it. The sound of the ceramic colliding with the doctor's skull had just the slightest concussive effect. It was like the vase simply dissolved into pieces, falling apart like a ten-dollar piñata.

But it hadn't happened. Ben hadn't picked up the vase. Ben hadn't hurled it into his therapist's head.

It was just a thought.

"Eight o'clock tomorrow morning?" confirmed Dr. Dhue.

"Right," conceded Ben, head lowered, sunglasses on, and not even shaking the doctor's hand. "8:00 A.M."

As Ben set out from the doctor's backyard office and walked up the driveway, he recalled the day he had first visited. At his wife-to-be's insistence, Ben and Alex had embarked on a special series of couple's grief sessions with Dr. Dhue. "A tune-up for marriage," the shrink had called it. The widow and the widower needed to make sure that their union was built on more than the sum of their combined losses. They would need to believe in the future. So they turned to Dr. Daniel Dhue, Zen Master in the art of mourning and recovery.

They believed in him.

At one point, Ben so believed in the doctor's advice to "reject the past in order to build the future" that, in what felt like an act of new-age chivalry, he offered to jettison his surname of Martin and take Alex's surname of Keller. Upon reflection, it was a silly gesture with little therapeutic results. But what was done was done. There would be no more looking back. From that point on it was all about looking forward.

As Ben walked to his car, he still wanted to believe in Daniel Dhue. He wanted to believe that he could still move on with his life. He wanted to believe in eight o'clock tomorrow morning.

But Ben would miss his appointment.

Ben would never see Daniel Dhue again.

"What's that noise?" asked Ben.

"What noise?" answered Woody.

"That *thump, thump, thump* sound."

"Can't hear it. Must be a sketchy cell connection," answered Woody, totally lying.

Woody Bell could not only hear the *thump, thump, thump*, it was so loud he could feel it. And noisier still just beyond the door of the janitor's closet where Woody was parked in his souped-up wheelchair. The only light came from the keypad on Woody's phone, revealing the faint but familiar shadows of mops, brooms, and stacks of paper towels and toilet paper.

"Maybe I should call you back," said Ben.

"My answer's gonna be the same, bro."

"That my request is illegal. You already said that."

Thump, thump, thump, thump . . .

"You wanna know if the guy did it."

"For certain," said Ben.

"Beyond a reasonable doubt and all that," said Woody.

"Yes."

"Then you're talking confession. Which has to come out of the bad guy's mouth. And lemme tell you, bad guys don't confess to capital crimes because there's no statute there."

"Statute of limitations," confirmed Ben.

"Damn straight, bro."

There came a wolf whistle and a smattering of applause from

outside the closet door. Next would come the fuzzy introduction of the next, slow-eyed stripper. His favorite girl, Siobhan, wouldn't be on for at least two more songs. This gave Woody time to wrap up the call from Ben and possibly return two more.

"Only way to get a real confession is to torture a guy," said Woody. "Are there operators out there who run that kinda game? Yeah. There's operators. Underworld guys that you don't want to be in business with."

"Guys you know."

"And what if I do know somebody?"

"Do you?"

"Here's the question you should be asking, 'What if it's the wrong guy?' Huh? What if I know somebody? And what if I pull some trigger for you and we do this dumb thing? What happens if you put the screws to an innocent guy?"

"You know he's not. You sent me the sheet."

"C'mon, Ben. This isn't you."

"Really? You know me that good?"

"Well enough, I think. Well enough that the Ben I know would rather peel off his own fingernails than do the wrong thing."

"I don't know about that anymore."

"That's right. You don't know. Which is exactly why you shouldn't be asking for this kind of trouble."

Applause. The next song began. But the beat never changed. *Thump, thump, thump, thump . . .*

"You hear it?" asked Ben. "That sound just started again."

"Ben. Go talk to somebody. Get your head right."

"If it was your family?"

"You askin' me about family? You know my story. Shit. All I had I left on the bottom of that pool when I was twelve fuckin' years old."

"Yeah, I know. Sorry," said Ben, his voice filled with sudden regret.

"You don't have to be sorry. You just have to be cool. You and me have had enough tragedy for ten lives. That means we know the pitfalls of courting certain disaster. You're the numbers man. You assess the risks. I'm tellin' you, what you're asking is a big risk."

"But you know people."

"'Course, I do. And sure as shit they can make the meanest man cry if that's the job. Pull off this fucker's skin and you'll have your confession. And then what? You can't use it in court. Because you broke the law in order to get it. And guess who goes to jail? You and me!"

Thump, thump, thump, thump . . .

"Lemme add one more fun fact," said Woody. Ain't no handicap access for me in prison."

Woody heard nothing but silence on the other end of the cell connection.

"Hey man, laugh," said Woody. "That was damn funny."

"On another day," said Ben.

"I hear you, bro. Now, go home to your safe family in your safe house. Remember, you keeping shit safe for everybody is what pays my electric bills. Need that juice to keep my batteries charged. Don't want you screwin' none of that up."

Ben clicked off, leaving Woody in a moment of worry. He felt deeply for Ben, his life and his losses. But Ben was also talking out of his ass. Speaking from his pain. And Woody knew plenty about loss and pain. Such was his daily grind. So apart from the private detective work that Woody performed from his wheelchair, the rest of his life was about self-gratification. Instant and immediate giggles. From *Seinfeld* reruns to strippers, Woody was all about the now.

Thump, thump, thump, thump . . .

"There. That's better," said Woody to himself as he parked his chair in the usual spot. Three feet from the neon-striped stage and slightly left of dead center. The owners of Smokey Blues strip club were such good pals to Woody that they had spray-painted a blue handicapped sign on the floor in the exact dimensions of his doublewide chair. They had assured Woody that every day, from the moment the doors opened until closing, that space was reserved for him and the never-ending supply of one dollar bills he twisted into the dancers' g-strings.

But due to California's overly strict secondhand smoke laws, Smokey Blues wasn't smokey anymore. The only haze found inside was between the ears of the inebriated customers, all male, each kept in check by the two beefy bouncers flanking the stage. Each bouncer was perched on a stool so spindly it appeared to defy basic physics.

"What do you like today?" winked Siobhan.

She wasn't near naked yet, with a bustier, fishnets, and panties still waiting to be peeled off. Siobhan split her legs then lay on the floor, propped up by her elbows, cradling her chin. Her teeth were like new porcelain.

"I like you, today," said Woody.

"You say that every time."

"But today I mean it."

"Tease," she said.

Siobhan was surely Woody's favorite.

Goodness, he mentally gasped. *She was utter perfection. Ceramic and creamy. Untouched by a plastic surgeon's scalpel.*

And she was a real dancer.

Sure, they were all real dancers. Probably were once little tyke ballerinas. Scared. Hanging onto their mommies' hands on the day of their first class. *First position*, he remembered. *Back straight, heels together, toes out.* That was when Woody was five and still too small to realize he was the only boy in the ballet class. *Thank God it didn't take*, he thought. Or that stupid accident would have cost him even more.

Siobhan removed her stockings and climbed onto the pole, her raven black hair tinged crispy blue in the backlight.

Woody missed the smoke. Too bad that public smoking had pretty much been relegated to parking lots and Porta-Johns. And not-so-ironically, Ol' Smokey himself had recently died from lung cancer. This made Woody think of Safety Ben. He didn't wonder if he had given his client the correct advice. Ben had no business endeavoring into a criminal enterprise. And it didn't matter how righteous it was. Ben wasn't wired that way. Thank goodness for that. He was Safety Ben. And Safety Ben was one helluva good customer.

"Somethin' on your mind?" asked Siobhan.

"Yeah. What's your phone number?"

"You know the rules."

"You knew I'd ask."

"Every time, lover."

The bustier came off, floating over the stage and landing in slow motion. Siobhan made sure to make eye contact with her favorite, crippled fan. Was he staring at her breasts? If he wasn't, Siobhan had screwed up the timing.

Woody fanned his stack of singles out of habit.

Siobhan twirled to the edge of the stage, stepped onto Woody's table, squatted and froze. A coquettish glance over her shoulder. She had expected to hear the familiar whine of the motorized wheelchair underneath the throbbing dance music. She had expected to see Woody with a fistful of dollars to slip between her skin and the elastic of her g-string.

"You didn't like that, lover?"

But Woody wasn't ogling her. He was lost in space, his eyes tracking the dust particles dancing in Siobhan's spotlight.

"Wood Man?"

"Smokin' hot," said Woody.

"I'll show you smokin' hot," she recovered, losing neither her attitude nor come-fuck-me smile.

Again, Woody fanned the stack of cash. As far as he was concerned, it was all hers. She could sweep the table, take the money, steal his wallet, and strut off the stage without so much as a thank-you.

He would love her no matter what.

But Siobhan wouldn't leave her Wood Man without something to write home about. After she had worked the stage, flexing her body for the chronic drunks and middle-aged masturbators, she returned to Woody's table. The colored lights gathered in her Lucite heels, displaying a constellation of rainbow-colored snowflakes across the paraplegic's face. Siobhan turned away from Woody, spread her feet, then folded at the waist until she was flat against her thighs.

"See anything you like?"

"'S'all good, girl."

"You're still not with me."

"Sorry," said Woody. I'm thinking of a friend."

"Anybody I know?"

"Naw. Just some customer who needs my help."

"And I'm sure you will help," she cooed. "Wanna help me, now?"

"How can I help you?"

"Make a deposit and you'll see something I saved just for you."

"Think I should help him?"

"Help who, lover?"

"My friend."

"Sure, you should. He's a friend, right?"

"Did I say friend? I meant customer."

"There a difference?"

No, thought Woody. *There wasn't*. Not in Woody's lonely world. He was her customer. She was his friend. And to think of it, Woody's customers were his friends. Who the hell else did he have?

Woody knew some guys. Operators. Men who straddled both sides of society's moral guidelines. If Stew Raymo was the demon in Ben's life, Woody had connections that could extract a confession, put it on the record, then do away with him. So what if Ben wasn't the wiser for it? He would do his friend a solid. His friend would be grateful. His friend would forever owe him for putting a lid on his nightmare.

Siobhan stroked her index finger along the only patch of fabric that kept her act legal.

"Right there, lover," she whispered. "Pull it and you'll get a private peek."

Woody rolled what must have been thirty singles, pulled her string, and looked into a world he could only imagine.

It was a typical winter's day in Simi Valley.

Sunny, seventy, with five-story palm trees swaying slowly in a five-mile-an-hour breeze. Every so often Ben was amazed at how unnaturally the palms dotted the local landscape, each tree equidistant from the next, perpendicular, and always perfectly placed to add vertical accents to some architect's vision of Southern California.

The tall palms were really quite beautiful. Elegant. It was like seeing queues of slender-necked giraffes on every horizon. Palm trees grew quickly and were common, shallow-rooted, easily transplanted, and required minimum maintenance, making them popular in most Southern California landscape designs.

But those damned shallow roots.

A recently transplanted thirty-foot palm didn't stand much of a chance in a fifty-mile-per-hour gust. And though such wind speeds happened only once or twice a winter, when they did scores of "new" palms would come crashing down onto power lines and parked cars.

Though already late for his lunch with Alex, Ben still took the extra time to search for a parking space that was safely out of danger from falling palm trees and fronds.

They had agreed to meet at Pane Dolce, their usual Saturday haunt. It was a sweet spot with a patch of outdoor tables, conveniently nestled between a pet salon and the neighborhood Jamba Juice. Across the parking lot stood a Target and Trader Joe's.

Nirvana for Alex, thought Ben.

"Sorry," he began.

He had glimpsed Alex as he had approached from the parking lot. She was inside the picture window, working her iPhone. *Probably making lists*, he thought.

"No problem," she said, accepting his lips on her left cheek.

As usual, Alex looked put-together, wearing tan capris and a black t-shirt. Ben always felt dressed down around her. Wearing his predictable uniform of denims, sneakers, and a simple polo, today was no different.

Alex already had a glass of iced coffee. Ben gestured to the waitress to please bring him the same.

"You ordered yet?" asked Ben.

"Waiting for you, hon."

"Got stuck on a call. Then discovered I'd missed the exit."

"Not at all like you . . ."

Alex let the rest of her thought just lie there.

She was so right about him. Ben wasn't at all like himself. Not even close to the man he had been just a month before. *The door had opened*, he thought. *She wanted to talk. She deserved an explanation.*

Ben sat back in the chair, scanning the simply decorated café. There were seven other diners. Two of them couples, the others singles, either reading or working a laptop. Two counters. One for gelato and the other for everything else from eggs to soup. Every song on the piped-in music sounded like it was by the Gypsy Kings.

"About the way I've been acting—"

"No," said Alex.

"No, what?" asked Ben. "I just wanted to say—"

"Please. I don't want to hear it. Really."

Alex held her palms up, fingers splayed full tensile. Her nails looked as perfect as all those damned palm trees Ben both loathed and admired.

"I owe you an apology," said Ben.

"If you apologize, then you're going to have to say why— and I just don't want to know."

"You're serious . . ."

Her eyes cast downward and her hands retreated to the tabletop, leaving the slightest streak of perspiration. A certain sign of nerves from a woman whose credo was to never let anybody see her sweat.

"Had this whole speech planned," she said before correcting herself. "Have this speech. So please. Just let me say it."

"Okay . . ." said Ben, worried. There was the tiniest tremor in his wife's voice—cause enough for concern.

"Okay," she began. "Yes. You've been acting strange. Not the first time. You and me, we've certainly both been through things. Bad things. Worse than anything that this can be."

"I can explain—"

"Ben, please! I don't want to hear anything. I just want to say what I need to say."

"Alright, then."

"What I want to say is that it doesn't matter. Whatever it is. I don't care. Just as long as you can tell me that it's over. You're done with it, through it, over it. Moving on, okay? Keep moving on, remember? Can we do that? Together?"

"Of course—"

"I'm not finished," she snapped, working hard to put a stranglehold on her nerves. "I'll have you know that I won't be embarrassed by it or you. Things happen. We both know things happen. Mistakes. We're human. I'd also like it very much if you started seeing Dr. Dhue again."

"Saw him this morning."

"Excellent. We're already moving on then."

Then Ben saw the tears. He could count on one hand the number of times he had seen her cry outside a therapy session. Alex was human steel wrapped around a softer middle. The trick was always about waiting for the armor to fall.

But what on earth was she crying about? How could she possibly know about Stew Raymo and Ben's recent, morbid obsession with his dead wife and girls? If so, who the hell had talked and breached his trust? Gonzo? Josie? Woody Bell?

The truth was, Ben hadn't the faintest, and it would never occur to him to sneak a peak into his wife's open email folder when he got home. If he had, he would have found a quick, anonymous missive from a concerned mom at Simi Canyons School. Contained within was a simple warning:

Did you know your husband was cheating with one of our "single" moms?

Not having read the email, how could Ben have possibly been clued in to his wife's fears of infidelity? A man behaving without indiscretion could not imagine being painted as such, unless of course, his wife either asks outright or fully accuses him. Ben's only defense would be the same truth he had guarded from her. The same truth he had planned, that very day, to confess to her.

The very same truth Alex insisted she didn't want to hear.

It was plain. Both husband and wife were certain they knew the other's secret. Yet neither knew anything at all.

"Very well, then," Ben relented. "We'll move on."

"I love you," she said. "You know that?"

"Yes," he said. "And you know I love you."

"And that's all that matters."

Ben touched her hand, leaned across and kissed her on the mouth. Then she wiped her tears and forced a smile.

"I'm famished. You?"

"Starving."

"Know what you want?"

"Just tell me what you want and I'll go order it."

Pam was up twelve pounds from what she called her "porn weight."

Her "porn weight" was one hundred and nine.

Not that anyone would notice. She had turned baby fat into lean muscle and seemingly trimmed all but her quasi-famous pneumatic breasts. Her hair was short and naturally blonde. A large pair of glasses and sweats and she would spend most days largely unrecognized.

That suited Pam just fine.

Not that she was entirely embarrassed by her sex-trade past. Given the opportunity, she would defend the decisions of her youth. Porn was a multibillion dollar business. Porn stocks were traded on Wall Street. If powerful Ivy League investment bankers weren't embarrassed to buy and sell porn equities, Pam sure as hell wasn't going to be ashamed of her own contributions to the skin-trade.

Twenty-two films.

Seven starring roles.

Over a hundred websites still dedicated to her sexy, baby-doll image.

So there were no surprises on those days she was recognized. Or even followed.

Example: the silver Lexus Pam noticed when she was rolling out of the Rite-Aid parking lot. She first looked left, then right before easing her foot off the brake of her Land Rover. That's when she first saw the car. It was parked across the street. The bright, but hazy sunlight spiked off the tinted windshield. As Pam made her turn, she had glimpsed the Lexus again as it surged into lunch-hour traffic, nearly running a red light in order to keep pace with her.

Since the Rite-Aid, the Lexus had been following her for three miles.

Pam was familiar with unsolicited attention. There were the usual sideways glances in restaurants, the occasional arm raised and finger pointed from across a busy boulevard, and the sleazy grins from supermarket checkers ringing up her groceries. Every so often, fans would be brave and approach Pam—to talk, ask for an autograph, or hit on her. But those were rare characters. And direct contact was always easy to deal with.

It was those times when she was followed that made her nervous.

Stalkers.

Perverts in cars who would do neck-wrenching double takes while parked next to her at a stoplight, then take it upon themselves to slide in behind her and tailgate for a mile or two. Usually, to shake a stalker, all she had to do was park and wait for them to pass. Or pull out her cell phone and pretend to be dictating the numbers off the creep's license plate.

If neither of those tactics worked, there was always Stew. At the drop of a dime, her Protector in Chief would stop what he was doing and run interference. Sometimes, the mere sight of the big man sent stalkers speeding away. One time, Pam had recognized the pervert parked outside her nail salon as the same man who had brushed by her in the lingerie department at Nordstrom. One quick phone call and Stew had come to her rescue. He had caught the stalker masturbating in his car. Incensed, Stew had yanked the car door open and dragged the scummy perv by the collar until he was lying in the gutter, exposed for all to see.

But the stalker in the silver Lexus was different. Miles ago, he had dropped two cars back. Then three cars to her rear and one lane over. At one point, the Lexus appeared to have vanished entirely, forcing Pam to second-guess her animal instincts.

Twenty minutes later though, the Lexus reappeared while Pam was waiting at the Handy J car wash on Ventura Boulevard. She paid $19.99 cash for the daily special: wash, quick wax, and leather cleaner. As she was flipping through a leftover copy of the *Daily News*, she caught the same sun-spike off the Lexus' windshield. Only this time the car was parked across the street on the south side, directly opposite the car wash, and facing east. For a moment, Pam felt vulnerable without the protection of the glass and steel of her SUV.

But she eventually found her customary reserve, straightened, and faced the vehicle with arms akimbo. She could barely make out the driver's silhouette behind the tinted window. The man inside hardly moved a muscle, let alone showed any sign of being intimidated.

Fine, she thought. *Be that way.*

She walked eighty feet to her right, down the sun-baked sidewalk until she had an angle on the Lexus' license plate. Through his side view mirror, the driver would get a damned good view of Pam, the ex-porn slut, wearing a sexless white sweat suit and sneakers. The driver was also certain to notice Pam using her cell phone to record the letters of his license plate.

5HJR8429.

That's when most stalkers would beat it out of there. But the Lexus driver didn't so much as twitch. This was when Pam spotted a second figure, a passenger, in the rear seat of the car. She couldn't recall car creepers ever working in pairs. Sure, there was the occasional carload of frat boys who spotted the former Misty Fresh. The more usually meant the merrier, with windows rolled down, whistles, catcalls, and peer-fueled illicit proposals.

These weren't frat boys.

A chill set in. Goosebumps rose from her moisturized flesh. Pam became so spooked that she turned and marched directly to her Land Rover. The Guatemalan man drying her rims wasn't given the chance to apply the wax or leather cleaner. He merely saw the five-dollar tip stuck in his face and handed over the keys.

Pam twisted the key, turned over the engine, hit the

windshield wipers, and charged westbound onto Ventura Boulevard, nearly causing a three-car pileup. The sound of skidding tires just scared her more. She pressed the accelerator and barely beat the red light. She felt a cold sweat erupt on her forehead as the air conditioner kicked in. Repeated glances into her rearview confirmed the Lexus was nowhere in sight. But Pam didn't feel the least bit safe. The creepy car had disappeared once before. Who knew when or where it could, or would, materialize again?

She drove aggressively until she had all four wheels on her own driveway and the gate closed and locked behind her. Once inside the house she knew what to do. Check the locks, draw the shades, and pocket the sleek, little, five-shot .38 Stew had given her for her thirtieth birthday. Despite the shiny, nickel-plated finish and mother-of-pearl grip, Pam thought the gift was demonstrably unromantic. And when certain he wasn't listening, she cursed Stew and called him "Shitferbrains."

Yet, every once in awhile, Pam thanked Jesus that big Stew had been thoughtful enough to buy the revolver, teach her how to punch hot little holes with it, and insist she keep it close and loaded at all times when he wasn't around to protect her.

Wheelchair conversion vans for paraplegics primarily came in three boring flavors. Honda Odyssey, Chrysler Town and Country, and Dodge Grand Caravan.

It pissed Woody Bell off that he couldn't test drive a vehicle like normies did. Kick the tires. Take it for a spin around the block, wrestle with the handling, and then haggle over the price with the salesman. Instead, Woody was relegated to shopping online, reading specs and bulletin boards and negotiating delivery costs via email. The closest thing to human involvement was the mobility technician sent to Woody's house by the conversion company. A tattooed former gangbanger had measured Woody's doublewide wheelchair, and given the private investigator a card for his brother-in-law's custom paint shop in nearby Panorama City.

Now Woody had flames.

What had started out as a white shell with four black sidewalls and a muscular Detroit engine had been, in the course of a month and $30,000, transformed into a shaggin' wagon for a four-hundred-pound paralytic. Ice-black base, spin-rims, red and orange flames licking the fenders, and a license plate rim on the rear door that read, *If this van's a rockin' don't come a knockin'.*

It was hardly inconspicuous. But Big Woody didn't give a rip, just as long as it disguised his infirmity. When Woody wheeled through the drive-through at Carl's Jr., nobody was ever the wiser. He could flirt, chitchat, and pay for his triple order of Western Bacon Cheeseburgers without anybody clued in that the fat man behind the wheel was disabled.

So what was the wisdom in driving a paraplegic shag-wagon to Stew Raymo's Studio City construction site? No wisdom at all, Woody excused himself. Just base curiosity. He had the site address. Hell, he had even accessed the building permits, architectural schematics, and the names and phone numbers of each and every subcontractor.

The mean February temperature had dropped eleven degrees and the winter breeze had stiffened to a steady wind, dusting the air with swirls of broken tree leaves. Woody rolled his van to a stop across the street and one address south of the site. A cyclone fence surrounded a frame Woody recognized from the plans. At one corner of the structure, he counted a crew of four men digging a shoulder-deep hole. All Hispanic. And strangely, all wearing bicycle helmets.

He observed a fifth man, also Hispanic, with salt-and-pepper hair and a fatherly demeanor. The man circled the hole, clapping his hands and barking Spanish. Woody saw the older man wave toward the rear of the property, whistle, and shout something that sounded like "*Jefe!*"

Woody felt a rush of adrenaline. He was, for the first time, mobile and on the job. Just like an old-school private dick, gathering information through his optic photoreceptors instead of via his regular, twenty-first-century drive down the digital highway. If asked, he would certainly cop to the efficiency of the new world order. That in a matter of seconds with a few simple keystrokes, a modern detective could score reams of pertinent information on any given subject.

But the efficiency of digital didn't hold the same rush as Woody's analogue whim. They used to call it "foot leather." A man on a stakeout. A job that spawned an entire genre of books and movies and television shows.

A flat-out, fuckin' gas, thought Woody. Even if it was for only a moment.

That and why should those hairy Anton Brothers have all the fun? The Armenian leg-breakers were all too eager to start the Raymo job by recording the comings and goings of the target's porno-licious wife. "Research through the lens of a silver Lexus," they called it. The need to know everything about a target before they made their move. First, leave nothing to chance. Then, when the moment was right, strike quickly and with decisive violence.

A dark room.

A taped confession.

Then the summary execution of the confessed murderer.

Maybe Woody would show the tape to Ben. Maybe he wouldn't. But the favor would be claimed. And Ben's pain would be, at last, forever vanquished.

Woody powered down the windows and let the wind brush his stubbled face. He deeply wished he could open the door, step to the street upright, his two feet carrying him down the crack-worn sidewalk instead of a motorized wheelchair.

Then Woody saw him. The fantasy snapped the instant Stew Raymo circled around from the back of the property in answer to the Hispanic man's call. But for the limp in his left leg, Stew appeared as advertised, closely matching the descriptions Woody had found in all the arrest records. Tanned and tall with a scruff of sunny blond hair topping his scalp. His carriage was like that of a retired pro athlete. A tool belt hung low on his waist like a gunslinger's holster. The man was impressive at a distance. Woody found himself imagining what Stew might look like close up and in a rage. If he would only turn around so Woody could see his face.

Instead, Stew had his cell phone glued to his ear, all the while half-listening to his site foreman. Without missing a step in his phone call, he gestured his instructions to the Hispanic foreman with a pointed index finger and flicks of the wrist. Then, just before Stew was about to disappear back inside the frame of the spec house, Woody thought he saw Stew take a sideways glance in his direction.

A sickening fear struck Woody.

Whatever silly-assed daydream the private detective had imagined was squeezed out in a flop sweat when he took a closer look at the killer. Woody's hammy fingers found the ignition key and turned over the Ford's engine. The rumble of eight, growling cylinders was loud enough to draw attention. By design. Along with the custom rims and the flames shooting off the fenders, Woody had splurged on a custom intake and exhaust package just so his shag-wagon sounded as nasty as it looked. That meant every engine start had an explosive quality that caused heads to turn and sent nearby birds into instant flight.

And Stew noticed.

At the sound of that guttural Detroit rumble, his eyes snapped from the double-door entry to the ruckus on the street. There he paid brief witness to the custom rig accelerating by his construction site. Stew didn't pay much attention beyond noting the chin-heavy black man in sunglasses and a baseball cap who was behind the wheel. *Odd*, he thought. *Not something you see every day. A fat black guy driving a custom fuckmobile. Takes all kinds*, thought Stew. *Some kind of white-trash wannabe—*

"You with me, Stewart?"

"Still here," said Stew back into the phone.

"Still a little confused on the picture you're painting me."

"Hang on," said Stew, who turned to Henry. "Don't care what the engineering says. After it's dug I wanna see every inch of rebar. Don't want no inspectors telling me to re-pour again. Hear me?"

"Gotcha, *Jefe*."

As Stew tromped toward the rear of his site, he continued his phone conversation.

"Picture is this. Having to re-pour my foundations on this thing has put me in a cash hole. You follow?"

"I follow. But what does this have to do with me?"

It was a woman he was talking to. A real estate agent with a distance in her voice. Stew could hear the clicking from the keyboard of her computer as she multitasked while on the phone with him.

"When you're done you're gonna sell this beast and make three points, right?"

"That's our agreement," she said.

"Right. Well, to raise the cash, I'm gonna sell my other house. And I want you to do it."

"Glad to."

"Tellin' you right now, there's nothing in the deal," said Stew. "I'll go up to four points on the spec house, but nothin' on the house I'm in."

"That doesn't seem fair at all."

"Fair hasn't nothin' to do with it. I need all the cash."

"Take a second on the house you're in."

"Mortgage?" asked Stew. "I already got two. Not gonna get another. I gotta sell. You're gonna do it."

"I'd like to," she said, sounding a bit more attentive. "But we all have to make a living. And I make mine on commission."

"I'm sayin' you'll make it on the spec house."

"You just said it. You got a cash problem. For all I know, you won't finish the spec—"

"Saying I'm not gonna finish it? Who the hell are you to—"

"Didn't say that at all, hon'. Just saying the market can go soft. You're already late. And my kid's gotta eat."

Stew stopped, kicked at a dirt clod, sending it flying into the bottom of the unfinished pool.

"So you won't list the house I'm in."

"I'll do it for two points."

"No points or you don't get the spec house."

"Hey Stew? Be a sweetie, huh. I got another call comin' in. Can we talk about this later?"

Stew answered by folding his phone closed and holstering it.

He stood still for a moment and tried to breathe. His left knee ached, the pain swelling as he strained to crush the rage inside. When he closed his eyes his vision turned the color of burnt orange, bordered by a black fog. He couldn't exactly see Jerome, the Sax Man, in his mind's eye. But he could feel his presence. And somewhere in his head Stew found himself smelling that putrid, sulfurous smell of the Stink Hole bathroom where he had killed the Sax Man.

"Fuck it," said Stew, spinning in the dirt and hobbling back toward the front. Then he shouted to Henry, "Goin' to the hardware store. Back after lunch!"

In a mere twenty-two minutes, Stew drove to a local hardware store, made his cash purchase, tossed the armload of goods into the bed of his truck, drove three miles, and cranked the parking brake after skidding to a stop at the curb outside his Morrison Street house.

And despite Stew's intent to return to the site that very afternoon, Henry, the site foreman and Stew's right-hand man, wouldn't see his boss until noon the following day. Not that Stew wouldn't return before then. He would visit the site later than he expected—around midnight—bloodied and under the cover of darkness.

"What the hell are you doing?"

"What's it look like?" answered Stew, dropping a heavy rubber mallet on top of a metal post.

Pam stood on the front porch, arms crossed, searching the recesses of her psyche for some explanation as to why her husband was posting a *For Sale by Owner* sign on their front lawn.

"For sale?"

"Taking too big of a hit on the job. Twenty Gs just to dig out and re-pour the foundations."

"You're not selling our house."

"No?"

Done with the mallet, Stew moved on to the bolts, fixing the red-and-white sign to the post. The spaces for price and contact numbers had yet to be filled in.

"Maybe you didn't hear me. We are not selling—"

"SHUT THE FUCK UP!"

Stew's color was pink and flush, a vein pushing the skin up from his neck. The last time Pam saw that vein bulge she had found herself in the emergency room with a broken jaw. The admitting nurse took one look at her and asked if she wanted to file a police report. Pam never wavered nor broke eye contact, softly answering, "No."

"You off the Program?"

"No. But you keep peppering me with questions and I'll sure as shit go bust me a couple drinks."

"I don't want you drinking."

"Neither do I. Guess that makes us even."

Pam took a single step toward Stew, off the porch and onto the walk.

"I want to talk about this."

"I don't."

"I love you and would like things to slow down. Just for a sec."

Stew dropped a bolt into the heavy grass. He bent down slowly searching for the silvery doughnut amongst the healthy blades of Marathon sod. It appeared to have vanished into the earth.

"Fuck."

"Stew?"

Stew lifted his eyes and looked at his wife for the very first time that day. To Pam it felt as if he was staring right through her. As if she wasn't flesh and blood, standing fifteen feet away.

His eyes, though, appeared clear and not dilated.

"You're selling our house."

"Make it simple, Pam," breathed Stew, his volume lowered to a notch above a whisper. "You go out and sell twenty large worth of your ass? Think that's about twenty high-class blowjobs for high-class dough? You can keep our house."

"Fuck you."

"Like that's gonna happen today."

"Apologize, asshole."

"Asshole? You just called me an asshole?"

"Dickhead. Cockweed. Shitferbrains."

Pam had her limits. And using the past against her was worth the fight. Even if he killed her this time.

"You gonna hit me? Go ahead, you fathead fuck!"

"Now, who's pissed off?"

"I am!" barked Pam.

Stew straightened and held his arms out in sudden surrender. At worst, he was amused. When Pam got mad it was damn funny to him.

"Honey. Listen to me. I can't make the vig on the loan unless we get some cash flow. No bank's gonna give us a third hump on the house. Only option we got is to get liquid for six months so I can finish. After, I promise, I'll buy you a bigger house in a better neighborhood."

"But I like our neighborhood."

"Right here, then. Bigger house right here."

Pam's arms were wrapped tightly around herself. And though she was shaking her head, it was more in disapproval than disagreement.

Stew took three steps nearer and then, a deep and cleansing breath. His normal skin color had returned and the bulging vein no longer appeared ready to explode.

"Bigger house, you know? Real family home."

"With a proper nursery?"

"With a proper nursery," answered Stew.

"No other options? We can't find twenty thousand anywhere else?"

"Unless you want me to rob a bank or something," joked Stew, limping the final few steps until she was in his arms, continuing to feign indifference.

"Cars are leased, babe. This house is our only real asset."

"Why couldn't you have just kept doing remodels?"

"Hey. That ugly skeleton in Studio City is our future."

"Our family's future."

Pam released her arms and let them wrap around her

husband. She pressed her head into his chest and listened to his heart thump. If he had lied to her and had been drugging or drinking, his heart rate would be elevated. Pam counted six seconds and did the quick math. Seventy heartbeats per minute. Stew was sober.

Sober forever? Or for now?

"Did you get my text?" she asked.

"What text?"

"Christ. Is your phone even on?"

Jack 'n' Coke.

"I'll pour," growled Stew.

The bartender left a double shot of Jack Daniels in a tumbler full of ice beside a second glass of Coca Cola. Stew had always liked it served that way. Seeing the soda pop fizz over the rocks of ice, the bubbles swirling within the liquor.

"Sugar and sin," he called it.

Ten years of sobriety were about to be smashed in a single gesture. All Stew had to do was lift the heavenly mash to his lips and sip. Instead, he let the tumbler sit there on the Outback Steakhouse bar. He ordered dinner off the bar menu and mustered some brief interest in the Sports Center updates on the pair of televisions flanking the triple-high shelves of booze.

"You should join the Carpenters Union," pressed the bearded drunk on the stool next to him. The man was fifty, bleary-eyed, and after getting a snort full of contractors' woes from Stew, had decided the best solution was for Stew to work as a construction dog on movie sets.

"High pay, easy hours."

Stew listened, but his eyes kept wandering to the Jack and Coke, full to the brim, but with fewer bubbles by the second.

"I know some fellahs. Young and experienced enough. Think they'd like you. Work swing on a couple of shows and bingo, you're in. Did I tell you the Union pays benefits? Health and dental, baby. Gonna keep my teeth 'til I'm ninety."

On any other day, Stew would have told the man to shut the fuck up. But distraction was key. For one, it kept his mind off his wife. With a great deal of self-control, Stew had curbed his anger and refrained from breaking her neck. He had even feigned affection when he was feeling nothing but rage.

"Something else about working movie construction. When you're building shit, ain't none of those pansy show-biz fags around. 'Cept maybe a production designer. But they come as fast as they go. By the time the cameras show up, we're on our stools, drinkin' our pay."

By the time Stew dug into his Bloomin' Onion and medium-rare rib eye, he had moved on to ignoring the blathering, show-biz hammerhead. He had assumed a prison posture, elbows on the table, arms circling his meal protectively.

The Jack and Coke remained untouched. All the fizz that was left was clinging to the shrinking cubes of ice.

Stew followed the meal with a pile of vanilla ice cream melting over the top of a steaming-hot chocolate brownie. A trio of college girls from Cal State Northridge was so taken with the looks of the dessert they considered ordering it themselves.

"Does it go down as good as it looks?" asked the freckled redhead, boldly swinging her swelling chest in Stew's direction.

Stew made a quick calculation.

She'd probably fuck me in the bathroom.

His straightened back and impish grin garnered giggles from the other two coeds. He let the trio measure him. He had had two women at once. Never three, to the best of his recollection. And college girls. That might be worth the marital infraction.

But inside, Stew still raged at Pam. Damn her for questioning my judgment—if even for a moment. And damn her for extorting a promise of a bigger house. With a proper nursery, for Christ's sake!

"Whatcha drinkin' with the brownie thingy?" asked the redhead.

"Jack and Coke."

"Mmmm," she replied. "Man's drink."

She didn't know shit, thought Stew. So what? She was young and willing, which meant her opinion was only as good as what she had between her legs.

"We're drinking . . ."

She had already had a few too many and had already forgotten. She turned to her compadres for assistance.

"Red Headed Slut!" chirped the short brunette, wearing jeans purchased before she had added on her freshman fifteen.

"That the name of a drink? Or a description your friend?" asked Stew, who was rewarded with a trio of willing giggles.

"*Jäger*, peach schnapps, and cranberry juice," answered the third girl, who was tall. Stew pegged her as the designated purse watcher. But he could tell by her pupils that she was also the drunkest, and when it came time to throw down, would probably be voted most likely to call him "daddy."

Turn you ass side up and you wouldn't say no.

Then the phone on his belt buzzed.

"That your girlfriend?" snipped the redhead.

Stupidly, Stew checked his phone. There, in bold letters against an aqua blue screen read a text message from Pam: CLD U PLZ BRING HOME 1 GLN NF MILK?

The text was punctuated by a yellow, smiley face emoticon.

Stew's anger swelled, his quiet rage turning his skin pink again. And that tell-all vein rose in his neck like an erection under tight denim.

For the trio of college women, the battle between instinct and alcohol was over in a heartbeat. Each of them quietly recoiled as dots of sweat bloomed on Stew's forehead while he stared unendingly at the text. Quiet nods were exchanged, handbags desperately clutched, and each of the coeds excused herself to the ladies' room.

"Cunts," groused Stew under his breath.

Then there was that jar of Jack and Coke, with the ice all but melted and the fizz diffused into the atmosphere. The drink found its way into Stew's grip. He could have crushed the glass, cut himself good and stopped his own madness from taking over. But it didn't happen that way. The cocktail touched his lips, slipped over his gums, and Stew swallowed. Gone were the years of sobriety, the promises, the amends to new and old associates.

Stew Raymo was officially off the wagon.

"Set me up again," demanded Stew, slapping the glass to the bar.

"Double shot?" asked the bartender.

"Four. Highball glass."

"You got it."

And with each gulp that followed, Stew remembered the times he drank Jack and Coke to get drunk and the times he merely used it to wash back handfuls of prescription narcotics. "The buzz and the after-buzz," he called it. It was all about the soda, sin, and see-what-the-hell-happens-next. Sometimes it was sex. Sometimes it was crime.

And sometimes it was murder.

By the time Stew settled into the seat of his pickup, raindrops were forming on the windshield. He kicked over the engine, turned on the wiper blades, then decided to recheck his phone for voicemails. The mix of Jack and Coke pumping through him felt warm and comfortable, all his angst momentarily eased by the booze. So when the first thing he read on his phone was Pam's last text, the venom never rose past a rehearsed apology.

CLD U PLZ BRING HOME I GLN NF MILK?

The wiper blades erased another sheet of raindrops. As Stew flicked on his headlamps, the beams landed squarely on the car parked opposite him.

A silver Lexus GS sedan.

Without any predictive thought, Stew popped his door and slid from the pickup, rotating clockwise across the parking lot and to his left until the Lexus' license plate came into his view. Stew checked it against the text sent by his wife earlier in the day.

The text he had ignored.

SILVER LEXUS 5HJR8429

There was no mistake. The tags matched.

Stew approached, more deliberate than bold. He remembered that about liquor. It stripped the rage and left him with a cozy feeling of omnipotence. Like Superman with a slightly malevolent side. Just don't piss off a man in tights.

The Lexus sedan was empty. The doors locked. Stew turned in place, doing a quick scan of the parking lot. The sprinkling of rain had left the tops of all the cars looking sparkling and new. Stew spotted a pair of aging Outback diners, one digging in her purse for keys. But they didn't seem to be heading toward the Lexus.

These guys weren't stalking Pam. Otherwise, why would they be following me? Then again, if they were following me, then where the hell were they? Still inside the steakhouse? *Must be*, thought Stew.

Then came the sudden urge for another round of Jack and Coke. With the push of a button, Stew locked his truck and set his bearings to return to the Outback.

6

GONZO DROVE IN circles. Four full revolutions around Ben's neighborhood, daring herself to drive up his cul de sac, park in front of his house, and ring the doorbell. The courage, though, wasn't coming. So she kept making right turns at nearly identical stoplights at nearly identical corners. Four times four times four times four. So many times, she had lost count. The only true gauges of how long she had been driving the square route were the clicks on the odometer and the gas her Chevy Suburban was guzzling.

If only the safety nut would return my call, she thought.

The hilly neighborhood was still Simi Valley. Just not Gonzo's Simi Valley. Ben's zip code had vistas, more square feet per house, and just about everything was newer—from the gutters to the trim paint, while Gonzo's streets sprung from an older development grid on the valley floor. Humble homes, cracked sidewalks, and a quantum leap more affordable to the dual-income cop families who had made the city famous.

Gonzo wondered if her worry about ringing the doorbell was nothing more than a class thing.

With her umpteenth right turn, she tried revising her speech, thinking the right sequence of sentences would explain her surprise visit to what she supposed was an already tense household.

I've heard the stupid rumors, she thought she would begin. *Stupid as in wrong. Stupid as in small-minded. Stupid as in I hope it hasn't caused you any undue grief.*

The word had gotten to Gonzo through, of all people, Travis, her kindergarten boy. At afternoon pick-up, he had climbed into the backseat of her car and breathlessly announced that he had already met his future daddy: Betsy's daddy. And that Carly's mom had told Carly that Betsy's daddy and Betsy's mom were going to get a divorce so that his mommy could marry Betsy's daddy.

It was an earful of trouble.

Gonzo's heart had turned sick, despite her logical side excusing the talk as silly shit six-year-olds say. But where on God's earth would a six-year-old get the notion without first hearing it from a parent?

Before approaching Carly's mom, whom Gonzo barely knew, she decided the best investigation was through the kindergarten teacher. Gonzo pulled her aside during a lunch-hour visit.

"Unvarnished," said Gonzo. "I need to know what's being said so I can undo it."

Uncomfortable, the wise old marm wearing a sweater hand-knit from neon-colored yarn and appearing as if she had stepped right out of a beauty shop and into the classroom, answered in the most politic way.

"Kids this age repeat what they hear from their moms and dads."

"But you've heard it," pressed Gonzo.

"Ms. Gonzalez—"

"Lydia . . . please."

"Fine. Lydia. Let me put it this way. You wouldn't be the first single mother who a jealous parent started a rumor about.

Mr. Keller is an attractive man. Please. I'm old enough to be his mom and I've noticed that there's . . . something about him?"

Gonzo could only sigh her response.

"So there's talk."

"There's always talk. I just choose not to listen. And neither should you," advised the teacher.

But there it was, thought Gonzo. She simply had to talk to Ben. Straighten things out. But after a week's worth of phone calls had gone unreturned, she had chosen to leave her boy with the sitter for an extra hour so she could politely rap on Ben's door. That was more her style. Direct. The thought of waiting until she bumped into Ben at school or some fund-raising function didn't so much as enter her mind.

But first she would have to turn up the cul de sac. When at last she had screwed up the courage to end her cycle of endless circling, the rain had increased from a mist to a drizzle. Gonzo set the brake with her two front tires in the driveway and the butt of her white SUV stuck into the street. She thought if she left the headlamps on and engine running, it would give the appearance of a visit that was less planned, informal, and something more akin to dropping a child off from a play date . . .

. . . instead of dropping a bomb on a marriage.

Gonzo stood momentarily in the rain, admiring the home. It was bigger than she had recalled from her one other visit. An inviting front yard, stone steps set neatly into perfectly mown grass curving to the arched front door. An arrangement of tropical plants framed a triad of vertical windows glowing with suburban warmth.

It was 6:37 P.M.

"Pasta mañana," announced Ben, wiping his hands on an apron with *I'm the Cook AND the Dishwasher* embroidered in bright red thread.

Thursday was leftovers night at the Kellers'. Since its inception, it had become one of Ben's all-time favorite family gatherings. Besides the opportunity to put his own culinary spin on the previous evening's meal, Ben so enjoyed the lightness that came with it. Thursday night was only a few hours sleep away from Friday and the relief that came with the weekend. And the kids could feel it, each energized with a look ahead to the future. Alex was simply happy that she wasn't stuck with the cooking.

When the doorbell rang, nobody thought it was the least bit strange. Solicitors often trolled the neighborhood at dinner hour. These were usually parents from down in the flats selling the likes of magazine subscriptions and Girl Scout cookies. Still, Ben had just set the last steaming plate of Pasta Mañana on the dining room's table. All but Elyssa and her new braces were thrilled at the entree. So Ben had also heated up a helping of chicken tenders.

"I'll get the door!" announced Nina.

"No, you won't," said Ben.

It was dark outside; most likely it was a stranger at the door, and Nina was only nine years old. Ben didn't have to be The Safety Expert to make that quick of a call.

"I'll get it," said Alex.

"Sit, eat," said Ben.

"Too slow."

Before Ben could argue Alex had pushed her chair away and left the room.

"Better that way," said Ben, after her exit.

"Why?" asked Betsy.

"Because your mom says, 'no thanks and goodbye' quicker than me."

Alex swiveled toward the front door without checking the video panel Ben had installed just inside the coat closet. A two-camera view: the front door and the rear gate. Alex rarely remembered to peek before unlatching and didn't much care at six-thirty in the evening.

She was mentally already rehearsing her all-bought-out speech when she first cracked the door.

"Listen, it's kind of a bad . . ."

Gonzo stood out of the dripping rain, wearing new denim and a black t-shirt under an LAPD windbreaker. Her cowboy boots added at least two inches to her five-foot-ten-inch frame.

Alex found herself looking up, momentarily stuck for a hello, and wondering if and when her anger would surface.

"Hey, Alex," said Gonzo.

"It's Lydia, right?"

Alex knew Lydia's name the moment she saw her. She didn't mean it as an insult. She simply couldn't think of anything else to say.

"I . . . I was just driving by . . . Kinda needed to talk to Ben," said Gonzo. "Is he okay?"

"He's fine. Listen, it's really not a good—"

"I'm sorry. I shoulda called the house first."

Alex opened the door wider. But it was more a territorial gesture than an invitation.

"What the hell are you doing here?"

And in that moment, Gonzo knew. The scorn in Alex's voice and posture spoke volumes. Gonzo's feminine instincts said, walk away, don't return, wait for time to pass. But the cop in her was more direct, to the point. Let's get this the hell over with!

"There's been some talk at school I wanted to address."

"You could've called. Left a note. It's our dinner time and you're interrupting."

"Think Ben should be here when I say this. Is he home?"

"I said it's dinner time."

"Whatever you think happened—"

"I don't want to know what happened!" snapped Alex.

When Alex heard her own voice rise she automatically stepped onto the welcome mat and closed the door behind her to mask her own volume. Gonzo eased backwards, one step down, thus leveling her eyes with Alex's.

"I'm sorry for whatever you assume—"

"Whatever happened is over, okay? So go home. You live down there. Ben lives up here with me and my girls. And when we see each other we'll be polite, but not friends. Is that so hard?"

On-the-job training had turned Gonzo into a patient listener, letting distressed civilians vent their emotions until they were too spent to be a danger to anybody but themselves. Later, when Gonzo replayed the tape of the conversation with Alex in her head, she realized she should have interrupted.

"What kind of stupid woman knocks at a married man's door at family dinner time? What is your problem? You in love with him? You think he's gonna leave us and take care of you?"

"What I think is Ben should be here to hear this."

"Well, Ben's with his family. This is about you and me."

"Alex. There's been a misunderstanding."

"As long as you're still standing here, there's a helluva misunderstanding. Just please! Go!"

"Lydia?"

The door widened, revealing Ben in that silly, stitched apron. His face was a baffled mix of concern and wonder. He stiffened, his eyes swiveling between his wife and his confidante. Neither woman looked happy to see the other. Or him, for that matter.

"Sorry," said Ben. "I step in something?"

It was in this moment that the pieces fell together in Gonzo's mind. It was like somebody tossed a jigsaw puzzle into the air and it fell to the ground, perfectly assembled as something painfully simple and obvious. It was a recipe in three painful parts.

- Ben hadn't informed his wife about Stew Raymo.
- Alex suspected Ben of having an affair with Gonzo, but had stuffed it.
- And Gonzo, more concerned about her reputation than her promise to protect Ben's privacy, had driven circles for an hour, then lost the battle with her better self.

Kept apart, the ingredients were relatively inert. Combined they were as combustible as a test tube full of nitroglycerine in the hands of a Parkinson's patient.

"I was just leaving," said Gonzo.

"You just got here." Ben widened the door. "Really wet out. Do you want to come in?"

"Better that she goes," said Alex.

"I agree," said Gonzo. "We'll talk some other time, okay?"

Something in Ben made him wisely go along with it. As he watched Gonzo retreat to her car, pulling her hood up to defend against a sudden and pelting rain, guilt crept over him for not returning her calls. Self-preservation was his excuse. That and he had made certain assurances to Alex that he would put behind whatever the hell was going on with him.

Ben was moving on.

As Gonzo backed out of the driveway, her headlights washed across the front door, igniting Ben and Alex in xenon white. Neither was speaking to the other as the door eased closed. Gonzo was both relieved and sickened. Her only consolation was that she had escaped the scene before it got ugly. The part that made her stomach sour was the marital fight that she was sure to have started.

Leftover night. It turned out to be a mostly somber evening, with both Ben and Alex defensively peppering the girls with hardly interested questions in a team effort to keep the meal from devolving into complete silence. The girls weren't fooled. They knew when things weren't right between their mother and Ben. It was a pure kind of instinct that only children possess. Still, they gamely played along then made quick excuses to exit the dining room. For the next three hours, Elyssa buried herself with her books, Nina climbed into bed with her iPod, and Betsy requested that both mommy and daddy read to her. Ben chose a short book with big illustrations and little story. Alex crawled into bed next to Betsy with a longer, chapter book and read until the child fell asleep.

Ben wondered if his wife would fall asleep too and whatever transpired between Gonzo and her would stay undiscussed until morning. But there was no such luck for Ben.

"You said it was over!"

"Said it was behind me."

"Then why the fuck was she showing up on our front stoop?"

"Probably because I wasn't returning her calls."

"She's still calling you?"

Alex's voice tipped the safety scale. As far as they knew, the children were sleeping. Ben checked the clock. It was 11:18 P.M.

"You could hold your voice down."

Alex leaned over the bathroom sink, wrung her freshly

washed hair, then twisted it into a towel. The makeup mirror's lights were on full blast. To look at her made Ben squint.

"You said you didn't want to know."

"I didn't," said Alex. "That, of course, was until I found out half the elementary school was talking."

The elementary school? Talking about what?

Alex stole a glance at Ben, expecting, hoping even, to catch a crack of remorse in him. Instead, what she saw was utter bewilderment. Ben was many things, but thick wasn't one of them. How in the name of Christ, at a moment such as this, could he believably feign looking so damn baffled?

"Do you think . . ." Ben's face split in an embarrassed smile. "You think I'm having an affair with her?"

"Have? Had?" Alex spun around to face Ben, pushing up only inches from his face. "Does it really matter now that everyone knows?"

"Everybody but me," said Ben, who released a laugh, both amused and momentarily relieved at what he was fast realizing was a massive misunderstanding. What he didn't calculate was the pain his wife was feeling.

Alex pounded her fists into Ben's chest.

"You're denying it?"

"She's a cop!"

"Oh. So cops don't screw married men?"

"Not me, they don't . . . Alex—"

"Don't Alex me!"

Ben tried to reassuringly place his hands on her shoulders, only to have them violently shrugged off. Alex spun around, then sat on the toilet, head in her hands.

"There's no affair. There never was. She was only helping me with a personal matter."

"Personal matter? What kind of personal matter turns into . . . all this?"

Ben squatted in front of Alex, his hands on her knees.

"Look at me," he said. "Please. Just look at me."

Alex looked at him, alright. Through a pair of teary red-streaked eyes that he hadn't seen since their early days in those Grief Relief group sessions.

"Now please listen," he said. "I was gonna tell you. I was acting weird and thought you deserved to know why. But then you said you didn't want to know. And I said okay—"

"So it's my fault I'm feeling this way? Are you fucking serious?"

"Not your fault. My fault for not telling you from the very beginning."

Alex focused through her tears, only to see Ben's guilty face, his own eyes wet and scared. His hands were trembling.

"Tell me what?"

"About Sara . . . the twins . . ."

Ben's shaky hands turned into white knuckled fists. His head tilted, facing the floor tiles.

"I know who did it," said Ben, his adrenaline surging as he released what he had been keeping from his wife for weeks.

The next words came with breathtaking excitement.

"I know who killed them. Know his name and where the bastard lives!"

Ben then recounted tale of his last month. From receiving the CD to his conversations with Woody Bell to how and when and why he had involved—then uninvolved—LAPD Detective Lydia Gonzalez. The only parts he failed to tell Alex about were his visit to the graves and his shaking hands with the devil himself.

Ben then played Alex the recording. At her request he made the trip out to his rear office and dug up what he had promised himself and her to keep buried. It was a quarter past two in the morning by the time she had listened to every raspy second of it, all without saying a word. During the entire time, she was curled up in the rain-streaked window seat, her mother's worn afghan wrapped around her shoulders, a saffron corduroy pillow clutched to her chest.

"I need coffee," said Alex, leaving the pillow, but keeping the blanket. She made zero eye contact with Ben as she crossed the bedroom, walked out the door, and thumped her way down

the stairs. Ben wasn't far behind. He found a chair at the kitchen
table and watched as she silently loaded a double shot of coffee
into the espresso machine, steamed a cup of milk, and poured
the froth into a ceramic mug.

Alex didn't ask if Ben wanted coffee. She held the cup under
her nose for a moment, but didn't yet take a sip.

"Stew Raymo," she said flatly, as if speaking the name aloud
would commit it to memory. Or once mentioned, it would be
purged forever. Ben couldn't tell.

"Short for Stewart Raymond," Ben found himself saying.

"And you know where he lives?"

"North Hollywood."

"Have you ever met him?" Alex sipped her brew.

"No," he lied.

"Haven't had any temptation to even get a look at him?"

"And then what?" Ben looked her dead in the eye, brows
raised in full emphasis.

"I don't know," she said, a hint of suspicion breathed over
the top of her latte. "You tell me."

"I'm putting it behind me. Why I saw the doc," said Ben.
"Why I didn't call Lydia Gonzalez back."

"So this . . . Stew Raymo . . . he doesn't know about you or
where we live? Doesn't know that you know. He's just going to
go on with his life while we go on with ours?"

"The way it's been."

"What if I don't like the way it's been?"

"You didn't like tonight? By that I mean the way it was
tonight before the goddamn doorbell rang."

"Before the doorbell rang I thought you were a liar and a
cheat."

"And you were wrong."

"Wrong about the cheating."

"Alex . . ."

She sipped at her coffee, crossed her feet and leaned against
the counter.

"I'd be lying if I didn't say this all made me extremely
uncomfortable."

"Me, too," said Ben, waiting for a glimmer of sympathy from her. She had been through her share of grief, done the hard work and moved on. As Ben read it, the difference between them was that Alex hadn't been reinjected with about a billion CC's of long lost anguish while she was daydreaming her life away.

"It's about trust, Ben."

"I was there, too. I was going to tell you and you said you didn't want to know."

"And you said it was over!"

"We're going in circles."

"I don't know what you want from me."

"I want you to understand. Is that so difficult?"

"Understand that you've re-obsessed yourself with your dead wife? Understand that for a month you've been sneaking around like you're screwing some other woman, but really haven't been screwing her? Jesus!"

"Would you be happier if I had?"

"No!"

"I said I've moved on and I have."

"Well, pardon me if I haven't!"

Alex jabbed a sharp index finger into her own chest, upsetting her mug and spilling her coffee onto the floor.

"Shit."

"I got it."

Ben was on his feet, reaching for some paper towels. He tore off a couple of sheets, but when he turned he found Alex crouched over the spill, wiping it up with a dishrag. She deposited the cup into the sink.

"I'm going to bed," she said, intoning that it wasn't exactly an invitation.

"We'll get through this," reassured Ben.

"Uh huh."

Whether Alex was being dismissive or just exhausted, she didn't let on. She never did after a fight. Time, along with sleep, was her constant ally. Even after a double espresso. *It was a good goddamned trick*, Ben thought. *Good for her.*

For Ben it would be a downstairs shower then a short night

spent on the couch in the den. He would probably fall asleep to an ESPN rerun of some damned Texas Hold'em tournament. Televised poker. It was a narcotic for Ben. Guaranteed slumber. A steady mix of professional and amateur players, each managing the risk of losing a little or a lot on the simple turn of a card.

Risk.

Ben plumped a couple of pillows and curled up under a fleece blanket. He settled in with the TiVo remote, unconsciously dialing the channels until he had found his drug. Unlike for Alex, sleep for Ben would come when the poker gods decided and no sooner.

There, under the high-definition blast of the big screen TV, he wondered.

For a man as averse to risk as Ben was, had he risked a little or a lot by waiting so long to come clean with his wife? What had he wagered by not informing her of every disturbing detail? And what would be the consequences of his soft deceit?

The answer came as a simple mantra.

Move on.

"Wise words," Ben said aloud to nobody but himself. After that he added a simple, "thank-you" to whomever or wherever the answer came from.

A suburban Mecca, the San Fernando Valley is a 345 square mile basin of sand and rock surrounded by mountains, only a few short miles from the sea. Were it not for the water siphoned in from the Colorado River, this most populous desert region would find it difficult to support a family of lizards, let alone the millions of families who had settled between the Santa Monica Mountains and the towering Santa Susanas. Where there were once endless acres of orange, grapefruit and avocado groves, now were neighborhoods and malls and seemingly every retail and restaurant franchise that could sprout under the sun. All of it was neatly divided by a mostly organized grid of streets—east and west—north and south.

But when the heavy rains came, each and every street funneled the water into fast-rising gutters. All the dirt, litter, and oil were washed from the roads and sucked into a series of deep, concrete channels known as the L.A. River. These arteries, so quick to fill with grime and debris, emptied themselves into the Pacific Ocean in places like Santa Monica, Playa Del Rey, San Pedro, and Long Beach. And as much as the city boulevards and sidewalks glistened after these rare drenchings, it was as if all of the valley got the stomach flu on the same day and vomited poison into the sea.

Few citizens were aware of the massive pollution to the ocean that followed every rain. And most of those who were aware felt helpless to do anything short of blasting their car horns when they saw the smoker in the vehicle in front of them flick his stinking cigarette butt out the window and onto the pavement.

Stew Raymo knew where the cigarette butts ended up. His answer was to let the fuckin' fish deal with them. With that, he sucked the last nanogram of tar and nicotine out of his Marlboro, then expertly sent it sparking across the sidewalk and into the gutter that fronted his construction site. Against the black of night, it looked like a tiny spray of Fourth of July pyrotechnics.

And Stew had always liked fireworks.

The rain had left the site misty and a little muddy, but not entirely slick. Under the glow of a nearby streetlamp sputtering and gasping to stay ignited, the wood framing glistened like a freshly peeled skeleton.

Stew had no clue what time it was. All he knew was that it was still dark. That, and that his fix of Jack and Coke had long worn off, leaving him tired and yearning for bed. But the job had to be finished. He had dragged the body into one of the many ten-by-six-by-five-foot holes that had been dug and framed for the new foundation pilings. The hard part was finding a way to fit the carcass through all the crisscrossing of rebar without dismembering his load.

The streetlamp continued to percolate, flashing on and off, barely allowing Stew to make out what was left of the man's face, one half bloodied and smashed, the other caked in mud.

This was the bearded one, he remembered. There were two men. One was stick-thin, dressed in an Izod polo, khakis, and thin sweater, heavily bearded with a circular bald spot at the back of his head. The other, younger and very clean-shaven. That one wore a starched shirt with gold cufflinks to match the gold watch, gold bracelet, and gold necklace. Both were olive-skinned. And neither, Stew guessed correctly, were cops.

Armenians, he figured. He had spotted them when he had returned inside the Outback Steakhouse. With one methodical scan across the restaurant, all Stew needed to do was match the faces with the silver Lexus. As Stew approached, they didn't exactly look like stalkers to him. Nor did they appear to have any interest in Stew. They neither saw him approach, nor were they focused on anything other than an oversized plate of nachos and their frosty mugs of microbrews.

"Hey, fellahs," said Stew.

When both men broke from the conversations and looked curiously up at Stew, neither man revealed the slightest hint of recognition. What they saw was that same winning smile Stew had shown Ben on the day they had met.

"Either of you guys driving a silver Lexus?"

"That's mine," said the skinny one with the beard in a heavy accent.

"Sorry to bother you, but you're kinda blocking me. Would you mind at all if—"

"No problem," said the skinny one, pulling out his keys and rattling them at his friend. He spoke something in Armenian that Stew deciphered as little more than, "Be right back."

"Thanks, man. Really appreciate it."

Stew stayed two strides to the rear of the man, politely shadowing him out of the restaurant and all the way to the car in question. As the Lexus chirped and flashed its headlights when the man activated the remote unlocking feature, Stew did a speedy pivot, checking for possible witnesses. The man was reaching for the door's handle when it dawned on him that he appeared to be blocking nobody at all.

"Which car am I supposed to be—"

The Armenian didn't see it coming. All he felt were Stew's fingers palming his head like a basketball, then slamming it hard into the door frame. Bones cracked. The man's knees buckled. But Stew kept him from hitting the ground by snatching hold of his polo shirt's collar. With that, Stew slipped his other arm around the man's waist and helped him across the parking lot.

If there had been witnesses, all they could have recalled was seeing what appeared to be a helpful friend carrying his drinking pal to his car for a safe ride home.

Meanwhile, as Stew hurried the man over to his truck, he whispered, "Fight me and I'll fucking gut you! Hear me? I'll spark up my chainsaw and slice you from Hollywood to Pacoima!"

The unlikely duo had to travel a short twenty yards. When they reached Stew's pickup, Stew lifted the man into the driver's side and climbed in after him, only to palm the man's head again, guiding him deep into the passenger-side's foot well.

"Please . . ." begged the man.

"Shut up!"

Stew popped the glove box, found a roll of duct tape, and quickly bound the man's feet and hands.

Through busted teeth the man groaned, "What do you want?"

"Like followin' pretty women? Shootin' yer video? You and your butt buddy with the gold chains?"

Stew reached across with his leg and lowered a steel-toed boot into the man's groin. Three hard stomps, then he had the pickup in gear and was easing out of the parking lot onto the six-lane, commuter-cramped Devonshire Boulevard.

A sudden cloudburst dropped a volley of heavy rain, each drop exploding against Stew's windshield. It came so fast the wiper blades found it difficult to catch up. All the headlights, taillights, and syncopated traffic lights blended with the downpour and beating wipers into a semi-psychedelic brainwash that Stew found pleasing.

He lit a Marlboro, cracked his window, and inhaled the mash of sweet rain, car exhaust, and cigarette smoke. But the moment was fouled by the faintest whiff of the tall man's heavy aftershave.

"Why you wanna follow her?"

Without waiting to hear an answer, Stew kicked the man once again. All he heard was the guttural wheeze of a man losing consciousness.

"Wake the fuck up, asshole!"

"Just a job," croaked the man.

"Since when's stalkin' my wife a fuckin' job, pervert?"

The man's eyes first widened, then focused as if truly looking at Stew for the first time.

"You're the husband," said the man, more thinking the words he spoke than expressing them to Stew.

"Fuckin' A I'm her fuckin' husband!"

"She was first . . . Follow her first, then you."

Stew braked for a stoplight, then swiveled his head robotically. In the darkness of the passenger-side's foot well, he could barely make out the man's features.

"Followin' me?"

The man's eyes blinked under Stew's hard gaze. Then he nodded yes.

"Who's the asshole that wants you to follow me?" The suspicion in Stew's voice was as heavy as wet cement.

"Paid job," whispered the man. "I dunno—"

The man howled in pain as Stew ground the burning end of his cigarette into his hostage's exposed calf. Stew punched up the local country station and twisted the volume knob until the music was just shy of earsplitting, masking the screams.

"Gimme a fuckin' name!"

". . . Wood . . . or Woody Somebody . . ." sobbed the man. "I didn't take the call."

"This Woody Woodfuck? He a cop?"

The man shook his head violently.

"No? What about Kashani? He work for Kashani?" pressed Stew.

Farrokh Kashani of Tarzana was Stew's money man. A first-generation Persian-American, he had hired Stew to remodel the kitchen of his hilltop home. Farrokh was so pleased he had kept Stew and his crew working for over a year and a half, renovating the entire hilltop property pillar by pillar. It was Farrokh who, after Stew had failed to secure a construction loan through conventional means, had floated him a personal line of credit for the Studio City property. And with the recent delays, Stew had entertained minor worries that Farrokh would lose faith and tighten the leash.

"Dunno..." muttered the man, once again, shaking his head in fear.

"Fuck!"

Stew pounded the steering wheel, causing the whole cab to shudder. If the man worked for Farrokh, Stew was doubly screwed. The other guy he had left behind at Outback would surely go back to this Woody Somebody and report.

"Wait, wait, wait," Stew said to himself.

The Jack and Coke was sending an instant message from his subcortex. It played like video, projected across his rainy windshield in widescreen. When Stew had approached their Outback Steakhouse table, both men had looked up from their microbrews in response to his question. Neither had revealed the faintest hint of recognition. Instinct was Stew's most trusted resource. And it was instinct that informed him now that neither the thick man with the gold chains and cufflinks, nor the tortured SOB stuffed into his passenger-side's foot well, clocked that he was the husband they had been assigned to follow.

"But why me?" wondered Stew.

"... Dunno."

"What I do to you? Or that Woody Woodfucker?"

"Please, sir . . ."

"You follow me to Outback?"

"... You didn't follow us?"

That's when it hit Stew between the eyes. It was coincidence. Pure and unadulterated. The same Armenian pair that had followed Pam, and were next assigned to follow him, had chosen to close out their day at Outback Steakhouse with some nachos and cold beer. Not at all unlike the way Stew had planned to lower the curtain on his lousy day.

Coincidence or fate?

The answer didn't matter a whit to Stew. Believing in fate

meant including higher powers into his mental conversations. And coincidence was just another way of saying "shit happens."

Just call me lucky.

Stew had always been lucky. He had wriggled out of most of the bad scrapes in his life. Enough, at least, to claim that he had been left with a winning percentage.

"Take me back. I will promise not to follow you again."

Stew ignored the man. He began thinking aloud, his voice elevated so he could hear himself over the blaring sound system.

"No going back, Stew."

"I got money," begged the man. The whimper escaping him was buried by the noise.

"Fuckin' boozer," barked Stew at himself.

"Jus' let me go—"

"Boozers are losers!"

"PLEASE!"

"YEAH, YEAH!"

Stew reached across and popped the glove box, fishing by feel until his fingertips brushed a cylindrical shape—metallic, cold and scored with a crosscut pattern for an easier grip.

And grip it he did, hefting it near the lens and letting the heavy barrel do the work. Sober Stew wouldn't remember how many cocks of his wrist it had taken to kill the man. But Jack and Coke never forgot. Jack and Coke counted twenty-two swings of the flashlight, each ending with a hard, whipping stroke to the man's ever-softening head.

That's how Stew found himself in the sticky shadows of his construction site, staring into one of those deep, concrete-ready foundation holes. His next order of business was to get rid of the body and deal with the bloody mess in his truck. That, and his clothes would have to be totally destroyed.

The dead man's thin body folded with surprising ease through the crisscrossing rebar, coming to rest at the bottom with a muddy splash. Next, Stew stripped down to his underwear, poked the remainder of his clothes into the hole with a shovel and began spading enough dirt on top to cover everything.

Six inches should do it, he thought. In a matter of hours, it would be covered by fast-hardening concrete. The remaining rain had a cooling effect, turning to steam nearly as quickly as it struck Stew's skin. He breathed in through his nose, exhaled through his mouth, and worked calmly, composing a list of chores he would need to accomplish in the hours ahead.

- Pickup truck. Hose and wipe down the interior, lose the carpet
- Golfer's rain suit. In the pickup's rear toolbox. Wear it.
- Drive the pickup into the barrio. East Los Angeles. Within the speed limit. Leave truck on a side street, door ajar, keys in the ignition.
- License plates. Removed and tossed into a dumpster.
- The Metro. Utilize city busses and railway for return home.
- Home. Shower, change. If Pam wakes, insist you'll explain it all to her later.
- Report pickup truck stolen.
- Back to site. Drive Pam's car. Oversee the Morales Brothers re-pour the concrete into the new foundation forms.

Showered, shaved, and warmed by his dry clothes, Stew stood in the exact position where he had built his mental checklist only hours earlier. It was a new day. And Stew was finally sober. He squinted into the morning sun and quietly watched Hector Morales and his four sons direct a fattened hose spewing wet, gray cement into the form. A gas-powered concrete pump droned loudly, splitting the morning quiet and fouling the air with the stink of burning petrol.

In that moment, Stew felt sorry for the neighbors. If he lived next door to the site, he could see himself complaining loudly, then later delivering a box of Krispy Kremes to the crew as an apology. After all, they were only doing their jobs.

And burying the evidence of a capital crime.

The yellow barrel of the cement truck made noisy revolutions, those brown sombreros turning one over the other. When the first form was filled to the brim with the gray mix, Stew turned the site back over to Henry and made a quiet exit. There was one last task for him to accomplish. A last minute addition to his list:

- Apologize to Pam. Admit falling off the wagon. Make amends and get to the nearest and soonest Alcoholics Anonymous meeting.

Ten years, three months, and eighteen days of sobriety. Flushed down the toilet. Strangely though, Stew felt renewed and full of confidence. He had cleaned himself up once before and sure as shit could do it again. With the love of a good woman and a clear head, not to mention the support of millions of his brothers in AA, he felt as if he could accomplish anything.

Next task for Stew to accomplish? Finding the man called Woody.

The drop-off line for Simi Canyons School was a certifiable traffic hazard. Every morning there was a line of gas-guzzling SUVs and luxury sedans backed up onto Tierra Rejada Road, a significant artery feeding both the 118 and 23 Freeways. Parents would queue up in the right lane, sometimes waiting as long as fifteen minutes in near standstill traffic, for their turn to pull into the campus' driveway. Once they had entered the Simi Canyons property, cars were divided into two lanes: one for elementary school, one for middle school and high school. Parents would then be directed by teachers and administrators, acting as traffic cops, to stop their cars, drop off their kids, and pop their trunks or hatches to unload backpacks so heavy with books they needed wheels. Both drop-off lanes would eventually merge again and horseshoe back onto the already choked boulevard.

The city fathers publicly screamed and blamed the school for the increased traffic, noise pollution, and elevated carbon-monoxide index. They even threatened to revoke the school's conditional use permit unless they came up with a viable plan to solve the problem. Quietly though, the politicians continued to curry favor with the upper crust of the parent body, assuring the headmaster and the board that the charter wasn't in any real danger as long as the school appeared to be making an effort to fix the problem.

Of course Ben knew otherwise. The problem wouldn't be fixed as long as the school continued to inch upward in enrollment. That, and slow traffic wasn't a true hazard. A car stuck in traffic was rarely in an accident worse than a fender bender, noise pollution was in the ear of the beholder, and the consistent offshore weather pattern essentially blew Simi's excess carbon residue into the yawning gullet of the San Fernando basin.

Ben treasured the time with the girls. While stuck in the conga line of cars he would spin vintage rock tunes for them, quiz them for their tests, arbitrate petty feuds, and play silly word association games.

And Ben had decided to expand what had formerly been a once-a-week event for him into a daily routine. At least, for the short term. It gave Alex a break from the drive, and Ben another way to reconnect with his adopted family.

"If you were a flavor, what would you be?" asked Ben.

Elyssa was first to answer because, well, she was always first. The oldest girl reserved that privilege along with sitting up front in the passenger seat. She always took her time and turn seriously, knowing she would be setting the bar high with her answer.

"Chocolate Fudge Brownie," said Elyssa, grinning broadly while looking to Ben for his secret wink of approval.

"Okay, Nina's turn," said Ben, withholding judgment.

Nina started with her usual "Ummmm." Because lately, Nina started every answer with an "Ummmm."

"Ummmm," mocked Elyssa.

"Ben!"

"Teasers will lose their turns," Ben reminded.

"Ummmm," began Nina, once again.

While Elyssa bit her lip, Ben reviewed the morning's drive. Simi Valley had dried out nicely since the rains. Beneath the golden scrub that blanketed the surrounding hills, Ben had detected a green undergrowth. *A good sign*, he thought. Green wild grasses significantly reduced the chance of the seasonal brushfires of fall and the mudslides of spring.

"Ummmmm, Cherry Garcia."

"Really," said Ben. "Why?"

"Because she'll say anything to sound different," mumbled Elyssa.

"Because I like it!" argued Nina.

"Then name one Grateful Dead song," said Elyssa.

"It's not about a song," said Ben. "It's about a flavor."

"And I'm a Cherry Garcia," said Nina. "It's like eating something tie-dye."

"Doesn't anybody want to know my flavor?" asked Betsy.

"I do," said Ben, squinting into the rearview mirror. The Volvo was angled east to west, allowing the morning sun to strike squarely in the middle of the back window. Ben slipped down his shade then twisted the mirror so he could meet Betsy eye-to-eye.

"Okay. I have lots of flavors that I am. Favorite flavors and fun flavors and ones I like because they remind me of Johnny."

"Johnny who?" asked Ben.

"Johnny Crismani," chimed Nina, "Betsy's boyfriend du jour."

"Is not!"

"Du jour?" asked Ben, amused at Nina's faux command of adult vernacular.

"I only sit next to him," said Betsy.

"I'm looking for your flavor?" reminded Ben.

"I'm Rainbow Sherbet, of course," said Betsy.

"Of course," added Nina. "Didn't we all know?"

"Because of all the things you love," answered Ben for her.

"Okay. Ben's turn," prompted Elyssa.

"Too old to be a flavor," said Ben.

"No you're not," said Nina. "Everybody's a flavor.

"I'm not a flavor," said Ben. "I'm an acquired taste."

"That's what Mom says," said Elyssa.

"And Mom would know," said Ben.

"I know," volunteered Betsy. "You're Rainbow Sherbet, too."

"Fine. Betsy said it," shrugged Ben. "I'm Rainbow Sherbet, too."

"Not fair," said Elyssa. "You have to come up with your own flavor or we'll give you one."

"Okay, then," said Ben. "Give me one. Betsy already says I'm Rainbow Sherbet. What do you think I am?"

"Ummmmm," said Nina.

"Vanilla," piped in Elyssa with a somewhat cutting understanding the flavor's social significance.

"That's what I was gonna say!" said Nina, disappointed her sister beat her to the punch. "But not because vanilla is vanilla. Because everybody likes it."

"Is there vanilla in Rainbow Sherbet?" asked Ben, hoping to be saved by either Betsy or the miracle of moving traffic.

"I don't know," said Betsy. "But vanilla's okay with me, too."

"Not even with chocolate sauce and nuts?" asked Ben.

"Sundaes aren't flavors," said Elyssa, sounding every bit the know-it-all.

And so it went. Two straight weeks of Ben driving his three adopted amigas to the Simi Canyons School, queuing up on Tierra Rejada with all the other private-school parents, partaking in the daily traffic jam, dropping the girls off with kisses and a "have a nice day," then not-so-promptly swinging onto the eastbound 118. Nearly each winter day was identical, a slight breeze from the west, and seventy-one degrees Fahrenheit.

Identical too was the order of freeway exits and interchanges. Like ticks on a clock, clicking all the way down to zero. Zero being where Ben stayed in one of the left-hand lanes, past where the southbound I-5 connected with the 170. After that, it was maybe ten minutes to the front door of his office. Ben could almost smell the hot coffee. And maybe, if he was lucky, Josie would have bought him some kind of pastry. A simple success, Ben decided. All temptation and curiosity would be averted for another day. His life was back on track.

Moving on.

But, if Ben were to let temptation flower—if while on the I-5 he were to inexplicably veer into the right-turn lanes, arch over the flood-control channels and find himself traveling south on the 170 —he would quickly be mere moments from the Burbank Boulevard exit.

North Hollywood.

Home of Stew Raymo.

As days passed, this became both Ben's figurative and literal crossroad. He would safely move along at the mean traffic speed, beginning his countdown as the 118 Freeway lifted him over the 405. Glancing to the distant north, he could see the water that fed the San Fernando Valley cascading down the California Aqueduct. Turning his gaze south, Ben could see thousands of daily commuters and truck drivers from places like Santa Clarita, Lancaster and Bakersfield, each waiting for his turn to merge onto the southbound San Diego Freeway.

Continuing eastbound, Ben would position himself in the centermost traffic lane, intently focused on keeping each wheel equidistant from the neat rows of Botts' Dots—those round, raised markers created by Dr. Elbert Botts, a California Department of Transportation engineer, as a warning system to sleepy or wandering drivers. "A genius invention," Ben would often remark, always crediting the man who, in many estimations, had saved tens of thousands of lives. When a car's tires ran over a row of Botts' Dots, the one-inch bumps delivered a distinctive, staccato vibration through the drivetrain to the steering wheel, and into the hands of the drifting driver.

Only when Ben had securely fixed his sights on staying dead in the middle lane, could he actually sense that he was straddling the line between his future and his past.

Stay left and his pledge to Alex would be kept.

Slide right and the promise would be shattered.

Left. Ben was moving on.

Right. A giant leap into his primeval past.

Left. Ben could taste his own limp flavor. Vanilla.

Right. Ben could taste blood.

So it was that on Friday, March 7 at exactly 8:32 A.M, four months and six days since he had first listened to that scratchy, dying voice utter Stew Raymo's name, Ben Keller decided that he would do something dumb and patently foolish. An act absolutely detrimental to the stitches that held his soul intact. As the 5/170 interchange approached, Ben chose to let fate— or God—decide which direction his life should take. And with that . . .

Ben took his hands off the steering wheel.

Whether it was the imperceptible canter of the road or the car's alignment or the slight wear on the treads of his Michelin steel-belted radials or even a meager gust of wind from the north, Ben would never, ever know the true cause.

But the car lingered to the right.

Only when the right front tire came in clear contact with Dr. Elbert Botts' Dots did Ben resume control of the vehicle. Then, without thought or true clarity of purpose, Ben instinctively clicked his right turn indicator, checked his mirrors, and entered the lanes designated for the 170 south.

Hell-bound, he thought. *Jesus God help me.*

"My name is Pamela."

Pam bit her lip and with it, her budding anger. The stupid Internet was down again. All she needed to do was determine from the DSL provider if the problem was on her end or theirs. After that, she could handle the next step. Unfortunately, she was stuck following a procedure laid out by some faceless phone tech in far-off India.

"Hello, Pam. My name is Roger," said the tech, adding insult to Pam's intelligence.

No it's not, said Pam to herself. Your name isn't Roger. It's something like Asim or Taj or Ganesh.

"For our records, can you confirm your full name and billing address?"

"Pamela Raymo. Two-one-two-three Morrison Street. North Hollywood, California."

That's right, she reminded herself. North Hollywood.

North Hollywood. A suburb within the City of Los Angeles. And it is, as its name would indicate, north of Hollywood. To the south, Studio City and the east, Toluca Lake and the City of Burbank.

North Hollywood, or NoHo as some real estate brokers had dubbed it in order to make living there sound chic, wasn't where Pam had wanted to invest in their first home. She had wanted Santa Monica, Mar Vista, or Pasadena, even. Wherever they bought, she had wanted to be far from the San Fernando Valley. More importantly, far from North Hollywood where she was born, schooled and recruited for her first movie role while still attending Grant High School. It was a student film, shot over two days for a wannabe director taking an introduction to filmmaking class at Valley College. And like so many young actresses who see the world through a prism made of stars, she had fallen hard for the young Spielberg, slept with him before the little film was finished, then dropped out of high school to move in with him in the guest house behind his mother's house.

She called him *College Boy*.

He called her *Misty Fresh*.

Within six months College Boy had convinced Misty Fresh that in order to fund their maturing cocaine habit, she could make easy money giving a few blowjobs on film. "Just oral sex," he had promised her. "Like Monica Lewinsky did for President Clinton."

Only Misty Fresh was way hotter than Monica Lewinsky.

Pam would later concede that her decision to make adult films had more to do with cocaine and curiosity than her love for College Boy.

"No," said Pam to phone tech from far, far away. "The power sync light is green, but the 10Base light is yellow."

"Is that the T2000 model modem?" asked Roger. "Or the T3000?"

"T3000," said Pam.

"Would you mind holding for a moment?"

Hell yes, I mind!

Stew would have hung up by now. Stew would have cursed, called poor Roger "Punjab" or "Camel Jockey," ripped the phone from the wall and stuffed it into the trash compactor.

Stew wasn't very practical. Pam was. And it was the

hardscrabble nature of the porn business that had educated her.

"Nothing like screwing on film," she had once said aloud in an Alcoholics Anonymous meeting, "to knock the stars clean out of a young girl's eyes."

Pam checked her watch. She had been in tech-hell for twenty-six minutes. Adding the hour prior to calling for assistance when she had jiggled wires, checked every connection, reconfirmed network settings, powered up and down her router, and waited on the multiple restarts of her computer, she had been two hours without a connection.

Two hours too long, considering that when Pam's Internet connection failed, she had been in the midst of adopting a baby boy without Stew's knowledge, let alone approval.

"Would you mind continuing to hold?" asked Roger. "We're experiencing our own technical problems."

Whatever.

Pam's one-woman adoption quest had begun the night Stew had disappeared. Only hours after she had discovered her beefy husband assembling the *For Sale* sign on the front lawn, fought with him over selling the house, and then kissed, cried, and made up, they had made plans to see a George Clooney movie that night. And he had turned around and stood her up. Not a call, not a text. Sure, Stew eventually showed his face the next morning with an armful of flowers and mea culpas.

She wasn't the least bit surprised when Stew confessed that he had spent the night with his old pals, Jack and Coke.

"I went out," Stew had said. "Fell off the wagon."

Pam was seated at the kitchen table, rimmed in morning daylight, grazing the *Style* section of the *Los Angeles Times* while spooning a cold soup of granola, sliced bananas, and soy milk into her mouth.

Stew talked. Pam never looked up.

"Not asking to be forgiven. I know that. I gotta get back into the rooms. This morning. Soon as I can. But I owed it to you to tell the truth. No hiding. I'm sick about this. Ten years in the shitter. So I'm sorry. I'm sorry. Real, real sorry. And I promise I'll get this done right. Back on the wagon. You'll see first, then you'll forgive when you're ready to forgive. Only then. Only when you're ready."

It was a good speech. And Pam really wanted to cry. She could feel the tears, the rumble of her nerves, and the plain sadness inside her wanting to override her emotional switchboard. But Pam wouldn't give Stew the satisfaction of witnessing a single tremor.

"Okay," was all she had said.

With that, Pam had risen from the table, rinsed her bowl in the sink and neatly placed it in the dishwasher. That was when she had decided. That was the moment. She was going to adopt a child. A baby. No more discussions. No more canceling of appointments with adoption lawyers. No more of Stew finding convenient reasons to delay. The decision to adopt a child had become painfully simple for one reason and one reason alone.

Pam had leverage.

The moral—and sober—high ground.

Stew could liquidate every damn asset to save his precious spec house. He could even liquidate their marriage, if he chose. What he wouldn't be able to liquidate was her resolve to be a mommy.

With the phone stuck to her ear, still on hold, Pam took in the little North Hollywood home she had first loathed. From the hardwood floors to the ceilings trimmed in molding to the custom-paint finishes she had personally applied to every wall. The old, country, hardwood accents were counterpoint to the soft, colorful fabrics she had chosen for every slipcover and cushion. Under protest, she had still made it her home, adorned by her own hand.

Suddenly, the thought of selling the house sickened her. With that, she briefly entertained an idea of how she could temporarily save her house and Stew. All it would take were a few simple phone calls. Surely there was some enterprising adult-film producer willing to pay her top dollar for a single comeback video. A three-day, one-off performance could make her as much as ten grand in cash. Why the hell not when she still had a body worth watching and abusing?

The Return of Misty Fresh.

Then Pam shook off the idiotic idea as quickly as it had snuck up on her. That was her former cocaine-addict-thinking. Or "Stinkin' Thinkin'" as they so often said in The Program.

And Pam thought Stew needed to get to some meetings? Hell, she should get to a few meetings herself if thoughts like double-penetration-sex-for-money were finding back-roads into her psyche. She blamed the long wait on hold with Roger the Indian Phone Tech.

Pam refocused herself to a single purpose. To the mission she had been engaged in when the Internet had crashed. Her thoughts returned to her new favorite website, *www.theadoptionoption.com*, a clearinghouse for all things related to child adoption. A baby of her own, or their own if Stew could find it within himself to step up and be a dad.

"Just another minute," said Roger. "I'm very sorry for the wait."

Pam had enough of waiting. She hung up, closed the notebook computer and shoved it into her backpack. She decided to speed-walk off her frustrations. It would take her about twenty minutes to break into a cleansing sweat. After that, she would duck into the nearest wireless-friendly Coffee Bean & Tea Leaf and plug back in.

Pam slipped into socks and pair of pink and white Adidas, matching golf visor and a wide pair of imitation Gucci sunglasses. She checked her appearance in the mirror hung opposite the front door.

See if anybody recognizes Misty in this getup.

She gripped the doorknob and twisted. The Baldwin hardware felt cold in her hand. Solid. Just like it did the day she had tested the sample model at Crown City Hardware in Pasadena. She loved the feel of the mechanism at work, the tumblers, the springs as they compressed, and the distinct click as the lock released.

She swung the door inward, only to be stopped by a stranger

on her doorstep. He was of average height, finely featured, with a shaggy haircut. He wore a pink polo shirt, jeans, and running shoes, though he looked nothing like a jogger. His index finger, frozen only inches from the doorbell's button, withdrew and quickly formed with the rest of his hand into an open, surrendering half-wave, half-Navajo "How."

"Sorry," said the man. "I saw your sign. For Sale by Owner."

"There's a phone number on it," said Pam, her voice abrupt and sharp as a knife.

"No cell signal," said the man, revealing the mobile phone in his other hand. He shrugged. "Truly sorry if I'm bothering you."

Funny thing about her address. It seemed to be smack in the center of a cellular void. Some carriers' signals would connect like landlines, others would vanish like the caller had stepped into the Bermuda Triangle.

"Was just checking around the neighborhood," defended the stranger. "Saw this house and . . . well . . . I'll call and make an appointment."

The man took a step backward off the porch, once again surrendering with that little wave. It was clear he wasn't a stalker. Otherwise, the instant the door opened, there would have been that telltale pause. A hiccup in time when the sexually possessed man, not quite prepared to be within spitting distance from the object of his desire, freezes, stutters, or even pisses himself with sudden, overwhelming anxiety.

"I know," said Pam. "Shoulda listed it through a real estate agent. But my husband . . ."

"Commission's too steep. I can relate to that."

"Too bad my husband's not here. You could relate together."

The man laughed. It was a healthy laugh. Real. Pam liked when men were genuine.

"Can I ask what you're asking for?"

"Six-hundred-fifty-nine thousand . . . I think."

"Sounds like a place to start."

"Look," relented Pam. "I've got a few minutes. If you want to see the house?"

"I'm already bothering you."

"Quick walk-through wouldn't hold me up. Then, maybe, you can call my husband if you're interested."

"Sounds fair."

"I should tell you we don't have a pool. Room for one, but no pool. If that's an issue."

"Not much of a swimmer," said he man.

"Then, well . . . come on in," said Pam, retreating a step and swinging the door into a more welcoming position.

"Thank you," said the man. "Really appreciate you doing this."

"I'm Pam," she said, hand stuck forward, as if ready to take a karate chop.

"Ben."

"Nice meeting you, Ben," said Pam, gesturing for him to enter. She made sure to leave the door open. Ben seemed harmless, enough. But experience had taught her to be careful.

"Very nice," said Ben, expressing his first impression.

"You married, Ben? Kids?"

"I was."

"So you're looking just for yourself?"

"Me and my accountant," joked Ben. "Says I need a bigger tax deduction."

"It was really nice running into to you."

"You too." Then thinking she sounded odd, Gonzo stammered, "I mean, me too. You know. It was a good thing it happened."

Alex smiled warmly, her glossed lips gliding across two rows of perfectly white teeth.

"See you 'round school," said Alex, flashing a set of newly lacquered nails with a finger wave.

Gonzo pulled the creaking passenger door of the Valley Checkered Cab closed. She had explained to Alex that she and Romeo were assigned the car as part of a robbery-suppression, undercover sting unit. As cabbie and passenger, the investigating duo could answer calls while cruising for pre-profiled armed-robbery suspects. It was a dull assignment. That, and no matter how much she complained or how many car deodorizers Romeo hung, the car still smelled of urine.

Still, Gonzo found herself unconsciously giving the same girlish wave back to Alex, then curling her fingers inward, embarrassed by her short mannish nails. She couldn't remember the last time she had a manicure. Or even the time to schedule an appointment.

All the while, Romeo was pleased to ogle Alex and her machine-cut ass as she skipped across Ventura Boulevard and vanished back inside Starbucks.

"You're staring," complained Gonzo.

"Damn straight, I am," said Romeo. "That's a fine—"

"She's got three kids, Romes."

"I can dig it. Makes her a smokin' hot MILF."

"A what?"

"M-I-L-F. Mom I'd Like to . . . you know."

Gonzo's face registered her disgust. "You think that up all by yourself?"

"MILF? You kidding me?" said Romeo. "They sell that shit on t-shirts. You seriously haven't heard that?"

"Maybe I'm looking in the wrong places."

"Not around the high-priced mommies you hang with?"

"Put it in gear, will ya?" asked Gonzo. "We're gonna be late for roll."

From that moment on, Gonzo's memory faded. While Romeo steered the cab north toward the Van Nuys Division, he ranted about everything from unnatural breast implants to city servants he would pay to taze, to videos he had recently tripped over on YouTube. But it was all a blur to Gonzo. All because she kept pressing the replay button in her mind.

It had begun with the surprise of bumping into Alex inside one of the hundred or so Starbucks that plagued the San Fernando Valley.

"What a surprise," said Alex.

"Small world," was all Gonzo could muster in response.

"Hey, you got a minute?" asked Alex after an awkwardly silent moment.

Gonzo had more than a minute. The line for coffee was backed up and in very uncop-like fashion, she had ordered a half-caff-venti-quad-180-latte. And according to Romeo, every hyphenated word in a Starbucks order added at least an extra forty-five seconds to the process. Romeo's order was simple, old-school. Coffee. Black.

Gonzo politely exchanged small talk while waiting for her order. Then, after texting her partner to please stand by, retired to a small corner table flanked by over-caffeinated singles plinking the keys of their laptops.

"First," began Alex, leaning nearly halfway across the two-foot table, "I wanna say how sorry I am for the other night. It must've been so awkward for you."

"I had no business showing up like that," apologized Gonzo.

"Ben explained all of it," Alex said. "I'm sick about misjudging the entire situation."

"So things are good?" Gonzo hoped to push the conversation to a quick conclusion so she could leave with her overpriced coffee and return to the comfort zone of her job, and even the smelly cab.

"Better," said Alex. "The truth hurts, but it helps. It's all about moving forward."

"Right."

"Let me add this. And if this sounds like unsolicited advice, well . . . I suppose it is."

Gonzo stiffened. She could swallow gratuitous guidance from her partner, PD superiors, judges, and occasional civilians when she was on the job. Other than that . . .

"Private schools can be really difficult to navigate. I'm not talking about the kids, either. It's school. They get it. It's the grown-ups who don't play nice."

"Oh," said Gonzo, only slightly relieved. After all, across from her was the woman who only days ago, was convinced Gonzo was sneaking around with her husband, exchanging body fluids and God knows what else.

"Especially for a single, working mom," added Alex. "There are just too many women with too much money and time on their hands. All they do is gossip. And when they're not doing that, they're getting in the faces of the teachers over why their kids aren't getting better grades or being challenged—"

"Listen. I understand. It was only talk, anyway. And now everything's good."

"Until the next land mine."

Alex took a cryptic tone and arched her eyebrows for extra emphasis.

Gonzo continued to replay the conversation through nearly all of the late-morning roll call. She sat in her usual seat at the rear of the cramped classroom. Nine rows back from the front. There were seventeen detectives in attendance. Only three were women, including the warrant officer breaking down the afternoon's business of warrants, weekly robbery clusters, and murders under current investigation. A fluorescent tube behind a water-stained panel sputtered above the corner opposite Gonzo. She stared at it like an epileptic waiting for a seizure.

"You're already a target," said Alex. "I'm not saying this to upset you. To the contrary. After all, you're a cop. If anyone's a big girl, it's you."

"Really," said Gonzo. "I'm not too concerned—"

"This is the part where it could affect your child, though." Alex was nodding in self-agreement. "People don't edit themselves in front of their children. They should, but we all know some parents don't. And the kids take all the stuff they hear back to school."

"Is there something you heard that I haven't?"

"No. I've just seen this before. And I don't want you to have to go through it. Or your child. It can be hell."

"So your unsolicited advice is?"

Alex splayed her right hand and pressed it against her chest.

"Use me," said Alex. "I'm your resource. I'm connected.

If there's a fire at school—with the moms or the kids or the teachers—I'm the one who can put it out."

"Wow," said Gonzo, taken aback and suddenly wondering if Alex's way of apologizing was through a promise of action. For a moment, she had misjudged the woman.

"I really appreciate that," said Gonzo.

"You hear anything, suspect anything. Your kid brings anything home or says something that you think is wrong, I want you to pick up the phone."

"I will," smiled Gonzo. "I can't express how appreciative I am, and you being so understanding about all of this."

Alex pushed her eco-friendly disposable coffee cup across the table until it kissed Gonzo's.

"I want us to be friends," said Alex.

"I can do that."

"One more thing."

"Yes?"

"My husband. If he asks you for any more help with this old business of his. Or just wants to bend your ear . . ."

It was as if all the moisture from Gonzo's throat was extinguished in a single gulp. The frizz behind her ears instantly turned wet and clammy, spreading across the back of her neck and forming a drip at the peak of her spine.

"You're talking about his deceased family—"

"We call it *old business*," repeated Alex. "It's part of moving on and building a new and productive life."

Gonzo caught the shine on those serenely lacquered nails. How with each gesture they caught the decorative lights. Now Alex gripped the lid of her coffee cup and twisted clockwise, as if shutting off a faucet.

"You asked how things were with Ben and I," continued Alex. "I said they're good and they are. But Ben has work to do. Counseling, that sort of stuff. If things are to remain on track, I have to know if things are just that. On track. Best for me. For Ben. My girls. You understand."

"And . . ." Gonzo groped. She needed wiggle room, not to mention oxygen. "If he volunteers something to me? In confidence?"

If the question aggravated Alex, Gonzo couldn't be the least bit certain. Alex did though, begin to twist that coffee cup in counterclockwise quarter turns.

"I can only make the request," answered Alex. "I want to be friends. I really do. Our children will be in school for a very long time, so . . ."

"So . . ."

"So we can't help but know each other, see each other, help or hurt each other. You agree?"

"Of course," said Gonzo, at last unfolding the tacit threat levied by her counterpart.

"Glad we had this talk."

"Me too."

Gonzo felt a pinch on her shoulder. Two fingers putting the squeeze on her left trapezius muscle. Her Pops used to call it the *Super Spock Grip*. Ever since she had told Romeo about her Pops' term, he had taken to employing his version of the shoulder squeeze whenever she drifted off.

"Ow," said Gonzo.

"You hear any of it?"

"I miss something?"

Gonzo returned to the present, noting the sliding chairs, murmuring, and shuffling feet of the other detectives. Someone told a joke that produced a short burst of laughter. Roll call was over. And like Romeo's rants in the car, Gonzo hadn't heard a word of it.

"Nothing unusual," said Romeo. "You feeling okay?"

"I'm good."

"You should eat something."

"Your cure for everything."

"Gotta feed the brain more than caffeine."

"Fine. Lead on," Gonzo relented with a nod.

As the room emptied, Gonzo remembered nothing more than that stupid, sputtering, fluorescent tube. If her brain had actually captured anything, she wouldn't immediately be able to access it. Too much information to remember anyway, she reasoned. Roll calls were all the same. Too many ad hoc descriptions of wanted criminals and stop-and-shop holdups and car-theft rings. The only wrinkle of the day was a repeat from the week prior—a missing-persons flyer describing an Armenian immigrant named Ara Djoumanian from Sunland. The man was described as tall, thirty-four-years-old, and was last spotted alongside an unidentified white male, leaving the Outback Steakhouse in Northridge.

Motorized wheelchairs that fit a four-hundred-pound private detective aren't found at a local medical supply storefront. Nor are they made in factories on an assembly line. Chairs like Woody Bell's are built in small, specialized factories akin to the custom motorcycle and chopper shops seen on cable TV reality series.

In fact, the engineer who designed Woody's newest set of wheels was a motorcycle enthusiast and part-time mechanic. This despite having lost the bottom half of his left leg when making the sweeping right turn from the southbound Long Beach Freeway to the brand-new, westbound I-105, the Glenn Anderson Freeway. He had laid down his Harley-Davidson Super Glide to avoid slamming into a rented U-Haul truck that was stalled in the transition lane. The six-hundred-plus-pound bike had severed his leg cleanly at the knee. He would have bled to death if the U-Haul driver hadn't been able to summon both a cell phone and the knowledge he had retained for twenty years from earning a first-aid merit badge as a Boy Scout.

Eventually, that same rider recovered and rehabbed. With a new prosthetic leg he entered the business of building custom, motorized wheelchairs. The name on his shingle was *Freedom Chairs*. The business grew as did the number of employees. Over time, some of his workers suffered expensive on-the-job injuries. Some injuries were real, others suspicious.

Enter Woody Bell, paraplegic private investigator specializing in fraudulent workmen's compensation claims, and Ben Keller, OSHA-inspector-turned-safety-consultant. Though each man was hired independently of the other, a marriage of sorts was made soon after the two met on a job for Freedom Chairs. Since then Ben had kept Woody on permanent retainer and Woody had gladly kicked back a fair portion of the fees generated from Ben's clients.

It was a double bonus for Woody.

Since the day he had met Ben he would never want for gainful employment or be denied the coolest and latest technological advancements in wheelchairs. His current chair was super-powered by a prototype rechargeable battery similar to those used in hybrid cars, custom-fit in a panel under his seat. The battery took a 220-volt charge and ran a cool 500-watt, high-torque electric motor. Due to the chair's size and heavy load, it was fitted with treaded ATV wheels, disc brakes, and an onboard computer connected to an active suspension system to compensate for unexpected G-forces generated from side-hill driving or speedy turns.

It even came with a safety belt.

Including its passenger, the super-chair weighed seven hundred and thirty-three pounds. Fully charged, it could deliver Woody across five miles of city sidewalks at a terrifying top speed of twenty-three miles per hour—plenty of juice for Woody to make the round-trip to one of a dozen neighborhood eateries.

Woody had dedicated this particular morning to a law firm client. Though Woody had never visited their Century City office, he imagined an entire floor filled with nothing but pinstriped divorce lawyers. A veritable New York Yankees with law degrees, dedicated to breaking up families for profit. Being a child of divorce, the thought of such a firm made Woody sick. But these lawyers paid retail. So after logging four morning hours searching for deadbeat dads delinquent in their child-support payments, Woody was hungry. Running his tongue between his lips, he tasted Chinese food. Mr. Gu's, he had decided.

Despite the overcast day, Woody donned a cheap black felt fedora he had purchased years ago at Disneyland and a pair of dark shades that would have made Roy Orbison jealous. Having called in his order ahead of time, Woody was subjected to no more than two minutes inside the poorly ventilated Mr. Gu's.

He paid with his gold American Express card, placed the plastic bag holding the boxes full of hot Chinese food on his lap, then began the return trip to his house.

Woody really enjoyed the mostly uphill ride home through the wooded streets of Chatsworth. He imagined his custom wheelchair to be a four-wheeled assault vehicle roaring through a post-holocaust wasteland. Woody busted across intersections, used those ATV tires to hop curbs, and every so often, swung wide and accelerated hard enough to loosen the new sod on a neighbor's fresh-cut lawn. Woody calculated the odds of anybody complaining as roughly nil. How stupid would some angry retiree look shouting down at a poor paraplegic? And how sweet would it be when Woody captured the moment using the video function on his cell phone? In minutes, the moving pictures of the shouting neighbor could be uploaded to the Internet for the entire planet's instant amusement.

Two blocks from Woody's driveway, though, the super-chair began to slow. A sure sign the battery pack underneath his seat was nearly dry. As Woody eased back on the joystick, hoping to conserve enough power to get himself home, he scoured his memory. Had he actually forgotten to charge the batteries the night before? Doubtful. The special power outlet was right next to his bed. It was his routine to plug the chair in before he winched himself into bed for the night. And yes! He distinctly recalled unhooking the cable that very morning.

Then he remembered something else—the blinking digits on his clock radio. The telltale giveaway that at some point during his slumber, the electricity had gone out. He didn't know for how long, but it was sure as hell long enough to short his wheelchair battery of a full charge.

Regret set in. He shouldn't have wasted juice on his off-road maneuvers. Or speed. Or taking a slightly longer route back to his house. Across a thin strip of street and a hundred yards ahead, Woody could see the pitch of his own cracked, concrete driveway peeking out from between the massive, unattended shrubs that spilled onto the sidewalk. The same deep driveway where, as a boy, he and his neighborhood pals would drag race on skateboards.

At fifty yards, the motor on the wheelchair began to whine and beg for more power.

"Shit," said Woody, working the joystick, hoping to trick the motor into stealing just enough power to get him through his front door.

Woody turned the wheelchair into the street, setting a beeline to his own address. He looked left, then right for approaching cars. And though none were visible, at the snail's pace he was moving, he might not be safe anyway. The huge, pneumatic wheels rolled heavily across the asphalt, making an excruciating dull crunching sound.

For drainage, the lane gently sloped away from the center stripe. So Woody was now hoping to reach the apex and disengage the chair's drivetrain. If he was lucky, gravity would propel him down the other side, saving him power, and leaving him with enough juice to finish the trip to his door. But the slope proved not nearly steep enough to deliver him past the two-inch lip of his own driveway. And after reengaging the gears, the motor only responded with the most impotent of hums.

"Goddammit!"

The curse, of course, fell on no ears other than his own. Woody flipped open his mobile phone and dialed up Freedom Chairs.

"I'm stuck," said Woody. "Where's Scotty?"

"Scotty's not here."

"Who's this then?"

"You got Rodrigo. Say you're stuck?"

"This is Woody Bell. Scott knows me and—"

"Hey, I know you, man," said Rodrigo. "I worked on your new chair, dude. That thing's got sass."

"Well," said Woody, bottled with frustration, "My fuckin' chair ain't got no more go."

"Sorry. Like is your motor dead?"

"Don't think so. Ran out of gas."

"Anywhere you can get a charge?"

"I'm stuck in the front of my driveway."

"That sucks, dude. So sorry."

"When's Scott comin' back from lunch?"

"No man. Scott's not in town. He's down in Cabo on vacation."

"Anybody there can come up here and help me out?"

"Yeah, sure. Where are you?"

"Chatsworth?"

"Where's that?"

"In the Valley."

"Oh . . ." said Rodrigo. "Is that like, near Reseda?"

"North of that," said Woody, leaking mental oil. "You got anybody who can come up and give me a jump?"

"Like Triple A? Hey, that's funny."

"I can assure you none of this shit is funny."

"Only guy here who lives up in the Valley is Chuck. And he can't cut out until five."

It was nearly one in the afternoon. Waiting for four hours wasn't Woody's idea of getting help. He clicked off without saying goodbye to Rodrigo, then quickly reviewed his options. There was his cleaning crew, but they didn't come but two days a week and Thursday wasn't one of them. After that, Woody thought of the home-care practitioners who on occasion would handle some of the messier nursing chores that paraplegics needed done. But most of these practitioners were women and past middle-aged. Getting enough of them to give him a proper push would be impossible on short notice.

Lastly, Woody saw two options that were essentially one in the same. Around his neck he wore a thin, stainless-steel chain from which hung a red button. In case of emergency, he could push the button, triggering an automated 911 phone call from his home landline. Woody regarded the button and the distance between himself and his little house set deep on the half-acre lot. By his own estimation, there was no way a radio signal that was only supposed to work within his house could travel those hundred and fifty or so feet. That left dialing 911 from his cell phone, an act that would certainly do the trick. But at what kind of embarrassing cost? The conversation ran in his head.

"Nine-one-one operator."

"Hullo. I'm a four-hundred-pound paraplegic in a three-hundred-pound custom moto-chair with five pounds of Mr. Gu's going cold on my fucking lap."

"Oh?"

"Yeah. I ran out of power because, well, the power last night kinda went out. Not my fault, see. So could you please scramble a two-man fire crew or some EMTs to come push me up my driveway so I can plug back in and eat my lunch?"

"Is this an emergency?"

"Technically, no. At least not until my colostomy bag bursts from WAITING FOR SOMEBODY TO FUCKING HELP ME!!!"

The imaginary conversation was followed by a silence in Woody's brain.

And suddenly, calling Triple A was sounding like less of a joke.

Then Woody heard a voice he didn't recognize.

"You need some help?"

"Hey, yeah . . ." said Woody, straining his neck to see who was behind him.

"Broke down or did you just run out of juice for that thing?"

"No power," said Woody. He twisted left and looked up toward the voice. Despite the fedora and Roy Orbison glasses, Woody still had to squint. The stranger was tall and wore paint-splattered overalls, a red Anaheim Angels baseball cap, and a pair of aviator-styled sunglasses. Other than that, the blast from the midday sun was too blinding for Woody to make out any of the man's features.

"That where you wanna go?"

"That's my house, yeah."

"What if we run us an extension cord?"

"The chair takes two-twenty. Unless you got that kind of cable."

"Two-twenty, wow. And no. I don't. Suppose one man pushin' won't work either."

"Unless you're named Superman."

"Sorry," said the stranger, offering a hand. "Keith."

"Keith?"

"Don't wear it out," joked the stranger, squatting and looking over the chair. "Can you steer it?"

Woody worked the joystick. The smaller, rear wheels turned slightly.

"Got a little somethin' left," said Woody.

Then came this moment of unnerving quiet. Woody, his neck in near spasm from trying to catch a clean look at the stranger, could feel the slightest vibrations through the chair, as if the stranger was running his hands along the sleek chassis.

"Really appreciate your help," said Woody. "Whatcha thinking?"

"If the steering works, maybe a push. Got my ride over there. If I could get square behind you—just a touch, see—then with a little gas, you steer yourself up the drive."

"Little push?" asked Woody, trying to suppress the nerves in his voice.

"Gentle kinda push," said the stranger, his voice trailing. "Of course, that's if you want a neighbor to give it a try."

"I'm sorry," said Woody. "But do I know you?"

"If it makes you uncomfortable, you can always call nine-one-one."

Woody heard a car door pull shut behind him. It had a deeper kuh-shunk kind of sound. But sweet. More like a new pickup truck than a car. Next he heard the starter whine, followed by the distinctive, husky rumble of a diesel engine.

"Gonna come in easy behind ya," shouted the stranger out the window of his truck. "Think it's a good idea if you raise your hand when you feel the touch."

Woody involuntarily raised an arm in worried acknowledgement. He squirmed, too. Then contorted to the right, trying like hell to get a better look at the help that was coming up from behind. At the very edge of his periphery where the corners of his eyes picked up little more than light and shadow, he saw what could have easily been mistaken for a white whale on wheels easing closer to his chair—the pickup truck's grill like silvery jaws ready to bite. Woody tried to read the California license plate, but discovered the harder he cranked his neck the more his vision blurred.

The sound of that heavy-duty engine? Throaty. Ear-numbing. Each piston cycle pulsed against Woody's skin. He felt the heat as the pickup edged closer. He smelled the residual, rich, unspent diesel.

Then came the first bump. Slightly more than a gentle shove, inching the chair up into the driveway, then releasing it back. At first, Woody wanted to steer. Then he suddenly recalled that he was supposed to signal with a raised arm. As he shot his left hand into the air, another bump came, this time a fair bit stronger, but hardly violent. Woody wiggled the joystick, but couldn't hear the servos working over the rumbling of the truck's engine. He could only hope he was steering, otherwise the pickup would roll him up into the untended tangle of rosebushes that edged the property.

"Y'okay?" barked the stranger behind the wheel.

"Okay . . ." squeaked Woody, the shout in him getting stuck in the back of his throat.

"A little harder now."

"Okay . . ."

Woody heard the engine rev and this time he was ready for the touch. So when the pickup's bumper made contact with the back of the chair, Woody was fully prepared to steer his dying machine, using the precious little battery power that was left.

It began like a roller coaster's uphill climb. An unexpected reminder of Woody's carefree times as a freewheeling, reckless adolescent. There was the first push of anticipation as the roller coaster's cars began climbing the track. The click-click-clicking sound. Ahead, the peak. And beyond, nothing but sky. Then at last, the release. Followed by the gut-thumping drop, where everything inside a thirteen-year-old's skin felt as if it was compressing into his brain.

Oh, the rapture.

Woody stretched his left arm high and gave the stranger an affirmative thumbs-up. Progress was a magical thing. Forward movement, a godsend. He was up the driveway's incline at the sidewalk and creeping along the twenty-foot wide strip of chipped brick and concrete. *Hell*, thought Woody, the Good Samaritan had come along so swiftly the damn Chinese food parked on his oversized lap was still warm.

Woody was overcome by shadow as he rolled under the green boughs of the towering eucalyptus trees that stood like a row of hundred-foot-tall sentries down his property line. It was as if all the sunshine had been swallowed up, leaving his entire property shrouded in shade.

Ahead and to the left stood Woody's house and flame-appointed van, parked on a slightly elevated pad of concrete that adjoined Woody's front-stoop-turned-paraplegic's-loading-dock. Directly in front of Woody was a flimsy old gate on metal casters that led to a detached garage full of junk and spiders. Above the garage doors was a cockeyed basketball hoop screwed to a plywood backboard where the remnants of a net hung from the last rusted loop.

Weird. Memories of youth were flooding into Woody's conscious. Memories that might have brought a melancholy smile to Woody's face were it not for the shove.

The shove actually, was closer to a jolt. So lost in his mental medley of 220-volt power cables and bare-chested boys playing backyard ball and the fragrance of shrimp fried rice, Woody hadn't heard the pickup's engine rev. All he felt was his four hundred pounds of flesh suddenly compressed deeper into his seat as his chair surged forward. Four feet per second suddenly became ten, then twenty-five . . .

Woody forgot all about the roller coasters. He even forgot about lunch. All Woody saw was the flimsy gate ahead, rushing at him like a barn door tossed by a tornado.

Sometime later he would only remember the strange silence. And the sense that he had actually been flying. The scenery tumbling, as if watching a video somebody had shot from a camera hidden inside a bowling ball. He heard the sound of his heart thumping at around two hundred beats per minute.

In the blackness that followed, he listened to his speeding heart fade until all sound appeared gone, extinguished in the crash. *This was death*, Woody thought. For in the faintest distance, he could hear his dead mother calling him inside to eat dinner.

7

"How many kids did you say you had?"

"I don't," said Ben plainly.

Pam looked puzzled.

"Weird," she said. "Back there I was pretty sure you said you had kids."

"I did have kids," said Ben. "Sorry. Maybe it came out wrong."

Pam stirred her soup, briefly looking past Ben at all the flavors of midday shoppers buzzing behind him. After showing Ben the house she had lingered for a bit, enjoying some friendly chatter with him. It softened her yen to readdress her Internet woes and her adoption obsession. She found herself craving the butternut squash soup served daily in the deli section of the neighborhood Gelson's.

Ben, on the other hand, needed drops for his dry contact lenses. So after thanking Pam for the house tour, he had driven away, breathed an exhilarated sigh of relief, then swung into the nearest market for a quick stop before setting his heading east for his Burbank office.

Pam had spotted Ben in the twelve-items-or-less line.

Of course her first instinct was that nice Ben might not be so nice after all. That after saying goodbye he had hung back and followed her. Experience had taught her that when it came to her and men, there was no such thing as coincidence. It was a rule by which she lived.

But as she carefully observed him from her spot in the salad bar line, Ben appeared exactly as he had first presented himself. Totally benign. Still, she watched and waited as the cashier rung up a blue box of contact-lens fluid. Ben paid with cash. Only when he had completed his single item purchase, walked by her without the slimmest of sideways glances, and was headed out the automated doors did Pam surprise herself by initiating their second contact by shouting out his name. Ben stopped, appeared as if he wasn't quite sure he had heard right, turned a full one-eighty, did a quick scan of the grocery shoppers behind him, and finally fixed on Pam's open palm, waving at him. Ben looked as surprised as she, flashed that genuine smile, then walked to her.

And in that solitary moment of mutual recognition, Pam actually began to believe that men and coincidence could coexist within her universe. That happy accidents were a possibility. She tested her new belief by inviting Ben to join her for lunch.

"Divorced, huh?" Pam assumed before sipping the soup from her spoon.

Ben looked at her directly with his head slightly cocked, lips pressed together. Then he let his eyes dip sadly out of view.

"I lost them all awhile ago." He choked up, cleared his throat, then found the easy save. "See. I kinda fibbed about the accountant and the tax deduction. Truth is the house I'm in is too big. Need to downsize for my own sanity."

"I'm so sorry," said Pam automatically. Her words were so quick and sounded so disingenuous that she suddenly felt ashamed. "That didn't come out right."

"Sure it did," excused Ben.

"No," she insisted. "I sounded as genuine as a condolence card."

"Really. It's okay."

"Can I ask . . ." Pam stopped herself. Now she was sounding morbidly curious. "Sorry. You don't have to."

"Sometimes I wonder if . . . roles reversed . . . if I would ask," said Ben. "Some people want to know, some people don't."

"Suppose it could also sound ghoulish."

"Suppose." Then Ben continued, "But I've found if you don't ask how and why bad things happen, then you'll never learn how to prevent things such as accidents."

"And that's what you do, right? You said you were a safety inspector?"

"Safety consultant," corrected Ben. Without thinking, he withdrew a business card from his wallet and handed it across to Pam.

"Safety First," read Pam. "Cool name."

Ben realized his awful mistake right after he made it. He had just handed Stew's wife a card bearing his name, business address, and office and mobile numbers. He couldn't imagine how he could possibly ask Pam to hand it back.

"Was it an accident?" she asked.

At first, Ben was so fixated on the business card in her hand that he thought she was referring to his mistake, his potentially fatal error.

Of course it was a goddamn accident!

But Ben shook his head no. She was asking about his family. Sara and the twins. Was their death an accident? Ben's eyes narrowed almost accusingly. He was so suddenly and acutely aware of what he was about to do and what he was about to say to Stew Raymo's wife.

"They were murdered."

Pam gasped.

"Random robbery thing. I wasn't home. They were." Ben shrugged off his anger. "No explanation, really. Other than bad things happen."

"I couldn't imagine . . ." said Pam. How could a man as kind and sweet as Ben withstand such an emotional body blow? Pam tried to spoon her soup, but found her hands were trembling ever so slightly.

"It's okay," said Ben. "Spent a long time getting over it. I'm sure you will, too."

"But they got the guy, right?" she tried to confirm. "The guy or guys. The ones who did it. Please tell me."

Under the table, Ben's legs began to drip with sweat. He hadn't touched his own soup, but the napkin in his hand was clenched into a ball.

"No," said Ben, his voice cracking. "Listen. It was nice running into you again."

"After so long a time apart," joked Pam, trying to laugh. She was sorry and wanted to compensate for making Ben uncomfortable.

"Maybe we'll run into each other again," said Ben.

"Or maybe you'll come back and make an offer on our house."

A nervous laugh escaped from Ben as he rose. He couldn't fathom the circumstances that would ever lead him to buy Stew Raymo's house unless it was to light a match and burn it to the ground.

"Good luck with the adoption thing," said Ben, making sure his palm was dry before shaking Pam's hand.

"Thank you," she said, a bit awkwardly. "Well . . ."

"Have a nice day," said Ben, who retreated and escaped through the automated doors.

"Christ Almighty, Ben. What were you thinking?"

Ben talked aloud to himself as he hurried to his car. If happenstance had brought him in contact with Stew's wife, how long before the big man himself made a guest appearance? Ben wasn't half-ready for that. His sortie into Stew's neighborhood was supposed to be nothing more than a drive-by. That was until he saw the *For Sale by Owner* sign on the lawn. And after ruminating in his car for twenty minutes, occasionally observing Stew's wife as she wandered throughout the house, Ben felt drawn to the front door. Just for a knock and a few questions, he told himself, first making sure there was no sign of Stew. Not to see if he could get away with it, but to discover if within himself, there was a soul brave enough to ring the bell.

The rest had been pure adventure.

The drop-dead woman, initially wary of the unknown white male on her doorstep, was eventually comfortable enough to let him through her door. She had willingly walked him through the layout of the house from stem to stern. All while Ben played the easy part of being himself. The Safety Expert. He cruised from room to room as if this were a job, complimenting the woman on her eclectic style while characteristically assessing and cataloguing the inherent dangers within the house.

But there was a new danger. One Ben had never recognized before. And that danger was himself.

When Ben had followed Pam, out the back door and fifteen paces across the backyard to the garage's locked side-door, he was oddly moved by how alone the two of them were. Then as Pam keyed the simple dead bolt and swung the door inward to her windowless, personal storage space, an idea formed in Ben's psyche in what seemed like an instant.

He could kill her.

Right then and there, inside that black garage, Ben could simply pick up any heavy object and smash it into her head. Payback, he rationalized. Stew would come home, find his wife had been brutally murdered, and he and Ben would be closer to even.

But before the evil thought was purged, a thought that would eventually scare Ben back into reality, Pam switched on the overhead light to reveal her private junkyard.

"Sorry," she had said innocently. "We don't use it for a car. It's like my own filing cabinet for stuff that doesn't have a place."

"You should have a garage sale," Ben volunteered.

That may have been the first time Ben had really looked at her. Or soaked in what a decadent, fuckable beauty she truly was. This woman, Stew Raymo's wife, sans any kind of makeup or come-hither clothing—was flat-out dazzling. The circumspect Pam he had met at the front door had cast off her armor to reveal sparkling, blue eyes underscored by a galaxy of Irish freckles.

"That open space over there's where I was going to move everything from the office," she had volunteered.

"What's going in the office?"

"I wanted it to be the nursery. Not that I'm pregnant or anything. My husband and I are in the process of adopting, though."

As Ben hurried from the supermarket to his car, he wrestled with both his rage and his jealousy. He hated Stew Raymo for all the atrocities the man had committed against himself and God knows whom else. Ben was also sick with a begrudging resentment. How dare Stew Raymo possess a human unicorn such as Pam, a woman so fresh and funny and earthy and sad. A woman who desired a child so badly that she was willing to adopt and make evil Stew the father.

Ben surely loved Alex. Alex was Ben's wife, his partner in rebuilding a life, not to mention the mother of his adopted children. But Ben hadn't been truly moved by a woman since meeting Sara, his first real love, whom he had married and with whom he had openly shared his heart. The twin baby girls were a gift. A double helping of joy that had ended in horror.

It was if as in destroying Ben's first family, Stew Raymo was about to be rewarded with a real family of his own. With Pam, a real woman not unlike Ben's Sara.

"The fucker!"

Ben kicked the side panel of his car door, leaving a Nike-sized-nine-and-a-half dent.

For once, Woody's dream had ended differently.

It had begun as always, filled with more memory than fancy. There was the cacophony of adolescents' laughter, shouts, and taunts. The hundred-degree heat blasting from a scorching, summer sun. And the dizzying spectacle of Woody's own pool viewed from the single-story rooftop. The tar and sand roof tiles were sticky hot and could burn the bottoms of the most well-calloused feet. The trick was to throw water from the pool up onto the torrid roof before a quick climb up the trellis. Hop-step into position, then run, jump, leap, or dive into the cool of the Bell family's swimming pool.

Woody had done this a million times, or so it seemed. His wild splashdowns were famous and in his friends' schoolyard accounts, usually scored the highest.

But in the dream and just like the day it happened, Woody didn't jump. At least not right away. He started, then stalled, changing his mind about the trick he wanted to perform. He had planned to run, push off his right leg, pivot, and spin his patented Double-Daffy-360 into the deep end. Instead he pulled back, regathered himself, then crept to the edge of the roof and let his toes curl over roof tiles made pliable by the heat. In Woody's dream, he could both see the steam rising from the last bit of water splashed upon the roof, feel the scorching heat through the thickened pads of his feet, and smell the tar as if the roof surface itself were freshly laid asphalt.

Then came the shouts.

C'mon! Jump! Hurry the hell up, Wood Dick!

Woody could usually see the faces, naming them as if it were the day. Johnny, Rufus, Kyle, Stevie, Jack. Then there were the dreams where the faces were different, a brew of friends, acquaintances, or clients. Each waiting, either patiently or not, for thirteen-year-old Woody Bell to perform his next, death-defying jump.

This was when the new trick had revealed itself to young Woody. He even had a name for it. The Death Drop. He could actually see it in his mind's eye, as if he were observing himself from a seat at the shallow end of the pool. Woody would first turn around with his back facing the pool. Like the Olympic platform divers, he would balance at the edge of the roof on the balls of his feet. Next, holding his arms out in the form of a cross, he would stiffen his body, lean backward and allow himself to tip. This would create the awesome illusion that Woody was sure to pancake against the wet, stone pool deck. In his head Woody could even hear audible gasps as he was falling. But before going totally horizontal, Woody would push off the edge of the roof, tossing his head and finishing with a feet first, back layout.

The second part of the dream never changed or was the least bit different from the awful reality. Woody stuck out his arms, leaned back, felt the rush of gravity taking control, looked up and saw wisps of clouds in an otherwise blazing blue sky. Then he began the push-off to his back layout. Only young Woody hadn't correctly factored in the speed at which Newton's Laws of Motion operated. By the time Woody fired with his legs, he was past horizontal and on the inescapable path to spending the rest of his life in a wheelchair. There was no time for prayers. The impact came quickly and without even the mercy of his blacking out.

That's where the dream would almost always end.

Occasionally Woody would remember added flashes from other moments—the explosion of young vertebrae, T12/L1. X-rays, MRIs and surgical photographs of a mangled spine, pins and screws protruding from bones like barbed wire wrapped around a broomstick.

Woody would usually wake up in an icy sweat, overworking his lungs, eyes swirling in their sockets until he had found a point of focus and what little relief came upon realizing he had only been dreaming.

Woody would never know why the nightmare had changed. Perhaps it was because of the unconsciousness brought on by the head trauma. Or from spinning nearly a hundred-and-eighty degrees when he and his wheelchair were catapulted through the listing gate, his chair's wheels eventually catching in the gravel, sending him tumbling backward. After nearly twenty years of the same dream, ending when his body slammed into the deck, Woody finally finished his trick. He tipped, pushed off, tossed his head backwards, and laid his body out in a perfect, backward fall. The Death Drop. Woody splashed into the deep end of the pool feet first, submerging all the way, embraced by the coolness. From the depths, Woody could hear traces of his friends' cheers. He couldn't wait to surface. Because maybe this was the moment he had always hoped for. That this was the day he would find out that his years in the chair were the nightmare. And that all he would have to do was kick off the bottom of the pool, break the plane between water and air, suck in a lung-full of San Fernando Valley atmosphere, and he would be thirteen again.

So Woody breathed in.

Only his lungs hurt like hell, a broken rib stinging him sharply just below his left armpit. Consciousness returned in a heavy-lidded haze. Woody lifted his chin and recognized his tree-shrouded backyard. He saw his swimming pool stretch out before him in all its decrepit glory. Gone were the crystal clear water and polished tiles. The pool was empty, the plaster either cracked or chipped down to the Gunite. Residual water from the sprinklers and recent rains had made a rusty, brown puddle at the bottom.

Woody coughed deeply. The broken rib dug deeper and he howled. Or at least tried to. His scream was muffled by the balled-up rag jammed into his mouth. The rag smelled of turpentine, but tasted like gasoline.

"You're a fat fucker, aren't you?" asked Stew. "If you weren't seat-belted all tight into that rig, don't know what the hell I'd have done with ya."

Woody twisted his head to the right. The stranger was seated on the pool's coping, his feet dangling over the edge. Only he didn't appear so strange all of a sudden, aside from the stained pair of heavy-duty, lumberjack's gloves he was wearing.

"You look at me like you know me," said Stew. "But guess what? Now, I know you. Not that it didn't take a little work. All I had to go on was some camel jockey sayin' Woody Somethin'. Had to look for private detectives named Woody. And, maybe you already know this, there's a coupla private detective fellahs around named Woody. Go figure."

Stew rose to his feet somewhat awkwardly, rotating his left knee just-so until he heard a couple of satisfying pops.

"Still wasn't sure you was the guy until I staked out your little mailbox place. But the second day I showed up, here comes the black shag-wagon with the flames. Then I knew, dude. I remembered those dumb-ass flames."

Woody noticed his right sleeve had nearly been shorn off and that his skin was scuffed and bleeding. Both his upper limbs were secured with duct tape to the armrests on his super-chair, the joystick and brake levers just out of reach of his chubby fingers. The chair itself was perilously close to the edge of the pool. In fact it was perched atop the coping, hanging over the edge of the deep end. Panicked, Woody swiveled his view every which way until he saw the 220v cable. It snaked all the way from his bedroom window to the power receptacle underneath his left armrest.

"Yeah," said Stew. "So the hard part was getting you from over there—where you wiped out—to over here—where I could plug you in. Like I said, you are one fat SOB."

Was it the concussion that made Woody feel as if he were picking up only one out of every three words uttered by the stranger? And what kept him from fully recognizing the man standing only ten feet away from him? Yet Woody's vision had been restored in Technicolor. His contact lenses remained intact. It was just that everything seemed like one of his nightmares. Reality hadn't completely set in yet. At least not until Stew asked, "Why did you have men following me?"

"Following you?" repeated Woody. Only Stew couldn't hear Woody's words because they were trapped by the rag balled in the fat man's mouth.

"Followed me and my wife," continued Stew. "Was it your thing? Somebody else's thing?"

"Stew Raymo!" blurted Woody, sounding like there was a pillow over his face. "Oh, Christ . . ."

Jesus! thought Woody. His chest began to rise and fall as his breathing turned rapid. As if the identity of the man in front of him had entered through a back door in his memory banks. There, only feet away from Woody, was a walking mug shot. A murderer. And he was live, in 3-D! The man whom Woody had paid those two hairy Anton brothers to follow. The man whom Woody had staked out himself at the Studio City construction site. The man who had coldly murdered poor Ben's first wife and twin girls.

Between those quick, painful breaths, Woody felt his heart thumping like a jackhammer from his insides.

"Oh," realized Stew. "Think you just put it together. Not until now did you figure who I was. Or are you still too dinged in your melon to know up from down?"

Woody shook his head.

"You paid for the camel jockeys," said Stew. "Now, who paid you?"

Though Woody's body went surprisingly slack, he sucked in air through his nose while his eyes widened in an obvious admission of guilt.

"Easier to talk if I take off the . . ." Stew gestured to the duct tape which secured the rag ball in Woody's mouth.

Woody nodded.

"Before I do that, I wanna show you somethin'."

Stew approached, stiffly extending his right arm all the way down to his gloved index finger that was aimed at the joystick that operated Woody's super-chair. Woody's view instantly swept back to the emptied pool and the sharp drop from where his chair stood, to the concrete bottom. Next, Woody bucked in his chair, straining to wrest his arms from their bindings.

"Uh uh," cautioned Stew, gently allowing his fingertip to rest atop the joystick. "Gimme a straight answer, fat man rolls back an inch. Lie to me, fat man rolls forward an inch. You get that?"

Woody nodded violently.

"And fuckin' scream? Shout out? Any shit like that? It's the skaters' pit for you."

Tears streamed from Woody's eyes as he rocked his head up and down in implicit understanding.

Pinching the corner of the tape between his thumb and forefinger, Stew peeled it slowly from Woody's face with little disregard for any pain it might induce. He then removed the spit-soaked rag from Woody's mouth.

Instantly, Woody began to wheeze and cough at the onset of an asthma attack.

"It's okay. Hack it up, first," said Stew. "Now, you ready?"

Woody nodded, then rasped a simple, "Yes."

"Who?"

"Don't know his name . . . Some dude on the phone who—"

The chair bucked ahead as Stew gave the joystick a forward prod. The audible gasp from Woody's mouth was caught by Stew's other glove, clasped across his face.

"Told you the rules, fat man. Need me to repeat 'em?"

Stew was so close that Woody could almost taste the flavor on his breath. A mix of sugar and whiskey. Stew slowly pressed the joystick forward while Woody shook his head.

"Alright," said Stew. "Who?"

"Guy named Ben."

Stew filed through the names in his head, quickly coming up with nothing at all.

"Ben got a last name?"

Woody's eyes remained fixed and unblinking on Stew's index finger as it tap-tap-tapped the top of the joystick.

"Keller," said Woody. "Ben Keller."

"Good," said Stew, reversing the joystick a lick until the chair jerked two inches backward.

"Where's Ben Keller live?"

"Simi . . . Simi Valley."

Once again, Stew pulled back a little on the joystick, moving the chair another few inches away from the pool.

"And why does Ben Keller from Simi Valley want to know about me?"

"Something you did to him."

"Really? Guy I never heard of says I did something to him?"

Woody nodded.

"You drove by my construction site, right? I know you did. You in your fuckmobile with the red flames and the noisemaker muffler. That was you. I remember."

"Sure. That was me."

"Then you saw what I do. I build homes. Homes for families. I'm a good guy, now. That means I am on the right side of things in this world."

"G . . . Gotcha," stammered Woody. "M . . . Maybe . . . maybe I can tell him that."

"Tell the Ben guy?"

Woody nodded.

"Oh, I think I'll tell 'im myself."

Stew tapped the joystick over and over again.

"Yes?" Woody asked.

"What's this guy think I did to him?"

The reflex was to gulp. But Woody's mouth was so dry he felt as if he might swallow his own tongue.

"I . . . I wasn't there so I don't know if it's true or nothing . . ."

Stew fingered the joystick and bumped the chair forward.

"No, please!" begged Woody. "Okay . . . The guy . . ."

"Said his name was Ben."

"Ben, yeah. Ben Keller," repeated Woody. "He says . . . He says you killed his family."

The heat sprayed up from Stew's feet, starting at his toes and spreading throughout his nervous system. A harsh surge that climbed his entire frame, radiating into his face and down all the way to the receptors in his fingertips. He straightened from the waist and unconsciously turned around in place while shifting his mind into recall. He remembered the recovery room and the surprise visit from that Amazon-sized Mexican cop. Then as if he had totally purged recent acts from his brain, the memory of visiting Old Jerome at the Stink Hole returned. The bathroom. The fire. He had killed Jerome, yes. And the Mojo Potato Cook, too.

Damn, thought Stew, thirsty for another sip of Jack and Coke.

"Killed the guy's family?" asked Stew.

"Like I said, I wasn't there . . ."

Stew shook his own head. Not in denial of the act. But because as much as he tried, he couldn't quite access a single image of the crimes he had committed prior to his life-changing stay in rehab. He knew he was a murderer. But knowing one did the crimes and being able to visualize the events from memory, were two completely different animals.

While Stew was twisting over his lousy memory, Woody made the desperate choice to give up any and all information in order to save himself.

"Do you want his address?" asked Woody.

"Where is it?"

"On my BlackBerry. Seat pocket right there."

Woody tipped his head in the direction of the pouch just inside his right armrest. Stew stepped over and reached in to remove the device. At the first touch of a button the screen came alive.

"Everything I have for him is on there. Just take it, please. Take it and go."

Stew scrolled and scrolled through the hundreds of names in Woody's electronic Rolodex.

"Don't see anybody named Keller."

"How about you let me?"

"There some kinda search function?"

"Yeah, okay. Button to the left of the scroller."

Stew had to take off a glove to type B-E-N on the tiny keyboard.

"Got cash, too," added Woody, trying like hell to sound businesslike and not like the panic-stricken, torture victim he was.

"Hey. How about I give you everything I've been paid so far . . ." begged Woody. "Plus some kind of vig, you know? For your trouble."

"Got three Bens in your list." Stew stuck the BlackBerry six inches in front of Woody's face. "See there? You got three Bens. Ben the Roto-Rooter guy with the North Hills address. Ben Washburn from up Bakersfield way. And . . . wait, I just had it . . . there it is. Ben Keller of Burbank. No Ben Keller from Simi Valley."

"Sure. Sorry. Made a mistake. It's Ben Keller of Burbank."

"You said Ben Keller of Simi."

"I don't know why I said . . ."

Woody's whole body went into a full-tilt shudder as he involuntarily emptied his bladder into a leaky colostomy bag.

"Really, really sorry, okay?" said Woody. "It's Ben Keller. He lives in Simi but I don't know where. That's his office. Burbank office."

"Wouldn't lie to me?"

"I'm just scared, okay?"

"Real scared?"

"Def . . . def . . ."

"Definitely?"

"Damn right."

"So I should believe you."

"Not lyin', dude. Swear."

Woody was nodding like a bobble-head doll on a bumpy road. As Stew mockingly began to mimic Woody, he laughed softly, then circled around the chair and began to slowly peel the duct tape away. This triggered an uncontrollable giggle in Woody as he witnessed his left arm being freed from the armrest.

"Thank you," squeaked Woody. "Thank you, thank you, thank you . . ."

Woody didn't need help ripping away the tape that bound his right arm. His left hand made quick work of it, peeling the sticky fabric from his skin and chair.

Laughter, being an infectious by-product of broken tension, caused Stew to join in. He even held out a friendly hand to take the tacky ball of silver tape from Woody.

"Thanks," said Woody.

"No problem," said Stew with a wink.

Stew hustled back to his new Ford F-250 Super Duty, coolly returning his sunglasses to his face and pulling the brim of his hat down low. He lingered for a minute in the cab, made a few meaningless scribbles on a clipboard for appearance's sake, then slowly backed out of the driveway onto the street.

Four blocks north of Woody's, Stew found a wooded lane and pulled over to the shoulder. To any casual observer, looky-loo, or dog walker, Stew would have appeared to be any old subcontractor who had stopped his pickup to check his tire pressure or tie down the contents in his truck bed. This was exactly how Stew wanted to appear. Ordinary. Part of the fabric that made up the average suburban background. He pretty much knew nobody would be watching him closely enough to see him pull off the stolen license plates he had acquired only hours before staking out Woody's home. Once again, the new truck sported chrome-framed dealer advertisements that read: *I Got Mine from Galpin Ford!*

Stew was certain that nothing in his actions betrayed the slightest hint to the truth of his circumstances. It was a sick truth that some poor soul would eventually discover when looking in on the reclusive private detective. It would either be a home-care practitioner, nursing specialist, or cleaning lady who spoke little English beyond, "How are you today, Mr. Woody?"

Whomever it would be and whenever that hour or day would come, it would be as if they had drawn an unlucky lottery ticket. They would first scour the house, then both yards, front and rear, calling out Woody's name until they thought to look into the barren pool. At the bottom they would find the body of the four-hundred-pound paraplegic, twisted around the mechanical wreckage of what must have once been a very cool wheelchair.

After Stew kicked the stolen plates into the storm drain, he climbed back into his truck and sucked back five quick hits from his Super Big Gulp. The ice had melted and the brew had warmed to car temperature. The kick, though, remained strong enough and finished with a slightly watered-down tingle.

Gotta love that Jack and Coke.

Stew was surprised he hadn't thought of it before. Even more surprised he hadn't heard of the trick before, considering the hours he had spent in Alcoholics Anonymous meetings. Pull into the nearest 7-11. Grab a Super Big Gulp cup. Load the cup with ice, then fill it halfway with Coke or Pepsi. Strap on a lid and straw. Pay. Back at the car, pop the glove box. Then dump a fresh pint or two of Jack Daniels into the mix. Perfect. And who the hell would be the wiser?

Stew sipped as he drove on. Next, he slid the Super Big Gulp into the F-250's much-improved cup holder and fumbled a bit with Woody's BlackBerry. He carefully scrolled the phone book until the cursor landed on Benjamin Keller. He pressed the autodial feature and placed the mobile device to his ear. After four rings came an answer:

"Hey, Wood-man," said Ben, sounding quite cheerful.

Stew only listened. One hand on the phone, the other on the steering wheel as he searched for the freeway on-ramp that would deliver him from the community of Chatsworth.

"Woody?" asked Ben again, before pausing for a count of three. "Listen man. This must be a lousy connection. Wanna try me again?"

And Ben hung up.

Stew stuck the BlackBerry between his legs, took another juicy hit from the Super Big Gulp, swung a hard left across traffic onto a busy freeway on-ramp, then joined a line of eleven cars waiting for a green light and the chance to merge. He returned to the mobile phone's directory. There were two telephone numbers listed under Ben's name. One was a mobile number, the other categorized as work. Stew autodialed again. This time, the phone rang only once.

"Safety First," answered Josie, neglecting to check the caller ID before answering.

"Yes," said Stew, his lips catching up with his imagination. "I'm looking to speak with Ben Keller."

"May I ask who's calling?"

"Keith."

"Yes, sir. Does Mr. Keller know what this regards?"

"Er, no," stumbled Stew. Realizing he had dialed without a glimmer of a plan, Stew thought of just hanging up. Instead, he thought maybe the best defense would be a stronger offense. So he asked her a question.

"Safety First," saved Stew. "And what exactly do you do there at—"

"Safety First?" finished Josie. "We're a consulting firm. I'm sorry. Did you give me your last name?"

"I apologize. My name is Keith. Keith Daniels."

"What can we do for you, Mr. Daniels?"

"I was just wondering if there was a way I could get some

information"

"On our services?"

"Exactly," said Stew, his voice trailing as he suspected the tapping he heard was Josie keying the name "Keith Daniels" into her database in order to do a proper search.

"We have a website that pretty much describes our services," she said. "It's w-w-w-dot-safety-first-consulting-dot-com. Would you like me to spell that?"

"Think I can handle that, darlin'," said Stew, deciding to turn on the charm.

"And who are you with?"

"Excuse me?"

"What company or organization do you represent?"

"I'm sorry," Stew lied. "But I'm in a bad cell area connection. Can I call you right back?"

Before Josie could answer, Stew cut her off, clicking the red end button and tossing the phone to the seat. Then as hunger nibbled at his insides, he wondered what Pam had in store for dinner. Of if she would be in the mood for eating out. *Strange*, thought Stew. He was in the mood for something hot and Chinese.

Five minutes was all it took.

The rare nights Ben dried Betsy's after-bath hair were some of his most mentally productive. As little Betsy sat on the floor, towel curled over her shoulders, having conversations with her menagerie of Polly Pockets, miniature farm animals, and Fisher Price family, Ben would brush her hair with one hand, the blow dryer in the other. All the while, Betsy would arrange the toys like pieces in a three-dimensional chess game that only she knew how to play.

She was in her world. And Ben was in his.

Here, he would risk-assess. Be it calculations on vision safety for drill-press operators in the Glendora factory he had walked through last month, or the astronomical odds that the Taiwan-built blow dryer in his left hand would explode into sparks and flames. Ben would crunch, divide, weigh, and quietly stress the numbers that would determine if an activity was safe or not.

He wondered why the numbers came more easily during the five minutes it took to dry Betsy's hair. Was it the white-noise drone of the blow dryer mixed with Betsy's tiny voice whispering words into the heads of her miniature playmates? Or the linear way the strands of Betsy's hair miraculously aligned as the brush cleaned out the tangles? *No matter*, thought Ben. *The numbers came. They were as much formulaic as they were instinctive.* And sometimes they were alarming.

Ben assessed the risks of his actions that day.

Odds that his car would have drifted left versus right? One to one. Risk? Negligible.

Odds on Ben actually having the gumption to knock on the door of Stew's house? Three to one. Risk? Ben was an unknown to Pam. Negligible.

Odds of Stew coming home while Ben was in the house? Twenty-five to one. Risk? Unknown because . . .

Odds of Stew recognizing Ben from the day Ben posed as an OSHA inspector? Three to one. Risk? Probable. After all, Stew was a murderer.

Odds that Pam knew Stew was a murderer? A hundred to one. Ben's estimations had everything to do with his impressions of Pam, the coziness and warmth of the home she had made with Stew, the pictures of the happy couple framed in silver and wood. Add in Pam's hopes of adopting a child and the odds elevated. Ben couldn't imagine Pam raising a child with a killer, let alone bedding down with one. Risk to Pam? Minimal short-term. But long-term?

Odds that Pam would one day discover Stew was a murderer? Ben figured four to one over a twenty-year term. The short-term was more of a maybe. That's because Ben was the question mark in the equation. With that assessment, Ben experienced a sudden sense of power.

It was weird too, that it was all tied directly to his foolhardy and patently unsafe morning. Every second Ben had stood inside Stew's house, he felt enmity. How dare the monster that snuffed out the lives of his wife and children live in such comfort? With such a sweet and beautiful woman? Consider raising children?

Yet Ben also felt a simultaneous sense of his own destiny. A strangely comfortable place within his own skin that was beyond any calculation. It reminded Ben of the foolish invincibility that adolescent boys often feel.

Foolish invincibility that gets boys killed.

"Ben?" asked Betsy.

"Yeah, sweetie?"

"Nina says I'm not big enough to sit in the front seat."

"Well, how much do you weigh?"

"Four, eight, and then another eight."

"You mean forty-eight."

"The thing in your and Mommy's bathroom says a four, then an eight then another eight."

"Oh," said Ben. "Forty-eight point eight pounds." That's almost forty-nine. That means you're getting big."

"How old do I need to be to be safe?"

"Depends on the kind of car, does the air bag turn off or not, stuff like that."

"What's a hair bag?"

"Air bag."

"Oh."

"It's like a big pillow that blows up in case the car gets in an accident."

"Your car or Mommy's car?"

"Both our cars."

The conversation stalled as Ben checked Betsy's hair to see if there were any strands left to dry. Betsy continued the chess game with her miniatures, hardly forgetting her original question.

Meanwhile . . .

Odds of stumbling into Pam in the supermarket? Three hundred to one. This was where the risks divided. And risks to whom? Ben or Pam? Direct dangers to Pam could be slid across Ben's mental bulletin board and subdirected under its own heading: *Risks to Pam*. But the dangers to Ben just got more complicated. After one encounter with Stew's wife, he might have been quickly forgotten. A memory as disposable as a used Kleenex. But a supermarket helping of Ben within an hour of their introduction, followed by an invitation from Pam to sit down for lunch? A connection had been made. Names exchanged.

You gave her your goddamn card, moron!

Ben could easily imagine Stew returning home from a day at work and inquiring if anybody had called about the house for sale. Pam would surely mention the nice man who had stopped by.

Or would she? The answer was unknown.

Unknowns weren't viewed favorably in Ben's mental game of *Safety versus Risk*. Unknowns demanded deeper investigation. Unknowns led to accidents. Unknowns got people hurt, even killed.

"Am I, Ben?" asked Betsy.

"Are you what?"

"Big enough for the front seat?"

"Not just yet."

"When?"

"When you weigh eighty pounds."

"Do you weigh eighty pounds?"

"Yes, sweetie. A lot more."

"So when I'm a grown-up?"

"Sooner," said Ben, switching off the blow dryer. "All done. Teeth, jammies, then stories. Let's beat those feet, puddin' face."

"I'm not your puddin' face. I'm your Betsy."

Betsy up and disappeared into her closet to search for the perfect pair of pajamas.

Ben reviewed his conclusions or lack thereof.

Unknowns: The risks Ben took spending another day living in both the present and past. The risks to Betsy, her sisters, and her mother as long as he continued to pick at his twelve-year-old scar. Risks of action, whatever the hell form that would take.

Known: The world was unsafe with Stew Raymo living in it.

"Hello. My name is Stew. And I'm an alcoholic."

"Hi, Stew," answered twenty-odd former abusers. Their not-quite-unified voices echoed through the sanctuary of the small North Hollywood church. It was five minutes after eight on a Monday morning and the light filtering in through the stained glass landed squarely on a loose circle of folding chairs filled by men and women who smelled of fresh, hot coffee and stale cigarettes.

Stew began to sweat. He must have shared a hundred times in his clean years. It was his turn to give of himself, reveal his fears and weaknesses to drugs and alcohol, relent to his higher power, relate the experience to the others present, and in return, find fortification in his comrades' unending support. So why the hell were there beads of sweat on his forehead to go with the words stuck in his throat? Was it guilt? Two weeks before he had admitted to falling off the wagon to fistfuls of whiskey and cola. And sure enough, his fellow alcoholics had rallied behind him. Pam was even there as a witness. All was good and well underneath the skin of Stew Raymo.

So why wouldn't all be good that day in the shadow of a Church of Christ altar swathed in sheets of white rayon to keep off the dust? The answer didn't come to Stew. At least not soon enough to keep him from shaking his head and bolting from his chair, nearly kicking it over as he twisted up the aisle and between the pews, headed like a bee-stung goat toward the double exit doors.

Stew was halfway into his shiny pickup truck when he heard the voice call after him.

"Stew! Hold it up, pal!"

Of course, Stew knew the voice. It had a ruddy face to match its timbre and more sand than the Mojave Desert.

"Whatever's goin' on, you don't have to share it," said Big Tony, Stew's AA sponsor. "You know you got me, right?"

"I gotta get back to my site."

"Sure you do. But you had another forty-five minutes blocked out for our thing, right? So let's go grab a doughnut and hear about the lump in your throat."

Big Tony Burns, a retired San Pedro longshoreman who now coached football at his high school alma mater, gimped around to the passenger side of Stew's pickup and hauled himself in, arthritic hip and all. Big Tony wasn't taking no for answer.

"You're an asshole," said Stew to possibly the only man he had ever truly respected. "Name your doughnut."

"Glazed ol' fashioned," said Big Tony. "And no place servin' fruitcake coffees, neither. Colorful as I get is black like my sister."

Big Tony Burns, born and raised on the suburban slopes of Burbank overlooking the flight patterns of the Bob Hope Airport, spent four years on the east coast where he played Division 1-AA football for Central Connecticut State. It was there he learned to love Dunkin' Donuts and the inky coffee they served to complement their daily lineup of sugary, quick-fried circles of dough. It seemed that in the northeast, there wasn't a city or town or four corners with a stoplight that didn't post a Dunkin' Donuts—for addicts, needy for a fix of sugar and caffeine. For the twenty years that had passed since returning home, Big Tony lamented that there wasn't a single Dunkin' Donuts to be found in all of Southern California.

"Everything's a latte this and a chai-cappuccino frou-frou that. All a buncha crap," griped Big Tony, settling into a booth at a North Hollywood Winchell's. "And do you know how much those assholes charge for a twenty-five cent cup of Joe? Three dollars, four dollars. Robbery, right? Criminals. The whole lot of 'em."

"This is where we sat," Stew remembered. "You and me. Before my first meeting. You went over the steps, man. All twelve. One, two, three . . . Took fuckin' forever."

"'Day by day. You and me will get there.' I said that. I remember, sayin' that and look. You slipped. So have I. We all do. But you just get back and do it again. Day one, day two."

"I'm there, man. You know I'm there."

"So what was that about back there in the church?"

"I dunno," said Stew, his face screwed into a question mark. "Ever have a thought in your head and you wanna say it, but your brain is like a TV set that can't stop changing channels?"

"Sure."

"It was like that. Brain kept switchin' channels on me."

"You're wrestling with somethin'," said Big Tony. "So relax and wring it out with me."

Stew nodded, trying to trust, then placed the heels of his palms against his eye sockets before rubbing his face.

"Okay . . ." said Stew. "Amends."

"Got some you need to make?"

"What if . . ." Stew began, trying to keep the channels straight inside his skull. "What if there was somethin' you did to somebody else? Somethin' that you don't remember doin' real good. Hard as you try, you just don't remember much about it."

Big Tony knew the answer. He knew Stew knew the answer. Still, he took a moment to make sure Stew could see the question had sunk in.

"Makin' amends is about takin' care of your side of the street. Blackout drunks don't remember nothin' they do. But they still gotta take care of business—"

"I get that," interrupted Stew. But what if by making this one amends I implicate myself in some kinda crime?"

"Then you take what comes. You still gotta clean up your side of the boulevard."

"But by making this one amends, I injure other people. Like the guys who work for me. They depend on me for their jobs. Or my wife . . ."

"See? That's the disease talkin'. If you don't make the amends, then living with that kinda guilt is what makes you slip up and use. And you'll keep slippin' again and again until you take care of your business. Know what I'm sayin'?"

Stew leaned back in the booth and stared down at his untouched cup of black coffee and jelly-filled doughnut. He shook his head.

"I swear, Tony. It was so long ago I wonder if it ever happened."

"But you know there's an injured party? Somebody you hurt?"

"Yeah."

"Know where to find this person?"

"Pretty much, yeah."

"Then lay it on his or her doorstep. Put it down, make your amends, and cross the next bridge. Power to forgive can be as healing to the injured soul as the soul that needs forgiving."

Big Tony stretched across the table and put that longshoreman's grip on Stew's forearm. "And I'll be there. I'll be there for ya no matter which way the shit flies. You know that?"

"I know," said Stew.

"You gonna eat your doughnut?" asked Big Tony.

"Naw," said Stew, pushing his plate across the table. "All yours."

Though Josie "enjoyed" her job, she did get kind of lonesome. Twice a week she would walk to lunch with a couple of the technicians who worked in the laser hair removal office down the hall. Ben was pretty good company—when he was in the office. But even then he was usually on the phone or reading one of the many papers and journals to which he subscribed. There was one week last winter when Josie counted seventy-two hours without actually talking to another human being face-to-face. Her choice of work puzzled her family as young Josie had always been such a people person.

Ben was just merging onto the I-5 when the new client knocked on his office door. He had arrived twenty minutes early giving Josie ample time to play the perfect hostess. Right off the bat Josie recognized something kind of sexy about him, though his shoes invoked a vivid and unwelcome image of her seventh-grade physical science teacher. It took a certain charisma in a man for a girl to forgive shoes like that. And Ben's new client had it. Josie popped a plastic "Donut Shop" pod into the coffee maker and in minutes the two were sharing stories like old friends.

Unsafe, thought Ben, in an endless mental loop.

The world was unsafe with Stew Raymo living in it.

In the thirty-six hours since he had made his conclusion, his own words repeated like a mantra. But was it a call to battle? Or a warning, demanding that Ben construct a stronger defense? After all, the caveat that Ben would always lay on each and every client was simple: danger was inherent to the universe. Accidents will surely happen. Surviving was simply a matter of implementing a structured set of proactive and passive safeguards, wisely chosen to fit each and every hazardous circumstance.

In a shift from his routine, Ben poked his car inside the office building's small, underground garage. It was early enough Monday morning that luck was on his side as he slipped into one of the three spaces that could not be blocked by another vehicle. Otherwise, Ben would have backed the Volvo out onto the street and attempted to score a two-hour parking meter.

Ben keyed the garage door that led to a cramped stairwell. As he climbed, his thoughts reflexively turned over the dirt clouding his most passive, defensive option. He could simply change his address, pull up stakes and settle in another state. Then, chances of a dangerous encounter with Stew Raymo would plummet to nearly absolute nil. The notion was ridiculous and nauseatingly weak. Alex would sooner divorce him than uproot her girls. And as much as changing area codes would make life safer for Ben, the world he would leave behind would still have to deal with Stew Raymo.

That option felt, at best, irresponsible.

Another defensive maneuver was for Ben to buy a gun. But for that to work Ben would have to carry it illegally, keeping it within arm's reach at all times. Then he would need time to hone the skills to use it effectively in case the deadly encounter ever happened. Cops were supposed to possess such finesse after months of training. Their abilities, though, were more myth than reality. Ben had cruised through pages of FBI reports on the true marksmanship talent of average police officers. Sure, they could accurately punch holes in paper. Yet when the moment of truth came, the adrenal glands took over, injecting an overdose of survival juice into their bloodstreams—lethal to anybody unlucky enough to step in front of a bullet. It turned out most street cops were not much better shots than your garden variety gangbanger on a drive-by, expending entire magazines of ammunition in the general direction of his intended target before the synapses in his frontal lobes caught up to his fuel-injected trigger fingers.

Ben rejected the idea of buying a gun for defensive purposes, but couldn't quite shake the exquisite thought of actually holding some kind of steely equalizer. Something he had never ever done. At least not a real gun. He imagined how heavy it would feel. And masculine. The thought also satisfied the bloodlust that welled inside him. A gun was at its core, a proactive instrument of death. And there was nothing more dynamic in Ben's new survival guide than the notion of walking up behind Stew Raymo, placing the muzzle of a loud and blustery cannon up against his skull, and splattering his brains into the atmosphere. In Ben's mind it was, of course, all make-believe and chock-full of special effects. A fantasy ending that lived only in a Hollywood universe. In the real world, Ben knew splashy revenge killings were punished with a ferocity greater than that of the original act. The news headlines usually demanded as much.

Ah . . . but revenge.

The word made Ben's heart instantly thump with an unexpected, but primal excitement. So much so, that before tilting left through his office door, he felt the need to stall a moment in order to gather himself, his thoughts, his composure. After all he was the Safety Expert. And in five minutes he had his first consultation with the regional health and safety organizer for the Transportation Workers Association, which represented over three thousand airline baggage handlers. Good impressions had to be made. Any lingering thoughts of red-blooded vengeance had to be stuffed and tucked away for a later date.

To avoid the electrostatic shock which came upon touching the door's handle after walking along the poly-blend carpeted corridor, Ben shouldered the door open.

"He's already here," said Josie, dispensing with a greeting. "In your office."

"My meeting? He's early," whispered Ben.

"Said traffic wasn't that bad coming up from . . ."

"El Segundo," finished Ben. "T.W.A. offices are next to LAX."

"'Least you didn't have to go down there to meet him."

"Offer him anything? Coffee or a Coke?"

"What do you think?"

"Sorry," said Ben, then leaning in so he could whisper. "What's his first name again?"

"Keith."

"Keith," repeated Ben with a nod. He ditched his coat and briefcase on the couch and reached for the door to his office.

Snap!

The electrostatic build-up stored in the soles of his shoes discharged the instant his skin made contact with the knob. Ben released a slightly audible, "Ouch," re-gripped the handle, then pushed through.

"Sorry I'm late," he began, fully expecting the new client who had been waiting in his office to politely reply with something along the lines of, "No, I'm sorry for being early."

But there would be no comeback.

When Ben pushed the door it hinged open. He crossed the threshold and glanced left, discovering the sofa and chair opposite his desk were unoccupied. Instinct demanded he look right.

Time suddenly switched into super-slow-motion.

It was as if Ben's life was a movie and by tripling the rate of frames-per-second, everything looked as if it was swimming underwater.

Standing perfectly erect, arms at his side, and facing that wall of framed family photos was none other than Stew Raymo. His six-foot-four frame filled a navy suit jacket that had been tailored eight years and thirty pounds ago. His feet were fit snugly into a pair of brown, lightly scuffed, size-fourteen Rockports.

Ben's legs instantly felt weak and screamed for oxygen, his quadriceps failing like a runner's at the finish of a marathon. Then as Stew turned a shoulder and swiveled his head in order to meet his host eye-to-eye, Ben knew what it meant to be a deer caught crossing a lonely two-lane at midnight. The car's headlights, sweeping around a bend. The glare. The on-rushing vehicle. And the legs, glued to the pavement, unable to do anything but twitch in fear.

"Please shut the door," said Stew, whose barreled chest rose and fell with a heavy breath. A sure sign of nerves. Not that Ben caught the cue. Ben's impulse was to retreat backward, nearly stumbling.

Stew took a quick step forward and gently swung the door closed. Next, he showed his hand, outstretched and open.

"You seem to know me, friend," said Stew. "But forgive me if I don't know you."

That's when Stew's head cocked a tick to the right, followed by a sudden look of recognition.

"Wait a sec," said Stew. "I do know you. You're the guy with the bicycle helmets. That's who you are. That was you on my site!"

Ben answered with a completely involuntary cough, expelling the saliva that was stuck at the top of his larynx. Between fading spasms, Ben hacked out a response.

"What do you want?"

"Stew Raymo."

Once again, Stew held out his hand in a strangely conciliatory gesture. Ben just looked at the open palm like Superman staring at a lump of kryptonite.

"Okay, then," said Stew, withdrawing his hand. "Let's get to it."

"Get to what?"

Again, Stew's chest rose and fell with a heavy sigh.

"Can I sit?"

Then without waiting for Ben's answer, Stew sat himself in the chair nearest the floor-to-ceiling, smoked-glass window. "Might be a good idea if you sat, too."

Ben nodded, then turned around his desk until his butt found his chair. He looked ahead and saw his hands laying flat on the empty desktop. Near his left hand was the telephone. Ben tried to calculate how long it would take to dial 911. Or hit the intercom button and shout for help. Only his subconscious told him Stew would wrap the telephone cord around his neck before he could utter a syllable.

. Near Ben's right hand was a coffee mug, hand-painted and kiln-glazed, with lemon-yellow suns and *Happy Fathers Day* scrawled in Nina's handwriting when she was five. Stuffed in the mug were an assortment of pens, mechanical pencils, and a sharp letter opener. If attacked, Ben could grab the letter opener and pray he found one of Stew's arteries before one of Stew's fists crushed his skull.

"I'll start with what we know, okay?" began Stew. "You've been lookin' for me. You been lookin' for me because you think I did somethin' to you. Is that about right?"

"You did somethin' to me," Ben acknowledged.

"Somethin' about your family?"

Ben nodded. He felt his face flush with heat.

"That family? In all the pictures on the wall?" Stew's thumb pointed back over his left shoulder.

"They're not part of this," said Ben, finding some grit in his voice.

"Oh," said Stew with a nod, working over the clues in his head.

"Why'd you come here?" asked Ben.

"Cuz you been lookin' for me," snapped Stew. "Well, here I am."

What followed was a brief, verbal stalemate. Then the slightest look of regret came over Stew's face. And in those ten seconds—when Ben was between panic and reaching for the letter opener—when he fantasized about crawling up over the desk and plunging the instrument into Stew's jugular—Ben unconsciously read the body language of the man opposite him. Stew appeared to withdraw ever so slightly into the back of his chair.

"That didn't come out right," said Stew. "And that's not what I came here to . . ."

Stew shifted uncomfortably. He let his fingers slip under the sleeve of his coat to briefly scratch an itch.

"I used to drink," restarted Stew. "Had a pretty bad problem for a lotta years. Liquor and pills, mostly . . . What I'm saying is that I'm an alcoholic. Recovering. Over ten years now, proud to say. Which . . . well . . . ain't too bad considering the failure rate. Ain't easy, either. Hell, you probably know that from your girlie out there . . ."

Ben filled in the pause.

"Josie?" asked Ben.

"I was behind her when she opened the door. Saw the one-year chip on her keychain. So you can understand how we—she and myself—got to talkin' . . ."

"You're saying my Josie's in AA?"

Stew clocked Ben's look of surprise. This time, Stew's regret took form in the shake of his head.

"My mistake. I owe her an apology. Program's supposed to be anonymous. Thus the name. Hey . . ."

Stew digressed a beat.

"Might be a good idea to send her out for something," suggested Stew. "Figure neither of us want this to be any more uncomfortable than it has to be."

Ben was still on his mental heels. He couldn't possibly decipher whether Stew was making a true suggestion, or a demand.

"And if I'm more comfortable with her here?" asked Ben.

"Suppose that makes some sense," said Stew. "But unless you plan to dial nine-one-one or come at me with that letter opener, ain't nothin' gonna happen in here but talk."

Without thinking, Ben removed his hands from the desktop, instantly noticing the prints left by his sweaty palms. He wiped his hands on his pants, then pressed the intercom button.

"Josie?" said Ben.

"Yes?"

"I uh . . . I skipped breakfast today. Mind running over to Mickey D's and getting me a McMuffin or something?"

"Anything for our guest?"

"No thanks. I'm good," said Stew.

"Nothing," said Ben.

"Gotcha, then," said Josie. "Back in a bit."

Josie clicked off. Then both men waited until they heard the door from the reception area thunk shut.

"Pretty girl," said Stew. "And I won't forget to say I'm sorry to her for the anonymity thing. Promise."

Ben rubbed his face, hoping he could wipe away the man seated across from him. Yet when he opened his eyes, Stew was still right there.

"You wanted to talk," prompted Ben.

Stew straightened in his chair and began speaking in a cadence that seemed half-rehearsed and half-baked.

"Like I said. I'm an alcoholic. And part of recognizing the disease is when you discover—or figure out—that you've injured somebody as a result of the disease... My case, the drinkin' and pills and all the shit that drags along behind it. Anyway, as alcoholics we make amends. And that's why I'm here. To make my amends to you, sir, for whatever I've done."

"You're here . . . to *apologize?*" Ben made no effort to disguise the incredulity in his voice.

"I am," said Stew. "But lemme go on, okay? See, when I used to drink, I did a lot of bad things. Evil things. Shit I did time for. But . . . and I say this with all honesty, man. Half the stuff I did I don't remember. Like, 'cept for the day you showed up on my site, I don't remember you."

"It's not me you should remember."

"I know. Was you who had the lady cop come pay me a visit, right? I'm right about the lady cop?"

For Ben, fear was in sudden retreat. He found he had the reserve to stare holes in Stew with no problem. All the while not answering the question.

"The lady cop?"

"I have friends who are police officers," said Ben.

"Me too," said Stew. "Lotsa cops in The Program. Lotsa cops."

"You were paid a visit . . ." cued Ben, desperately wanting to get back to the point. The issue. The murder.

"Right. Big tall lady cop. Mexican gal. Forgive me, but I was kinda doped up after this surgery thing I had done on my

ACL. Drugs, by the way, was the doctor's deal. Swear to Christ, I wouldn't let him prescribe me shit. I ate Advil for a month and believe me, the Advil ate my stomach to shreds."

"My family was murdered," said Ben in a tone much flatter than he had anticipated. He considered standing and screaming the fact. Only Stew continued.

"That's what she said. She was investigating some old thing down in Culver City. And here's the part where, after the surgery and I flushed all that Demerol from my system, I got to thinking and trying to remember. And I don't remember doin' no job down that way. Not a thing. I don't remember nothin'."

"So because you don't remember," said Ben, volume slightly elevated. "That means it didn't happen?"

"No, sir. Not at all," said Stew. "Why I'm here, you see? Somethin' or somebody led you to me. Maybe I did the thing, maybe I didn't. Do you know for sure? I mean, I don't know. I truly don't know. But if I don't remember, that doesn't mean I didn't do it. So here I am takin' care of my side of the street. I'm here to offer my hand and say I'm sorry. I apologize for your loss and whatever hand or part I had in it. Sincerely."

There it was. Stew Raymo had apologized. Then he stood and leaned across the table, once again offering his open palm for Ben to take, grip, and shake on the promise to forgive and forget.

"I can't . . ." said Ben. "You can understand that—"

"I understand just fine. That's your side of the street and you gotta do what you gotta do. That, and I had all weekend to work on what I was gonna say and how I was gonna say it. Take your time. Accept my amends or don't."

Stew stepped around the chair. It appeared that he was considering a quick exit. Instead, he turned to the wall of family photos.

"This must be your new family," figured Stew. "You got remarried?"

"I said they're not part of this," Ben repeated.

"I'm married myself," said Stew. "Five years ago. Number one, for me. Aside from stepping into my first AA meeting, best thing I ever did."

Stew scanned the black-and-white photos. Snapshots of perfect moments. The joyous children. The beautiful wife. It appeared to Ben that Stew was absorbing the pictures. Sucking them into his sick psyche. And that made Ben very uneasy. He stood.

"Please," said Ben. "I think we're done."

"My wife and I," ignored Stew. "We're starting a family. Gotta say, I was worried that I'd make a lousy father. Not anymore, though. That's cuz I've moved on. Out of the past and into today. You know what I mean, right?"

Then Stew held his palms toward that collage of family images and made a swirling gesture.

"I can see here that you've moved on, too," smiled Stew. "And that's awesome, man. You and me. We've both done it. Changed. Moved on, yeah?"

"Sure we have," said Ben, just wishing Stew would grab the door handle, pull it, and be gone.

"In The Program we advise to learn from the past. But once you've learned, always look ahead."

"Important safety tip," said Ben a bit too glibly.

The smile on Stew's face faded marginally as he tried to interpret the intent of Ben's jibe. Then Stew broke into a laugh.

"I get it," said Stew. "Safety tip from the Safety Guy."

"That's me," said Ben weakly.

"Hey, man. You have a good day," said Stew with an affirmative nod. He reached for the door, yanked it wide open and walked out.

Stew was gone.

And Ben suddenly felt as if he had the flu. His muscles ached. He was chilled to his ever-tightening ligaments and tendons.

He found himself manically leveling the rows of framed, family photos to their former, uniform and squared-to-the-ceiling positions. After that, he walked as if half-drunk into the outer office and snatched the men's room key from the soap dish on Josie's desk. The dish itself was a Disney collector's curio, emblazoned with a cheerful message: *Greetings from the Happiest Place on Earth.*

Ben had himself a powerful urge.

Not that he actually needed to use the toilet. He merely desired to lock himself inside a cave where nobody could touch him, hear him, or see or smell the fear on him. The men's room was the nearest place Ben could think of for isolation. He needed to work his bearings back into place.

It was a quick step out the door, a hard left, eleven paces, then a ninety-degree right at a slivered window that overlooked the exit to the underground parking structure. Ben fumbled and jiggled a key that felt as if it couldn't possibly turn the lock. Wondering if he had mistakenly grabbed the women's room key, he checked and found it was attached to a tiny, plastic Mickey Mouse keychain. If it were the ladies' room key, it would have been dangling on an equally cute Minnie Mouse keychain. Both the charms and the soap dish, whimsical mementos from a brief consulting gig handed Ben by the Burbank-based Disney Corporation.

But right now the happiest place on earth for Ben was going to be inside the men's room. If he could only get in.

He tried the key once more. And the lock turned like it had been greased. In an instant, Ben slipped into the bathroom and locked the door behind him. The motion-controlled sensor flicked on a double-strip of cool-white fluorescents revealing a bathroom that hadn't received much more than a basic facelift since the sixties. There was a urinal and a toilet in a stall. Double sinks set into a Formica countertop below a large mirror. One waste can, one paper-towel dispenser. All surrounded by stacked white tiles rising from a polished concrete floor with a collection drain at the center.

Ben avoided his own reflection as he turned on the faucet and splashed cold water up into his face. He then withdrew his mobile phone and scrolled for Gonzo's telephone number. He had to tell someone. Purge himself of what had just happened inside his office. Most of all, he needed advice on what to do next. Should he call the police? Was he a witness to a confession of sorts? And if it had been a confession, would it be anything more than Ben's word versus Stew's—

"You've reached the voicemail box of Lydia Gonzalez. Please leave a message."

Before Ben could think, there was a beep, followed by an unconscious flow of broken sentences.

"Lydia. It's me . . . Ben. I was just . . . He knows. He knows about me and was here. The sonofabitch showed up at my office and . . . He was just here when I arrived this . . . It's so weird. I don't know how or what to think about the apology. Did I say that? He came to apologize. That's what he said . . . apologize for his side of the street. But he says he doesn't remember any of it . . . Remembered you, yeah. Remembered you. Says he changed. Says we've all changed and we've moved on. Christ, I wanted to kill him. Right there. How the hell he found me I—"

Beep.

And like that, Ben stopped, realizing how much he was babbling. He thought of redialing her. Starting over from the beginning. Less panicked. More cogent. But most likely that would lead to another voicemail beep followed by yet more verbal diarrhea.

The water gushed from the spigot. Ben placed his cell phone on the counter, grabbed a handful of loosely stacked paper towels, then as he dabbed at his face he unwittingly caught himself staring at his own reflection. He appeared weary with broken capillaries overpowering the whites of his eyes, his skin a shade paler than an albino stripper's. Then came the convulsion. His stomach was preparing to flip-flop and send his breakfast back over his gums. Ben spun and dove for the stall.

He loathed vomiting. Not just the vile smell and taste of regurgitated food. But the idea of handing over momentary control of his bodily functions to a return-reflux system while kneeling at a toilet bowl? It was nine parts repugnant, one part relief until the act was finished and he had gargled with Listerine and was chewing twin sticks of spearmint gum.

But in this purge, Ben felt no relief whatsoever. He held his nose, pressed the handle on the toilet, and puked a second and third time until his stomach had scraped itself clean. With his head hanging over the bowl, the constant sound of flushing was akin to that at the base of Niagara Falls.

So overpowering was the rushing noise in his ears that Ben hadn't heard the key in the lock, the bathroom door swinging open, or the leather footfalls of size fourteen shoes.

"Shoulda figured a guy like you wouldn't have the stomach."

Ben heard the voice, but couldn't make out the words, let alone place the voice.

"Sorry," said Ben, still squatting, embarrassed, wiping his mouth on his sleeve, and then lying, "must be some kinda food poisoning."

Ben's memory sped backward to the moment he had entered the bathroom. He couldn't recall the part where he fumbled with the key, let alone throwing the privacy latch.

"Need the stall?" asked Ben. He anchored himself on the seat, stood, and opened the stall's door while wiping his hands on a wad of toilet paper.

Then Ben's eyes lifted.

Standing before him was the same Stew Raymo in the same sadly-tailored navy jacket. Only his chest strained at his shirt buttons as it heaved in and out and his face had turned to the pigment of a feral pig. The vein that forked above the bridge of his nose pulsed as if he had sprinted up ten flights of stairs.

"How'd you get—"

"You're a mother fuckin' skunk," interrupted Stew. As Stew punctuated his own curse with his left middle and ring finger, Ben's question was answered when he saw the key with the Minnie Mouse charm wedged in Stew's palm.

The women's room key.

If Stew had been interested, he could have explained to Ben that most commercial contractors and building supers were too lackadaisical to key men's and women's restrooms with different keys. It was a better than fifty-fifty shot that the Minnie Mouse key would open the door to the room stenciled "Men."

Ben's error had been in not sliding the privacy bolt closed.

"Said you'd think on it," said Stew as he angled closer. "But I could see your face. That's right. I read you, mister. After I come to you like a man and apologize. But no. You're not forgettin' shit, are you? You're gonna push this until it gets ugly."

"Nobody here's lookin' for trouble."

"Called your cop friend?" nodded Stew toward the cell phone in a puddle on the countertop. If Stew had looked harder he would have seen the sink had begun to overflow, the drain stopped-up by the fistful of spent paper towels left there by Ben moments earlier.

"Please," said Ben in full defensive mode, his hands thrust forward, palms squared in the universal sign of "stop." The man closing in was clearly bent with rage. Ben braced himself for the imminent attack.

As the big man lunged, all Ben could manage was a quick retreat backward into the stall. He slammed the door shut and locked it, only to have the latch snap and explode with a ping. A flying screw scored Ben's left cheek. Ben felt a massive hand reach in and snag his hair, jerking him from the stall.

If not for those size-fourteen Rockport shoes with leather soles. Worn leather soles built for style. Leather soles that weren't designed for traction on a wet, polished, concrete floor.

The sink had bubbled over and produced a drain-seeking, lazy stream across the restroom's floor. The spill was at the precise spot where a man of Stew's weight and structure needed a solid purchase to both kick in the stall's door and remain vertical.

Stew's left food slipped from under him. Gravity took over and sucked the big man to the floor. Making matters worse, he hadn't let go of Ben's hair. Stew's skull slapped the concrete surface a microsecond before the full weight of Ben landed on his chest.

Thud. Wheeze.

Ben felt the man's entire body vibrate as Stew groaned and rolled in a momentary daze. Ben scrambled away, found his feet, and considered running.

Considered?

There was nothing in the human body's primitive, fight-or-flight response that accounted for weighing options. It was a simple axiom. And automatic. To advance or retreat didn't require permission from any of the brain's logic centers. Still, as Stew struggled to recover, Ben was making the choice. And in that perplexing instant, he felt as if he had all the time in the world to choose.

Fight or flight?

Stew was temporarily immobilized, straining for air as his lungs hadn't yet fully inflated. All Ben needed to manage were those three steps to the door and he could then flee to the nearest phone to dial 911.

Only Ben found himself drawn closer to Stew. And as he neared, his fingertips curled up into his palms until his knuckles turned white. Ben had never hit a man in his life. Not a blow or so much as a drunken, roundhouse, swing and a miss.

"Motherfucker," growled Stew, sitting partway up, dizzy, in a bout to find his equilibrium. His eyes were glazed and unfocused. Then as if his neck was the ball-and-socket-joint to which his head was attached, Stew's mandible turned robotically up and to the left. Through an obvious haze, his eyes leveled and focused on Ben's balled fists. This is when Stew's eyes lifted, swiveling up the length of Ben's body until he had reckoned with the owner.

"Huh," said Stew. "You're still fuckin' here."

Ben didn't need to think another second. The rest came either naturally or from his tangled database of movies and television shows. Ben swung the laces of his left shoe into Stew's face with a force that returned the big man back to the concrete. Next he circled counterclockwise and followed with three—correct that—five swift kicks into Stew's rib cage. Each strike landed with a satisfying thud. Stew wheezed and cried out in pain while trying to roll away.

Ben lowered himself. He spiked one knee into Stew's shoulder, thus pinning his target to the floor while he dropped a heavy fist into Stew's face. The adrenalin thrust into the nerve endings of Ben's white knuckles masking any pain, allowing him to cock, reload, and punch again and again. All the while, Ben found himself huffing with the mantra, "Welcome to my side of the street, motherfucker!"

Then a word popped into Ben's head.

Bloodrite.

A word that was all his own. A word that seemed to justify each successive lick he pounded into Stew who, unnoticed by Ben, had stopped flailing, lost consciousness, and gone totally limp.

But Ben didn't stop until the pounding on the door got louder than the bestial grunts he was uttering from a place deep in his solar plexus.

"Everything okay in there?" shouted the voice. Distinctively Irish. Ben clocked it as one of the software testers who shared an office suite at the other end of the corridor.

"Call nine-one-one," said Ben, his voice so raspy it bordered on laryngitis.

"What did you say?"

Ben swung off of Stew, took a moment to find his balance, then lunged for the door. He threw the privacy bolt and pulled it open.

"Call nine-one-one," repeated Ben, sucking for air.

"What happened?"

"There's been an assault."

Then as Ben leaned into the jamb, the young software tester pushed at the door until he saw big Stew, fully prostrate on the floor, soaked in a sour-looking mix of sink-water and blood.

"Please call!" said Ben, exhausted, plunging out of the restroom and into the corridor where he crashed against the opposite wall. That's when Ben's knees turned to oatmeal. He slid all the way to the carpet, head in his hands, trembling.

8

BARELY SIXTY-EIGHT MINUTES had elapsed from the time Ben had crossed the threshold of his office that Monday to the moment the Burbank PD flooded into the building. As coffee breaks unfolded and tongues wagged, rumors swirled that a man had been brutally murdered in the third floor men's room and the killer was still at large within the property.

Ben excused Josie for the day without much explanation. Upon her return from McDonalds, Ben had asked her to leave in order to spare her from feeling as if she needed to care for him and his bloodied right hand. From Ben's perspective the battle had been his. He was the underdog, had been attacked, and he had won. He made his initial statement to the uniformed officers upon their arrival with the EMTs, before he was asked to wait until detectives arrived for formal questioning. With an officer posted outside his office door, Ben gladly agreed to wait inside. There, alone with his turbo-charged brain, he paced the spartan interior, never once sitting while he hatched an entire list of new worries.

He made no phone calls.

Foremost on Ben's list of concerns was Alex. He had promised her that the whole Stew Raymo issue would vanish and be gone from both their lives. He had broken that vow the day he let the 170 choose his fate, knocked on Stew Raymo's door and met the man's tawny wife, Pam. But what Alex didn't know might not hurt her. After all, Stew Raymo had showed up at *his* office. Stew Raymo had attacked *him*. The sympathy quotient alone should be enough to wash away Alex's feelings of betrayal. Or so Ben hoped. He hated having to calculate on his wife's emotional reactions. And it felt dishonest as hell.

Because you were dishonest, Ben.

Between worrying about everything from the effect of the attack on his home life to prayers that the case file on his first family's murder would be reopened, Ben's scattered brain surfed from his upcoming calendar—to taking stock of his life choices—to a critical rundown of his office's dated décor. He should remodel, or even move. While his thoughts ran on, Ben would have to peel a bloody Kleenex off his knuckles and replace it with another every five minutes. His hand throbbed and felt heavy, sending him into Josie's desk in search for bottles full of any over-the-counter anti-inflammatory pills. It was in the midst of this mission that Ben was visited by a pair of plainclothes Burbank PD detectives. They entered, noted Ben's injured hand, and took up separate positions opposite Josie's horseshoe-shaped desk. One asked Ben if he would mind if his answers were recorded.

"Of course not," said Ben, who glanced at his watch. It was 11:20, better than an hour that Ben had been waiting in his office.

"You got someplace to go?" asked Detective Grossman, who was in a brown, polyblend suit and shaped more like a bodybuilder-turned-couch-potato than what Ben imagined a modern detective should be. Grossman's partner was a younger, freckled fellow named Phillips who wore khakis, a blue-black threaded sport coat, and a tie that looked as if it had been picked out by his four-year-old. Phillips placed a pocket recorder on the table in front of Ben, and returned to his near-silent post, leaning back against the closed door.

"This your place of business?" asked Grossman.

"Yes," answered Ben.

"What do you do?"

"Safety consultant," said Ben.

"Business good?"

"No complaints."

"Better safe than sorry, huh?" added Phillips.

"Shut up," said Grossman, revealing an unguarded smile. "Bet he's heard 'em all. Isn't that right?"

"Yeah," confirmed Ben. "Heard 'em all."

"Can we talk about that statement you made?"

"I'm all yours."

"In your statement, you claim that while in the men's restroom, Mr. Raymo entered and attacked you."

"A few words passed between us before," corrected Ben, "But yeah. He seemed intent on—"

"Did he intend to attack?" asked Grossman. "Or did he attack you?"

"He attacked me," said Ben. "Just looked to me like that was his plan, so . . ."

"You didn't say anything that would make him attack you? Provoke him into . . ."

"What in the world could I say to make anyone assault me?"

"You tell me," said Grossman. "It's a men's room. Men are exposed. Stuff gets said."

"You get a lot of assaults in men's rooms?" asked Ben.

"You'd be surprised."

It made sense. Just about every bar on the planet had a men's room. A small space where men who had consumed overwhelming amounts to drink were suddenly in close proximity. Too close.

"I didn't say anything to provoke him," said Ben.

"So you'd be surprised if Mr. Raymo tells a different story?"

"I wouldn't be surprised at all," said Ben, his voice rising with a taste of incredulity.

"Said he came here to apologize to you. Is that correct?"

"I guess. Did he tell you what the apology was for? Or did he conveniently leave that part out?"

"I read your statement," said Grossman. "And for the record, however long ago it was, I'm sorry for your loss."

"Appreciated—"

"That being said," interrupted Phillips, "Mr. Raymo claims that, despite some of his misspent past, he doesn't recall having anything to do with your family—"

"To do with?" repeated Ben without much restraint. "He goddamn murdered them!"

"So says you."

"Why then would he apologize?"

"He claims that if he did so—he thought—you might refrain from harassing him."

"I'm harassing him?"

"First things first. Did the man apologize? Yes or no?"

"Yes. Here. In my office. But after that . . . after he said goodbye, he jumped me in the men's room—"

"What were you doing in the men's room?"

Ben shrugged at the question. As if to imply what men did in the restroom was obvious. Even if that wasn't why he had been in the restroom.

"Aside from having to pee?" said Ben. "I went in to gather my thoughts. The whole encounter really shook me."

"Why?"

"I dunno. Maybe cuz the guy who killed my wife and baby girls suddenly shows up at my office. Unexpected, uninvited. Out of the goddamn blue. Asks me to excuse my assistant, then lays out this dumb Alcoholics Anonymous apology."

"My old man was in AA," said Phillips. "Saved his life. Lotta cops, too, in the Program."

"Lotta cops," added Grossman.

"Not knocking it," defended Ben. "Just giving you my state of mind. That's what you were asking, right? My state of mind? Why I went into the men's room?"

"What's your assistant's name?" asked Grossman.

"Josie Jones."

"Where is she?"

"I sent her home."

"Contact information?"

Ben found a pen and a Post-it. He wrote down Josie's name and mobile phone number, then handed it to Detective Grossman.

"You know, we checked with LAPD and Culver," spoke Detective Phillips shifting his weight but keeping his back pressed against the door as if relieving a knot in his left trapezius. "This unsolved thing with your family? It's been closed a long, long time, right?"

Of course, it had been closed. Twelve years it had been closed. Ben felt flush.

"Yes, it's been closed. And I think maybe what happened here is a reason to reopen it? Do you?"

"What my partner wants to know is if you have any new evidence," said Grossman, "that points to Mr. Raymo."

"I have a recording," said Ben.

"A confession?" asked Grossman, inching forward in his chair.

"A deathbed confession," said Ben. "From some inmate who'd shared a cell with Stew Raymo."

"So," said Phillips, not hiding his naturally cynical predisposition, "some dying inmate gives you a name and . . ."

"And I did some checking through a private investigator."

"P.I. got a name?"

"Woody Bell."

"Contact info?"

Ben started scribbling Woody's contact information on another Post-it.

"Besides the recording, did the P.I. come up with anything incriminating Stew Raymo?" asked Grossman.

"No."

"No," repeated Phillips, directing his look to his partner, eyebrows raised.

"Mr. Keller," said Grossman. "It's not difficult for me to

understand your frustration or anger. How it can fester. We see it all the time. Marry that with this recording you received. Hire a detective. That detective does a little digging. Discovers Mr. Raymo has a criminal record."

"You saying it's not him?"

"Got proof that it was him?" asked Phillips.

"Not saying it is or isn't," added Grossman. "I'm saying I—we—the two of us here—understand where you're coming from. Your anger."

"Guy's an alcoholic," said Phillips. "Wanted to make an amends. Not necessarily an admission of guilt. AA guys will make amends to the mommy who abandoned them if it keeps 'em another day sober."

"Okay, fine," said Ben. "Stew Raymo made his amends. He left. I went to the men's room. He followed me. He attacked."

"Attacked *you*. But got the shit kicked out of *him*," said Phillips. "You a fighter? Good in a throw-down?"

Ben looked at his right hand. It appeared at last to have stopped bleeding. He could feel both detectives looking right through him. *Men could sense it*, thought Ben. *Men could sense when another man hadn't truly been in a fight.* And until today, Ben had gone zero for zero in lifetime fisticuffs. Truth was, Ben had been fortunate beyond description in his first real act of defensive violence.

"No," answered Ben. "Hadn't ever had to defend myself before today."

"Not even in grade school?" joked Phillips, feigning a fighter's stance. "No schoolyard shit?"

"Suppose I was lucky that way," said Ben.

Damn lucky.

Ben understood luck. Understood it to his bones. Who didn't? Be it good luck, bad luck, hard luck, dumb luck, or something as sticky sweet as a person being lucky in love. Luck was part of the human condition. Luck was part of life. Just don't ask a self-respecting actuary to pencil luck into any kind of risk equation. Statistically speaking, luck wasn't a factor in life. That's because luck couldn't truly be quantified. Throughout human history, mathematicians had tried and failed to make sense of luck, despite that they themselves as human beings knew in their calculating hearts that luck had to exist. That's because they had experienced luck. Or seen it with their own damn eyes.

For Ben, luck was like God. He knew God existed. He just couldn't prove it.

Grossman produced a small digital camera from his coat pocket. He switched on the power, then turned the small, one-and-a-half-by-two-inch screen toward Ben.

"Want you to look at these, okay?" said Grossman, handing Ben the camera. "You advance it with that button there."

As Ben took possession of the camera, he was immediately struck with little square images of Stew seated on the rear bumper of a Burbank Fire Department's paramedics' van. Closer shots revealed Stew's face riddled with contusions, scrapes, and swollen welts that nearly shut both the man's eyes. Stew's left ear was so bloody and mangled he looked as if he had been in a Dixie dogfight, hardly in one with a rookie like Ben Keller, the man who had never seen any action before.

The photos were a sharp contrast to the mere scrapes on Ben's right hand.

"I remember this one time," said Grossman. "Back when I was just in the Navy. San Diego. Bunch of us had been drinkin' and hell if I didn't get into it with a couple of jarries from Pendleton. One got me so mad I had to put him down. And I did. Wasn't until later, after my pals pulled me off the guy and I got sobered up that they told me the way it really was. Dude was down, but hell if I didn't stop. Kept beatin' the dude silly until three guys got me wrapped up and out the door."

Ben listened to Grossman's words. Heard the fullest intent of the speech. All the while, he kept moving forward and backward over the short set of eight digital photos. Soaking in the extent of the damage he had inflicted upon Stew. Something in Ben wanted to feel guilty. It was a conditioned response. After all, why else the speech from the detective?

Guilt be damned.

"It was self defense," said Ben.

"Maybe," said Grossman. "Maybe he started it like you say. But there's a line, you know. Because I pop you one in the mouth don't necessarily give you the right to back up over me with your car, know what I mean?"

There was a soft knock. Phillips turned and cracked the door wide enough to receive a single faxed page. Ben's eyes twisted to the document, quickly zeroing in on the small box in the lower right corner, containing a scribbled signature.

"That a warrant?" asked Ben, his voice lowered an octave.

"Part of a set. Goes with the signed complaint from Stew Raymo," said Grossman, unfolding another piece of paper for Ben's perusal.

Ben gave the documents a cursory examination, lingering only on the obsessively neat signature at the bottom of the warrant. The judge's name was Juan Albert Lemus. Ben free-associated a memory of a childhood pal named Juan Albert. But was his surname Lemus or Leonidas? His mind already muddy with the nature of his luck, Ben couldn't recollect.

Good luck could be defined as the moment Stew's foot slipped on the bathroom floor. Otherwise, that digital camera might have been rich with photos of a badly beaten Ben—or worse.

Bad luck could be characterized as the moment Ben was asked to stand and face the wall in order to be fitted with a pair of handcuffs.

And if handcuffs were bad luck, what kind of luck was it when your beautiful wife and kids were murdered?

Shit luck.

Miranda rights were half-whispered into Ben's right ear by Detective Grossman as Ben was efficiently escorted to the stairwell by two more uniformed officers. Phillips led the way, plunging the tight quintet down three flights to the garage where a pair of radio units was waiting to deliver Ben to the Burbank PD for booking. The official charge was aggravated assault and battery. Strangely, Ben wondered if his mug shot would be an improvement over the screwed-up expression captured on his California drivers license. And would it reflect badly on his case if he were photographed with a shit-assed grin, proud as hell that he pounded the prick who murdered Sara and the twins?

A wide shaft of dusty light flooded into the crowded underground parking lot. The rear door of the nearest black-and-white unit was opened for Ben. He felt like Lee Harvey Oswald waiting for Jack Ruby—in the guise of Stew Raymo—to slip through the ranks, stick a revolver between his ribs, and pull the trigger.

"Watch your head," said Grossman, placing his hand atop Ben's skull to guide him safely into the backseat.

"Wait a minute!" echoed a voice from the street. A shadow appeared, large and limping, descending the ramp, followed by the smaller shadows of two EMTs.

Stew appeared in a bloody dress shirt. He was bandaged, one side of his face packed and strapped with a wad of instant ice packs.

"Said wait!" slurred Stew, trying to shout through his inflamed lips.

Grossman shifted in front of Ben, his hand reaching back to touch the butt of the pistol snugly holstered inside his waistband.

"Stay right there, Mr. Raymo," barked Phillips. "Fight's over."

Stew kept his distance at thirty feet, arms held wide in surrender.

"Wanna drop the charges," said Stew.

"'Scuse me?" said Phillips.

"Don't wanna press charges," repeated Stew. "But I got a condition."

"He on anything?" Phillips pointed to the EMTs for an answer.

The chief paramedic shook his head.

"Mr. Raymo, we got your complaint. We got us a warrant. Let us please do our job."

"Begging your pardon," pleaded Stew. "Just let the man hear me then you can decide."

Grossman reached out and touched Phillips' shoulder.

"Okay," said Phillips. "But the fight's over. You can stay right there."

"Just as long as he can hear me," said Stew. "Can you hear me, Ben?"

"What do you want?" said Ben, somewhat emboldened inside the safety of the police vehicle.

"Right here," said Stew. "In front of everybody. I'm apologizing like I did when nobody was around. Making my amends. Taking care of my side the street."

"Okay . . ." said Ben, overcome by déjà vu. It wasn't the scene in his office all over again. There was something else to it that he couldn't place.

"Accept my apology and I'll tear up the complaint."

Grossman heard Ben suck in a lung-full of air, hold it, then exhale. He turned to Ben.

"Strongly suggest you say yes to this," said Grossman. "Save all of us a lot of paperwork. And save you some uncomfortable chitchat with your wife, knowhatImean?"

"I'm supposed to forgive him for killing my wife and kids?"

"I'm waiting, Benjy-man," said Stew, louder, and as if were a time clock ticking on the offer.

"Not forgive," continued Grossman's whisper to Ben. "Accept the apology then stay the fuck away from him for as long as you live."

Pressure built inside Ben's skull. He squeezed his eyes shut and in a heartbeat, he was back in the men's room prepared to vomit all over again.

"He apologized," whispered Grossman. "Just say you accept."

"Don't you see what he's doing?" asked Ben.

"Versus what he can do to you if you don't accept?"

"Last chance," said Stew. "I'm saying sorry. And I got witnesses—"

"Alright," shouted Ben. "Alright . . . I accept."

"Hallelujah," said Stew. "And you all heard it. I made the amends. And he accepted."

"You can leave now," said Phillips, still wary of Stew

and his posture. This whole business made the detective very uncomfortable.

"And you can tear up my complaint, okay?" reminded Stew.

"We'll do that," said Phillips.

Stew nodded with his chin and before pivoting back up the ramp, tilted his head upward in order to give Ben one last look through his almost-shuttered eyes. The gaze chilled Ben. Then it was over. Stew was gone. And Ben felt a key working the lock of his handcuffs.

"That's it?" asked Ben.

"No complaint, no charge," said Grossman. "Meant what I said, too. If I was you I'd keep my distance from that dude."

"What if I can't? What if he comes for me again?"

"You get into it with him again?" Grossman smirked and gave Ben a once-over. A mock assessment that acknowledged that whatever luck Ben had stumbled upon in the men's room wasn't likely to materialize again. At least not when it counted.

"If the shit hits the fan?" finished Phillips. "Just make sure it doesn't happen in Burbank."

"Lydia. It's me . . . Ben. I was just . . . He knows. He knows about me and was here. The sonofabitch showed up at my office . . ."

Gonzo replayed the message Ben left on her cell phone. While she tried to measure the level of panic in his voice, she unconsciously wiped the thin veil of sweat that had broken out on her forehead, leaving a skid mark of chestnut colored foundation on her white linen sleeve.

"Crap," muttered Gonzo, loud enough to draw glances from a few of the thirty or so other Federal Air Marshal candidates.

The disparate gathering of Southland cops was spread out across the mint-painted fourth-floor lobby of the Federal Transportation Safety offices in El Segundo. They were on a break from evaluation exams offered to a new crop of potential part-time air marshals. It was phase one of an experimental program to train cops in the art of defending against terrorist attacks at 36,000 feet. In exchange, the airlines would provide their peace-officers-in-the-sky with a stipend and two free round-trip tickets to any destination to where a cop was willing to carry a gun.

Exhausted from listening to stories of every other school mom's family holiday in paradise and concerned that young Travis would feel left out if he, too, didn't return from school breaks with stories of Cabo or Sun Valley or Maui, Gonzo had set on a mission to show her boy the world. At first glance, the air marshal program seemed like a tidy fit for Gonzo and her boy. She merely needed to get past the initial evaluations. But now Ben was leaving creepy, panicked voicemails on her cell phone.

She dialed Ben's mobile phone and left what she hoped was a calming voicemail. Then she called his office, got a recording, and left a second message. With five minutes to go before she had to return to the classroom, Gonzo chose to make a quick dial to the Burbank Police Department in lieu of stepping outside for a cigarette. Though she knew a couple of guys on the BPD gang suppression detail, she chose to go the official route instead. She would dial the main number, identify herself as an LAPD detective checking on a disturbing voicemail left by a Simi Valley neighbor, and probably get pinballed from desk-to-desk until she either got some real intel or convinced somebody to send a unit over Ben's office.

What Gonzo got in return was a speedy transfer to the patrol desk and the watch sergeant who was quick to pepper her with questions.

What is your relationship with Ben Keller?

Can you tell us if Ben Keller has a history of violence?

Do you know anything about a crime involving his family?

What is the nature of his relationship with a Mr. Stewart Raymo?

Gonzo politely answered the questions as quickly as she could, trying to be succinct, and sneaking in a question of her own when she could. But before she could receive any quantifiable answers, she saw her competitors shuffling from the lobby toward the classroom.

"Sorry, but I have to go," apologized Gonzo. "I really can't talk anymore. By the way. You haven't answered a single one of my questions."

"What would you like to know?" snipped the watch sergeant.

"Is Mr. Keller okay?"

"As far as I know, yes. It's Mr. Raymo who may have been seriously injured."

"How seriously?" asked Gonzo, walking crisply toward the classroom with none of her classmates in sight.

"Unknown."

"Can I call back?"

"You're welcome to. My name is Sergeant Dowd. D-O-W-D."

"Thanks."

Gonzo flipped her cell phone shut, rammed it into her pocket, then shoved the door to the classroom open. As if synchronized to a microsecond, every head in the room twisted to stare at her. This ballet included the redheaded instructor, a forty-year-old, pixie-like dynamo who, in Gonzo's initial appraisal, wasn't stout enough to pass the Los Angeles Police Academy's simple grip-strength test. She had also pegged the woman as an L.I.D., or Lesbian In Denial.

"Keeping to the schedule is important for Federal Air Marshals," said the instructor without missing a blink. "The TSA workers, the flight attendants and crew need to know to the minute when you are coming and going in order to maintain the level of security to which we all aspire."

"I'm sorry—"

"So in the spirit of evaluation," interrupted the instructor, followed by a spunky cock of the head, "let's accept that you're not Air Marshal material and call it a date, okay?"

Gonzo was shaken. But not so bad that she couldn't put on an air of indifference. She stood in the doorway, nodding as if she had expected as much.

"Okay," said Gonzo. "I'd like to tell you where to shove your evaluation. But even if I did, you're probably so uptight you couldn't find it with a flashlight and a magnifying glass."

The rest of the candidates broke out in laughter. After all, they were cops and practiced at sizing people up. Gonzo may have been out. But as far as the students were concerned, the instructor would never be in.

Women, Gonzo griped to herself. They could talk until they were hoarse about issues like sexual discrimination. Glass ceilings. Equal rights and equal pay. At the end of day, though, Gonzo couldn't recall a single woman in the ranks that wasn't dangerously competitive or flat-out venal to her working sisters. In Gonzo's not-so-clinical experience, the truth was the truth. Women didn't help other women. At least not those they considered a threat to their personal power.

So why the hell was Gonzo wrestling with calling Alex? Was it her loyalty to Ben? A man she thought she trusted? Or her fear that Alex might follow through with her threat to make Gonzo's life at Simi Canyons miserable if she failed to inform on Ben? As she trudged out of the FTS offices, she kept flipping her mobile phone open then closed. Daring herself to dial. She was angry, yes. She was also practical. Travis loved Simi Canyons School. He loved his classmates and sometimes asked his mommy to buy a bigger house so all his friends and teachers could move in with them.

Gonzo slid on a pair of Ray Ban Aviators as she stepped into the sunlight. When she flipped open her cell phone again, she saw the photo saved on the tiny screen as wallpaper. There was her gap-toothed boy, joyously smiling back at the camera. His world was hers and vice versa. And damned if she wouldn't do everything within her womanly power to protect it.

Still, Gonzo flip-flopped until she was behind the wheel of that Valley Checkered Cab she had been driving for over a month now. The vehicle was, in Gonzo's eyes, on permanent loan from the LAPD while her Chevy Suburban was technically in the repair shop. "Technically" meant the SUV would be in her garage, resting from the normal wear and tear of commuting to Van Nuys until the motor-pool sergeant caught on that Gonzo was using the cab for her own personal use. Seven miles from El Segundo, Gonzo was northbound on the 405 Freeway and cresting the pass that split the Los Angeles city basin from the San Fernando Valley. This is where the area codes changed, and come summertime, temperatures were always elevated. Gonzo gripped the wheel of the cab with her left hand and scrolled her cell phone's memory for Alex's number. With a press of her thumb on the DIAL button, she made a choice that would most certainly screw over her friend, Ben Keller. But what could possibly happen? wondered Gonzo. A little extra marital discord? Maybe a three-month stint in couple's therapy? She was rationalizing to make herself feel better and she knew it. But this was about her little boy. And Travis was her sun and her moon.

"Hello, Alex? It's Lydia Gonzalez. How are you today?"

Strange. At that precise, fixed moment in time—while traffic was slowing—and Alex and Gonzo were engaged in full-tilt school chatter—if Gonzo had glanced out the driver's window a mere thirty degrees to her left, she would have seen Ben, alone and shell-shocked in his car, southbound on the same freeway. Not that she could have noticed. She was traveling forty-five miles per hour while Ben was pushing seventy in the opposite direction. The measure of time was barely more than a blink of the eye. And Ben's silver Volvo didn't exactly stick out in the constant flow of L.A. traffic.

But if she had looked—if Gonzo had clocked Ben as they passed each other—would she have altered the tenor of her dialogue? Would she have told?

"Listen, Alex . . ." said Gonzo, switching conversational gears. "Do you recall our talk? You know, the one where I promised to inform you of Ben's . . ."

"I remember," said Alex.

How Ben began looking for a church and ended up in a bar was beyond any rational explanation. It simply was.

"Another?" asked the bartender.

Ben gestured. And a fresh Cadillac margarita was assembled, shaken, and poured over a six-inch tall tumbler full of ice.

"On the tab?" asked the bartender.

Ben nodded, made no eye contact, all the time keeping his gaze fixed on the drink.

After the handcuffs had been removed and the police vacated his Burbank office building, it was barely past noon. The day was still young. But what to do? Ben couldn't imagine returning to work. Josie had been excused, and understandably, Ben's ability to concentrate on anything more complicated than putting one foot in front of the other was all but shattered. When he had climbed in behind the wheel of his car, he started shaking so violently that he feared operating the vehicle would lead to certain catastrophe.

So Ben decided to walk off his case of the shakes. It was on the walk down 2nd Avenue that he happened upon a neighborhood house of worship. An Episcopal church. Ben assumed the doors would be open. And inside he might find a man of God. Someone kind and wise. With a good ear and welcome advice. Yet there was something uncomfortable about entering a strange sanctuary no matter how inviting the unlocked door might seem. This is when Ben remembered The Calvary Christ Church of Santa Monica. Oh Lord, how he and Sara loved the room the moment they stepped through the sanctuary doors. It was a living antique from old California, styled in oil-rubbed floors made from heavy, foot-wide planks. The twenty rows of pews were a deep brownish red, quarter-sawn oak polished clean of human fingerprints. And the ceiling was open beamed, carved to appear like the hull of Noah's Ark.

In five month's time, Ben and Sara had been married at Calvary Christ Church before God and some fifty of their closest friends and family. Though the church was a non-denominational Christian church, young Ben and Sara were still required to attend some premarital counseling with the Old Sage of a minister they had asked to perform the ceremony. As confessed agnostics, the couple entered the three two-hour sessions with equal amounts of mirth and cynicism. But somewhere within the course of saying "I do," Sara's quick and unplanned pregnancy, and the births of twin baby girls, both Ben and Sara were drawn back to the same Calvary Christ Church and the same Old Sage pastor with his soft words and plainspoken morality. The twins were baptized in the very same sanctuary where their parents had promised to love and cherish each other through whatever unkindness life could possibly invent. These slights of nature were the sort that went unimagined by young couples experiencing love and success and the early joys that come with two beautiful babies.

Though Ben had clearly endured, and over time, conveniently learned places he could stuff or hide his pain, he hadn't forgotten. Nor had he, in the purely therapeutic sense, actually moved on. As Ben set his car on a heading for Santa Monica and the old Calvary Christ Church, he came to wonder what to call the life he had led since his family's destruction. A second chapter? A non-Catholic kind of purgatory? A lie?

Suddenly, only one hope existed within Ben. It was the hope of finding his way back to the old church and for just a moment or two, sitting silently in one of those perfect pews. Once there, he would pray and he would listen for answers from either that Old Sage . . .or God.

Instead, the only answers Ben had found were from either the bartender or at the bottom of another glass of lime, triple sec, and Jose Cuervo Gold.

Ben had spent nearly an hour driving around the Santa Monica neighborhood in search of the old church. Certain that he had remembered the location, he turned a corner and found a three-storied apartment building lathered in pinkish stucco. From there, Ben drove in a series of right turns, block after block, in an ever-increasing circle in hope of stumbling upon the familiar steeple. He eventually found himself parked in front of a different address, yet equally well known to him.

The Sham Rock.

The restaurant/bar—Ben's former pride and joy—had been painted over and reupholstered to clearly reflect some Irish-American's fantasy of the modern Dublin sports bar. What wasn't slathered clover green or tan or white, or tuck-and-rolled in cream or red Naugahyde, was worn and dinged from the older days of Prague '88. And the walls, once hand-aged to perfection and adorned with magnificent old bullfighting prints, were mounted with either flat-panel or projection TV screens. In the odd spaces in between were placards advertising the virtues of mixing Guinness with everything—from golfing to hurling to salmon-fishing to Gaelic football.

The only thing that hadn't changed was the bar top. Though not nearly as lustrously preserved as when Ben was operating behind it, the bar remained its original wooden self. Deep-grained with a rolled edge, a comfortable perch for a man to rest arms weary from lifting too many pints.

"Yeah, I remember that church," said the bartender, who was nearly too thin and tall for description. Ben guessed his waist size to be somewhere short of twenty-eight. A hard fit to find for a man six-foot-six.

"Like somewhere around 24th Street and Broadway, right?" he continued. "Yeah, yeah. All white on the outside, kinda woody inside? Cavalry something?"

"Calvary," corrected Ben. "Calvary Christ Church."

"Think they moved someplace closer to Venice," said the bartender. "Yeah, yeah. Bulldozed it and put up, like, an apartment building, right?"

"How long?"

"Dunno. Maybe eight, nine years ago. More?"

"So awhile ago," said Ben, not that it mattered much anymore. The church was gone forever.

"By more, I meant Cadillac? You're looking low."

"Go Rob."

"Name's Bob," said the bartender. "No worries, though. Rob, Bob, Blob, Slob. All of 'em work for me."

It was nearly three in the afternoon. Both the bar and restaurant were empty but for Ben and Bob, who was already mixing the liquor. The lunch rush—or whatever passed for a lunch rush at that odd location—had long since passed. Not a single afternoon alcoholic was in sight.

Bob seemed damned glad to have somebody to talk to. Ben wasn't so sure that he himself was. But he still tried.

"How's business?"

"Between you, me, and the rats the Health Department don't know about?" said Bob. "Pretty damn crappy."

"Your place?"

"Ten bucks an hour. That's my real name. You can call me that, too."

"Been open how long? Three, four months?"

"A year. Just took down the grand opening sign last week when they figured all the local Irish were already in on the joke."

"Good joke. Funny."

"Tell me about it. Before it was The Sham Rock, it was this black-satin club called Therapy. Velvet Rope. Bouncers at the door. But two weeks in. Forget it. Went bust-ola."

Bob shook Ben's cocktail and poured.

"Before that," continued Bob. "Was a place called Curtains. You can guess what that décor was like. Lemme see. Before that it was some kinda Russian nightclub. Forget the frickin' name, but they had this kinda kitschy house band I will never forget. Khazak Pop. Real hottie behind the mic, too. She looked Russian but I ran into her one day at Whole Foods and found out she was just Polish. Think her name was Carolina."

"You must live close."

"My whole life. Three blocks east, one block south. I walk to work."

"Four-block commute. Sounds like an L.A. fantasy."

"Lemme see. Before it was a Russian joint, I get a little fogged in. Think it was . . . yeah, yeah . . . fancy fine dining, Wolfgang-Puck-wannabe-sushi kinda blah, blah. Never even came in for a drink. That's when double-bar whammies cost fourteen bucks . . . before they cost fourteen bucks, know what I'm sayin'?"

Ben remembered well. When he began his bar business, he fought to keep the basic urban double-shot mixer at seven dollars. It was the local Johnny Walker rep who convinced Ben that unless he charged ridiculous prices on his call drinks, there would always be an open stool at his establishment. Bargain prices would attract only drunks and tourists. That and the top-shelf liquor reps wouldn't sell him their most posh bottles unless Ben charged well into the double digits.

The Johnny Walker rep was right. The more Ben edged up his prices, the deeper the crowds grew, with everyone running tabs or tossing hundred-dollar bills across the bar. So much cash flowed through his till that Ben thought it was wiser to buy a safe and install it in his Culver City home.

Whoops, thought Ben. *Brain fart.*

An error in foresight that eventually cost his wife and daughters their precious lives. Not that Ben could have actually foreseen the oncoming tragedy. Still, nothing prevented him from assigning himself more blame. The alcohol, in fact, promoted negative thinking. The effects of which had already lassoed Ben. The liquor was beginning to retool his gray matter—exactly what Ben had in mind.

"Only time I can remember this address drawing any kind of a crowd?" recounted Bob. "Back when it was a joint called Prague '88."

As Ben politely nodded over his drink, Bob's wispy goatee, possibly the only hair on the man's body, reformed around a wide, memory-stuffed grin.

"Actually, got truly laid for the first time there. After I met some banker slut. I was seventeen."

"Seventeen?" asked Ben.

"Okay. Sixteen. I was tall for my age and was already losing my hair. Only upside was, with the right pair of glasses? I looked like twenty-five. Never got ID'd. And you think I told her? Hell no. She was drunk and I had such a boner in my pants. She took me right into the ladies' restroom and like wham, man. My cherry was so fuckin' popped."

"Things you never knew," said Ben, amused.

"Like I saw that, comin', right?"

Bob shook his head, not really believing his own memory. The grin, seemingly unshakable from his face.

"Well, here's to your first time."

Ben raised his glass in a toast, then gulped back a good twenty-five percent of his cocktail, hoping to temporarily purge himself of all his mental data. He would have preferred not discussing his former restaurant.

Bob changed the subject for him.

"What happened?" Bob was pointing to his own right knuckles, hairless and unscraped.

The skin on Ben's right hand had clotted into a scabby mess, looking like that of a mechanic who had lost an argument with a radiator fan.

"Suppose I should say something clichéd," said Ben. "Like, 'You should see the other guy.'"

"Would only be clichéd if it were true."

Ben sucked back the rest of his margarita and pushed his empty glass forward.

"Go Bob."

"Seriously."

"Go Bob." Now, Ben raised his empty glass and shook the ice in it from side to side.

"Nope. You're already over the limit."

"Unsafe to drive," said Ben, laughing, tickled by his newfound inebriation.

"Seriously, dude."

"I'll call a cab."

"Just slow down, tell me a few stories, then maybe I'll uncork a bottle."

"How's this?" negotiated Ben, hearing a wee slur in his voice. "I'll tell you all about the other guy if you keep the bar open."

"Then you'll take a cab."

"Course I'll take a cab. Wouldn't be safe if I didn't take a cab."

"Safety first," quipped Bob without a clue.

"My middle name," joked Ben.

"Cadillac?"

"Go Bob."

Like a mother worrying over her preadolescent son, Alex stared over Ben as he slept. It was almost 6:00 A.M. Daylight was just beginning to overtake the dark and filter through the shutters. And despite the early hour, Alex was already showered and dressed with her makeup expertly applied for the day. She had been unable to return to sleep after being disturbed at nearly two in morning by Ben's ruckus in the kitchen. She lay in bed for some time, awake, at first planning to feign sleep if Ben proved brave enough to enter their bed. But while she rolled to the side and gathered under the covers, she found herself listening to a constant clatter from the kitchen. If she could hear it, she worried, so would one of her girls. Then came the charred odor of burning raisin toast.

Damn it.

And even more to the point.

Damn him!

Alex found Ben downstairs, passed out on the sofa she had rearranged to fit underneath the big kitchen window. He was splayed across it, shirt half-exposing his stomach, pants unbuckled, with one shoe on and the other who knows where? He also stunk of booze. Her initial instinct was to leave him there. Her second instinct was to remove the water pitcher from the refrigerator and tilt the entire half gallon onto his lying face. That would surely cause a reaction. Though since she couldn't gauge exactly what kind, or how violent his response, she chose to save their inevitable altercation until after Ben had sobered up—even if meant he would be at the nadir of his imminent hangover.

Always thinking of the girls first, and not caring for any of the young trio to discover Ben in his inebriated state, Alex decided to gently wake Ben and encourage him to quietly sleep it off upstairs.

"Ben?" she said quietly. "Ben? Come on. Let's get you to bed."

When neither nudging nor shaking him proved successful, Alex resorted to a trick she had seen her mother use on her oft drunken father. She placed one hand over his mouth and used the other to pinch his nose. This created an involuntary breathing spasm. Ben's eyes popped open wide as saucers and his lungs gasped for air as if he had been held under water for thirty seconds, not for the measly four Alex had applied gentle pressure.

"What was that . . ." said Ben.

"Let's get upstairs, Ben. Don't want the girls to see you like this."

"Yeah, right . . ." Ben said, not sounding the least bit sauced.

"Musta closed my eyes when . . . Sorry."

With that, Ben stood and gripped Alex's hand and pulled her to him.

"Bad timing," said Alex.

"Just wanted to say I love you, Sara."

Ben clutched Alex's head, kissed her forehead, and walked with one sneaker on, one sneaker off, out of the kitchen and made a sharp left turn up the stairs.

Sara?

Drunk or not, Ben's utterance made Alex's sense of betrayal feel nearly complete. She didn't follow him upstairs. Instead she paced the kitchen for five minutes, rummaged in the downstairs bathroom for a double dose of Excedrin, and chased the caplets with some Sunny D and the dry remnants of Ben's burnt raisin toast.

In those last hours before daylight, Alex made lunches, brewed coffee, weighed her marital options, plotted and replotted how and when she would eventually lock horns with Ben. But mostly observed and listened to the strange conversation that was produced from her sleeping husband's dreams.

"Go Stew," was what Ben kept saying between fits and mumblings. Most of his words were indecipherable. But every so often, words would find articulation with both emphasis and subtext.

"Props," said Ben. "S'all just props. After Sara I mean..."

"Move on ... move on, *move on!* We've *all* moved on and on and on. But where we goin', huh? Where's it all supposed to lead ..."

"Wife's a hottie. Not my wife. *Your* wife. Hot hot hot hottie ..."

"Ssshhhh. Alex don't know about Sara and Sara sure as shit don't know about Alex. I mean, really Stew. How the hell could she? Right? Right? I am right!"

After that, Ben uttered a laugh so creepy, from a place so unholy, deep in his solar plexus, that it exhausted the very last lick of Alex's curiosity. She unfolded herself from the chenille-covered chair and in a final tender act, quietly closed every shutter in the room before disappearing into the walk-in closet.

All the while, Ben kept right on dreaming.

And inside the dream nothing had really changed since his fifth Cadillac margarita. Not the time or the location or the characters. It was just Ben and Bob at the bar inside The Sham Rock. Only the roles are reversed. Ben pours while Bob consumes tumblers of liquor, paying with handfuls of crumpled cash. The conversation itself is abundantly genial, bordering on familiar. It's as if Ben is having a chat with a long-lost pal. An old buddy who somewhere between shakers of lime juice, Triple Sec, and Jose Cuervo, morphs into a youngish Stew Raymo.

"What's with the margaritas?" asks Stew. "How 'bout one of those Ice Breakers?"

"Sorry," said Ben. "Don't serve 'em anymore. Not since it was Prague '88. And that was, jeez, how many restaurants ago?"

"Gimme a Jack and Coke, then."

"Go Stew," smiles Ben, mixing a quick cocktail for his friend then pouring the Cadillac margarita for himself. Tumbler, rocks, no salt.

"You thinkin' of drivin' home, pal?" asks Stew.

"Nope. You're calling me a cab."

"That's because driving wouldn't be safe."

As if cued, each man points his index finger at the other and says in comic unison: "Safety first!"

There follows a brief pause, after which both men explode into bellows of laughter. When it fades . . .

"Okay, okay. If I call you a cab then you call me a cab," says Stew.

"How's this? I'll call us both a cab."

"Drink to that."

And they do. It's presently as collegial as a frat beer-bonging race. Ben and Stew gulping their liquor until their glasses are dry, then slamming their tumblers on the bar.

"Go Ben."

"Go Stew."

More laughter follows. Then as Ben shakes up fresh margaritas with his left and pours Stew a Jack and Coke with his right . . .

"Hey. Where'd Bob go?" asks Stew.

"Best friends come, best friends go," says Ben.

"You and Bob?"

"Me and Sara."

"That's right," says Stew, revealing a hint of sorrow. "Man needs a best friend."

"Alex says if I want a best friend that I should get a dog."

"So why don't you?"

"Allergies."

"Cats, too?"

"Hate cats. You?"

"Hate everybody."

"Well, that says it all, huh?"

Stew raises his drink in a toast. Ben clinks glass with him. But this time, there are no laughs. There is no competition for either man to be first to the bottom of his glass.

"I have an idea," says Stew. "I could be your best friend. You could talk to me."

"Naw. You've got Pam," says Ben.

"Sure I do. But you 'n' me. We got history."

"We do go back a ways, don't we?"

"Right here," says Stew, his arms held out wide. "It all started right here."

"Was the Ice Breaker," says Ben. "I did that, didn't I?"

"Shoulda never served me that drink."

"You were sick all the way back then, huh?"

"Know what? You should come to a meeting with me."

"Alcoholics Anonymous?"

"V.A.," says Stew. "Victims Anonymous."

"You're kidding me. There's a twelve-step program for victims?"

"Hey. If they got a twelve-step program for Trekkies. They got a twelve-step program for you, friend."

"I'm not a victim," insists Ben, drink down, both arms braced against the bar and leaning.

"Sure you're not," winks Stew.

"I'm absolutely not," insists Ben.

"Get a good look at yourself lately?" grins Stew. "Makes me wonder what happened to the other guy."

Ben raises his right hand to examine his scraped fist, only to find a young man's skin stretched over a neat row of pink knuckles. Next, he touches his face and gets no feedback from a single cranial nerve. His fingertips, though, report to his brain stem that he's touching some kind of silicon mask—the kind employed by Hollywood makeup wizards. His nose feels crooked and these bloody, crusty welts have sprouted around his eye. Lastly, his fingers find his gums, discovering teeth so loose that a simple sneeze would send them to the floor like marbles spilling from a broken jar.

And when Ben wheels to check his reflection in the mirror behind the shelves of liquor bottles, he screams at what he sees.

Ben awoke from his nightmare to a bedroom cast in mostly grays. Following the relief that comes with the realization that the bad dream was just that—a bad dream—Ben lay in bed and stared at the ceiling until his eyes resumed their ability to focus. Tiny shafts of sunlight filtered through cracks in the shutters. Each one was closed. *Unusual*, thought Ben. *Alex hated when the shutters were closed.* She claimed it made the room feel claustrophobic. In fact the only time the shutters were ever shut was when Alex figured Ben needed the sleep.

He could easily have remained still and returned to the dream. Not necessarily by sleeping. But analytically. That idea was erased the moment Ben moved his neck muscles in order to get a look at the clock on his nightstand. Whatever time it was, Ben didn't care a whit after the chain reaction of pain that started at his left ear and radiated all the way down to his kneecaps. It was as if every joint in his body had turned cripplingly arthritic overnight. And his muscles, too. They ached from the seeming gallons of poison Ben had poured into himself the day and night before.

"Christ," Ben moaned, startling himself.

Ben was unaccustomed to speaking aloud when there was nobody to hear but himself. He swung his legs over the edge of the bed and forced himself upright. *Any moment now*, he thought. First, the pain would rush to his skull. And after, he would surely feel the need to puke. It would prove the perfect one-two punch, finishing with a haymaker of a hangover. And though it had been a good long while since Ben had punished himself so—years, in fact—the memory of what to expect remained as intact as his own name.

So he waited.

Surely, the pain in his skull was there. Yet it wasn't anything compared to the soreness inside his body. Nor did the urge to puke come readily. That's when Ben took some account of the day before. After he had purged himself completely in the men's room at his office, he couldn't recall eating anything whatsoever. Had he been drinking on an empty stomach? Usually, at such a moment Ben's mind would instantly summon scores of esoteric safety trivia. Presently, the subject was: *The Dangers of Drinking Too Much Alcohol;* sub-header: *Empty Stomach.* But the best Ben could muster were snippets of some Swedish study . . . something about blood alcohol levels being inhibited by proteins, fats, and dense carbohydrates.

"Blah blah blah . . ." said Ben to himself as if bored by his own obsessive recall.

He stood slowly, allowing for the aching twinges to shift within him, re-radiate and suggest that a return to a horizontal position might prove more comfortable. Ben ignored his body's better judgment, instead choosing to spy on what kind of day it was by peeling open one of the wooden louvers that covered the window above his bed. Through his protective squint, Ben registered a sunny, cloudless sky. Tilting his view downward, he caught a glimpse of the neighborhood mail carrier returning to the sidewalk via the driveway.

"What the hell to do," Ben said to himself, no more consigned to his next move than he had been the day before. Before turning away from the window, something made him look once more. And yes, just as his instinct had subconsciously confirmed only a split second earlier, Ben spotted his Volvo parked right next to Alex's car.

"Jesus, no," said Ben. "No no no no no . . ."

Ben thought back to yesterday morning. As if in fast-forward, he ran through everything until he was seated at the bar in The Sham Rock, chitter-chatting with Bob, ordering another shaker of margaritas and . . . blank. But for the lousy, ugly dream, every scintilla of memory, every etch, every sound, every thought, from the last "Go Bob" up to the second Ben awoke only moments ago . . . all of it appeared to have been erased.

Blackout.

He spun and looked at the clock. 11:52 A.M. Despite the clanging of thunder beneath his skullcap, Ben did the third grade math. Nineteen hours in the dark. Nineteen hours unsupported by any recollection. Sure, he had slept off some of it. But not all of it. Worst of all, he had driven drunk. Not just the legal definition of driving while intoxicated. That number was .08 percent of blood alcohol. As Ben stood at the bedroom window, his kidneys continuing to filter the poison in his veins, his bet was that he was still in violation. That meant at the time he had driven, whenever the hell that was, he was well beyond the law. Beyond inebriated.

Shit-faced for sure.

The thought of having driven so awfully drunk just added to the queasiness that resonated from his core.

"Dumb fuck," Ben said.

What followed, though, was that oh-so-human feeling of relief after having dodged a deadly bullet. Luck had been, again, on his side.

Ben forced himself to shower, shave, then dress, trying impossibly to organize his thoughts, let alone the next hour of his life. Working wasn't an option with his brain on the back burner, so he would have to call Josie and make up another lame excuse for pushing meetings or canceling another factory walk-though. Most importantly, he had to find Alex and start his laundry list of mea culpas. Surely, she had seen him the night before, smelled him, possibly assisted him without his even remembering a lick of it. But Alex certainly wouldn't forget. Not for a long time. If there was a marital doghouse, Ben had hammered his own out of splintered wood and furnished it with barbed wire and thorns.

First things first. He needed food to protect his stomach lining from the fistful of Excedrin he desperately needed to wash back with a gallon of electrolyte-loaded Gatorade. Soon, the aches in his joints would marginally subside, the fuzz in his brain would evaporate, and options would appear.

Ben's plans lasted as long as it took for him to descend to the first landing above the front-door entry. There, standing at the bottom of the stairs was Alex, hair pulled back under a white fleece cap. She held a matching down parka. At her feet were two suitcases and a stuffed backpack. For a queasy moment, neither knew what to say.

"You going somewhere?" croaked Ben, before rolling his eyes at the stupidity of his assumption. "Or maybe I should ask if I'm going somewhere?"

"Van Gores just bought a place up in Mammoth. Invited us up for the weekend. Thought it would be a good idea to take the girls after school."

"It's Tuesday," said Ben.

"They'll bring their homework."

Ben squeezed the bridge of his nose. As if that could possibly quell the pain under his dome.

"I owe you an apology," began Ben.

"Please. I really can't right now."

"My cell phone got doused and I couldn't call —"

"Ben. I have something to say, so—"

"I don't know what you saw last night . . . or what I said. Just want you to know that I understand what a mistake I made—"

"Please!" said Alex, her voice as sharp as a fresh axe. "I've been rehearsing this speech I've had. Over and over, Ben, okay? I really need to say this, so please . . ."

Ben answered by holding his hands up in surrender and seating himself on the landing. He rested his bare feet on the steps, his elbows on his knees, and cradled his head in his hands.

Alex took a deep breath, but didn't move her feet from first position. Once a ballet dancer, always a ballet dancer, thought Ben, who used to marvel at how long Alex could stand, stock still, heels together, toes at ten and two o'clock. Her style was always about having more patience and steely resolve than just about anybody else.

"You broke a promise, Ben. You broke the promise that you wouldn't pursue this . . . this . . . sick agenda with this crazy man who you think did something—"

"I don't think, Alex. I know."

"Ben, please."

"He came to me, Alex, okay? My office! Okay?"

"How'd he find you?" she said, voice full of rancor.

"Don't judge me," said Ben. "You don't have a goddamn clue what I've been through the last . . . months! Not to mention the last twenty-four freaking hours!"

"I talked to Danny Dhue. You said you were going to see him. You promised to see him and get this under control—"

"And what's he gonna do?" asked Ben. "He's gonna give me another exercise where I can learn to both contain myself and eat more shit."

"That's what life is, Ben. Stuffing things and moving past them."

"And sometimes . . . sometimes you find out what's behind you isn't exactly over."

"What's in the past needs to stay in the past."

"You know what? That sounds all well and cheery."

"It's true."

"It's a goddamn Hallmark card!"

"Ben—"

"Sometimes the past sneaks up behind you and kicks your ass. Ever think of that? Sometimes the past moves in right next door to you."

"I said, Ben—"

"Or you find out the past is living thirty miles away, okay? Thirty fucking miles! He's breathing the same air. Living it up while I'm welding another lid on another emotion which, in order to move on, is more shit I have to swallow."

Alex still hadn't moved a millimeter.

"Can I say what I've been waiting to say? Please?" asked Alex.

"Right. Sure."

"It's unsafe, Ben. All of this. Unsafe for you, your well-being. Unsafe for your family." At last, Alex broke from her dancer's pose and eased to the bottom step. "Don't you care about us? Your family? Or were we just props for you until you finally discovered that your past life is more important that your present?"

"That part of your speech?"

"Comes with a big finish. You want the big finish?"

"Sure. Bring it."

"I'm taking the girls to Mammoth. We'll be back Sunday night. That should give you enough time to gather what you need and get out."

"This is our house, Alex."

"It's my house. In my name, paid for by my trust."

"Got a speech for the girls, too?"

"They've already lost one father. Maybe, after you work out whatever you have to work out—maybe you can see them. I don't deny they're gonna want to see you. We'll work something out as long as you're not in jail."

"You talked to somebody, didn't you?" Ben stood. "About yesterday. Who did you talk to?"

"I'm leaving now." Alex reached for the door and began to swing it open.

"Hey," complained Ben. "Don't I get to make a speech?"

She was already lifting the luggage when she stopped and twisted a quarter turn.

"In fact," said Ben, descending two steps. "It's not a speech, really. Questions. Just a few. You can answer or not."

Alex shrugged, but didn't release the handles of the suitcases.

"First question," said Ben as he lowered himself one more step. "Why don't I have any close friends?"

"I thought I was your friend."

"Male friends," corrected Ben. "Guys have guy friends. They play cards. Smoke a few cigars. Tell sex jokes—"

"Complain about their wives. Yes, guys. I don't know, Ben. Never really cared for that kind of man. Maybe that's why I liked you."

"Liked me. Right. That's my second question. You liked me more than you ever loved me. Yes? Come on."

"Did you love Sara?"

"Yes?"

"And me?"

"You first."

Alex thought for a moment, lowered her luggage and clasped her hands together.

"I loved you more than I loved any man. As I still do."

"But am I a man?" asked Ben. "Really, Alex. Does a real man spend his waking hours assessing the risks of others without ever taking a single risk himself?"

Alex kept her eyes fixed on the bottom of the staircase. She looked to be both exercising patience and carefully choosing her words before she committed them to speech.

"I don't know," she finally answered. "You were man enough for me. Man enough for my daughters. And you came along when we needed you most. If that's not a man . . ." she shrugged.

"Fair enough," said Ben, who sat once more, this time halfway between the landing and Alex. "But I wasn't there for Sara. I wasn't there for my baby girls."

"You know what Danny would say to that —"

"That I woulda died, too," answered Ben. "I'm no longer sure. See. Yesterday. I shoulda died. Stew shoulda killed me."

"Instead, you nearly killed yourself driving home drunk—"

"I'm here, aren't I? And isn't that the point? I'm still here! And so is he!"

"We can move, Ben! Santa Barbara. San Diego!" Alex climbed the stairs. "You can still do what you do anywhere we decide. Together!"

"Do what I do," Ben repeated. "And what is that?"

Alex kneeled and cradled Ben's face.

"Keep us safe," said Alex. "Keep us all very, very safe."

"Then it's not so much about what I do," said Ben. "It's about what I don't do. Or haven't done. Or should've done when this all started."

Alex straightened. Then she blinked her brown eyes once,

then again, very slowly.

"I can't be here if you're going to do something stupid," she said. "Or foolish or criminal. I can't expose myself or the girls. I won't."

"It's good that you're going," said Ben. "A good time to be gone."

Gracefully, Alex returned to the open door and re-gripped the suitcase handles.

"Remember what I asked," she said. "We'll be back Sunday. You should be gone by then."

"Never answered your question," said Ben.

"Which one?"

"Do I love you."

"You just did," Alex smiled sadly. "You just did."

Alex, her last words capping the argument, shouldered the backpack, hoisted the small suitcase, then rolled the larger bag out the door and down the path. She clearly needed no help from Ben. Nor wanted any. At least that was her intention. Ben was left to wonder if she had left the door wide open just so he could watch her leave. The sun streaked in and was so damned bright, Alex practically disappeared into the day in her white-on-white snow togs.

"Last year's Ben" would have chased after Alex. He would have begged her not to go, made quiet and copious acts of contrition while adding the kind of promises that he could and would surely keep. Hell, thought Ben. Last year's model of himself wouldn't have gotten his life into such a stinking twist.

As for "this year's Ben?"

He needed that fistful of Excedrin. That would require some form of food to protect his stomach. And Gatorade to hydrate and replenish fluids. The plan was simple, had clarity, direction, and the practical endgame of curing his crusher of a hangover.

Ben's next move would come later.

9

"IF YOU UPGRADE to a new plan, we can discount you on a new phone."

"Just the phone I had, please," said Ben, trying hard to tie a noose around his frustration. He had stood in line for twenty minutes at the closest Verizon Store to his house just to replace his BlackBerry. And all the porky, pimply, nineteen-year-old salesman could manage was to push new phones and longer contracts on him.

"I know you're just trying to help me," said Ben. He snapped his credit card on the counter like it was a playing card. "I also understand it's your job to sell new contracts and upgraded phones and all that stuff. But really. All I can deal with today is giving you this credit card, and in exchange, you replacing the phone which admittedly I am responsible for drowning."

"Yes, sir," said the salesman. "But you understand I can't give you a discount on the replacement phone."

"You said that twice already."

"It's less expensive for you to upgrade your contract and—"

"Credit card. New phone. Now," said Ben, emphatic. "Or I'll walk across the street and talk to the nice people at Sprint."

Ben waited for eye contact from salesman, whose lowered lids and long lashes hid a pair of dilated pupils that constantly darted behind square-rimmed glasses.

Drugs, thought Ben. The pimpled pork chop behind the counter had probably been up all night playing computer wars against scores of other socially inept gamers in places as far away as India. Normally, Ben would have cared, showed more patience and empathy. But with the sickening hangover still lingering beneath his skin, he found himself short of most human niceties.

"Here's your phone," said the salesman when he returned. "I've already programmed it to your old number. The battery's only on about a quarter charge, so I recommend . . ."

Ben didn't hear the rest. The moment the phone was in his hand, he had it turned on and was retrieving all the voicemails he had received since the day before. Twenty-one in all. Ben used the "skip" function for the business calls. He listened to mere seconds of the only two calls left by Alex, either because he couldn't stomach hearing her messages or because it felt like they had already said everything that needed to be said just an hour before. There was a pair of calls from Gonzo, concerned, trying to reach Ben after the frenzied voice message he had left her prior to his being attacked by Stew Raymo.

There were six voicemails from Josie. The first message, one that she had left only minutes before Ben had arrived at the office the day before, was a simple head's up that Ben's 9:00 A.M. meeting had shown up early. Josie's subsequent voicemails began with curiosity about the events she had missed while on her errand, then quickly escalated past worry and concern into flights of paranoia, the likes of which Ben had never heard from her. She asked if Ben was in jail. Would he need her help in order for him to post bail? Was Ben even alive? Would this be something she should call Woody Bell about? Is this the same Stew Raymo Ben had asked her to Google three months back? And would she be fired if she called Alex?

Clearly, reasoned Ben, *that's how Alex knew all about yesterday*. Josie, being the good egg that she was, first worried about protecting her boss' privacy, but at last couldn't help but inform his wife of her grave worries.

The final message left by Josie was somber, haltingly delivered, and left at 7:58 that same morning.

"Ben, hey. Josie here. Think it's almost eight in the morning . . . I, uh . . . was thinking of calling in sick but . . . not that I feel great . . . but I don't feel bad enough to lie. So I'll just say it. I think I need to take a break. Maybe just quit. I don't know. Feeling really uncomfortable with everything. Especially yesterday, you know? It's been too hard lately, with all the cancellations and making excuses for you and all the stuff I do . . . or don't know what you're doing. Uh . . . yeah. If you want, I suppose I can say this in a letter of resignation. I guess I'll call you in a few days and we can talk about things. Till then, I've texted you the number of the temp company I used that last time I was out with the flu . . . Really, really sorry. I hope you understand, and well . . . Okay. Bye."

Given the context of Ben's day thus far, what should have been a surprise gut-punch felt like little more than a stubbed toe. In fact, Josie taking a break, even quitting, made strange and instant sense to Ben. He had been inconsistent as both a boss and safety consultant. How long could he expect her to make excuses for his acts in absentia? And then on the last day Ben had showed up in the office, he nearly got hauled off to jail for beating the tar out a man who, as for as Josie knew, was a certified advocate for the safety interests of union baggage handlers.

Thoughts of Josie quitting were crushed the instant Ben's shoes hit the sidewalk, new phone held tightly at his ear as he listened to the last voicemail, left not an hour ago.

"Ben. Hi. It's Pamela Raymo," said the soft voice.

Ben's heart nearly stopped. Then, like a pump that momentarily lost its prime, overcompensated by swallowing an extra valve full of blood before expressing it back though his aorta.

"I just wanted to call you and thank you for last night. I mean, well, I suppose I should be asking you what in the world possessed

you to call me so late? Jeezus. Couldn't tell if you were a devil or an angel. Of course, now I know. And Lord help me, you are a godsend. So thank you, thank you, thank you. And . . . and this is the important part . . . I just wanted you to know that I took your advice and kicked the son-of-a-bitch out of the house. My lawyer friend says the restraining order should be in effect by the end of the day, too, so . . . I can't . . . I . . . Wow, I can't believe I did it. And for you? I guess I have no more words. Other than I can't thank you enough. So. Well. Wow. Guess it's bye for now."

Standing stock still on the sidewalk, Ben was bumped by the cross traffic of pedestrians and those trying to enter or exit the Verizon Store. What the hell else had he done during his blackout? Either to whom or with whom? *Christ*, thought Ben. *Did I really call Pam Raymo? And in my drunken stupor I gave advice?!* As he looked down, the sidewalk began to spin. He needed to sit. And think. And as much as it may hurt, remember.

It was the most pivotal moment of Pam's life. And she understood it to be exactly such. The digital clock on the bedside table read a number just short of midnight. And at the primal instant Pam was inching the muzzle of her shiny .38 caliber revolver closer to the grotesquely swollen cheek of her sleeping husband, the house phone rang with a loud, electronic whistle. Stew, lying naked and semi-fetal, stirred, groaned, and rolled a quarter turn on the bed. The snore that followed was equal in decibels to that of the telephone's second ring. It was decision time for Pam. Pull the trigger and end the abuse. Maybe even take her own life afterward.

Or answer the fucking phone.

It wasn't as if the telephone never rang that late at night. But it was always Stew's mobile. Never Pam's cell phone. And certainly not the house line. Pam's thoughts instantly swerved from murder to the well-being of her long-since divorced mother and father. God, she worried, was calling to tell her someone else in her family had died before she could pull the trigger on Stew.

On the third ring, Pam pocketed the revolver and grabbed the wireless handset from the cradle. She didn't answer until she had left the bedroom and shut the door.

"Hello," she had answered.

"Hi," said the voice. "Is this Pam?"

"Who's calling?"

"Don't know if you remember me," said the voice. "Ben . . . Ben Martin. I looked at your house a coupla weeks back. Then we sorta bumped into each other again at the market—"

"I remember," said Pam. "Why are you calling?"

"Don't really know," said Ben, bold, and sounding as sober as a Sunday judge. "Was just thinking of you . . . how you are . . . so . . . Well, how the heck are you?"

"It's nearly midnight."

"Did I wake you?"

"No," answered Pam, her right hand wrapped firmly around the grip of her .38. "No, I was up. It's just—"

"Sounds like I called at a bad time."

"No," said Pam, surprised at how her answer seemed to burst from her chest. "No. It's good to hear a different voice."

There followed a pause at the other end of the phone call. So long a pause that Pam worried that the connection was lost.

"You still there?" she asked.

"Yeah, yeah. You alone?"

"So to speak," said Pam.

"Husband home?"

"Sleeping it off."

"Oh," said Ben as if he understood. "Got tanked tonight, did he?"

"He's way off the wagon," said Pam, sad, her voice signaling her distress with a faint quiver.

"How far?" asked Ben, sounding both earnest and curious, just like the man he had pretended to be. A stranger. A man barely known to her and a nonentity to Stew.

"Too far," admitted Pam, finally cracking. "Too fucking far."

She began to cry.

And seated on the living room couch with her sweaty hand cradling the revolver in her lap, Pam kept her eyes squared on the shadows of the bedroom corridor in case Stew were to rise from bed. All the while and in vivid detail, she recounted the awfulness of her evening. From the hour Stew returned home, sticky and stinking from the mix of sugar and whisky, to just shy of the moment she had crept into their bedroom, revolver cocked and loaded, with every intent to kill her husband.

"I don't know what happened to him," she said. "He wouldn't say what happened. But it looked like he had been in some kind of fight. Half his face was all swoll up. From there he went right to the booze. I mean, I swear I didn't even know there was liquor in the house. Otherwise, I woulda poured it all down the drain before . . ."

"Before?"

"I was afraid for him. He was already drunk and I didn't want him to drink anymore. So while he was in the garage looking for a liter of Pepsi, I popped the cap and poured it down the sink. All of it. The whole fifth of whisky."

"Stew," said Pam. "He took the bottle and hit me with it. I don't know how many times. I think my cheekbone's busted and there's some glass under my skin—"

"You need to go the emergency room right now."

"I know, I know."

"Then why don't you?"

"Because I was going to go after."

"After what?"

"Just after—" said Pam, her voice cutting off.

Stew had lost control when he had discovered that Pam had poured an entire bottle of Jack Daniels down the kitchen disposal. And when she stood up to face his obscene drunkenness, he picked up the bottle and backhanded it across her face. Pam slid down the counter, but Stew kept swinging until the neck of the bottle had snapped.

Pam was still kicking, shouting for help, as he rolled her over and sodomized her on the kitchen pavers. When he was finished, he lay on top of her, his teeth biting her ear between breathless rants about what a whoring, worthless . . .

"Cunt," said Pam. "He kept calling me that over and over again."

"That's horrible," said Ben.

"Not like the first time I was called that. Or raped, you know? But he's my husband. And a husband's supposed..."

Pam's voice trailed and for more times than she could remember, was overtaken by sobs.

Ben convinced her to locate her car keys, exit the house, and drive to the nearest emergency room. Once she had explained her situation to the admitting nurse, the police would be called and a rape kit assembled. Ben calmly cautioned Pam not to return home until a restraining order had been issued and Stew had been arrested and removed from the house.

Somewhere between the door and the car, Pam hung up on Ben without recalling if she had said thank you or goodbye. Safe inside an old girlfriend's condo, but yet unable to sleep, Pam called Ben's cell phone and left her grateful message. Never once did she question why Ben had called her so very late the night before. Nor did she imagine he was, or suspect that he was, drunk. To her, Ben was an angel, sent by God himself to deliver the instructions that prevented her from committing a deadly sin.

Stew awoke to the sound of a doorbell. He groaned, shouted for Pam to answer the goddamn door. Moments later, there was a hard rapping on the French doors that led from the bedroom to the backyard, then a rattling as if somebody was twisting the handle.

"What the fuck?" said Stew aloud.

Through squinted eyes, he recognized the deep navy-blue uniforms of the LAPD. This is when he knew.

"Bitch," he muttered, detecting within his own tone more than a spoonful of regret.

In a matter of hours, Stew was cuffed, booked for battery and rape at the LAPD North Hollywood substation, and then transferred by cruiser to the Van Nuys Division. He had his blood drawn for a DNA test by a Ukrainian-accented nurse with forearms nearly as big as his and was bussed downtown for a meeting with a public defender. The day was topped off by a smelly night inside the L.A. County Jail. Because Stew hadn't been subject to anything heavier than a traffic fine during his sober years, the arraignment judge set bail at a mere twenty-five thousand dollars. The ten percent fee to the bail bondsman was covered by Stew's new American Express card.

So by Wednesday morning, with a copy of Pam's five-hundred-foot restraining order clenched in his fist, Stew was released back to the free world less than twenty-four hours after his arrest. Now came his hardest decision. He could either have the turban-wearing Sikh cabby deliver him to the nearest bar—or the nearest Alcoholics Anonymous meeting.

"You have an address?" asked the cabby.

"Hold on to your fuckin' diaper," snapped Stew, hung up on his dilemma.

Stew fished into his rear pants pocket and came up with a yellow Post-it folded in quarters. Scribbled in thin blue ink were a phone number and a pair of cross streets in Los Feliz, just south of Los Angeles' gargantuan Griffith Park.

"Awright, I got it," said Stew, pushing the Post-it through the coin and bill drawer hinged in the bulletproof glass.

Back in February, Gonzo had made a request for e-notes to be deposited into her electronic in-box if Stew Raymo's name ever rang up on the LAPD's digital blotter. The request was still in effect two months later. So she was officially pinged when Stew was booked, again when he checked into L.A. County Jail, and a third time upon his arraignment and release.

If only she had been at her desk.

Instead, having already heard through the Simi Canyons' grapevine that an actual separation between Ben and Alex was in the works, her mind was more occupied with Ben's marital fate than her cop job. The weight of her culpability had pulled Gonzo deep inside her own guilty skin. So on that fateful Wednesday, Gonzo called in sick.

But what of her partner, Romeo?

It was Romeo's habit to cover for Gonzo and that duty included running through her inter-office memos. If he had checked in to his desk on Wednesday, he would have read the news of Stew Raymo's overnight incarceration and surely forwarded it on to Gonzo's personal email. But Romeo had chosen to turn Gonzo's sick day into a golden opportunity to impress the lieutenant who ran the downtown division's Gang Suppression Unit. So instead of a day in his low-backed swivel chair writing and filing e-reports from the gray windowless detectives' cubicle he shared with Gonzo, he drove to downtown's Parker Center and volunteered to assist his new homies in the G.S.U. A transfer, promised the lieutenant, would come with a reduction in both pay and estrogen, and a decided increase in adrenalin.

And since Ben didn't appear interested in picking up his cell phone and nobody in his office was answering calls, Gonzo went patrolling for him disguised in that Valley Checkered Cab she had borrowed from the PD. She first went by Ben's home, then the nearby coffee haunts, followed by the gym where they first met and became friends.

Gonzo reasoned that Ben was merely underground and licking his marital wounds. Or maybe with a therapist, working some healthy mental exercises. Gonzo even tried to picture Ben in a rented Mustang convertible, top down and roaring up Pacific Coast Highway to air out his newfound loneliness in the ocean breezes. None of her thoughts, though, quelled the pit that was growing in her gut. Gonzo liked to think she could trust her instincts. Cops, after all, survived on training and intuition. And Gonzo's intuition was scraping at her stomach lining, forming an acid reflux tsunami—all reminding her that Ben was on some dangerous, self-destructive collision course with a psychopath. Why had she visited Raymo in the hospital? And why had she confirmed Ben's suspicions about the prick?

"Dispatch," called Gonzo over her radio.

"Identify," replied the dispatcher.

"Gonzalez. Six-Mary-Zebra-Two-Four-Seven-Seven."

"Go ahead."

"Requesting North Hollywood street address. Raymo, first name Stew or Stewart. R-A-Y-M-O."

"Subject is listed at two-one-two-three Morrison Street. Cross street is Lauren Canyon."

After a warmish Southern California winter, where rain had come in fits and starts, those perma-tanned TV weathermen were predicting that come Wednesday, the skies would darken and unleash something on par with a mild hurricane. Winds, thunder and heavy downpours, flooding intersections and increasing the possibility of mudslides. But until the first raindrops fell, experienced Angelenos would likely keep the tops stowed on their convertibles, umbrellas in the broom closets, and favor outdoor recreation over the certain depression that came with days bunkered inside their workplaces and homes

Outdoor malls—or destination sites as city planners called them—were popular. Themed mosh pits of retail stores, pricey chain restaurants, nightclubs, hotels, and movie theaters advertising state of the art, ear-crushing sound and cushy, stadium seating with loads of legroom. City Walk was such a junction for commerce and crowds.

Annexed to the hilltop Universal Studios theme park, City Walk at night was Blade Runner-esque, its thousands of linear feet of colored neon second only to New York City's Times Square. And with parking aplenty, the tourist attraction seemed to draw an equal concoction of locals and international visitors alike.

Increasingly xenophobic, Stew hated the place. He hated sharing the same oxygen with so many Asians and Hispanics, none of who, to his ear, spoke a word of English. He hated the noise. He hated paying for the parking. He hated the twisting sea of constant foot traffic. So if there were twenty square acres of San Fernando Valley real estate where Pam felt relatively safe from her husband, it was City Walk at night.

"I'm thinking of keeping the baby," said Pam. "I mean, I know I don't have the baby yet. But I want to go ahead with it, you know? The adoption part."

"Of course," said Ben, finding it difficult to fully concentrate on Pam without constantly scanning the parade of humanity that meandered by their dinner table as if caught in the flow of a muddy river.

"Can I ask you something?" said Pam. "Do I make you uncomfortable?"

"No," answered Ben. "Why do you wanna know?"

"Is it hard to look at me? The big glasses and all?"

Though it was nighttime and the light at the sidewalk-styled table was dim enough to make young eyes strain just to read the menu, Pam insisted on wearing a pair of oversized sunglasses she had purchased during her stay at the nearby Universal Hilton. *Understandable*, thought Ben. Despite coats of heavy makeup, the wide shades and a blazing white bucket hat with an embroidered yellow sunburst, there was little hiding the damage Stew had done to Pam's face. Ben felt silently responsible—an accessory to the crime—as if Stew had passed along the beating he had received from Ben to Pam.

"Force of habit," said Ben. "Always on the lookout for danger."

"I told you. This is the last place on earth he would ever come look for me."

"Been awhile since I've been up here," shifted Ben. "Any more people and we could start a new area code."

"Makes me feel invisible," said Pam. "Not the getup. You know, the glasses and the makeup. All the people. They make me feel like I can disappear."

"You're pretty hard to miss," complimented Ben. "Even with the . . ."

Pam nodded. She understood Ben's inference.

"Once a sucker, always a sucker," smiled Pam.

"Sucker for what?"

"Compliments. I like compliments."

"And your taste in headwear," quipped Ben, quick on the uptake. "Cutting edge. Next year's fashion."

"Are you . . ." Pam leaned across the table. "Are you flirting with me?"

Ben straightened. Was he flirting?

"It's okay, you know," said Pam. "Flirting is good."

"Been awhile," said Ben, uncertain.

Before either could think of something witty to add, the square-jawed server-cum-actor appeared with a tasting platter of shrimp. Fried, sautéed, skewered, sizzling in butter.

"Yum," said Pam. "Smells awesome."

Pam's invitation for Ben to join her for dinner was less a request than an insistence to somehow repay him for saving her from her own deadly thoughts. Not that she had fully told Ben what kind of precipice she had been teetering on the moment her phone rang. Nor did Ben feel inclined to explain to Pam that he had made the rescue call when he was blindly drunk and had zero recollection of doing so, let alone what he might have said or why in God's name he had dialed her number in the first place.

"You still staying at the hotel here?"

"Just last night. I'm over at the Beverly Garland now. Burning up Stew's credit card at two bills a night."

"I can understand not wanting to go back to your—"

"Enough about me," interrupted Pam, forcing a girlish voice. "On my way here I was thinking, *What the hell do I know about this Ben the Safety Dude?*"

"Oh. So now I'm the *Ben the Safety Dude?*"

"Unless you mind being Ben the Safety Dude?"

"No no. I've been the Safety Man, the Safety Guy, Mister Safety. Guess I can add Ben the Safety Dude to the lexicon. Of course, only if it suits your purpose . . ."

"And what do you think my purpose is?" grinned Pam, eyebrows raised. She clearly enjoyed the playful banter. It had been some time since she had allowed herself.

"Now who's flirting?" asked Ben.

"I am sooo busted!" Pam peeled a large steamed shrimp, dipped it in sauce, then sucked it before popping it into her mouth. "But I'm also curious."

Ben paused, making sure he appeared more thoughtful than terrified that she would see through him.

"You want to know if there's more to me than being a widowed repository of useless safety tips."

"No such thing as a useless safety tip."

"No?"

"Bring it, Safety Dude."

"Okay," said Ben, hardly challenged, but maybe allowing himself to get a little lost in her charm, which was direct without coming off as pushy or controlling.

"After beefsteak," quizzed Ben. "What would you say is the number one choking hazard for a woman?"

If only Ben could have seen Pam's eyes behind those dark shades. Her face slackened just enough. Her eyes, narrowed. Her lips were suddenly pursed and stiff.

Could he know about me?

At least, that's what Pam wondered. Could Ben have known all along about her porno half-life? Was that why Ben was brave enough to call her at home—where she lived with her husband—at midnight of all hours? Pam looked harder at Ben, dark as it was through the smoked lenses, certain that if he was some kind of perv, she could read it on him.

"What?" asked Ben, innocently.

"You think that's funny?" she asked, sounding a bit harsher than she had planned.

"Funny how?" Ben shook his head.

"It's not like I'm some kind of prude. I mean, it is funny, I guess . . ."

"Not without a punch line," said Ben, completely clueless of his own rude suggestion.

"There is a punch line?" asked Pam, forcing herself to soften. She liked Ben. She felt she had read the fine print. Her instincts instructed her as much. "A punch line I gotta hear. See, I thought the question was the joke. Women. Meat. Choking hazard."

And Ben finally got it. He had been handed the key to his own subconscious vault of bad double entendres, yet still needed some stunner of woman to unlock it for him.

"Oh, crap," announced Ben, his ears flushing red with embarrassment. "Did I ask what I think I asked?"

"Did you?"

"No," said Ben, laughing aloud at himself. "Wow. Not at all what I was thinking."

"So there really is a punch line?" asked Pam.

"Yes, of course," he said, shaking his head. "Shrimp. Other than beefsteak, the second most common choking hazard for women is—"

"Shrimp?" Pam joined in with the laughing, but still not entirely certain that Ben was genuinely chagrined at his gaff.

"Something to do with the shape and the size of the air shaft . . ."

"You did not just said shape, size, shaft," she pointed in a mock accusation, eyebrows raised high above those wide, black rims.

"You asked for a useless safety tip."

"And the tip is?"

"Chicken," said Ben. "Eat more chicken."

Ben shrugged and cut into some of the sautéed shrimp.

Pam leaned a little bit forward.

"You don't really know, do you?" she asked. "About me. Who I am. Where I'm from. What I've done and all that."

"Guess that makes us a little bit even."

Pam agreed, nodding. But before returning to her meal, she had to ask:

"Do you believe in God?"

"Big question," answered Ben.

"Big subject."

"Suppose," began Ben before doubling back and rethinking his answer. "Suppose I do. But there's a lotta questions I'd want to ask Him before I'd vote Him in as the one and only true deity."

"Like why do bad things happen—"

"Something along those lines, yeah," finished Ben, feeling wholly uncomfortable with the subject. So he retreated into glibness with, "And if God answered my initial question satisfactorily, I'd follow up with who killed JFK? I'd also ask Him to explain the popularity of golf and NASCAR."

Though Pam laughed willingly, she wasn't yet ready to let

the subject die.

"I believe," she said. "I believe He rescued me from my addiction. I believe He wants me to have a baby of my own. And I believe, for whatever reason, He sent you to rescue me from Stew."

"A nine-one-one operator would've given you the same advice," said Ben, matter-of-factly.

"The nine-one-one operator didn't call me," said Pam. "But you did."

"You're not eating," said Ben, desperate to shift the conversation.

"Neither are you."

"Guess I'm not hungry . . ." said Ben.

"You like movies?"

"Sure," said Ben.

"Wanna go? I feel like I could eat a tub of popcorn."

But Ben didn't answer.

From Pam's perspective, Ben was locked-off at the neck, staring into space, appearing as if he hadn't heard her offer.

"I said, 'Do you want to go to the movies?' You, me. Dark room. A box of five-dollar Junior Mints?"

"Will you . . ." Ben pushed his chair out, left his napkin on his plate. "I'll be back in just a minute."

Without so much as looking at Pam for permission or even acknowledging her invitation to the movies, he was climbing over the chain that separated the diners from the flow of pedestrian traffic.

"No problem," said Pam to nobody in particular.

With Ben gone, Pam fought the sudden sense of abandonment, looking to flag down a waiter to refill her glass with iced tea.

It was a tattoo that stole Ben's attention.

A flash-frame moment that tripped Ben in the middle of his conversation with Pam about God and movies. Amid the constant wash of City Walk visitors cruising past their sidewalk table, Ben thought he had seen a Wile Coyote cartoon character peeking over the back of a woman's red blouse. In his life, he had seen only one other tattoo like it. And that was on Josie on the rare day she pinned her dyed black hair into a curly updo.

But the minute Ben had jumped the chain and pushed into the crowd, he thought he had already lost her. It was a disorganized mass of flesh that moved in all directions. And with every step, regret crept in about leaving poor Pam in an uncomfortable lurch. All because he had wanted to apologize to Josie for sending her home without an explanation on that awful day and for his months of inconsistent behavior. He couldn't even remember the last time he had asked how she was doing, an obvious failure at *Employer 101: How to Keep and Care for Your Valued Workers*.

Sum total: Ben had been a lousy boss and wanted to say, "I'm sorry."

Ahead, Ben caught another glimpse of his ex-assistant in a spot where the walking lane widened. He saw her wobble slightly on a pair of stiletto heels. Not her usual footwear. In truth, he couldn't recall having seen Josie wear anything other than Converse All Stars.

"Josie?" Ben shouted out. His voice was swallowed by the music pounding from a giant screen playing music videos mixed with live camera shots of the crowd. So Ben shouted her name, "JOSIE!"

Josie heard him, twisting and nearly tripping over her own tangled feet, all while trying not to drop her neon pink, frozen strawberry daiquiri served in a foot-long plastic tube. Josie released the straw from her mouth in surprise.

"Ben?"

Ben's mind rehashed the last day he had seen her. Monday. The day Stew came to apologize for murdering Ben's family. Ben recalled Stew using Josie as an example of recovery. That Josie had a year of sobriety under her belt. And later, when Ben was letting Josie go for the day, he had taken note of her keychain, and, indeed he had seen something that looked like a recovery chip. Not that he was any kind of expert. Not until Josie was standing feet from him, teetering on her unusually high heels, and sucking on what looked like a gallon of frozen rum and strawberry mix, had the short memory been reborn in living color.

"Josie," began Ben, uncertain of his next words, what he wanted to say or how in the world he would say it.

Then somebody from behind squeezed Ben's arm. *Pam*, he thought. She had bounced out on the check and chased him through the throng. But the grip on his arm was less than feminine, with a force that spun Ben around.

Stew Raymo stood inches from Ben, one large hand gripping Ben's arm, the other holding an equally obscene concoction of frozen blue booze.

"What the fuck?" said Stew, not necessarily directing the comment at Ben.

"We just bumped," said Josie, stepping up. "Just this second."

Heat rose in Ben's face, turning prickly across his skin and radiating inside until he felt his shock turn to fear. Ben's fight-or-flight instinct manifested in a clockwise swing of his arm that broke Stew's viselike grasp. Only Stew released his blue tube, gathered handfuls of Ben's shirt and stuck his face close to Ben's, grinning through his black-and-blue complexion.

"'Bout that apology," growled Stew. "Takin' it back."

"Murderer!" hissed Ben. And in the utterance of that single word, Ben was never more convicted.

"Ready for Round Two?"

"Go fuck yourself!"

The next ten seconds were a blur.

Stew drove the peak of his forehead into Ben's skull with such efficiency that, in what seemed like a mere blink of an eye, Ben was on the ground and unable to force his eyes to focus. First he saw shoes. Then streaks of neon. And then Josie pushing herself in between him and Stew.

"What you do that for?" asked Josie, angrily.

"That was nothin'," said Stew. "Stick around, honey, and watch me do a helluva lot worse."

"No! I won't let you!"

"Let him," shouted Ben, staggering to his feet and pointing to the ground. "Let him kill me right here!"

Stew shoved Josie aside. And with clenched fists and a drunken resolve, he approached Ben with a tunnel vision so extreme—so deviant—that he hadn't yet noticed the crowd drawing a wide circle around him.

"Do it!" goaded Ben. "Got me a thousand witnesses. Got camera phones all around. I may die here and now, but you're gonna spend the rest of forever in prison!"

Ben stood his ground. Defiant, determined, and—though it may have been only for that adrenalin-fueled moment—fully prepared to meet his death if it meant justice and the end of Stew Raymo.

This is it. Our mutually assured destruction.

Stew, so hell-bent on crushing Ben's skull, didn't hear the challenge. Or the warning. What gave him pause were the camera flashes. Not from just one digital pocket shooter, but a veritable paparazzi blast from a flock of Korean tourists caught up in what was shaping up to be the highlight of their American holiday.

A sudden self-awareness broke through Stew's rage. His eyes panned away from Ben to the growing ring of spectators. Making the situation even more surreal was the moving image on the giant video screen. There was Stew, twenty feet tall, looking like a grainy, live-action version of Marvel's Incredible Hulk.

And Josie?

She stood only a few yards away, shocked, her hands stuck to her face in fear at what she had wrought. Two days ago, slipping off the wagon had never crossed her mind. If anything, her part had begun as a kindred act from one recovering alcoholic to another. While Stew had waited for Ben to arrive at the office, he had instantly noticed Josie's sobriety chip on her key ring. A conversation had followed. The kind shared only by those belonging to the Brotherhood of Bill W. Then Josie, charmed by Stew's blue-collar smile, had invited him to attend her morning AA meeting. She had scribbled the address on a Post-it along with her telephone number, folded it, and given it to Stew. Yes, she would admit. It was a sexy come-on that only a fellow twelve-stepper would understand.

God, I am such a stupid bitch!

Stew and Josie had strolled from the AA meeting, climbed the steps to her Los Feliz apartment, and between bouts of sweaty, un-showered and unprotected sex, had broken into her roommate's stash and smoked bong-loads of Humboldt County weed from a vase Josie had turned into a water pipe. The hunger that had followed was quenched by pizza, beer, and even more sex. From there, the day had spun out of control. Both were off whatever wagons they had rode in on and it seemed that all bets, narcotic or otherwise, were off.

It was Josie's bright idea to drive up to City Walk, order a pair of silly frozen tourist drinks, and go bowling. It could be said that Stew was just along for the ride. Who could have predicted the events that came after? Least of all Josie.

When the blinding camera flashes subsided and the gawkers started to recede, Stew regained his few remaining wits that weren't owned by his unchecked rage. Stew thought he caught a brief flash of Josie disappearing through the doors of the Hard Rock Café.

Ben, though, was nowhere in sight.

One particular cell-phone jockey—scruffy, sixteen-years-old, and still curiously capturing video of Stew through the screen of his mobile device—was caught unaware when Stew lurched at him with a death scowl.

"Which way'd he go?"

So terrified was the teen that he just dropped his phone and ran away. Frustrated and punching at air, Stew wheeled a speedy three-hundred-sixty degrees before he bent over, picked up the mobile device, and working the menu with his thumbs, brought up the video. Stew wasn't as interested in his own moments as much as he was keen on Ben's, especially the direction in which his prey had run. West, it appeared, past the escalators and underneath a hanging, blue and black neon King Kong.

"WE GOTTA GO!" urged Ben.

Ben didn't think to ask before he grabbed Pam's wrist after letting a couple of twenty-dollar bills flutter to the table.

"I already paid," Pam said. "Stew's card—"

"Doesn't matter. Let's just move." Ben just wanted to get Pam moving toward the valet stand in the parking garage.

"What's going on?" stalled Pam before twisting out of his grip. "Where'd you go, anyway?"

Then she saw the thin stream of red trickling down Ben's face from the cut just beneath his hairline. A large knot was forming. And the blood looked black through her dark shades.

"It's not safe—"

"What happened to you?"

"Your husband!"

He held his hand out for her to take, hoping to get through to the eyes hiding behind those large sunglasses.

"Stew?" asked Pam, half rhetorically, the other half in utter disbelief. "How—"

"You want answers now? Or you wanna move?"

Pam got the gist and her hand into Ben's. Together they hurried through the mob, never losing the other, until they reached the crowded first-floor valet stand. Ben paid cash and offered an extra fifty dollars if the cashier would agree to bring his car first. The cashier, a thick man with an equally indistinguishable accent, took offense at Ben's bribe and chastised Ben accordingly. Not even the blood on Ben's face got a reaction from the angry cashier. When the notion of arguing appeared pointless, Ben retreated and sought secondary options. While Pam was dabbing his face with tissues from her purse, he grabbed her yet again and started walking toward the exit.

"We'll walk," he said. "Down to the boulevard and grab the Rapid Bus."

"What about a taxi?" asked Pam.

"This is the Valley. Too long a wait—"

Pam tugged Ben to his right.

"I said . . ." Pam was pointing east, through the valet entrance to a drop-off circle. There, two hundred feet away, a Valley Checkered Cab stood idling as if waiting to rescue Ben and Pam.

"Run!" said Ben.

Stew, in fact, had given up the chase once the faces of the Wednesday night horde had began to muddy and dissolve, one into the other. It was dizzying, and surprising to Stew, who grew exponentially claustrophobic with every hurried step. Stew blamed the frozen blue cocktail, blamed Josie for suggesting that it was fun to bowl while tanked on booze, blamed City Walk for merely existing, and blamed Ben for the fact that he badly needed oxygen and a few extra yard's distance from the constant swarm of foreigners.

So Stew cut in the direction of the nearest exit sign as if he were deep underwater and needed to kick extra hard to the surface just for a lungful of air. He rushed, stumbling past strangers, and flattened a poor little Latino boy who had broken loose from his father's hand. The father, a heavily tattooed gangbanger, a true O.G., chased a few steps after Stew, loudly cursing him in Spanish. But after getting frozen by an over-the-shoulder glower from the big white man, the father threw Stew a sideways middle finger, then wisely returned to his family.

Ahead of Stew was a yellow, checkered taxi. *Just the ticket*, he thought. *An easy ride home*. Though the restraining order was still in Stew's pocket, he hadn't given it any mind since he had stuffed it there shortly after he had been served. It may as well have been delivered on a platter to a paper-chewing goat.

Stew waved at the taxi thirty yards away.

"Hold up!" shouted Stew.

Next, Stew saw a blurry flash as a couple climbed in ahead of him. He saw the door close, followed by the flare of brake lights as the cabby put the car into drive.

"My goddamn ride!" yelled Stew.

Whether it was the mist in the air, the distance from the crowd, the flush of O_2 in his lungs, or the frustration of feeling like dirt had just been kicked in his face, Stew's visual acuity returned in a matter of seconds. And in that precious instant, he focused on the couple in the cab as it pulled away.

Framed in a rear window dappled with fresh rain was Pam, clear as day, her short blonde mane as distinct as the cut of her jawline. Stew saw her remove her sunglasses to reveal glistening tears of fright. He also watched in awe as she willingly folded her arms around another man . . .

. . . the man Stew knew as Ben Keller.

Neither Ben nor Pam had paid the slightest attention to the cabdriver. Ben had merely slammed the rear door closed and curtly said, "Just drive," before the question of "Where to?" could have conceivably been asked. The driver paused, regarded the passengers through the rearview mirror as they settled into the backseat, then dropped the transmission into drive. The cab rolled away from City Walk and toward Ventura Boulevard.

Pam was nearly hysterical, but quietly so, trembling in Ben's arms.

"I don't understand," she whispered, her voice wavering at the same frequency as her shuddering body.

"He must've seen me with you."

Ben was already spinning another lie. And without much forethought, either. Why did the lies come so easily to him? How many tales, he wondered, could he fabricate before his stories unraveled into pile of spent thread?

"But he hates this place," said Pam. "How'd he know where to find me here?"

The truth was screaming inside of Ben. The truth that so desperately wanted to be released. She deserved to know. Everything. From his Santa Monica restaurant to the murders to the deathbed confession to the truth of why he had rung her doorbell on that sunny morning.

"He was drinking," said Ben. "I could smell it on him."

"The sonofabitch," she cried. "He's gonna kill me, now. I swear to God he's gonna kill me."

"That's not gonna happen," calmed Ben, clueless, of course, as to how or why he would be able to prevent her death.

"Yes he will!"

"There's the restraining order, remember? You've got the police."

"After he's seen me with another man? Like that's gonna help me. He'll kill us both!"

"Where to?" asked the driver. "Left or right."

The cab was idling at a stoplight. When Ben looked away from Pam he could see the rain was getting heavier, sheeting from the blackness that hung above the skyline.

"Where's your hotel?" asked Ben.

"Can't go back there. He might know."

"Another hotel, then. The Radisson."

Pam thought for a brief moment, then nodded.

"Encino," said Ben. "The Radisson."

"Mind if I take the freeway?" asked the cabby.

Finally, Ben's eyes met the driver's through those sixteen square inches of rearview mirror. Of course, Ben registered no recognition of the driver, nor did the driver show the faintest hint of having ever seen Ben. That's because the driver was not Gonzo. He was a middle-aged pug of a white man, with an unshaven face and a resplendent right earring.

"I need my gun," Pam whispered.

"Your *what?*" asked Ben. He wondered if he had heard it wrong.

"I have a gun," she said. "Stew gave me a gun. Just in case."

"In case of what?"

"Sometimes I get attention," she said. "You know, the wrong kind. From fans."

"Fans?"

"You don't know," said Pam, grateful, but still crying. She shook her head. "You don't want to know."

"Okay," conceded Ben, more interested in Pam's gun than her past. He kept his voice below the hum of the cab's tires against the street so only Pam could hear him.

"Where's your gun?" he asked.

"I should've taken it with me when I left for the hospital."

"It's at home?" Ben guessed. "So Stew has it?"

"No," Pam shook her head. "He couldn't find a clean pair of socks without me telling him . . . I hid it. I hid the gun."

"You hid it in your house?"

"It's in a tampon box under the sink in our bathroom."

Ben gripped Pam's shoulders and lowered his head to hers.

"And you would feel safer," Ben asked, "If you had your gun with you?"

"You tell me. You're the expert. Would I be safer?"

Statistically, yes, flashed the answer. A loaded gun against a home invader or an assailant without a gun was a decided advantage. But a weapon out of reach, let alone hidden in a tampon box underneath the bathroom sink? The odds tipped dramatically to the attacker.

"You can't go home," said Ben. "That wouldn't be safe."

"You're right, you're right," repeated Pam before turning up her volume for the cabby. "How far to the hotel?"

"The Radisson?" asked the cabby. "Five minutes."

Pam nodded and relaxed a little, settling back into the seat and feeling more assured that, at least for the moment, there was a safe cushion between herself and Stew. Ben joined her, leaning into the seat and facing ahead. The taxi's windshield wipers were churning at maximum speed, swatting at the pouring rain. Then Ben felt Pam's fingers intertwine with his. There followed a good minute of quiet comfort before Pam asked:

"Why are you doing this?" she asked softly.

"Why what?"

"Helping me. You don't know me. You don't owe me . . ."

"I don't know," said Ben, not exactly lying this time, but still not telling close to the truth. "Sometimes, I think we find ourselves in unfamiliar situations . . . and maybe it's just instinct or survival. But I think we kinda reach out."

"You talking about you?" asked Pam. "Or me?"

"Both of us," said Ben.

When the cab arrived at the Radisson Hotel and parked under a protective awning out of the rain, Pam was quick to slide out first. She was reaching into her purse for cash when Ben touched her hand.

"No," he said, still inside the cab. "You check in. I'm going back to get my car."

Pam exhaled and let her face fall, downcast, pouting like a rejected teenager.

"Stay?" she pleaded. "Please?"

"I'll come back," said Ben.

"I can't be alone right now."

"You're safe here," said Ben. "And I will be back. Promise."

Pam leaned in close enough for Ben to smell her.

"I know I'm not much to look at right now," she said. "But maybe . . . maybe we can take care of each other. Just for tonight?"

"And in the morning?"

"Whole new day," said Pam with a hopeful snuffle, her ruby lips gliding back over her teeth. Inviting.

At the split second before Ben imagined kissing her, he was overcome with the same sense of release he had experienced when he had let go of the wheel of his car and let fate—or God—or the road itself—decide the path he would take. It was the same path that had led him to Stew's house, the doorstep where he had stood and waited to meet Pam. And had brought him to this critical moment where, parked in front of the Radisson Hotel, there was nothing for Ben to decide or calculate or risk assess.

All there was for him to do was put his lips to hers. But Pam made the first move. She kissed him. And he neither recoiled nor gave any message that he was surprised. In fact, he kissed her right back.

As Ben later reflected, there was no revenge in the act. At least no feeling as such. Since meeting Pam, Ben had experienced moments where he had fantasized about sleeping with her. Pam was, at the jump, as sexually attractive a woman as he had ever met. What sweet and twisted justice—if only partial—would it be for Ben to screw the wife of the man who had murdered his family? But the thought itself was always dashed against the rocks at the sheer sickness of it all. Ben was a married man, responsible for three young girls whom he cared for dearly.

Ben wasn't out for revenge. Or so he rationalized.

Ben's was a practical problem.

That his world wasn't safe with Stew Raymo in it.

Still, there he was. Kissing Pam. Liking it. Accepting the tingles that came from having her mouth linked with his. As if Stew Raymo hadn't a bloody thing in the world to do with it.

"So you're coming up," said Pam, taking a breath, then kissing him back.

"I need to get my car," said Ben.

"Get it tomorrow."

"You're safe here," repeated Ben, retreating back into the cab. "I'll be back soon."

Ben shut the door, rapped the glass partition and said to the cabby, "C'mon, let's go." He made sure to turn and wave confidently back at Pam as if to take the sting out of his rejection. He wanted her to understand he had every intention of returning. Just not quite as soon as he had implied. The plan unfolding in his head was not yet fully formed. But it was still a plan of action. A plan that would, at last, resolve all conflict.

"I have a gun," she had said.

Pam's words formed an audio loop in Ben's head. And with each trip around his brain, the pieces of a plot fell into place. Not necessarily neatly. But in such a fashion that an actual endgame was suddenly in plain sight. All of this in the course of a short cab ride, between the moment when Pam had said, "I have a gun" and when Ben had shut the cab door and promised, "I'll be back soon."

The immediate future unfolded on Ben's mental white board in simple bullet points.

- Retrieve Pam's gun.
- Return to the hotel.
- Wait for Stew to discover that Pam is sharing the hotel room with him.
- An enraged Stew arrives at the hotel, thus violating his restraining order.
- Ben shoots and kills Stew with Pam's gun.
- Ben claims self defense. The court rules justifiable homicide.

Ben only needed to reach out, embrace the scheme, and execute it without fear. His heart pounded with an adrenalized brew of excitement and terror. He was well beyond his uncanny abilities to calculate and assess risk. His precious numbers and odds weren't available to give him any kind of handhold on reality. It was as if he had leaped off a high bridge, consciously ignoring all basic laws of physics, plummeting face first into the danger zone.

"Where to now?" asked the driver.

"Back to where we started," said Ben.

10

RAGE, BETRAYAL, AND heartbreak.

The first emotion was familiar. That other pair of feelings was mostly foreign to Stew. Stew was familiar with rage. Rage could be tempered, molded, turned into satisfying action, negative or otherwise. And the first action Stew had chosen was to march onward and leave City Walk behind by putting one foot in front of the other. Get downhill, he told himself. Walk down to the boulevard and damn all the rain and the man who sent it.

Betrayal, though. That one sucked Stew so far back that he was recalling his first middle-school crush. She had curls of red hair, freckles to match, and was adored by every boy in the class, especially Stew. But she didn't know about Stew. She assumed Stew was her tall, skinny friend. The only boy to whom she could tell her secrets. Stew listened, then one day screwed up the courage to tell her a secret of his own. His most important secret. That he loved the red-haired girl and wanted her to be his girlfriend. Then moments later, after she had acted flattered and interested in the content of Stew's confession, she had told all her other friends of Stew's romantic intentions. For a week after, Stew stayed home pretending to be sick with the stomach flu. Then he begged his mother to allow him to transfer to another public school. He remembered his mother gently smiling at the request, then sprinkling a thimble-full of hashish into little pile of tobacco. She rolled the mixture into a joint, expertly twisting the ends, and before putting flame to it, smiled at her crushed son and promised, "I'll look into it."

Stew's mom never did look into the school transfer. In that one week, Stew had been betrayed by the two most important women in his life. From that day forward he vowed to never let another woman get under his skin.

Then came Pam.

Stew met his first and only wife at the end of a painful rehab. Both were vulnerable and needed someone of the opposite sex to hang on to. In that window of life they both appeared to have discovered love and redemption in the same fix-it package. Eighteen years after Stew had pledged to himself he would never be vulnerable to another woman, he had exchanged that personal promise for the vow to love, honor and obey.

As for the heartbreak? Stew hadn't a glimmer how to soothe that kind of wound. To shake the image of Ben with his arms wrapped around Pam, Stew thumped himself in the head with alternating fists. Motorists driving past saw an aimless, rain-soaked behemoth, shuffling down the sidewalk, looking like a homeless veteran who had lost his shopping cart.

None could have known that Stew was fast forming his own agenda. His single plan of action was to walk himself into the first open establishment serving liquor. That turned out to be a Ventura Boulevard bar called Gaby's, a twelve-stool joint with scattered tables and booths with a single six-foot pool table in the rear.

Stew didn't bother to sit before he pushed up to the bar and ordered.

"Double Jack and Coke!" he said hoarsely.

Stew started hacking like he had been struck with a case of pneumonia. Then he spread a wet hundred-dollar bill on the bar to show the smoky, boozy-looking broad behind the bar top that he meant big business.

"I gotcha, hon," said the woman. "But you gotta stop drippin' on my bar." She found a clean bar rag, wiped the bar clean then tossed the towel to Stew.

"Sorry," croaked Stew in a voice that sounded nearly humble. "Wet out there?"

"What do you think?"

The woman stuffed a tall glass with ice and set it on the bar in front of Stew, poured four fingers of Jack Daniels, then used a soda gun to top it off with a carbonated RC Cola mix.

The instant she retreated, Stew had the tumbler in his fist and was guzzling the entire cocktail without so much as a breath.

That's one to settle the nerves.

"Another?" asked the woman, though it wasn't much of a guess.

Stew nodded, she poured, then he pounded the brew back just as quickly as the first.

Two. To ease my fuckin' mind.

"Again," said Stew.

"You drivin' anywhere?"

"If I was drivin' somewhere, you think I'd be this fuckin' wet?"

"Point taken."

There was a threat to Stew's voice that some, if not most, bartenders would have taken as a reason to cut a fellah off. But the woman bartender revealed a crookedly wicked smile, then fixed Stew another drink exactly like the first two.

"Last one," she said. "But what's left over is my tip. You with me?"

Stew pushed the drenched hundred-dollar bill across to her, then pumped the last drink into his body. The wash of foam and syrup coated his throat. The pinch between his shoulder blades slackened. His core began to warm.

Three. To clarify the rage in my soul.

"Bathroom?" asked Stew.

"Left at the felt," she said with a head-tilt.

Stew's next move was to find a drug dealer.

Every dive bar had a local narcotics seller who sometimes doubled as a pimp. It was only a matter of spotting the guy. Or of being spotted, as Stew already had been by the poseur-looking elf in a paisley shirt seated on a stool at the opposite end of the bar. The man was sharing a Mai Tai with a hooker in black go-go boots, a rubber dress, and a blonde, faux-fro wig.

On his way to the men's room, Stew simply nodded with an ever-so-subtle jut of his jaw. Stew had barely enough time to unzip his pants before the dope dealer walked in from behind and locked the door.

"Need air for my tires," said Stew. "Got any tweekers?"

"Are you, by chance, a cop?" asked the dealer.

"No," said Stew. "So now that the formalities are over, is it a yes or no?"

"How do I know you're not Johnny Law?"

"Saw me walk in, didn't ya? Wet and stupid and thirsty as fuck. What more do you need?"

"Show me the money."

Stew zipped his pants, never bothered flushing the toilet, and pulled another wet hundred-dollar bill from his front pants pocket. But the dealer merely held his hands up in disgust.

"Dude. You wanna wash your hands first?"

Before the dealer could so much as yelp, Stew had him pinned against the door, his knotted forearm wedged underneath the little man's chin. Stew fished around the dealer's coat pockets and came up with a set of car keys with a nifty blue and black BMW remote button.

"That's right," choked out the dealer, scared enough to nearly pee in his pants. "Tweeks 'n' shit's in my car."

"Where's the car?"

"In the back alley."

"Okay," said Stew. "Stay at the bar, I return your car. Leave, and well . . ."

Stew helped the threat sink into the dealer with an extra few square pounds of pressure from his forearm.

"I got friends," squeaked out the dealer.

"Sure you do," sneered Stew. "But what good are friends if you're dead already?"

Stew left the bar without looking back.

As he made a hard right turn out of the men's room, he barely acknowledged the biker wannabes playing pool. He steered himself for the rear door marked with a red-lit exit sign, made three long strides into the alley, then hit the remote button on the car keys until he heard the high-pitched chirp from a black, BMW 3 series. The head and taillights of the Beemer flashed twice.

And that quickly, Stew was behind the wheel, starting the German engine, and splashing through every pothole in the back lane corridor.

The booze in Stew's bloodstream finally reached his skin, warming him all the way to his fingertips. But like a soup that needed to simmer before adding the last measure of ingredients, Stew craved both the tingle and tangle of alcohol merging with methamphetamines. To Stew, it was the addict's way of splitting the atom.

In an effort to make his actions appear normal, Stew pulled into a nearby gas station and feigned that he was buying fuel by loading the delivery nozzle into the Beemer's gas receptacle. He popped the trunk, figuring that like most respectable drug dealers, the owner of the BMW hid his stash somewhere in the wheel well under the trunk mat. Stew's theory proved correct. Just underneath the spare tire was a gallon-sized Ziploc bag stuffed with a potpourri of drugs, mostly prescription meds like OxyContin and Percocet. Scattered amongst the unmarked bottles of pills were tubes of colored Ecstasy tablets and tiny, thumbnail-sized jewelry bags filled with two different textures of powder. It had been ten years, but even under the trunk's pale twenty-five-watt bulb, Stew recognized the brownish-white powder as heroin, and the glassy, crystallized substance as the meth he was craving. But without a proper pipe to smoke it in . . .

Damn!

Stew shook the bag then flipped it sideways. There, he saw one small bag that appeared like something akin to processed sugar. It was pure methamphetamine. More expensive and refined enough to snort. With two fingers, Stew extracted the tiny baggie of pure meth and slipped it into his shirt pocket. He slammed the trunk lid, returned the nozzle to the pump, and folded himself back into the black leather car seat.

If anybody was watching what he did next, Stew didn't much care. He pried the baggie open, made a seal between the baggie and his right nostril, and inhaled every last granule. At first, it burned his sinus cavity, then scorched at the lining of his lungs. Stew's blood vessels would soon absorb the chemical and put the evil mix to work on the receptors in his brain. What few fears Stew had stored would be temporarily vanquished. And what morals he had earned from his ten years of sobriety and marriage would be flushed forever into the dark recesses of his psyche.

The sky gushed, turning each street and boulevard with the slightest pitch into a culvert for channeling water. San Fernando Valley storm drains were already overwhelmed, and in some neighborhoods, six-inch city curbs were the only defense against millions in costly flooding. Cars on the freeways were in danger of serious hydroplaning. During the downpour, Caltrans officials scrambled to respond to reported pileups on almost every major artery.

And now with the wind becoming a factor, sectors of the city's electrical grid were losing power as downed trees compromised power lines. The danger was, if outages occurred in any number of sequences, the Valley could be plunged into a nearly total blackout.

Stew sat inside the safety of the stolen BMW, staring across the street to his beloved construction site. From there he watched the power transformer attached to a pole behind the unfinished house arc, spark, then blow, dunking the street into sudden darkness. Through Stew's toxic prism, the blue flash was a beautiful sign that affirmed just why he was there.

First my house, then her house.

No longer was the construction site just a skeleton on foundation pilings. It now resembled something closer to the architectural schematics, a two-story, single-family, dream home complete with a pool. The roof was fully installed and window frames had been cut into shearing walls nailed with plywood. For looks, Stew had even had Henry hang a proper entry door to sit atop a temporary stoop formed from old brick and cinder blocks.

For Stew, the timing couldn't have been much better. While the neighbors were surely scrambling for flashlights and candles, Stew stepped from the stolen car and strode across the street. It was misting the last time he had made a nighttime visit to the site. He had stripped naked and buried both his victim and the evidence of his crime in a five-foot deep foundation form. Then, the wet air had carried with it the sting of relief.

No longer.

Stew, workman-like in his gait, yet narcotically impregnable from pain, peeled away the chain-link, ducked inside the fence, and felt his way down the property line toward the backyard. Along the way, he tripped over a leftover piece of half-inch galvanized pipe, reached down for it and dragged it with him to the pair of refrigerator-sized supply boxes parked beyond the pool. After feeling around a bit, Stew wedged the pipe between the padlock and the latch on the first container and let leverage do the work. *Snap!* Stew heard the padlock hit the dirt. He pushed up the lid and breathed in the heady mix of lubricant and gasoline. Inside the box were a compressor, air hoses, and a gas can.

The second box was just as easily peeled, but required a frustrating five minutes of prowling with his fingertips and whispered gripes until he found both the flint sparker and the propane torch.

Now Stew hurried.

He wanted to get the first half of his chore over and done with. He carried the tools inside the house where, considering the volume of rain, the slab floor remained mostly dry, but icy cold to the touch. Then he uncorked the gas can and began splashing the liquid between studs stuffed with fiberglass insulation and pre-stubbed electrical wiring. The wind howled through the upper floor and sent a chill down the stairs where Stew set the propane torch. He opened the valve and scratched out a spark. A flame issued and with it, just enough illumination for him to give one final regard to the sum total of nine months of his righteous handiwork.

It was good house, solid, full of promise and prosperity for the man with the vision to construct it.

Or the desire to destroy it.

Stew pulled the front door toward him, exited onto the temporary doorstep, then wheeled and bowled the propane bottle back into the entry. The torch rolled, then spun and skittered across the concrete floor until it slapped against a gas-soaked wall.

I'm on a rampage! And this is what it feels like!

As Stew rushed to the car, he found himself imagining how the newsmen would describe his actions. Not that he gave a flying rat's fuck about anything those talking TV blowhards had to say about him. They could spew whatever they wanted and Stew wouldn't care. He would likely be dead by then. Put down, and out of his misery, by a stranger's bullet. Most likely by a cop.

But not before he had his revenge.

Stew never looked back at the house. Not even once to see if the fire had caught. He had glimpsed the flames in the rainy reflection off the windows of the stolen BMW as he climbed in. But that was all he ever saw of it. He started the engine and drove on, preferring to remember the unfinished house as it was, and not as a burning shrine to his unrepentant rage.

Despite the heavy rain, the fire Stew left in his wake was fed enough oxygen and dry fuel to overcome the buckets of water that fell from the sky. Neighbors rushed from their homes. In awe, under umbrellas and rain jackets held securely over their heads, they watched the pyre roar. They jawed with each other about whether the fire was caused by a downed power line or even, possibly, a million-to-one lightning strike delivered from

the angry sky. Not a single man or woman suspected arson or
foul play from the kind and solid contractor-cum-speculator
they had come to know as Stew Raymo.

"I know I said I'd be there by eight," said Gonzo, "but something's
come up and I won't be able to get him until I don't know."

With her weak plea, Gonzo hoped the kindergarten mom
who had brought her son home for an afternoon play date
would respond with minimum grief. Better yet, the kindly mom
might offer up an extra pair of jammies and invite Travis for a
midweek sleepover. But there was no such luck for the LAPD
cop. Instead of understanding, Gonzo got an earful from the
frustrated mother, who appeared at her wit's end from dealing
with two little boys who had failed to get along since dinner.

"I really understand," said Gonzo, trying like hell to sound
appreciative. "Let me see what I can do about getting out of
here, okay? Really get it. Sorry for any inconvenience—"

The frantic mother cut Gonzo off, muttering something
curt and unintelligible before hanging up.

Getting out of here now!

"Here" was Jack in the Box, where Gonzo splashed a
pocketful of quarters onto the counter in exchange for a Jumbo
Jack and Diet Coke. She danced between raindrops and cars
waiting in the drive-thru in a dash to her checkered cab. She
would eat and drink on the way back to Simi Valley.

But not before one last sweep by Stew Raymo's house.

What would her final fool's errand accomplish? Most likely,
the same disappointing result. She had now slowly rolled the cab
past Stew's North Hollywood house too many times to count,
parked, watched, knocked on the door, poked around the back
under both daylight and dark and even jimmied the door to
Stew's spanking new pickup truck in hopes she might uncover
information as to where the hell Stew might be.

And while waiting for Stew to magically appear, she had
burned up her cell phone minutes, calling anybody whom she
could imagine might know or have seen where Ben Keller had
disappeared.

All the while, Gonzo continued to rehearse her speech. She had composed it in her mind and repeated it aloud to herself until it was pitch perfect. Her agenda was to leave no room for improvisation. Her only question was whether or not she would need to insert the muzzle of her Beretta 9mm into Stew's mouth to ensure his inability to argue.

Stew Raymo? Remember me? Lydia Gonzalez, LAPD. We met when you were post-op. Remember me now? Yeah? Got two words for you. Ben Keller. I want you to stay the fuck away from him. Understood? And I'm not talkin' ten feet. I'm not talkin' ten miles. I want you gone. The fuck out of the Valley, the city. Out of the fuckin' state. Otherwise, me and every cop I know—and I know a lot of 'em—we will drop a heavy fuckin' hammer on you. And just so we're clear, I'll tell you how. You drivin' to work? Maybe you get pulled over. Maybe we find a paint bucket in the back of your truck and that's fulla crack. Or maybe you got a concealed weapon in your toolbox that's a dead-fuckin' ballistic match for some unsolved murder. You hearin' all this? You better because I am one dedicated bitch! And if you don't make this happen, I'm gonna personally grease the pole that slides you into a tub of boiling hot fuckin' hellfire. You hearin' me? Nod if you get me? Yeah? Yeah? Good.

For the last time, Gonzo maneuvered the cab into a right turn onto Morrison Street. She instinctively cracked both the driver's and front passenger's windows. It was a trick she had learned as a rookie while patrolling the boulevards of South Central. By slightly lowering car windows and keeping the speedometer under twenty miles per hour, cops could employ their eyes and ears. And in the case of sudden gunfire, hearing the direction from where bullets were flying could save a smart cop's life.

Gonzo listened as her tires slowly splashed through potholes and crunched across asphalt loosened by the downpour. The rain had momentarily eased from a tumult to a steady drizzle. Without so much moisture, the cab's windshield wipers began to squeak with every cycle. The air smelled fresh and sweet and green.

Ahead on Gonzo's right, was Stew's home. It was a house

that reminded her much of her own little Simi Valley residence. The modest pale green stucco house sprouted from the neatly landscaped yard behind a white picket fence. As the cab approached, the home appeared exactly as she had left it before her dinner dash to Jack in the Box. The windows were dark, as were all porch lights. The only illumination was on the path and driveway, each dimly trimmed by rows of twelve-inch, solar-powered garden lamps in the shape of bent tulips. The same three newspapers lay un-retrieved on the driveway near Stew's pickup, yellowed and disintegrated from the deluge.

But as Gonzo rolled past the house—as she cast one last and final flick of her eyes before pressing on the accelerator—a glimmer of flame caught her attention. Or was it just a reflection? Or even a trick of the optic nerve? Gonzo cranked the wheel, made a three-point-turn, and guided the cab into a dark, curbside spot on the opposite side of the street and one address to the west. She killed the lights, rolled down her window, and stared into windows so black and opaque that they looked as dead as a doll's eyes. Then she saw it again. A small, yellow flame, tracking deep inside the glass. And quite possibly, the outline of a man.

What is that? A candle?

Gonzo was already out of the car. She turned smoothly in place, sweeping the landscape with her eyes in an attempt to sight down strangers, potential witnesses, or dog-walking bystanders. Thankfully, the rain appeared to have shuttered every living being in the neighborhood but her. The sporadically spaced streetlamps were glowing, as well as windows dotting other homes. This meant that, despite the storm, electricity was obviously intact and being fed to the neighborhood by healthy power lines.

Then why the hell had Gonzo seen a flame inside Stew Raymo's house?

Troubled but yet undeterred, Gonzo checked the safety on her pistol, tucked the muzzle into her jeans between the small of her back and her wide leather belt, covered the weapon under her letterman jacket, and crossed the street as if she were going to ring the bell of Stew's neighbor to the left. Once she had crossed the sidewalk, she made three great strides across the lawn and did a one-armed vault over the fence to Stew's driveway, ever careful to keep the pickup between herself and the house. There, Gonzo paused to recheck her surroundings and the street. She listened for sounds such as windows opening or the muffled strain of raised voices. Any sign that she, the stranger amongst them, had been identified as a prowler.

Breathe, bitch, breathe. And don't forget your fucking speech.

With that thought, Gonzo muttered her opening lines to herself.

"Stew Raymo? Remember me?"

She tucked her nearly six-foot frame against a five-foot Cyclone gate faced with a privacy screen. In the dark, she couldn't see the grease spot. Nightly oil drippings from Stew's truck had left a puddle that, when mixed with the rainwater, left parts of the pavement slick. So as Gonzo, half-crouched, touched her Vibram boot sole to the unseen spot, she slid, spun, tried like hell to maintain her balance, then fell backward and absently thumped hard against the stucco siding of the house.

Mother-fuck!

Gonzo clenched both fists and gave a disgusted yet inaudible shout-down at herself. She knew what sounded like a gentle bump outside had to come across as an audible *whump* to anybody inside the house.

Above and to her left, Gonzo made out a small, garden window attached to what she expected was the kitchen. And despite the dark, she thought she detected movement somewhere within the three-way reflection. Gonzo pressed her ear to the wall. Were those footsteps she heard? Or her heart pounding? No! Footsteps followed by a clatter of something spilling to the floor. She unholstered her pistol, pressed herself flat against the wall and made a coin flip of a choice. Back door or front door?

Or just retreat to the damn cab!

Gonzo imagined Travis. She saw her son in tears, ignored by the frustrated school mom in charge of his care, bawling for his mother. Gonzo gave herself permission to cut and run. She should return to face Stew another day. Then again, she was an experienced cop with a gun in hand. Her better instincts calculated that she still had a partial element of surprise.

And your speech, Gonzo. Don't forget your fuckin' speech!

She chose the back door. She hunched her shoulders and pushed at the gate that opened easily, but squeaked loudly. So with both hands gripping the 9mm, she ran hell-bent along the length of the house.

But who saw whom first?

A broad, darkened figure turned the corner. It was at close range. Barely ten feet separated her from him. Gonzo could have raised her weapon and emptied her clip. Instead, she used her momentum, lowered her left shoulder, and drove hard with her legs.

Contact!

Gonzo felt the pop of her shoulder separating—the A.C. ligament twisting over the top of her collarbone. What would usually be a searing, knife-like pain was masked by a chemical spell of human adrenalin. As the pair spun to a patch of wet earth, Gonzo kept moving. She swung backward with a bone-crushing elbow, then rolled atop him, knee spearing his chest and her pistol tattooing his bloody cheek with the shape of a muzzle.

"Right there, motherfucker," hissed Gonzo, "or so help me I'll punch smoke holes in your face!"

"It's me," wheezed the man, working to push air over his tongue. "It's me, Ben."

If there had been the opportunity for someone—anyone—to ask Ben if there was a flaw in his plan, he would have replied with the question:

"Isn't there always a flaw?"

But the plan had been formed so damn fast and with so little regard for anything but his own prismatic sense of justice, there was no time for his usual applied logic or assessment of risk. In the past seventy-two hours, his nerves had received such a beating, merely breathing had felt like a risk. And if he could get over that hurdle, how big of a leap was it for him to figure he could get away with executing Stew Raymo?

Somewhere between leaving Pam in a lusty lurch outside the Radisson and retrieving his car from the City Walk valet Ben had even found a moment to laugh at himself, reminded of what he used to tell his clients about the importance of planning before executing any safety plan. Avoiding costly injuries was five percent planning, ninety-five percent sweating out the plan. Such was the way Ben had spent the last ten years of his life with, in his former interpretation, much success.

No longer.

At least, he thought, *not until Stew Raymo was vanquished from the planet.* Maybe afterward, if Ben wasn't dead or rotting away in incarceration, he would revisit all his misconceived concepts. Until then, he needed to execute his scheme.

After paying the valet for his car, Ben had made a quick visit to Target where he had picked up a set of black sweats and a matching rain jacket and knit cap, plus a box of disposable rubber gloves. He donned the new duds in the restroom, returned to his car, and drove unnoticed directly to North Hollywood. It wasn't until he had parked around the corner and walked onto Morrison Street that he had realized he had forgotten to purchase a flashlight. Of course, he could have easily returned to his car and driven to any convenience store and the problem would have been solved.

But would his nerve have remained intact?

Without an answer, Ben had forged ahead armed with a handful of dangerous knowledge only criminals and paranoids like himself would possess:

1. The police, after removing Stew from the premises, would most likely not have reset the alarm. And in the unlikelihood that Stew had returned to set the alarm, Ben knew that the LAPD no longer responded to home alarm calls. More pathetic than that was the over-thirty-minute average response to home alarm calls by security companies offering patrol services.

2. Ben also knew the top ten most likely places people hide house keys, and if no key was found, the easiest and most silent means to enter a suburban house.
3. The location of Pam's hidden gun.

The only real dangers, Ben figured, were the possible actions of dogs, pedestrians, and neighbors. The odds, though, were also with Ben. Neighborhood watch programs in L.A. were poorly attended with little or no follow-up by visiting officers or even those who hosted the gathering. That was why Ben lived in Simi Valley with nearly every other LAPD cop. In that way, North Hollywood seemed more like an entirely different country than a different area code.

So it followed that, but for the flashlight, Ben's execution of the first part of his plan had been nearly flawless. He had trespassed onto Stew's property without notice. He had found a back door key hidden above the nearby window trim. The alarm had not been set, so no alert was triggered and phoned to the security company. Ben had quickly found matches and a candle in a kitchen utility drawer. And lastly, under the sink in the master bath, Ben had found a half-filled box of Tampax, at the bottom of which was a small, nickel-plated revolver with a mother-of-pearl grip.

Ben had found an odd surprise upon the realization that he had never held a gun before. And as much as he knew about guns, their history, the crunchable numbers concerning gun violence, or more accurately, the violence and harm that, statistically, people with guns could and would continue to perpetrate— only the most base of human thoughts entered his head once the gun was firmly gripped in hand. The first revelation had been how heavy such a small weapon was to heft. The second had been how stirred and potent he felt just holding the gun. As Ben pointed the revolver into the scant streetlight filtering into the house, the second and final act of his plan had played out in full, living color.

Then came a sound that startled Ben. A sort of *whump* had rippled through the house. Ben stood frozen for a moment, one half of him wanting to analyze the sound while the other half yelled pure and simply . . .

Run!

Ben pocketed the gun, felt his way out of the bathroom into the master bedroom, fumbled horribly with the locks on the French door, and hurried down the rear steps into the backyard. Walk fast, he had told himself. Chest out, shoulders wide, with your head titled down, as if you were Stew. In the dim light, no self-respecting witness would have been able to testify if the dark figure walking alongside the house was or was not Stew Raymo, let alone somebody as unknown and vanilla as Ben Keller.

He had not seen her coming.

Right at him, shoulder down, and rushing like a linebacker. It wasn't until Ben was flat on his back with her knee in his chest that he heard her voice, and against the clouded haze from a million city lights, had placed that patently curly hair. He knew it was Gonzo.

"It's me . . . It's me, Ben!"

"What the crap?"

Gonzo bared her teeth and shoved Ben's head back into the sod.

"Can't breathe!" coughed Ben.

Gonzo climbed off, breathing as if she had just finished a ten-mile foot race. Ben gagged for air.

"Why the hell . . ." Gonzo didn't finish her question. That's because she knew why Ben was at Stew's.

"Fuck it! Roll over! On your stomach!"

"What'd you say?"

Gonzo didn't ask a second time. She kicked Ben in the gut, forcing him to contract into a fetal ball. With that, she spiked her other knee into his shoulder blades, thus turning him to a surrendering, prone position.

"Lyd—"

"Shut up! Hands behind your neck. Interlace your fingers."

"You're arresting me?"

"For your own goddamn good," hissed Gonzo. "Put you in jail for as long as it takes to keep your dumb ass alive."

It was when Gonzo reached back to withdraw a pair of handcuffs from her back pocket that the tender tendon in her shoulder did a reverse loop, jolting her with a deep, searing pain.

"Mother fucker!" howled Gonzo.

"You don't wanna do this—"

"I said shut up!"

Gonzo cradled her left arm, then with her right hand, stuck her pistol back into her waistband and went about working the handcuffs. Once the restraints were snapped into place around Ben's wrists, she stood, fought back tears of pain, then yanked Ben upright and kicked his feet to shoulder width. She instinctively frisked him as if he were a common perp.

"You're screwing with a really good plan," urged Ben.

"Guess that means the day's not a total loss."

"Would you listen to me—"

"What the hell . . ."

This is when Gonzo discovered the revolver in Ben's pocket. She pulled it clear and gave it a once-over in the slim light.

"Where'd you get this? This yours?"

"No."

"Whose, then?"

"Pam Raymo's," said Ben with a defeated sigh. "The gun belongs to Stew Raymo's wife."

All the while, Stew watched.

From a spot equidistant between the granite countertop and the stainless steel refrigerator, Stew stood like a rampart, screwed into his own kitchen floor as the chemicals in his brain collided with the receptors in his eyes. At first it was the odor of spent sulfur and candle wax that had given him pause. After, it was muted voices that drifted in from the backyard. He tracked the voices with his ears as they moved up the driveway, then his eyes caught two shapes passing by the kitchen windows, left to right, one person trailing close to the other. As the figures moved onto the street, their outlines became more defined, their wet hair glistening under the streetlamps.

A man and a woman.

The woman was tall and walked with the glide of authority. The man appeared slightly slumped and suffering from the familiar gate of an arrestee with hands bound behind his back by a pair handcuffs. A prowler? Caught by a woman cop dressed in tight jeans and a letterman's jacket and walking him to a checkered taxicab?

The methamphetamines in Stew's bloodstream had more lasting power than the ethanol. Stew's warm, boozy buzz was fading while the meth argued that it would feel good to grind his molars down to each respective nerve. Yet, there was the benefit of a heightened sense of time and place and Stew was convinced, a greater visual acuity.

Or maybe it was just that the woman cop was checking her prisoner into a goddamned, yellow-checkered cab. She opened the rear door of the taxi, triggering the dome light, and gestured for her prisoner to get inside. Stew witnessed a brief struggle, followed by an argument that ended with the prisoner relenting and slipping butt first into the backseat.

Then Stew saw Ben.

The moment Ben's face became illuminated it was, for Stew, as if a snapshot had been taken and etched with laser precision into each cornea.

The bastard!

The man Stew had last seen in a tearful embrace with his precious Pam, had somehow returned into his orbit without so much as an invitation. Captured and arrested? And for what? A flash of memory pushed through the synthetic static between Stew's ears—and with it came a prickly heat to the skin on his face. It was the picture of a woman detective who had visited him during his hours of post-operative recovery. She had pressed Stew about a set of twelve-year-old murders in Culver City.

That's her, Stewy. The cunt that started this shit!

Ground zero, reasoned the rationally-inhibited killer. The downward spiral Stew was on hadn't begun with Ben. It had begun with . . . *Her!*

The short respite from the storm was closing in a cascade of heavy rain that lowered like a curtain at the end of a final act. As the rain pounded hard against the house, growing louder by the microsecond, Stew's picture of Ben and Gonzo in the checkered cab, framed by the generous kitchen window, quickly dissolved into a watery blur of amorphous and benign contours.

Stew's right hand gripped a two-gallon gas can. In his left hand he clutched rags to use as a wick for the firebomb he planned to set in the bedroom. He dropped the contents of both fists in a synchronized clatter, then swept his arm across the kitchen counter until he heard the familiar jangle of his truck keys landing on the floor.

"I'm going to uncuff you for a second," said Gonzo. "Turn 'em this way so I can see 'em."

Ben rolled his eyes, then twisted in the seat to show Gonzo his hands. Gonzo keyed the lock, releasing one of Ben's wrists.

"Okay. Buckle up," said Gonzo.

"You're making a mistake," pressed Ben.

"You already said that," Gonzo shot back. "How's this? If my big mistake is stopping your even bigger mistake? I can learn to live with that."

Ben wanted to resist. With his own hands free and Gonzo's left shoulder clearly compromised, how hard would it be to grab a handful of Gonzo's hair and slam her head into the Plexiglas safety screen, retrieve Pam's revolver, and run? Would Gonzo dare shoot him? Would it be a kind relief to have bullets sting him from behind and cut the motors to his brain? Ben would never know, wisely deciding to comply with her command. He reached across and snapped himself in with the three-point harness.

"Run the open cuff underneath the lap belt," ordered Gonzo. "Then snap the cuff back on."

"I'm not gonna run."

"Just do it for me, will ya?" said Gonzo.

Gonzo tested Ben's handiwork with a tug, making sure he was secure. Satisfied, she slammed the door shut and climbed in behind the wheel with an audible groan. Her left shoulder felt like someone had dropped a sledgehammer onto it. She tossed both her 9mm and Pam's revolver onto the passenger seat and started the engine. She shook her hair so violently, it left a symmetrical pattern of watery droplets across the safety screen.

"I know you think you're helping," said Ben. "But all you're doing is prolonging the inevitable."

"Half my job is prolonging shit. The other half is hoping that by prolonging shit, people's better angels prevail and they forget what got 'em pissed off in the first place."

"Right. Like I could ever forget."

"Shut up. Most of what you're hot about right now is Alex kicking you out. You just don't know it yet."

Ben shook his head in disagreement. "Guess word travels fast in Simi," he said.

Gonzo flicked a guilty look into the rearview mirror before making a hard right, surging south onto Laurel Canyon Boulevard and through a changing stoplight, then swinging into northbound traffic on the Hollywood Freeway with the accelerator pressed to the floorboard. After all, Gonzo still needed to get back home to rescue her boy from that impatient mom.

It was 9:32 P.M.

"Take a picture," said Gonzo, trying to lighten the moment. "If a year ago, somebody told me that I'd be driving a cab with Ben-the-Safety-Expert handcuffed in the back, I woulda told them to get their head checked."

"Would be two of us," said Ben.

"There you go. A little perspective. Now we're getting somewhere."

"It could work," said Ben.

"Perspective? Or you talkin' about something else?"

"All I need is the gun."

"Swear, Benjy," said Gonzo. "I will cuff your ass to my bedpost and make you watch Oprah reruns—all night—if that's what it takes to talk you down from the idiot tree."

"He beat the shit outta her," said Ben. "And she's got a restraining order!"

"Who?"

"Pamela. Stew's wife."

"And what the hell would you know about her? And how would you get her gun? How deep into her shit are you?"

Ben looked sideways. He couldn't imagine a succinct answer, let alone one that could explain feelings that he hadn't yet even begun to sort out.

Gonzo moved on.

"So that's a surprise? That Stew the Dipshit beats his wife?"

"You don't know what I know," Ben said sotto voce. He rested his head on the seat back, his eyes swirling behind closed lids.

"Okay, okay," said Gonzo. "I'll bite because we got a ways to drive. So we'll talk for a while. You say what you need to say. Then we pick up my boy, go to my house, and that's when we stop talkin' shit and start talkin' about tomorrow. Waking up, taking a shower, moving on. Remember that? Those were your words, right? It's all about 'moving on.'"

Gonzo turned the wipers on full. But no matter how quickly they cycled, the rain and spray from all the other cars and trucks were almost too overwhelming to safely keep the car in the fast lane.

But Gonzo had opened the door. She had invited Ben to explain himself. Yet in thinking of how to recount his clandestine relationship with Pam, he realized he would be admitting to lies on top of deceptions, not to mention the potential for indiscretion. All in the name of a plot, just two hours old, that had hinged on his breaking into Stew's house, stealing Pam's gun without her knowledge, and returning to Pam's hotel room. All that had been left for Ben to figure was how to tell Stew where he was and who he was with. Ben knew enough about the law that if Stew were to violate Pam's restraining order, Ben would be well within his legal rights to shoot and kill him in Pam's defense. And using Pam's gun to end Stew's life would make the case all the more airtight.

"Oh," said Gonzo. "So now you don't wanna talk. Can I take this as a positive? A moment of self-evaluation? That the adrenalin in your veins and the testosterone in your pants are no longer ruling your senses?"

If Ben were to answer honestly, it would have been a resounding, "*No.*" Though Gonzo had suggested something that made him think.

What about tomorrow?

Ben had no Plan B. That and fate had him on a return trajectory to Simi Valley. He was sure that once Gonzo had tongue-lashed him until she was convinced he was no longer a threat to himself or Stew or the general public at large, she would deliver him to a flower shop and then his own front doorstep with advice on how best to make things right with Alex. But what after that? What of Stew? He certainly wasn't going to move on until Ben or Pam or both of them were dead.

"Gotta question," asked Gonzo. "What happened to the sensible Ben Keller? Nice guy, smart mouth, wiseass cocktail party flirt that makes all those Simi Canyon mommies feel so safe and secure and wish you were the one they were sharing carpool with?"

"Vanilla Man," Ben found himself whispering.

"Come again?"

"That guy was one hundred percent bullshit," said Ben, loud enough for Gonzo to hear him through the perforated holes in the Plexiglas.

"Well, I liked that guy," said Gonzo. "That guy was sweet and funny and . . ."

Gonzo's eyes moved with sudden intuition.

She flicked a look into her right side-view mirror as a blast of high-beam fury exploded from the pack of cars behind her. The closing headlights cut back across three lanes and crowded her rearview mirror like an oncoming locomotive engine. The cab ignited with light. A collision was a matter of certainty. In her single defensive maneuver, Gonzo floored the accelerator. Then while letting go of the wheel, she reached with her good arm in a last attempt to string the seatbelt across herself and into the buckle.

Crunch!

Ben heard the ugly sound of mashing sheet metal and

thermoplastic polymer, felt his body violently compressed into the rear seat, then experienced the world spinning in a momentary panorama of streaking white and red lights.

The blow from the new white pickup truck sent the cab hydroplaning, leaving little to no traction between the tires and the road. When the cab hit the concrete divider it was traveling eighty-two miles per hour in a pouring rain. The force of impact was so great it reversed momentum and sent the cab twirling counterclockwise back into traffic. Airbags were deployed, barely cushioning the teeth-shattering wallop from a ten-ton semi-tractor trailer rig. The force lifted the cab onto two wheels, tipping the vehicle into a watery tumble across four lanes of traffic until it punched clean through a guardrail, snapping off the six-by-six-inch wooden posts like matchsticks, and twisting the metal barrier into a forty-foot ribbon of skyward-reaching sculpture.

The pileup of cars was like a Russian ballet or a synchronized swimming exhibition. Cars didn't collide so much as they glided and spun, sending great red-lit rooster tails of water spraying into the air.

A Caltrans traffic camera caught the entire event in digital color. In later months, then years, it was studied by traffic experts and eventually replayed in slow motion video all over the Internet. First came the attacking white pickup truck, the initial collision, the cab's impact with the center wall, the reverse spin, the crush from the semi-rig, then the cab tumbling out of the picture's frame. Meanwhile, the white F-250 pickup bucked off the concrete meridian and got caught with its wheels stuck behind the divider sliding along with a display of trailing sparks. The rest of the show looked as if it had been story-boarded by a second-unit director. The subsequent cars were all braking and spinning like pinwheels in opposition, yet miraculously, not a single innocent vehicle came in contact with another. The video ended with ten seconds of no movement whatsoever but for the steady pour of rain.

Stew didn't miss a moment of the wreck.

He was conscious from the initial surge across three lanes of traffic, the satisfying strike as his shiny new pickup impacted the checkered cab and the explosion of the airbag in his face, to the sensation of being airborne as his rear wheels took flight before straddling and skidding along the top of the concrete divider for a good hundred and seventy feet.

All the while, Stew had fully expected to flip at any moment and re-enter traffic as a target of heavy-metal death. Instead, his truck hopped and skidded and sent incandescent embers into the black night. From his driver's side window, Stew caught the last sparks from the impact of the semi crushing the cab, which only added to his vindictive pleasure. He did his level all to grapple against his steering wheel so he could remain fixed on the yellow checkered cab as it tumbled end-over-end across traffic, stripping the guardrail before disappearing into the dark beyond the wash of headlights and streetlamps.

But when the stillness came, the noise inside his skull got louder and ugly, as if he needed mayhem to quiet the grinding gears gummed by the residual methamphetamines. What he needed was booze. A super-sized shot of Jack and Coke to set him straight.

But not until he was sure both the bastard and the dyke cop were dead.

Stew shouldered his door open and slid into the rain. When his feet touched the pavement, his left knee screamed with pain. Was it just a memory from his last accident? Or had he re-injured his ACL during the crash?

"Fuck it," mouthed Stew.

He slid a twenty-pound fitting wrench out from underneath the seat. So what if he was slightly busted up? He had suffered worse injuries. And a hellish limp would sell the illusion that he was just another victim of a weather-induced freeway mishap.

Not your fault Stewy. He started it.

Using the fitting wrench as a crutch of sorts, Stew began a dead-reckoning gimp across the five freeway lanes. A graying Indian man, stuffed into a dress shirt soaked and buttoned to his Adam's apple, stood at the open driver's door of his stalled Chevy

Malibu with a helpful arm held out in Stew's direction.

"Are you okay, sir?" asked the Indian man, shaken to his core. "I . . . I just called for nine-one-one assistance. We should sit and wait, you think?"

Stew's eyes swerved, regarding the Indian man with a glare so menacing it sent the would-be Good Samaritan recoiling back into his vehicle. Stew never changed direction or altered the painful hitch in his step. The drugs were fading on him. If there was finish work to be done, Stew would need to do it on resolve alone. The hole where the cab punched through the guardrail and disappeared lay ahead—beyond the asphalt, the freeway streetlamps, and under a relentless assault of rain, a backdrop of utter blackness—a void where Stew and that twenty-pound fitting wrench were headed.

The best Ben could figure was that he had lost consciousness somewhere between the collision with the semi and the time it had taken the cab to come to rest. He had somehow missed the part where the cab had tumbled end-over-end and snapped that ribbon of guardrail like a worn shoelace. When Ben awoke, the cab lay inverted on its half-crushed roof, teetering on a sandy precipice. He was hanging upside-down, turned backwards, cuffed and tangled in his seatbelt harness, his bloody scalp scraping against torn upholstery.

Beyond the shattered windows, he could make out the tips of trees and scrub growing up from around ramparts that lifted the freeway over what he reckoned was the Sepulveda flood plane. Then he thought of Gonzo.

Ben tried to choke out her name, but found his larynx clogged with spit and phlegm. He coughed and twisted toward the driver's seat. His neck stung. Pain, he recognized, was a good thing. He wriggled his fingers and toes, feeling the handcuffs and the seams inside his sneakers. There was no obvious sign of spinal distress, the single most common injury in vehicle accidents where cars become airborne and flip.

"Lydia?" whispered Ben before finding the bass in his vocal chords. "Lydia!"

Ben pushed with his knee and swiveled himself toward the driver's compartment. The yellow-tinted Plexiglas partition was partially dislodged and looking as dangerous as a guillotine blade. The steering wheel had snapped at the column and was at rest in the passenger-side's foot well, hanging by the spent airbag. But for the jagged, toothy edges, all the glass from the windshield had been blasted out.

"GONZO!" screamed Ben

He hoped to hell she would hear him and answer back. Just like he had prayed that when he had finally turned himself around he would find her equally strung up and alive. Instead, she was nowhere to be seen. Not a body or severed limb or bloody trail to be seen in the bare gleam of light coming from the opened glove box.

What did catch Ben's eye was the slick glint off Pam's revolver. The gun lay in a spray of bejeweled safety glass, mere inches away, but on the other side of the now-slanting, see-though partition.

A thick blackness filled his eyes, obscuring his vision beyond the simple blink of his eyelids. Ben wiped at them, smearing blood across his sleeve. He was bleeding from somewhere unknown and it was draining into his eyes. He cleared them again, blinked and blinked, trying to focus again on the brightest light, a metal halide streetlamp that hung over the freeway, some sixty-plus feet away.

Under the lamp, Ben saw a single, silhouetted figure.

Praise Christ. Help has come.

The figure limped and appeared to be using some sort of heavy stick for a crutch. Ben wiped his eyes once more, strained to focus, and made a more honest assessment. The savior with the faltering gate was no savior at all. It was, indeed, Stew Raymo. And Stew was coming to finish the job.

Ben's instincts flared. He fought with the seatbelt, seeking places where it was slack so he could untangle himself, then looked for a cut or a weakness in the fabric where he might slip the handcuffs free. But the cab was a late model Chrysler, and just moments after his struggle began, Ben surrendered when his mind recalled the latest goddamn study on modern seatbelt safety by the National Insurance Institute. His brain swamped with survival statistics of accident victims using the old No Locking Retractor recoiling lap belts versus the Emergency Locking Retractor harnesses. The latter technology was sensitive to vehicle rollovers, thus working as a decelerator during momentum shifts, keeping the wearer locked in position until all life threatening movement had ceased.

Once again, Ben's view swung to Stew, steady on the approach. Next, his bloodied eyes keyed on Pam's revolver. If only he could reach it. He had to release the inertia reel of the seatbelt tensioner. That meant un-weighting himself in order to release the clutch in the mechanism. So with all that he had in his weakened abdominals, he pulled himself upward until, with his cuffed hands, he was able to sink his fingers between the cushions, find a handhold and slowly pull until he felt the click. The shoulder belt eased enough for Ben to depress the buckle release. That's when gravity took over. And though Ben fell only inches, when he landed on his head it felt as if he had been dropped five feet onto solid concrete.

The car shuddered, rocked, slipped across the sand for nearly an entire yard, then stopped again.

Ben caught his breath, but couldn't slow the feeling that his heart was about to burst from his chest. He rolled to his stomach, fully intent on slipping his cuffed hands under the Plexiglas to retrieve the gun. But a shadow fell across him, blocking the light from the distant streetlamp.

"Anybody left alive in there?" growled Stew, before hammering the big pipe wrench against the chassis.

Clank!

Ben steadied himself, focused on the gun, and lunged ahead with both hands, only to have the belt tensioner seize and stop him cold.

"C'mon, you cockroaches. Crawl the fuck out!"

Clank! Clank!

With each resounding blow of the wrench against the car, Ben flinched. So Ben took a painful breath, calmed his nerves enough to refocus on the revolver, and this time, ever-so-slowly reached forward and unwound the remaining inches of seatbelt left wrapped around the inertia reel.

"Anybody home?" yelled Stew

Stew began gouging around with the wrench, stabbing it though the shrunken windows and working it around like he was trying to stir up a bed of snakes.

"C'mon, lady cop. Tell me all about the trouble I'm in now!"

Inches from the revolver, Ben flattened his hands and slid them underneath the partition, stretching with his fingertips until his middle nail actually brushed the muzzle of the gun. And that was it. As far as the belt would allow.

Christ, no!

Ben withdrew his hands, rolled up onto his shoulder, angling his arms differently with desperate hopes of releasing another inch of the harness.

"I hear youuuuuuuuu!" shouted Stew.

Stew swung the wrench into the rear passenger door.

Clank!

Last chance, thought Ben. He reached under the partition, fingers flexed to their tensile . . .

"Whatcha lookin' for?" asked Stew, soft, throaty and almost playful.

Ben's sights lifted from the gun to the dashboard. There was Stew, propped on his hands and knees, head stuck through the windshield. Stew's eyes immediately tracked from Ben, half-obscured through the tilted Plexiglas, to Pam's gleaming, five-shot revolver.

The gun may as well have been a blood-red bone that lay between two angry dogs. One rabid, the other desperate to survive. Stew left the wrench behind, scrambling onto his stomach, and with astonishing speed, wriggled his thick torso through the crushed and jagged window frame.

Ben extended himself for the gun, uncoiling the belt to the very last thread—the gun, the sole core of his focus. Using the tips of his index and middle fingers, he pinched the muzzle into a weak vise and began drawing the gun nearer.

Stew kicked and howled and snaked closer. The cab rocked. The earth moved underneath and the cab tilted and slid a foot sideways. The gun slid, too. Away from Ben. Out of reach and directly into Stew's grasp. A gift.

Stew grinned.

Fight or flight?

As Stew twisted into position, poking the revolver forward and training the muzzle at Ben's face, Ben was overcome with a sense of calm and clarity. *It was all physics*, he thought. *To fight I must take flight.* The adrenaline in Ben surged, firing every fast twitching muscle fiber into a single vicious retreat. With all his force, Ben threw himself rearward, cramming into the space between the shattered rear window and the seat's back.

The rest was up to Newton.

Stew pulled the trigger in three rapid bursts. Each bullet deflected off the Plexiglas, piercing the seats.

The cab rocked, slid and tipped. Then came the free-fall.

The Sepulveda Dam was built by the Army Corps of Engineers in 1941. To the north of the barrier were parks and lakes and public golf courses, all constructed in a natural collection basin. When the gutters and flood channels of the San Fernando Valley were overwhelmed, the water pooled behind the dam and was released by a spillway into a gravel-based trough. The trough tilted south, passing underneath the Ventura Freeway.

The cab's fifty-foot drop between the muddy shelf and the rocky bottom was broken by a pair of large birch trees that mitigated the total force of the fall. The car twirled before it landed on its side in five feet of swift, rising water. The cab settled, pinned against a tree trunk by the sheer force of moving water.

Then the river entered the car.

Somehow, with help from those handcuffs still strung through the seatbelt, Ben hung on through the half-flip and touchdown without losing consciousness. He feared drowning. Swallowed by the swirling water, Ben was lost, uncertain which direction was up or down until he let the bubbles blowing from his nose show him the way. He eventually found air and a handhold near the left passenger door. As oxygen filled his lungs, Ben experienced a stab in his side, a sure sign of broken ribs. He coughed up blood, looked for a second handhold, and tried to orient himself in the darkness that, at first, seemed absolute. Ben's right leg felt mangled, possibly fractured.

"Can't move," gurgled Stew. "Can't feel nothin'."

Ben swung himself in the direction of the weak voice to find himself only inches away from Stew. Still, it was hard to hear over the roar of the water surging against and through the car. Ben's eyes adjusted to the ambient light. He could see Stew's shape, wedged between the Plexiglas partition and the driver's door. While Stew's head and neck were supported, the rest of his body swished and flapped with the movement of the current.

"Anybody there? Can't see ya but I hear ya coughin'."

"Water's rising," said Ben.

"So why don't you just swim?" said Stew. "Don't tell me you can't swim?"

But Ben was still cuffed with that infernal seatbelt between himself and actual safety.

"Stuck," said Ben. "Handcuffed to a safety belt."

"Don't that beat it," chuckled Stew, weakly.

To Ben it was a goddamned safety paradox. He kicked with his left leg until he found a foothold against the headrest.

"What's it mean . . . when you can't feel shit?" asked Stew. He spoke with heavy breaths between phrases. "That's bad, right . . . ? Spinal and shit . . . yeah?"

"Yeah," said Ben, not exactly relieved that Stew no longer appeared to be a threat. The river was moving upward. He was handcuffed and would be drowning soon along with Stew. Ben stuck his head out the busted window, tugged at the belt, unwinding it until there was nothing left. He pulled, hoping against hope that he would be the million-to-one customer that experienced seatbelt failure. But there was no give to the reel. And most of Ben's strength felt as if it had been expended, never to return.

"I remember," said Stew, even more haltingly. "Tried to forget . . . But . . . I remember most of it."

Ben was half listening, half trying to devise some kind of secondary plan that ended up with him surviving. That was until Stew continued.

"Remember she... was blonde... Kinda pretty... Stuck to her guns, too... Her little girls... she kept sayin'... 'Let my girls live'... So fucked up, man... so... fucked up, I... I didn't listen... listen to shit from... nobody."

The water was close to overtaking the entire car. The cabin was totally swamped but for the inches of air Stew was still breathing. Ben had the window. That meant he had more time before his inevitable end.

"Shoulda done it there... first night... in the bar... Showed you my piece... took what was in... register."

"What bar?"

"Yours... You 'n' me... we talked 'n' talked... Served me... Ice Breaker, remember?"

My bar? Stew came into my bar?

"I don't," said Ben. Through the trauma, through the years, Ben had done everything he could to put it all behind him. To move on. Some memories were lost... or still locked away.

"No matter..." said Stew, his voice near a whisper.

The water was up to Stew's ears, only an inch or so from submerging him forever.

"I remember... tried to... forget... But you... you made me 'member... so good... good for you."

"I moved on," said Ben. "I tried to move on."

"Yeah..." said Stew. "Was doin'... was doin' so good... so good for awhile there... legit... Think, see... I moved on, too..."

Stew's words were stopped with a surge of water that rolled across the top of the river and smacked the car like a rogue wave in the middle of the sea. The car tilted and went completely under. Stew. Ben. Drowning in a churning tempest of leaves and soil and litter.

The busted steering wheel clunked Ben in the jaw, then swirled around him, dragged by that spent airbag. Ben thought he heard a muddled jangle of keys. Without the slightest aforethought, as if by pure, unconscious instinct, Ben grabbed for the wheel. He found keys, still stuck in the ignition switch.

Gonzo's keys!

With his lungs bursting, crying to inhale anything in order to end the ordeal, Ben touched on a tiny, cylindrical peg, gripped it, and jammed it at the handcuff lock—over and over again—until it slipped into the hole.

All he had to do was twist the key. The cuffs released from his wrist and away he went with the current, bouncing through the cab, sucked out through the back window.

If Ben was to be rescued, the work would have to be done by the river, the rain, and God.

epilogue

IN SIMI VALLEY, the arrival of June summoned warmer temperatures, a change of color in the wild, winter grasses that were sketched in and around the surrounding rocky slopes, and the end of the Simi Canyons school year.

Most of the Simi Canyons students, from growing kindergartners to graduating high school seniors, experienced a far greater sense of giddiness than concern at the prospect of moving on, anticipating three months of summer holidays. Parents, on the other hand, were far more apprehensive, wondering how the hell they were going to manage both their own time and their children's. Some moms and dads queued up in double pick-up lanes, and when they weren't ignoring the safety rule of no texting or talking on cell phones while driving on campus, worried over summer camps or vacation plans or how they were going to budget for the next year's tuition increase.

Alex, though, in her usual cool and organized style, was looking to solve a more immediate problem. The recently dismissed high school principal was dogging her for a dinner date. Alex wanted to say yes. He was attractive, attentive, and now that he was no longer a school administrator, available to romantically socialize without any attached stigma. Alex's problem, though, was threefold.

Though officially separated from Ben, she had only just hired an attorney and filed for divorce.

What would her girls think?

And why was the principal's firing still shrouded in mystery? The rumors had been flying for months about the terms of the man's release, yet despite all the efforts of those gossipy Yummy Mummies, the school had successfully followed their lawyers' advice and remained mum. A date with the tainted man would, at worst, solve the mystery. Alex would get the truth out of him. Or so she reasoned.

A car honked from behind. The pick-up lanes were, for some reason, not moving at all. When Alex looked around for someone to ask what the holdup was, she noticed that, behind the wheel of the car to her right, was none other than Lydia Gonzalez.

Alex could see that Gonzo, slightly obscured behind the tinted window of her Suburban, was still healing from her reconstructive surgery. Her hair was butch and short, only recently growing back after the initial hydrocephalus. The bandages on her face were clean, covering the harsher realities of the pins that held her shattered jaw together. Through the grapevine, Alex had heard that Gonzo could only take her meals through a straw, a sight better and more convenient than the feeding tube that had fed directly into her stomach.

But seeing Gonzo behind the wheel gave Alex comfort. It meant the broken bones below her neck had healed sufficiently enough to allow her to drive to school and pick up her little boy, Travis, a graduating kindergartner.

Alex rolled down her window and gave a polite shout.

"Lydia?"

At first, Gonzo didn't respond. So giving it one last chance, Alex upped her volume.

"Lydia!"

Alex watched Gonzo's eyes swerve in her direction. The tinted glass made their brown pigment look black and piercing until Gonzo lowered her window.

"How are you?" asked Alex.

Gonzo answered with a slight pause, then a subtler nod as if to say, "Okay."

"I see your hair's growing in."

Gonzo didn't hear the question, so she shrugged and hung her ear out the window.

"I said you look well," said Alex. "Your hair is growing in nicely."

Gonzo nodded a thank-you.

"Travis looking forward to summer vacation?"

Gonzo nodded again, and despite all the metal in her jaw and the wiring that kept her teeth clenched, mouthed a simple: "We both are."

Though it didn't hurt for Gonzo to speak, to an observer it appeared uncomfortable as hell. Sometimes Gonzo wondered if and how she had used it to her advantage. Simply put, there were certain people she didn't care to talk to. Parents, neighbors, colleagues. Conversations could carry on only so long when all Gonzo could do was shrug, nod or offer a thin smile.

Ah, the upside of disability.

On that fateful night, had Gonzo not been driving home in a cab that, in the terms of her union-negotiated settlement, was part of an active LAPD investigation, the accident would have remained uncovered by the insurance policies protecting officers from on-the-job injuries.

None of that explained why her passenger and friend, Ben Keller, was handcuffed in the backseat. *Protective custody*, her lawyer had argued. Before the compensation review panel, Gonzo's attorney successfully argued that her passenger was, despite his objection, in her protective custody from the clear and present threat of the man named Stew Raymo. The lawyer's theory was proven by the ensuing deadly attack on that rain-drenched freeway.

Remember the positives, girlfriend.

Gonzo was spending more time with Travis now. And forever would be at school for every drop-off, pick-up and parent-involved activity that landed in between. No more long days with the baby sitter. At last, mommy belonged to Travis.

Stew Raymo, a blessing in a scary disguise.

Of the attack itself Gonzo drew pretty much a blank slate. She remembered the contact from behind, then smacking into the concrete divider. Because of the angle of impact and the stupid fact that she wasn't wearing her seatbelt, she had sailed over the airbag, snapping off the steering wheel at the column as it collided with her pelvis, hurling her through the windshield as if it were candy glass. Gonzo didn't remember landing on the asphalt, but insisted she could still see the underbelly of Stew's F-250, rear wheels stuck behind the barrier, sliding over her and spraying sparks into the rainy sky.

While Gonzo was in the hospital recovering, Romeo appeared with a portable DVD player. As he replayed the enhanced version of the Caltrans recording of the accident, her faint memory proved correct. Frame by frame, they could track Gonzo's limp body as it was ejected from the cab to the pavement, followed by Stew's truck, bucking up onto the meridian and sliding right over her.

"What dumb fucking luck," Romeo had repeated over and over.

Gonzo kept thinking about the seatbelt. Had she been wearing it, she wouldn't have been sent flying into the street. And with the airbag already deployed, there was no imagining that she could have survived the second impact with the semi.

But Ben had.

Gonzo thought of Ben often. Not missing him so much as wondering about him.

So with Alex only yards away, Gonzo braved her question.

"How's Ben?" she asked, forcing her voice to carry over her wired jaw.

"What's that?" asked Alex.

"Ben," forced Gonzo. "How . . . is . . . Ben?"

"Have I seen Ben?" asked Alex, misreading Gonzo's question.

Close enough, nodded Gonzo.

"We're separated," said Alex without much pause whatsoever, let alone a trace of sadness. But that was Alex. Usually matter-of-fact, bordering on cold. She was dependable that way, purposefully keeping her problems in the rearview mirror. Always moving on.

"He sees the girls sometimes," continued Alex. "It's mostly Betsy, though. She misses him most, and well . . . it's nice that Ben makes the time. He's good that way."

It was answer enough for Gonzo, who nodded her appreciation. When Alex's queue began to move, she waved her trademark lacquered nails and smiled brightly.

"Have a great summer!" said Alex, rolling ahead.

Gonzo waved back and hit the button that automatically returned her window to the fully closed position. Silence filled her car. Her emotions rumbled underneath her skin. With the emotions came a recurring guilt. What could have been? Had she not succumbed to Alex's blackmail, Gonzo never would have made the call that set in motion the couple's separation. And if the relationship had still been intact, would Ben have climbed out onto that dangerous limb that led to, well, that god-awful Wednesday night? Gonzo would never know. All she could hope for was that someday, maybe, she would have the chance to apologize to Ben in such a way that he might actually forgive her.

Josie Jones had retreated to her mother's house in New Mexico. After the week long booze and cocaine binge following her twelve-hour fling with Stew, she got scared for her future, hopped an overnight train to Albuquerque and checked herself directly into a twenty-eight-day recovery program. The events of that rainy night remained a mystery to her. When she finally called Ben's office, the number had been disconnected. The same was true for both Ben's cell number and home phone. Her brightest idea was to contact private detective Woody Bell. If Woody didn't know how to contact Ben, he would surely have the resources to find him.

But Woody's number had also been switched off.

An eventual Google search proved shocking to Josie as she read a single blurb that had appeared in the Valley's *Daily News*. It told of the stymied police investigation into Woody Bell's murder. The rough details were that Woody had been found with his wheelchair, dead at the bottom of his empty pool. Foul play was suspected. And there were persons of interest within the Armenian mob with whom the police were seeking to speak.

Josie could find nothing more on the murder.

In late May, she finally received an email reply from Ben that read simply:

Glad you are recovering in Albuquerque. All is well and as it should be. Be safe. Ben.

The baby cried.

Pam, in denial that she was sleep-deprived, snapped awake from her twelve-minute nap, oriented herself on the couch, and made her way back to the baby's room.

How the hell did I just fall asleep so fast?

Stew's former office was unrecognizable. After the funeral, it had been quickly remodeled from a cramped space of un-filed papers, dirt stains and clutter, to a tastefully simple nursery. Crib, bureau, changing table, and rocking chair. Swedish pine all. The walls were painted in calming pastels, complete with ascending cherubs and silly jungle animals, all hand-painted with loving care by mommy.

"What's all the fuss?" smiled Pam, sweetly whispering to her baby boy. "I just changed you so you're not dirty. Are you the only one in the house who doesn't want a nap?"

Pam reached into the crib and picked up the ten-week-old baby. *Her gift*, she called him. A joyous dividend of fate and love. Wannabe parents wait months, even years, before placement with a newborn. But timing and luck had been on her side. A young couple in Fairbanks, Alaska, had registered with an adoption site at nearly the precise moment Pam had finished her first phone interview with the online adoption attorney. Maybe he had been wowed by his eighty-minute talk with Pam. Or could he have recognized her from the photo she had attached to the e-application, and as an ardent fan, moved her up to the top of the baby list? Pam didn't know nor did she care. She had a baby of her own and that was the end of that.

The *For Sale by Owner* sign was gone, trashed, left for scavengers to resuscitate from a landfill. As was every remnant and reminder of her dead husband. Curb to property line. Vanished, dismissed, and with a prayer, someday forgotten.

Pam lifted her boy, named Michael after her favorite, fifth-grade homeroom teacher, cradled him to her left shoulder, and went about preparing a warm bottle of Enfamil. She still wasn't used to every drawer and cupboard being locked in place with safety catches for both earthquakes and the day in the future when young Michael would stand on his own two legs and attempt to explore every imaginable hiding place, crevasse, and electrical outlet, all already protected from a toddler's probing nubs.

The baby, briefly pacified by his attentive mother, expressed himself with another complaint.

"Sssshhhh," soothed Pam

She married a nipple from the drying rack with a collar and plastic bottle. All she needed to do was fill the bottle from a container in the fridge, nuke it for twenty-five seconds, and the meal would be ready to serve.

Only the phone rang.

Catch it before the second ring, thought Pam. *Grab the handset quick and answer in a calm, clarifying voice*. She shifted Michael to the opposite shoulder, reached for the telephone, pressed LINE 1, and spoke.

"Safety first," answered Pam, professional and proud.

Michael couldn't wait. He had seen the bottle, watched it being filled with thick, sweetened, luscious, sand-colored goo, then heard the oh-so-familiar beep-beep-beeping of mommy's fingers setting the timer on the microwave.

So Michael wailed.

Pam quickly placed the caller on hold.

"Sssshhhh. You wanna wake the dead?"

"The dead are already awake," said the voice from behind her.

The baby's eyes widened in sudden recognition.

Pam turned in place and smiled apologetically with the phone still at her ear.

"Please hold . . ." she said, "for Ben Martin."

She held out the phone to Ben.

"Sorry."

"No apologies necessary," said Ben with sleepy eyes.

He was only half-awakened from his nap, barefoot, bare-chested, wearing nothing but a pair of old Levi's. He kissed Michael on the forehead, then Pam on the lips, and accepted the telephone.

"I'm sorry," said Ben to the caller. "This is Ben Martin. What can I do for you?"

Pam rubbed her knuckles sweetly against Ben's soft belly hair, then returned to serving Michael his baby formula. She sat comfortably in a kitchen chair, tilted the bottle into Michael's little maw, and watched as another chapter in her new life unfolded before her eyes.

Ben shuffled over to a quiet corner of the living room to carry on his phone consult. But for the healing limp and some leftover scarring on his torso, Ben showed no signs from the accident. As far as Pam knew, he had confessed everything to her—not a solitary detail of the accident left for guesswork. Up to, and including, the miracle of his rescue by a fire crew who had been posted above the rushing river channel, practicing exactly the kind of extraction that Ben had required. Had the fireman not already been nearby, Ben surely would have drowned.

On the day Pam had visited Ben in his hospital room, he had concealed nothing. He included all his prior dishonest behavior. He even retold the events leading up to the morning he had knocked on her door and totally misrepresented himself.

Pam was initially sickened by his disclosure, arms wrapped around herself, pacing at the end of his bed, silently nodding as every additional piece of the puzzle was laid bare. Nearly every fiber in her wanted to bolt for the door and never, ever look back.

Maybe it was her own guilt that kept her from running. The guilt of her marriage to Stew. The guilt of her past. So when Ben was finished, Pam began. She confessed to him the sorry horrors of *her* past. Her addictions. Her sordid porn career. Her occasional moonlighting as a high-priced call girl, an embarrassing act she had never disclosed to a solitary soul. Especially, not Stew.

And when she was finished . . .

"We're both gonna need a lot of therapy," Ben had joked from his hospital bed.

Pam was instantly reminded of how she had always laughed with Ben. Unguarded. Safe. Easy. She visited him daily and she wondered if she was falling for him. Though not yet brave enough to use the "L" word.

So as Ben limped back and forth across the living room, phone fixed to his ear and selling his rare and unique expertise to another needy customer, Pam looked her new man over yet again.

With Ben sleeping over more nights than not, she hoped her bad luck may have finally turned into good luck. Her sin into salvation. And now, she at last had a baby she could call her own, not to mention the prospect of a man in her life the baby boy could one day call *daddy*.

For his part, Ben hadn't yet found himself comfortable with the sleeping arrangements. It seemed too soon to be at ease, especially when it had been barely more than a month since Alex had told Ben she was moving on. With some hard-core counseling, Alex had imagined that the old Ben was worth the effort of resurrecting. But this new Ben? He was dangerous. More reflexive than reflective. And as much as Alex said she could appreciate Ben's newly minted sense of emotional liberation since that awful rainy night, that wasn't the Ben she had fallen in love with and married. Alex said she missed the forever-mourning Ben. The sweetly-moving-on Ben.

The Safe Ben.

Once the lifestyle changes began, Ben discovered, they became easier and easier to accept. He found it relatively simple to scale back his business clients to just a few that mattered. He gave up the office in Burbank with plans to work out of his new home, that for a time, was a furnished apartment in Northridge, complete with a pool, gym, and a crate full of other divorced or soon-to-be-divorced men. It was when he was thinking aloud about hiring a part-time college student as a research assistant that Pam asked to be considered for the job.

Things moved fast from there. Maybe too fast for Ben. He hadn't a clue. He had never been there before. He did, however, take a pinch of solace in something Pam had uttered in the wee hours of their first night together. She had said that true affection had no set incubation period. Whether it happened fast or slow, real love was real love.

"I like the sound of that," Ben had whispered. "But would you mind if I wait awhile and see?"

"Not at all," was Pam's sweet answer. She understood their situation wasn't perfect. Nothing was perfect. But for now, maybe even forever, it was safe.

Acknowledgments

As solitary as most writing endeavors are, not a word gets published without enormous faith and support from a bevy of outstanding individuals. So it is with thanks and appreciation that I mention these very fine folks.

Marge Herring and Gary Cramer. You know what you've done for us. I am and will remain eternally grateful.

Valarie Phillips. It's rare when people who aren't your next of kin believe in you. You believed in me. Please don't stop.

Alan Wertheimer. People laugh when I say my attorney is the most honest man I know. They can laugh all they want, because it's true.

Candy Dooley and Carolyn Herbertson for their eyes and ears.

Doctors Noreen and Ivan Green. Your love and generosity are boundless. I'm grateful to have you in my life.

Special mentions to my good pals Lexi Alexander and Anthony Rodriguez for the only kind of advice that comes from friends who care.

Also extra cool "chick" props to Jeanne Bowerman and J.T. Ellison who, though late to party, have been key in the publishing of this book.

My two children, Henry and Kate. I love you. My world revolves around you. You both are my moon, stars, and inspiration.

And lastly, but certainly mostly, my wife and partner, Karen Richardson. Your love, effort, and attention to every detail are more than appreciated. They're cherished. None of this happens without you.

Thanks to you all. dr

About the Author

Doug Richardson is the author of two previous novels—*Dark Horse* and *True Believers*. A well-known, respected screenwriter, his film credits include *Die Hard 2: Die Harder*, *Bad Boys*, *Money Train*, and *Hostage*. He lives in Southern California with his wife, two children and four mutts.

You can learn more about Doug at www.dougrichardson.com. You can contact him at bydougrich@dougrichardson.com. You can also follow him at www.facebook.com/bydougrichardson and on Twitter: @byDougRich.

Made in the USA
Charleston, SC
13 June 2013